THE COMPANION

SARAH DUNNAKEY

First published in Great Britain in 2017 by Orion Books,
an imprint of The Orion Publishing Group Ltd
Carmelite House, 50 Victoria Embankment
London EC4Y 0DZ

An Hachette UK company

1 3 5 7 9 10 8 6 4 2

A CIP catalogue record for this book
is available from the British Library.

ISBN (Hardback) 978 1 4091 6855 3

Typeset by Deltatype Ltd, Birkenhead, Merseyside

Printed in Great Britain by Clays Ltd, St Ives plc

MIX
Paper from
responsible sources
FSC® C104740

www.orionbooks.co.uk

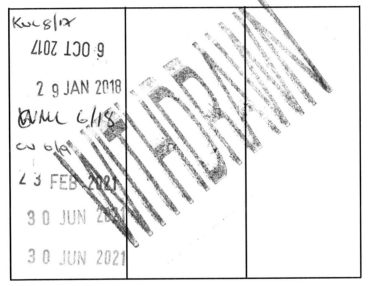

THE COMPANION

To Tim and Eliza

Ref:	AckerdeanColl / Box 23 / Oakenshaw / St Johns/ AH
Content:	Correspondence between Revd Anthony Haste, St John's, Oakenshaw (incumbent 1933–69) and Revd Jonathan Netherwood, St Michael's, Halifax (inc. 1933–82)
Date:	1935–1969

Oakenshaw Parsonage, 22nd July 1936

Jonathan

I plan to include a few words about the Harpers' deaths in the service this Sunday (the funeral itself is to be in Hertfordshire as you may have read in the papers). Not the easiest eulogy I have wrestled with and I am still uncertain. Your thoughts as always are most welcome.

~~"Our parish has~~ "We have suffered a dreadful tragedy. Through the word of God the Father we will find comfort.

We all carry burdens. The passing of Charles and Edie Harper reminds us that at times those burdens can seem impossible to bear. Remember that Jesus himself once told his disciples that his soul was overwhelmed with sorrow even to the point of death. We pray for the strength to be steadfast through days of tumult.

That I, in the company of Miss Harper's young son Jasper, found them, too late, that evening, and bore witness to the tragic path they had chosen, has touched me personally, but I stand before you now as your minister and as theirs.

I

~~The Harpers were our brethren family.~~ They were our brother and our sister. Mother and uncle to a boy, now left bereft and alone. ~~They knew this and still~~ God does not judge any of us on our final act, whether good or bad, but on the totality of our life and heart. None here shall judge them. We can only pray for their souls."

[Here I struggle. To preach forgiveness and acceptance, when I saw with my own eyes what they did. I do judge them. They abandoned that boy. No word of comfort in the note they left. Just indulgent doggerel.]

"There is sadness here today, and questions too. How could this happen? Could any of us have done more? I offered them an open door, a listening ear. I wish I could have given them more: the hope, the faith, they needed to carry on. ~~Should I have~~ But today is not about guilt or recriminations. Our thoughts must be with those whom they left behind, in particular young Jasper who, on the brink of becoming a man, will have to take his next steps without the guiding hands of those who loved him most."

As we stood there together, the only living souls in that bleak house, the boy shed no tears. His eyes reflected neither sorrow nor anger, not even fear. They were filled only with a darkness that I could not read. All I could do, then and now, is hold on to the promise of God's grace, and to pray.

Anthony

2

CHAPTER I

Billy: 1932

I grew up in a palace. God's own truth. And the best thing were, it were mine. The crowds they came and went, but at the end of every day when they traipsed back to the ordinary lives they'd escaped from, I were the one still there, looking down from the top window, waving them goodbye.

So all right, technically it belonged to Mr Nathaniel. But he didn't live there. He had the Big House up the hill. He came and went in his motor car. Never slept at the Palace, never ate a full meal, did a day's work or took a shit there. No more owned it than the day trippers did.

It were no fairy-tale palace. There weren't no turrets or towers, chandeliers or fancy staircases. But we had the biggest swingboats this side of the Pennines, and you can't swing a lass till she screams off a chandelier, well, not without a bloomin' big ladder. The charabancs that rollicked up in the yard might have been shabby but they were full to busting with smiley-faced, pockets-bulging trippers. All up for a day of 'First Class Entertainment – Guaranteed!'

'Potter's Pleasure Palace' – that's what Old Mr Potter had my da paint on the wooden sign nailed to the mill wall. Except it weren't a mill no more. Ackerdean Mill, like dozens of others, closed before the Great War. Cheap cotton fabric were being made all over the world and there were less of a call for the English stuff. But old Jeremiah Potter saw the way things were going. When he died, instead of a worn-out mill, his son Mr Nathaniel inherited a palace.

Folk came from miles. From over the border and as far as Burnley and Leeds. They'd pile out the train in Sowley and pour up the road like slow treacle. I went to watch 'em one Whit Monday with David, the Palace handyman. We stood on the wall at the end of the track looking down the road to town.

'Like wood ants swarming up an anthill,' David said, and he grabbed hold of my pullover sleeve as they passed as if to stop me being carried off, like ants carry off leaves and crumbs.

Some came by bus and walked down from the top road through the woods in their weekend best. The lasses carrying their dancing slippers and their roller skates as they trogged down in their boots and their clogs. The nobs arrived in motor cars, honking their horns through the crowds.

I spent my days dodging round the legs of the suited and booted, the stockings and frocks. Watching 'em when they didn't know they were being watched. Catching their change when it spilled from their pockets, taking the pastries they left on their plates. Made sure they saw me when I needed them to. They tipped me well when I ran an errand, fetched a drink, took a lass a message or held a horse. I'd even fasten up their skates if they asked.

Ma were in charge of the tea rooms and always wore a clean pinny and her hair up smart. My sisters Maud and Peggy helped serve up. I learnt my numbers when I were a little'un, counting out spoons and plates, and chanting the 'one-two-three-four, one-two-three-four' of the foxtrot stepped out on the dance floor, above my head. All the decent songs I knew were ones I'd heard the skaters bellowing above the roar of their wheels as they circled the roller rink. The indecent ones were those carolled by the lads as they left the dances of an evening, arms around the lasses, faces tilted to the sky.

4

The Palace were only open weekends and holidays. Ma said if it had been seven days a week she'd be dead on her feet in six months and my sisters worn to nubbins. I didn't have any fixed jobs but there were always errands to do and generally keeping an eye on the place for Mr Nathaniel. Getting ready to be his assistant when I left school. I had a load of ideas for how we could match the likes of Blackpool and Morecambe that were starting to draw people away. Racing and games with prizes on the field, and reopening the miniature railway with me as the train guard. Mr Nathaniel had said they were 'splendid notions' and promised to 'give them some serious cogitation'. He hadn't finished cogitating yet, but it were only a matter of time.

It were February, cold and wet and the trippers scarce. Mr Nathaniel turned up on Saturday morning, as usual, for one of Ma's scones fresh from the oven. But instead of taking his plate over to the table by the window where he could spy down onto the yard below, he stood by the counter, resting his elbow on the 'Today's Hot Specials' chalkboard. If he weren't careful he'd have 'PIES' written back-to-front on his best tweed. Crumbs speckled his moustache, which like his hair were the colour of well-baked pastry. His cheeks were flushed a ruddy red and the fingers of his left hand were dancing, playing an invisible piano by his side. A sure sign that he'd got some new scheme in mind.

He said there'd been a 'turn up for the books', 'an opportunity not to be missed'. Words that usually meant he'd got a new plan for bringing more trippers in – two skaters for the price of one, private dancing lessons, discounted meals. I prayed it would be the miniature railway this time, though I carried on slicing the ham for the sandwiches as if there were no other thought in my head. The ham had to be extra thin or we wouldn't get enough out of it. I didn't want to face the wrath of Maud if I didn't get it right.

'How old are you these days, Billy Shaw?' Mr Nathaniel asked. Which were a daft question seeing as how he'd been there the day

I were born. Ma nearly popping me out in the mill yard and Da shouting what in hell were happening.

Mr Nathaniel looked out for Ma and us after Da came back from the war. Da had been a piecer at the mill before it closed and general handyman when it became the Palace. Then there were the war, and Ma said he came back only half himself. Gave me nightmares that did, imagining the Huns had blown half his body away, till she put me right, that it were summat inside his head that were missing. He died of the pneumonia in '24 when I were a tiddler and I could scarce remember him, only his whistling of the birds' songs and the autumn smell of him that he had all year round.

Mr Nathaniel let us stay on in the cottage in the mill yard. Said my ma were the star attraction in the tea rooms and my sisters were a pair of sunbeams, by which I reckoned he'd never looked at them proper, cos I've never seen anything less like a warm shaft of sunlight than our Maud's face of a morning. He never said what bit of the sky I were.

'I'm eleven, sir,' I said. 'Almost twelve.' My birthday being but two months off.

'Perfect, perfect.' He supped his tea, then dabbed at a spot of leftover jam on his plate with his finger. 'Y'know the Harpers, up at High Hob, Mary?' Ma stopped her buttering and wiped her brow with her arm.

'The brother and sister writers?' she said.

'Aye. That's them. Charles and Edie Harper. Big in the world of litera-choor they are.' He nodded to us all. 'Did you know that? World famous authors living on our very doorstep.'

Of course we knew. Everyone knew about the Harpers. But no one hardly saw them. Must be all that writing keeping them busy, that and the wind up on the tops stopping them from going out the door.

Peggy who's the middle one 'twixt me and Maud piped up, 'Mrs Trimmer up at Thurcross Farm has seen Miss Harper wandering out on Oakenshaw Moor in her nightgown. She reckons she's trying to catch summat romantic to die of.'

Ma said, 'Hush now,' and Maud groaned and muttered under her breath. She'd read one of Mr Harper's adventure books. Maybe she fancied herself as one of his heroines – Maud of the Jungle. It made me chuckle and the knife slipped and cut a chunk off the ham.

'Billy!' Maud wrested the knife from my hand and rolled up her sleeves. 'I'll do it myself.'

'Never you mind, Billy,' said Mr Nathaniel. 'Come here. We need to have a serious talk, you, me and your mother.'

Ma hated being interrupted when she were working. But she always said it made life easier for everyone if we just did as Mr Nathaniel asked. She put down her knife, though she started faffing with the curls of pale hair that had escaped from her cap. It were her way of saying, 'Well, get on with it then, some of us have got work to do.'

'So, Billy-almost-twelve,' Mr Nathaniel's moustache twitched and his fingers danced out a string of notes in the air, 'how do you fancy going up to that big fine house?'

'What big fine house?'

'High Hob,' he said. 'Come on, lad, keep up. Where the Harpers live.'

I thought mebbes, 'Why the blazes would I do that?' weren't the answer he were after.

'Is it a job?' asked Ma. She'd stopped playing with her hair.

'Not quite.' He pulled out a scrap of newsprint from his jacket pocket. 'Saw this in the *Echo*. I was up there faster than you can sing Jack Robinson.'

He passed me the paper.

I were good at reading. Miss Offat at the school said if I kept at it I could have the makings of summat. Though she never said what that summat were.

It were an advertisement. I read it out for the sake of the others:

Child companion wanted, age 11–12, for boy, 11.
Chas. Harper Esq,
High Hob House,
Oakenshaw, Yorkshire

'I've heard tell of that child,' said Ma with a frown. 'Some trouble in the graveyard at St John's. A lad left tied to the railings at night.'

Mr Nathaniel waved his hand. 'Boisterous high spirits. Boys will be boys, you know how it is.'

'He howls at the moon,' Peggy burst out. Which got all our eyes on her. 'Martha Marsden's sister told her and she works up there so it must be true. The Harpers found him in the heather one stormy night. A wild bairn all wrapped in rabbit fur and they fetched him home to bring up as their own. It's true, Martha Marsden ...' She caught Ma's eye and her voice trailed to a whisper. 'She told me so.'

Ma weren't one for raising her hand to us, but I swear right then she were ready to give our Peggy a slap.

'Young lady,' said Mr Nathaniel in the voice he used for giving orders to David or the lads who serviced the turbine: reminding them who he were, 'you must learn not to heed such ridiculous gossip. You'll be telling me next that you believe in the giant wildcat that the gamekeepers and shepherds bleat on about. The boy is Edie Harper's son. He was born in Paris and I believe his father died over there. Though it really is none of our business.' He peered down at Peggy like Miss Offat does over her spectacles when she's asked a right hard question that she thinks you should know the answer to. Peggy said 'yes sir, no sir' and sat down.

'It must be mad lonely for him up there,' said Ma.

'Exactly!' said Mr Nathaniel. 'Hencewith and for why the advertisement.' He shook his head. 'I told Mr Harper yesterday, he was lucky I spotted it. He could have ended up with some noddy from who knows where. Told him Billy was just the boy for them.'

I knew the stories about the wild beast that attacked newborn lambs and such on the moor, but this were the first I'd heard of there being a half-wild lad up there too. And now Mr Nathaniel's telling me I were to go and be his companion. Never mind him saying, 'Don't worry, he was born in Paris', which I knew were the capital of France. That didn't make him any less strange. How would I understand what he were saying if all he spoke were foreign?

'How often would they want him?' asked Ma. She were looking from him to me as if weighing it all up, like pounds of flour and sugar for her cakes.

'He'd be there full-time. Live in.'

'Live there?' I said. 'Leave the Palace?' Next they'd be telling me I had to ride up there on an elephant, then I'd know this were all a horrible dream. My throat felt so thick and dry I could hardly swallow. I hoped I'd wake up soon and have a glass of water and everything would be all right.

'That's the gist of it,' said Mr Nathaniel. He clapped his hand on my shoulder that hard, I knew I weren't dreaming. He drew his face close to mine till I could smell the fresh strawberry jam on his breath. 'There's no silver spoons going begging in this valley, lad. The Potters started off as farmers and spinners. It's taken two hundred years of hard graft to get my family where we are today. You put your back into this and who knows where you'll end up. It's your big chance. To step up. To get out into the world.'

'Or at least to the top of the hill,' said Ma with an odd not-quite smile. She folded her arms. 'What's his work to be? And what about school?'

Trust Ma to worry about that. Never mind the French lad who howled at the moon.

'There'll be no work as such,' Mr Nathaniel said. 'They're just wanting company for the lad. And Billy's schooling,' he added, 'is part of the deal. Their lad's between tutors at the moment, but they're on the lookout for a new one. You'll be educated like a proper young gentleman, Billy. It's not to be sniffed at.'

The thought of leaving the Palace for High Hob House made me feel sick in my stomach, like being at the top point of the boat swing just before the rope goes slack and you fall. But Mr Nathaniel's words struck at something I'd been worriting at. I wanted a Palace of my own one day. For all his talk of hard graft, Mr Nathaniel had been handed his Palace like a present from his da. I were going to have to work for every stone and roof slate of mine. Getting to know London folk like the Harpers and being educated by a tutor could give me a hoick up. Would it be worth it though, having to live with a mad lonely boy who had to advertise for a friend?

It were all sorted. Mr Nathaniel would drive me up to High Hob on Saturday morning. He had a fine and dandy motor car, and a driver with a cap to go with it. But most times he drove it himself, honking the horn as he came down the main track whether there were anyone in the way or not.

I waited in the yard with Da's old knapsack, that Ma made me promise I'd look after, kicking my clogs in the dust by the 'Prentice House storeroom, half an hour before he were due.

I'd made Ma a lot of promises over the last week: not to be late, not to be rude, not to make a fuss. 'It's a big opportunity,' she said as she snipped at a length of cotton with her scissors. She'd been sewing up a rip in my second best pair of trousers, sat upstairs on her bed by the back window where she said the light were best. 'Half the mills in the valley have gone and those that are left are struggling. When the last of them go, what will there be for you? A shop job in Sowley, if you're lucky. Make the most of this and who knows where you might end up.'

She paused to shake out the trouser legs and check the hems. 'But life up there. It'll be ... different to what you're used to.' She seemed to struggle for the words, which weren't like Ma at all. 'I've been talking to Elsie Trimmer,' she continued. 'She says the lad has some funny ways. He treats that stretch of moor as if it's his alone, with no regard for fences and walls, or even doors. She's caught him in her barn more than once. I don't want you getting into trouble. Remember the rights and wrongs you've been brought up by.' Her face twisted and I half thought she might cry. So I quickly promised I'd be good, and I wouldn't let her and Mr Nathaniel down. Which made her smile.

'It's but eight weeks till your birthday. We'll have a good catch-up then.'

'So long as they don't send you packing before,' Maud added as she came in with my jersey and vests slung over one arm fresh from drying by the fire. 'When you've driven them all mad with your wittering about trains and birds.'

'Don't take any notice, Billy,' Ma said, with a nod at Maud. 'She'll be missing you before the week is out. We all will.'

I kept checking the mill clock, which were daft cos it hadn't told right since the war. David said it stopped dead the night Old Mr Potter died, the day before the Armistice, and it would be bad luck to right it. Maybe Mr Nathaniel believed that too, cos he did nowt to fix it.

So the clock said twenty past four when I set the knapsack down by my feet and it were still saying twenty past four when Lizzie Potter came running over the bridge, her dark bobbed hair bouncing. She stopped when she reached me and took a breath.

'Father's had to go to Halifax on important business,' she said. 'He won't be back before supper. He said you'd be all right walking up, you being a healthy young lad with your head screwed on right.' She were staring at me as if checking for herself whether my head were on right or wrong.

I stared back. She were long-limbed and skinny. Nearly taller than me, though we were of an age. I stood up straighter now like I always did when she were near. I wanted to tell her that her eyes were like the flash of blue under a mallard's wing, and her hair all soft and dark 'minded me of the moss at Wicken Falls. But instead I just said, 'Bugger!' And her eyes flew wide and she put her hand to her mouth to hide her grin.

My sisters said she were full of herself since her ma took her out of our school at Draper's Cross and sent her to a fancy place over Ripponden way. But I knew she hadn't changed. I'd seen her watching the swingboats when they were full of squealing lasses and I wanted to ask her to hang back till the trippers had gone home and have a swing with me. But my words jumbled when she looked at me, so it had never happened. Mebbes now it never would.

Ma came out into the yard, brushing the flour from her hands. She'd brought out some butties and a slice of pie wrapped in paper, to 'keep me going'. When she heard about Mr Nathaniel not coming she said it were probably for the best and the walk were only a little way compared to the long drive round on the road.

'Shouldn't take you longer than an hour. Go straight up the track to Haworth Lane, then up on to the moor for another mile or so. You can't miss the house. It's on its own at the top of the hill, above Oakenshaw.' She paused and I knew she wanted to say something and I hoped it weren't going to be a whole new long list of promises. But she just licked her thumb and rubbed at summat on my chin. 'We'll see you on your birthday.'

Then she gave me a quick kiss on my cheek and started shooing Lizzie into the Palace to get a bite to eat before her walk home. Lizzie dragged her feet and I didn't blame her, having to face my sisters in their lair. I smiled at her for encouragement, and she gave me a smile right back, a full-on cheek-to-cheek one.

I shouldered my knapsack, like I imagined Da did when he went off to war. I waved to Ma but I didn't say goodbye to the Palace. I weren't going off to France or nothing, only to the top of the hill to be a companion for a bit. My birthday were two whole months off. I couldn't stay away that long. I'd bring the Harper lad down with me if I had to, and the tutor. What's the point of algebra and geography if you haven't heard a dance floor clatter with a quickstep, seen skaters race around a rink chanting 'Bluebells cockle shells', or got seven skims from a single stone on the dam? It would be an opportunity for them to learn something too.

*

It were a fair haul up the hill, must have been half an hour before I reached the top. I stopped once I got to the highest point and looked back across the valley, which were nowt now but a dark cleft of green. On the other side, straight up from the Palace, the Big House stood out proud as a boil, its gardens sketched out with trees and the long drive like a yellow tongue licking up to the top road.

I waved, though no one could see me that far, and unless she'd belted back up Lizzie wouldn't even be there yet. I'd half a mind to sit down and eat my butties but I weren't sure how far I had still to go and what if I missed the house and spent the day and mebbes the night wandering on the moor. I'd never been much of a one for the tops, except for watching the birds, the curlews and the plovers and if you were lucky a peregrine, waiting to see it dive. All that sky and the endless heather, rolling out in every direction until they met so far away you couldn't see the join. Made me long for the valley sides and a rushing river and the cover of trees. Two fat grey clouds formed above my head and I got to thinking they were following me. Every few minutes I stopped to look over my shoulder to check if they were still there. They just hung in the pale blue, giving nowt away.

I knew High Hob well enough once it came into view. It were one of them places that I've always known were there but never thought much about. It had its back to the Ackerdean valley, like it had no interest in us either.

It were a heck of a big house for three people. Sharp-edged, with its gables and chimneys prodding the sky. Stubby trees and a low stone wall looped round the side and front to make a sort of garden. Though what could they grow up there? All that grew natural that high were heather and sheep, and them clouds.

There were a gate in the wall at the front, 'twixt two of the trees, and then I were walking up a path with grit and scabby grass on either side and lumps of stones scattered about like bodies. I got to thinking of bodies cos I'd have sworn there were someone watching me.

The windows of the house were blinded by the sun on them, and there were no twitching curtains. It were more like I were being watched from the garden. But the stones weren't blinking and nor were the trees. I kept going, cos so what? I had a right to be there. Then the door opened and a lady were standing there, all in grey, her short waves of hair pinned back from her face. I say lady, but my first thought were of a bird. She 'minded me of the heron who hung around the top dam, still and watchful.

'Come in,' she said.

I stepped into the house and felt like I was being swallowed up, especially when the door closed behind me. The room was dimly lit, with dark wood and crimson paper on the walls. I started to follow the lady, who surely must be Miss Harper, across the black and white chequerboard floor. A screech stopped me mid-step, a cold shiver jagging from my neck to my fingertips. The noise came from behind a door to our left. It were followed by a deep belch and another burst of screeching. Miss Harper just kept walking like nothing had happened, past a fancy staircase with knobs on the banister rail. I hurried past the closed door and the stairs and followed her into a long room. There were books and sheets of paper everywhere, covering tables and chairs and even the rugs on the floor. It were as if a cow had done a rampage. Like Maud when she couldn't find her favourite hair ribbon and turned the bed linen out. The lady's face didn't twitch at it, so I reckoned she must have seen it like this before.

'I'm Edie.' She put out her hand and I took it and said, 'Billy Shaw, ma'am' as I'd been taught. I were still shook up by the sounds in the hall and now I were flummoxed by her being 'Edie'. It were too chummy for someone so solemn. Then she smiled, and it made her younger and softer and more Edie-like after all.

'Sit down.' She pointed to a fat velvety chair. It had a stack of books on it, but she leaned over and lifted them off, dropping them on the rug. 'Would you like some tea?'

I nodded. I were fair starved after that hike. I hadn't had even a nibble of my butties.

She went to the open door and shouted, 'Livvy! Tea for two,' and came back scratching the back of her head.

'Charles wants a bell but he'll have to fix one up himself because neither I nor Livvy will be doing it.' She sat on the edge of the chair opposite. Looking at me, though more like looking through me, as I gaped back not knowing what else to do. I always beat Maud at staring contests, though I've never out-stared Peggy because she starts tickling me when she's had enough. For a moment I almost missed my sisters and my throat felt dry and so did my eyes. I couldn't blink even though I wanted to. I were thinking I might never blink again and I'd have to join a circus as the amazing non-blinking boy when Miss Harper, Edie, looked away. I blinked and blinked until my eyes felt properly wet again.

A grey-haired woman came into the room. Her face were so still it seemed frozen and her mouth such a thin line I'd swear she had no lips. She put a tray down on the little table between us, ignoring the sheets of paper that were already there. The tray had a teapot and milk jug on it and two cups. But nothing to eat, not even a biscuit.

'Thank you, Livvy, that will be all.' She filled the two cups and passed me one. 'Jasper will be here shortly,' she said. 'I told him you were expected.'

I gulped at my tea. It were milky and barely warmer than my breath. Who the heck were Jasper? Mr Harper? No, he were Charles. Were Jasper the lad I were to be a companion to? I wished I'd asked more questions when I were at home. What did a companion do anyway?

Behind Miss Harper there were a big window, lattice-paned, like the ones at the Palace and in our cottage, with long dark curtains either side. I counted four by four squares of glass. There were two more windows alongside, the same except the middle one were arched at the top. Something blurred quick and dark at the bottom of the middle window. A bird, I thought, daft buggers are always flying into glass. But then it popped up again and it were a head of black curls, as long as a lass's, but them weren't a lass's eyes beneath. I drank more milky tea.

Miss Harper sighed. 'Where is that boy?' She tweaked her face into a little smile. 'Potter says you're bright. I'm sure you and Jasper will get on famously. Like Don Quixote and Sancho Panza, Achilles and Patroclus.'

'Do they live here too?' My first proper words since I'd got there. I wanted to show the glaring lad outside that I weren't scared. Look at me having a natter and a cup of tea. When I glanced back at the window he'd gone.

Miss Harper gave a sharp laugh. 'Bright but lots to learn. You'll be good for each other.' Somewhere a door slammed. She cocked her head to one side. I've seen the heron do that too, just before it takes flight. Then her face cracked into a full smile.

'There you are!' She was looking past me as she put down her still full cup of tea and rose to her feet. 'Jasper, this is … I'm so sorry, I've forgotten your name.'

She frowned and I wanted to tell her there'd been a mistake. I weren't the boy she were expecting. I'd just been out for a wander on the moor and had popped in for a drink. I'd be off now, on my way.

'Billy,' I said instead, feeling the black-haired lad's eyes on my back. I straightened my shoulders.

Her forehead was still scrunched up. 'Billy,' she repeated. 'Would that be William then?'

I shook my head. My da were William. I were Billy, always had been.

'Well, I'm sure we'll settle on something. Jasper, you'll show William around and get him settled in.' She turned to the big desk by the window and picked up a sheet of paper with one hand and scratched at the back of her head with the other.

I knew I should turn and face Jasper but it were like a dare and

I weren't giving in first. Then summat sharp stung the back of my head and I spun round. He had his hands behind his back.

'All right?' He were shorter than me, stockier too. His eyes were a challenge.

'All right,' I said, accepting it.

He jerked his head and went out into the hall. Miss Harper were hunched over her desk scribbling. I picked up my bag and left.

He were leaning against the post at the bottom of the stairs, stretching the rubber of a catapult to its full and letting it ping back. A crimson smear marked the back of his hand.

'She's got nits. Don't get too close or you'll catch them.'

A rapid ratcheting noise broke out from behind the closed door to the left. I jumped at the sound and Jasper smirked.

'That's just Charles. You'll get used to it.' He stuffed the catty in his pocket and kicked at my bag. 'Got any food in there?'

'Butties,' I said. 'And a slice of tatie pie.'

'Any meat in the butties?'

'Ham.'

He grunted. 'That might do it. Come on.'

He headed for the front door.

'Where are we going?' I asked.

'The moor,' he said. 'And bring the ham. We're going to set a trap for the Beast.'

CHAPTER 2

Anna: October

Anna locks the door of the cottage and steps out onto the cobbled yard. The mill looms over her, its rough gritstone dark against the pale sky, its many-paned windows blank and steely grey. The double doors to one side are wedged open with a couple of large rocks. One of the doors bears the sign 'Ackerdean Heritage Centre' and below it hangs a smaller one saying 'Open'. A dog tied to a post next to a metal water bowl barks when Anna looks its way.

She shifts the empty rucksack on her shoulder. Filled with wood it should provide enough for a decent fire tonight. The cottage, her new home, sits at a right angle to the mill. Cosy-looking from the outside, with its flower-sprigged curtains and newly painted door. Inside, it is dark and damp, with chalky plaster walls and bare flagstones on the floor. The sparsely furnished rooms stacked with unpacked boxes and bags.

A sharp breeze whips at her hair. She hugs her puffa jacket to her body and stamps her feet in their rainbow-striped wellies. The boots were part of her leaving present from her workmates at the Tyneside People's History Museum, along with a book of Yorkshire dialect poems, inscribed with the words 'To help you blend in'.

A chill across her back. More than just the Yorkshire air. No challenge to someone born and bred in the north-east. It's the same chill she'd felt this morning after she waved the removal men goodbye and stepped into the cottage for the first time on her own. Excitement, she hopes, not fear. She shoves her hands into her coat pockets. A fresh start. On her terms, her choice. The threat of redundancy had made it easier. 'Better to jump than be pushed,' as her dad had said more than once since she told her parents about her decision. Her mum had been more cautious, concerned about her apparent lack of a 'career plan'. But this is her life and she doesn't intend to have any regrets. Not any more.

The clock above the entrance to the mill says twenty past four, although Anna knows it's only half past one. Already the yard is in shadow. When night falls it will be in total silent darkness. No street lights. No city glow in the sky. No whoosh of passing cars, no sirens or alarms. But there will be stars, she reminds herself. She will learn the names of constellations she hasn't seen before.

Four women with gaiters over their boots and a walking pole in each hand stride over the bridge. They nod their 'Afternoons'. Anna smiles and nods in return as they head to the café in the long low building opposite her cottage.

As she passes the open doors of the mill she peeks inside at the reception desk, with its display of souvenir pens and postcards, but there is no one there. A man's voice carries from further inside. It sounds like Trevor, the Friends of Ackerdean volunteer who had given her a tour of the centre on the day of her interview. Now, as then, he isn't pausing for breath or for questions.

On the other side of the reception area a door leads into the single-storey weaving shed that had served as a roller rink during the mill's time as an entertainment centre. A plaque on the wall welcomes visitors to 'The Harper Room. A unique exhibition devoted to the lives and works of Charles and Edie Harper. Donated by Lawrence Harper-Low, 1948'. When she had been shown round the room after her interview, Anna had lingered over a newspaper article from 1936, blown up to poster size: a photograph of the two writers under the headline 'Tragic Deaths Shock Literary World'. The same small smile on both their faces, as if they were remembering a joke that only they would understand.

Between the café and the mill a cobbled humpback bridge spans the river. Anna pauses at the top to watch the foam-specked water rushing below. Its orange-red tint and metallic smell make her think at first of blood. Iron, she tells herself, leached from the peat of the moors above. She carries on over to the other side and takes the path to the right, following the rim of the millpond.

The water is glass smooth and the mill, its windows, its blackened stone, its redundant chimney, are perfectly mirrored. There would have been rowing boats at the beginning of the last century. Men in hats at the oars, women trailing their hands over the side. Now there are only fallen leaves at the edges and nothing to ruffle its stillness.

She follows the track up through the trees, inhaling the spice of rotting leaves and the mustiness of hidden fungi as she gathers sticks of fallen wood. The valley side climbs to her left, threaded with steep paths, outcrops of rock and slender waterfalls. She reaches a fork in the path, one track zigzagging up the hill and the other disappearing into an overgrown arch of holly.

Her rucksack is half full and she's left some sizeable pieces along the way, to collect on her way home. Enough for a fire tonight with some spare to start the wood store she'll need over winter. Head back or carry on? A bird swoops past, too fast for her to identify, and flies through the holly arch. Just a bit further. She carries on.

Dan would have loved this. Foraging for fuel. Storing up for winter. The thought of having someone to hunker down with in the cottage brings an ache to her chest. She clears her throat. *Get a grip, woman.*

She follows the track under the holly, emerging after a short while from cold shadow into cold light. The path flattens out and widens as it meets an unmade road that leads down from the hillside to a metal gate, half open onto a rutted track.

The farmhouse on the other side of the gate is a surprise. She thought her nearest neighbours were higher up the hillside. She approaches, feeling like a trespasser even though there is no obvious sign of occupation.

The windows of the house are blind with dirt, the yard filled with discarded racks of metal, the remnants of disused farming equipment, and an old Land Rover, with one door hanging open.

She has just decided the place must be abandoned when a border collie lopes from behind an outhouse. It throws its head back and barks.

She starts to step backwards.

'Don't move or she'll have your hand off!'

He is tall, wiry like his dog. The sleeves of his red-checked shirt are rolled up over veined and freckled forearms. Grey hair plasters his forehead above blue eyes like broken china.

'Get in your bed,' he growls, and the collie slinks back towards the house. He watches it go then turns and winks. 'Only kidding. She's soft as muck.' He looks Anna up and down. 'Lost, are you?'

'No, I've been gathering wood. I've just moved in at the mill. I'm going to be the custodian of the heritage centre.'

'Oh aye, I'd heard they'd taken a professional on at last. Never told me it were a lass. How're you finding it down there?'

'Cold,' she says. Her first impression of the rough walls and stone floors that shape her new home.

'Aye, I'll bet. Tight-fisted so-and-sos haven't spent owt on that cottage in years. There were talk of doing it up as a holiday let years back, but it never 'appened.' He extends a knotty hand. 'Frank Chambers. You need a cup of tea. I've got the fire going. Get yourself in here for a warm.'

It's more of a command than an invitation, but the prospect of a hot cup of tea is appealing. Anna shakes his hand, leaves her rucksack by the back door and follows him into a small kitchen, past yellowed walls and stone shelves, and a dark wooden table set with a half-eaten plate of baked beans and an empty glass. He motions her through a low doorway.

'Make yourself at home. I won't be a minute.'

The room is warmer than anywhere she's been since she left Jesmond that morning. A sofa and a chair both covered in blankets face a three-bar electric fire set in front of an empty grate. A bookcase filled with novels covers most of one wall. A name repeated on several of the spines catches her eye. Sam Klein. The best-selling crime writer who rents the Harpers' old house up on the moor. She pulls one of the books out. On the cover, under the title *Seven Down*, the figure of a man stands alone by a railway track. The *Sunday Times* has described it as 'electrifying'. She places it back on the shelf.

'Aye, you have a good nosey.' Frank enters the room. 'Curiosity might have killed the cat but it's a good trait in a young'un.' He hands her a tumbler of whisky, the glass smudged with his fingerprints.

'No milk,' he says, by way of explanation, as he lowers himself onto the chair and takes a drink from his own glass. 'Sit yourself down. I can't be done with folk hovering about.'

The whisky smells of cleaning fluid and the first sip sears her throat. She perches on the sofa cradling the glass in her hands.

'Tight as a duck's you know what,' Frank says, returning to the subject of the Ackerdean board of trustees. 'Potter left them enough to see them right, with the land and whatnot that they were allowed to sell off. You'd think they were down to their last farthing, the state of the place.' He screws up his eyes. 'Have you fought your way up the stairs in the mill yet, past that mess of tape and "Enter ye at your peril" signs?'

'The upper floors?' Anna says. 'I haven't had a chance yet. When I was shown round at my interview, Trevor, the volunteer, just said they were out of bounds to the public.'

'Humph. Bet he fed you the whole health and safety spiel. Handy that, for when you want to keep people out.'

'He did mention that the stairs were very worn,' Anna says. At the end of her interview she had asked the panel of trustees if there were plans to expand upstairs in the future. She had been given a sharp 'No' from Erica Walker, the chair of the board. 'That's a shame,' Anna had said. 'All that space going spare. It could be used for interactive displays and changing exhibitions. Give our visitors a reason to keep coming back.' But Erica had started discussing potential start dates and the subject was dropped.

'You make sure you have a good poke around,' Frank says. 'See if you can figure out why they're so keen to keep folk out. There's some say the place is haunted. But I don't have any truck with such notions and I can't see Erica paying it any heed neither. She's got her reasons but whatever they are she's keeping them under that tidy grey bun of hers.' He leans forward. 'Bloody waste, if you'll pardon my French. That floor at the top. Properly sprung, it is. Used to be one of the finest dance floors in the county.' He drains his glass and gives a low whistle. The collie trots into the room and settles across his feet.

'It must have been a fantastic place to go dancing.'

'Before my time.' Frank sniffs. 'But the tea room were legendary. May, who runs the café in the old Apprentice House, she can knock out a decent bit of cake and a hot cuppa, but it doesn't compare with Nana Shaw's empire.'

'Nana Shaw?'

'My mam's mother. Ran the first-floor tea room for years. Would have won awards if they'd bothered with that sort of thing then. Part of the fabric, she were, and my granddad when he were alive. Bless her, that cottage of yours were her home right till she died.' He examines his empty glass. 'Wouldn't know it from the board's version of history. You'd think it were the turbine and the machines alone that kept the place going.'

'I agree,' Anna says.

He raises an eyebrow.

'People's experiences and stories. It's what draws visitors into

23

museums. That and dinosaurs or tanks but we don't have either of those.' She smiles. 'Though I won't know that for certain until I've got stuck into the contents of the storeroom.'

'Well, good luck with convincing the board,' Frank says, returning to the contemplation of his empty glass. 'And I'll be keen to see what you turn up on them writers. Another one of Erica Walker's protected areas.'

'The Harpers?' Anna asks. 'What do you mean?'

'Well. There's the official story of what happened to them, their supposed suicide, and then there's the what-do-you-callits, the alternatives. But the board won't hear any talk about third parties or cover-ups.'

'You don't believe it was suicide?' There had always been speculation about the Harpers, the nature of the siblings' relationship and their hermitic existence in Yorkshire. This was the first time she'd heard doubt cast over the cause of their deaths.

'Not just me,' Frank says. 'There's plenty round here would say the same, but them in charge don't want to hear it. The Harpers were well connected. Maybe not blue blood, but old money anyroad. Suicide's a pretty neat verdict.'

'Not for the family,' she says, but she feels a tingle of excitement, an awakening of the curiosity that had steered her into a career sifting through remnants of the past. Two young gifted writers taking their own lives was tragic, but was there an even darker side to the Harpers' story?

'Depends on the alternatives, don't it.' Frank wipes his mouth with the back of his hand. 'And whether or not you wants the police poking around in your business. The truth ain't always what you stick on your mantelpiece.'

'But they left a note. The farewell poem signed by them both.'

'Aye, there is that.' Frank is gazing into the fire now as if trying to see images in the glowing bars. Anna wonders how much whisky he's already had.

She has read the Harpers' official biography, *Siblings in Arms*, written by their friend Bunty Baxendale. It makes only a brief reference to their deaths, but it has the two verses that comprised their suicide note as its frontispiece. The simple words and rhythm of the first verse have stuck in her mind:

> *If I should say 'farewell'*
> *It would be too short.*
> *A single word, a tolling bell.*
> *A gunner's last retort.*

It's almost jaunty, Anna thinks now, not something you'd want to read aloud in case you seemed to be mocking the sentiment. She has a sudden memory of Dan's best friend Nat at the funeral, the nervous giggle as he read out the lyrics from a song Dan had loved. His mortified face, reddening cheeks, tears welling in his eyes. She feels the familiar tightness in her throat.

'Married?' Frank asks.

The question jolts her. Had she spoken Dan's name out loud?

'He died,' she says.

'That's a bad do at your age. At any age. I lost mine too.' Frank puts his hand in his pocket, draws out a stained leather wallet. 'Go on,' he says, throwing it to her. 'Have a gander.'

Inside the wallet two photographs lie behind dulled plastic. The first a faded shot of a middle-aged woman in a jumper and work trousers kneeling by a newborn lamb, squinting up at the camera. The other shows a man and two boys grinning on a beach.

'Oz.' Frank points to the second photograph. 'Our John buggered off there to teach soon as he qualified. Married a local. Them's his boys. My younger one Michael lives down south, but might as well be the other side of the world for all I see or hear from him.'

He gnaws at his lower lip. 'They've forgotten this place. The valley, the moors, the bleedin' mill. Forgotten what it means.' He shakes his head as if to clear it. 'My dad's family have had this farm for over two hundred years. Mam did well to marry in. There's been Chambers' sheep in them fields since before Victoria were born. Only got rid of mine back end of last year. Betsy weren't up to it no more, were you, you useless hound?'

The collie's ears twitch. She shifts her position on his feet but doesn't open her eyes.

'It must have been hard for you. Farming here by yourself.'

'Not as hard as it will be to leave it.'

'You're leaving?'

'Our John is after me selling up and moving into the old biddies' place in Sowley. Halcyon Haven, it's called. Sheltered housing. Doesn't trust me here on my own. "What if you have a fall?" he says. I told him I haven't been in the habit of falling over in seventy-odd years and I don't intend to start now. Then it's "What if you couldn't get to the phone? No one would even know."' He shakes his head. 'Jim and the lads would soon kick up a fuss if I weren't there to get my round in at the Red Lion of a Thursday night, and the woman at the paper shop knows to expect me every weekend. But John won't give up. Gets his stubbornness from my mam. She were never a one for turning. The Iron Lady had nowt on her.' He gives a wheezy laugh and raises his empty glass, then frowns at it. 'I'll fetch us a top-up.'

Anna gets to her feet. 'Thanks, but I have to be getting back.'

'Fair enough. Got to get yourself settled in, I s'pose. Don't want to be wasting your time nattering to an old man. But don't forget what I've said about stuff being covered up. There's summat to it. I might be old but I'm not daft.'

The path through the woods is in near darkness on the way back. She stumbles a couple of times over tree roots and as she nears the millpond an overhanging branch catches on her rucksack and tugs her backwards. She is relieved when the old bridge comes into sight.

Later, in the narrow kitchen at the back of the cottage, as she fills the kettle at the white Belfast sink, she challenges her reflection in the window. Are you up to this? Bringing order to chaos. Untangling the truth from speculation and red tape. The sash window is closed but a draught stirs the pulled-back curtains and the wooden frame rattles.

Frank was quick to dismiss talk of ghosts, yet he seems convinced that the board's refusal to open the mill's upper floors is an attempt to hide something. Is it linked to his suggestion that the Harpers didn't kill themselves? They were both at the height of their careers when they died. Charles's books were bestsellers. Edie had written two critically acclaimed novels and was believed to have completed a long-awaited, though now lost, third. What could have happened to tip their world?

A pale blur flickers across the image of Anna-in-the-glass, pulling her out of her thoughts. It is followed by the hoot of an owl.

She tugs the thin curtains closed. 'Shut the buggers out.' Something Dan used to say at night. She is surprised at the quick memory of his voice. As if he is letting her know that unlike her old job and the flat and her Geordie friends, he isn't going to be that easy to leave behind.

CHAPTER 3

Billy: 1932

We didn't catch the Beast that day. Jasper reckoned the ham were off.

'The Beast only wants fresh meat. The bloodier the better.' Then he ate a long strip of it, straight off the rock we'd left it on. Gobbled it down like I once saw a hen eat a mouse, the tail disappearing last. Wiped his mouth on the sleeve of his jacket when he were done.

He'd been hunting the Beast ever since he came up to High Hob from London three years ago. That first night he'd heard something snuffling at the front door. He knew straight away it were a wild creature that had crept over at the first scent of humans. Human meat were the Beast's favourite and it only ate lambs and birds for convenience.

He'd asked around among the farmers and the folk in Oakenshaw. Some said it were a great cat descended from a tiger that escaped from a circus fifty years ago, others reckoned on it being an ancient breed of beast, neither cat nor wolf nor bear, that had prowled the hills since prehistoric times. A shepherd called Abe Bartlett had met the creature and lived to tell the tale. 'We'll visit him in the summer, when he's up with his sheep,' Jasper said. 'There's still fear in his eyes when he talks about it.'

I asked him about the noise we'd heard in the house earlier, and the one when I first arrived that had sounded like a wild creature in pain.

'Was it like this?' He let out a fair imitation of the screeching.

I nodded.

'Could be a llama,' he said. 'Or maybe a desert fox.'

'In the house?'

'Nah. They're recordings. Charles plays them on his gramophone when he's writing about Africa or wherever.' He started fidgeting with his catty again. 'Let's see your scars,' he said.

'Which ones?'

'How many have you got?'

Without waiting for a reply, he sat down on the heather and pulled down his left sock. A long pale welt ran from the side of his knee almost to his ankle.

'Sheet of glass,' he said. 'Left in the outhouse from when they fixed the kitchen window two summers ago. It was white inside, like a gutted fish. You could see the bone and everything.'

He took off his jacket and lifted up his pullover and shirt. A dark scar crossed his ribs on one side.

'Came off Scaling Crags. I got back on and reached the top though.' He pulled up his sleeve, twisting his arm to show the back of it. A criss-cross of jagged lines. 'Slid down the wall of the reservoir they're building out at Walthorpe. Had a corker of a bruise on my head. But bruises are no good. They don't last.' He tugged his sleeve back down. 'Go on then. Show me yours.'

I were lost for a minute. I'd done my fair share of climbing and tumbling but I hadn't got anything like a proper scar for the proof of it.

'Bin lucky, I suppose,' I said. His blank face showed what he thought of that. Then I had it. 'I were dead once, mind. For ten whole minutes.'

Jasper tilted his head back, eyes narrowed.

'I got knocked on the head by a swingboat. They couldn't find my heartbeat. A lady held a mirror to my mouth but there were no breath to mist it. David, the Palace handyman, were all for measuring me up for my coffin and my ma were crying and saying her prayers.' My throat tightened at the tragic scene I'd painted. 'Then I just sat straight up and asked for the football I'd been chasing. David said it were a bleedin' miracle. I got free sweets from the kiosk for a month.'

Jasper passed me his catty. 'First to hit that rock five times gets a head start home,' he said. I'd passed the test. For now, at least.

He beat me to the front door, but only just, cos I ran like hell with the thought of the Beast close on my heels. 'Dinner will be uneatable,' he said, once he'd caught his breath. 'It always is.'

We had dinner, which turned out to be their name for tea, in Miss Harper's room at an oval table that had been hidden behind a fancy screen. It were set with silver candlesticks and red napkins that were grubby at the edges. The food weren't as bad as Jasper made out, though the meat took a fair bit of sawing through. Mr Harper sat at the head of the table wearing a fancy dressing gown, all red and green swirls, and gold-coloured slippers tied to his feet with an embroidered thong between his toes.

I'd said 'Thank you, Mr Harper, thank you, Miss Harper' for about the millionth time, trying to remember what I'd promised Ma about my Ps and Qs, when Mr Harper put up his hand, the wide sleeve of his gown just missing his gravy.

'My name is Charles,' he said, with a twitch of his thin black moustache. 'And my sister is Edie. Let's not have any of this Mr and Miss, it makes me feel like an old man, or worse, a schoolteacher.'

So Charles and Edie it were and I got so used to it I were flummoxed if I heard them called owt else.

After that first night Jasper and me ate our meals on our own in the kitchen. Livvy putting the food on the table and letting us help ourselves while she or Sally, the lass who came up to help most days, took a covered plate to 'the missus'. Edie preferred to eat alone, though she sometimes let Charles join her. Mostly he ended up 'eating out', which according to Jasper meant a pie and a couple of drinks down at the Drovers' Rest in Oakenshaw.

Livvy and Sally called us Master Jasper and Master Billy. Though Sally said 'Master William' to try to please Edie. It were cracking either way. I'd never been called Master before.

My room sat at the top of the house, across from Livvy's. It had a bed with a flower-sprigged eiderdown that smelled of camphor, a wardrobe and a set of drawers with a bevel-edged mirror and an oil lamp of my own. The rug on the floor 'minded me of the ones Ma made from knotted strips of rags. Next to the bed an uncurtained window stuck out over the roof. If you knelt on the deep wooden ledge you could see out to the open moor and the pale line of the road down to Oakenshaw village.

On that first night I sat cross-legged on the rug avoiding the bed and the gaping darkness of the window. I tried not to think about home as I listened out for Jasper's feet on the stairs, fearing he might burst in any minute to try to catch me blubbing. The house creaked as if it were shifting itself comfy. There were clankings and gurglings that I kept telling myself were just the pipes from the bathroom on the first floor. What if Charles played one of his animal recordings in the night? How would I know if it were an African elephant or the Beast baying at my door? What if even just a part of Peggy's story were true – did Jasper really howl at the moon? Summat humped and shuffled on the landing and I huddled my body tighter and smaller until a cough told me it were Livvy making her way to bed. Only after her door clicked shut did I dare to scuttle to my bed. My feet frozen solid and pins-and-needles in my legs, still I fell asleep before I'd a chance to say my prayers.

There were more than one Edie Harper. That's one thing I learned quick. There were the one who met me on the day I arrived. Voice all gentle and her eyes hazy as if you were a distraction, but one she didn't really mind. She had that face a lot. Then there were the bright and brittle Edie. Sharp-edged and ready to crack like thin ice on the dam. Her mouth a tight beak, eyes glittering and a lash to her tongue even when her words were gay. She were like that mostly around Charles, who scarce seemed to notice her moods and rarely showed any more surprise at the things she said than a twitching of his moustache. And there were sad Edie too, who locked herself away all day, coming out moth-like when the lamps were lit and flitting through the house without lifting her eyes as she passed.

When she were being gentle Edie she said everything in a tired voice, as if it were all she could do to speak, and to do any more would finish her off. 'Fetch Jasper, will you, sweetie.' 'Go and find Jasper, there's a dear.' I felt like a dog rounding up the sheep. Except all I were herding were Jasper. Him and whatever beast he were after catching that day.

Cos the Beast kept changing too. Jasper could never settle on its shape and form. Most times it were a cat, with an ancient bloodline that made it bigger and fiercer and more cunning than any lion or tiger. But then he'd announce it had wings, which explained how it could move so fast, and he wouldn't be surprised if they were tipped with gold cos he'd once caught a glint of it high in the sky. Another time, imitating its call, he howled like a dog abandoned by its master, and it made me wonder again at Peggy's tale of the wild bairn found on the moor. I told him I reckoned the Beast were something like the Jabberwock that we'd read about at school. But Jasper said that were a kid's story and nothing like the real thing at all.

Jasper were keen enough to take me with him hunting and trap-setting. Showing me the rocks and clefts and abandoned buildings that made up the landscape of my new home. It made each day an adventure and I'd even taught him a thing or two about the birds and their songs. But every game of his had an edge to it. If he did something you had to do it too, or he'd call you a cissy or a baby and make a show of pretending to cry. So I balanced on rocks and climbed the broken walls of old barns and held my face under the thick water of a bog while he counted to twenty. Dreading the day when he'd do something I couldn't or wouldn't copy. Not knowing what the limits were to what he would try next.

I were that busy exploring my new world and watching out for Jasper that I didn't hanker much after my old life, sitting with my classmates at Draper's Cross, or running errands for Mr Nathaniel or Ma. But at night on my own in bed, I missed it all – Ma's singing while she worked and her quick cuddles, even my sisters' silly chatter and their endless teasing – with a hard ache in my chest. I missed my old bed and the rough stone of the Palace walls, the clatter of clogs on the cobbles and the rush rush rush of the river. I'd tell myself that the very next day I would go home. But in the morning there'd be Jasper and the Beast traps and a new route to follow across the heather. I would remember my promise to Ma and I'd swear to stick with being a companion. I'd show her and Mr Nathaniel that I could do it. I weren't going to let anyone down.

'If we catch the Beast,' I said one day when we were whittling wooden spikes to line a trap, 'we could show it at the Palace. People'd come from miles to see the Beast of Oakenshaw Moor.'

I could picture the whole spectacle. There'd be a fancy cage, painted gold. I'd sell tickets from a booth and I'd wear a cap and bellow into a megaphone, 'Roll up! Roll up!' They'd be able to hear me in Wakefield. It would be the biggest attraction in the whole of Yorkshire and Lancashire. Mebbes in England.

'It's not "if" we catch it. It's when,' Jasper said, the tip of his tongue showing as he worked his knife. 'And who says there'd be anything to show in a cage?' He held up the stick and examined its point. 'We might just kill it and skin it.' He rolled the sharpened wood between his fingers. 'What did you do down at this palace then? Did you polish the throne? Or were you the king's jester? Can you do juggling and somersaults?'

Before then he'd showed little interest in the Palace. He'd yawned and looked bored when I started telling him about the rink and the rowing boats and hadn't even blinked when I described the chops and ale and Ma's famous pies.

'It's not a king's palace,' I said. 'You know that. It's Mr Nathaniel Potter's and I were his assistant.' It were almost true. I hurried on, 'You've never seen anything like it. There's the dragon swingboats that fly higher than any rope swing, and there's the boating and skating and dancing.'

'Dancing's for nancies.' He'd done dancing at his last school and he'd had to bite one of the other boys who held him too tight in a waltz. I didn't tell him about how I used to sit on the landing and watch the dancers on the top floor and wish it were me twirling a lass round the room. I bet Lizzie Potter would know all the steps and could show me what to do.

He kicked at the pile of whittled wood. We'd have enough spikes for three or four traps if we set them right. 'What about the skating?' he asked. 'Do they have races?'

'Only when Albert's not there. He's on the door most days and he throws out anyone who's causing trouble. But he lopes off early on Sunday afternoons. When it's not so busy you can get the ramps out and do tricks.

'But the Beast would top it all,' I added. 'It would be the star attraction. If we catch it.'

'I told you it's not if, it's when.' Jasper's eyes had darkened. A sign that he thought I were mocking him.

'We'll charge people extra to have their photographs taken with it,' I said quickly. 'Extra extra if they want to get in the cage.'

Jasper closed one eye and squinted at the half-sharpened stick he'd started working on. I barely saw the quick flick of his wrist as he hurled it past my head, just missing my ear. I didn't flinch; I'd been half expecting it. 'We need a bigger trap.' He got to his feet. 'Come on, there's a shovel in the outhouse. We'll take it in turns to dig. You can go first.'

When it tipped down outside, which it did a fair bit, we holed up in the kitchen and did experiments. We raided the larder for ingredients or brought in finds from the moor – rodent or bird carcasses mainly – to dissect, or burn or try to dissolve in vinegar (or once in a bottle of Charles's cologne which at least disguised the smell). Jasper sketched everything and got me writing down the methods and results. Livvy worked round us, her face stiff as ever, so I never knew what she made of it all or whether she ever tried to complain to Edie or Charles. Sally kept out of our way.

I'd been promised my schooling. Ma said the inspectors would kick up a fuss if not. Jasper had been to school in London before they moved up to Yorkshire. He didn't want to talk about London. It stank and he were glad to see the back of it. He'd been to school up here too though that hadn't lasted long. He'd been told school didn't suit his temperament. Jasper's temperament had seen off two tutors as well. The last one had left at Christmas.

'He was meant to come back in the new year but he wrote them this long letter instead.' Jasper screwed up his face. 'Said I'd be better for the company of a boy my own age. That's how they came up with the idea of you.'

About a month after I arrived Charles announced that there were no tutors to be found. Word must've got round about Jasper. Them tutors and teachers and dancing masters probably all met up in special clubs, like the bar over at Robin's Bridge where the hands from Hawksclough Mill got paid of a Friday. David called it a den of iniquity, a word I'd not got round to looking up but it reeked of smoking and drinking and complaining about the bosses. I imagined the tutors in their clubhouse comparing notes on the different lads they'd taught. I'd happily sit among a bit of iniquity to hear all they had to say about Jasper.

But Ma were right; the law said we had to have schooling, at least till we were fourteen. To keep the inspectors happy Edie decided that she and Charles would teach us themselves until other arrangements – a tutor from another country, mebbes, where Jasper hadn't been heard of yet – could be made.

Charles grumbled about it at first, saying that if he didn't get his next novel on the shelves sharpish we'd be living on bread and water. His books had this hero in them called Garth Winter who kept getting into scrapes in places like Africa and South America. Jasper said Charles hated Garth but he had to stick with him cos he had no other way of earning money. Mebbes that were why he found time to teach us after all, so he could escape from Garth for a bit. He'd take us for three mornings for natural history, geography, British history and arithmetic. Edie would cover literature and art.

She'd had enough after a week. On the first day she read us a poem about geese on a river. Her voice sounded all angry, like she were having a boxing match with the words. Then she told us to write down how the poem made us feel. When we'd done she sent us away without reading our efforts, which were a shame cos Jasper had written a brilliant story about a two-headed man-eating bird that terrorised the riverbank. It were heaps better than my effort, trying to say the poem made me feel sad without sounding soft. On the second day she read from a book about painters in Italy. It were pouring down so hard outside it looked like the window glass were melting. When she finished she put the book back up on the shelf and frowned at us and particularly at Jasper's left foot, which had been kicking the table leg all the time.

'I think,' she said, 'that the very best thing you boys can do to educate your minds is read.' She waved at the bookshelves that lined the far end of her room. 'Everything and anything. We'll gather together every Friday morning, over a pot of tea, and discuss what you have read. Yes?' And we were dismissed.

On our first morning with Charles he explained his 'Theory of Education'. While he paced the length and breadth of his study, his hands clasped behind his back, I just gaped around me. The room were like a story, lots of stories, emptied out into real life.

A black-skinned warrior hunkered in one corner, almost as big as

Charles, naked except for a skirt and boots of fur; across from it in the other corner was a hideous thing in red robes and plated armour that Charles called 'a Mongol from the East'. His gramophone were there and a stack of records in cardboard sleeves, an elephant's foot that he stuck umbrellas in, a ship's wheel and the nameplate off a locomotive, *Palatine*. A globe, a great curved sword, a model of a human head covered with lines and symbols and wearing a deerstalker hat, a dried monkey, all tiny and shrivelled like a starved bairn, a couple of guns propped on stands, and a whole tray of lenses and levers and springs.

It felt hard to breathe, as if the objects were sponges soaking up the air and not leaving enough for the human beings. My arse got numb from sitting while Charles talked and talked and talked. Jasper beside me hummed all the way through, just low enough for Charles not to hear, though he stopped a couple of times mid-talk and cocked his head as if listening for an insect or a motor car trying to drive up the path. We ran out of the door soon as he were done, flying so fast onto the moor you'd think the Mongol from the East himself were after us.

Charles paced up and down for most of our lessons, his head bent so we saw more of his brows than his eyes. Every now and then he would pick up an object and thrust it at us asking, 'Do you know what this is?' Then he'd tell us it were a ball of rose marble hewn from an Italian mountainside and had been formed millions of years ago deep under the ground. Or it would be a spear tipped with steel and wound with ribbon and feathers and he'd tell us dates and names we had to remember if we were ever to understand the struggles in Africa. We never knew one day to the next what we would be learning and we had to remember it all too. At any time, catching us crossing the hall, having our supper in the kitchen or heading out the front door, Charles might suddenly ask, 'What was the date of Inkerman and who commanded the British force?' or 'What two metals make brass?' and we had to have the answer fast if we didn't want the whole lecture all over again. And in my case I had to make sure I answered in 'proper English'. Charles said it hurt his ears to hear me talk Yorkshire. To which I could have answered what did he expect, us being on top of a moor in the heart of the county and it weren't my fault he were nowt but a southern incomer. But I kept my trap shut, cos I was there to learn like a gentleman, after all, and I opened my ears to the way he and Edie and Jasper talked.

One day we did capital cities of the world, calling them out from memory as Charles spun and stabbed at the multicoloured globe. I got my twenty before Jasper had twelve.

'Very good, Billy. We'll make a geographer of you yet. Now remind me. Who was Sir Walter Raleigh?'

'He were, I mean, he was, an explorer who sailed to America in Tudor times. He was a favourite of Elizabeth I and if it wasn't for him we wouldn't have no, that is, there'd be no taties ... potatoes or tobacco and so England would be a poorer place.' Which must have been at least half right because as we were leaving his study Charles handed me a brown leather box.

'Observation, Billy-boy,' he said, 'is what makes life rich. Stops you just skating the surface.'

It was a pair of binoculars. Heavy, with a thick brown leather strap. Perfect for spying on grouse in their nests or curlews and peregrine on the wing.

Jasper grabbed them from my hands soon as we were out of the gate.

'I've been after these for ages. We'll be able to spot the Beast a mile off and be clear of his scent range. We can watch for his weak spots. Figure out how best to bring him down.'

CHAPTER 4

Anna: October

If she sticks to her plan she'll be fine. The three 'Rs' – Relabel, Re-file, Reject. Two weeks into the job and it has become her mantra.

Her office is in a corner of the old engine shed, jutting out from the back of the mill, with a window overlooking the pond. Her desk is wedged under the window between a bank of grey filing cabinets and two huge wickerwork baskets stacked on top of each other, marked 'AM' in black letters, for Ackerdean Mill.

The rest of the room is filled with boxes. Some labelled – 'Local History Guides', 'Geology Finds', 'Bunting', 'Cotton Bobbins (mixed)' – some not. Behind the boxes lies an assortment of bigger items including an ornate coat stand and a signpost with 'This Way' painted on the arrow. Anna has already mentally marked them both 'Reject'. The filing cabinets hold most of the paper archive: the history of the valley and the hilltops, Ackerdean as cotton mill and pleasure palace, and documents relating to the Harpers, all crammed in together.

When the Harpers died High Hob had been reclaimed by their distant cousin, Lawrence Harper-Low who owned it. After the war he decided to rent it out to aspiring writers and artists and at the same time donated much of the contents to the museum run by the Sowley Literary and Scientific Society in a small building attached to the town hall. When Nathaniel Potter bequeathed the mill to the society in the 1960s the Ackerdean board of trustees was formed and the museum's collections were moved into their new home. Until Anna's appointment the museum and archives had been maintained by a succession of volunteers with varying degrees of competence and commitment.

This morning Anna had found a flyer from the 1930s advertising skating lessons on the Palace rink and a menu for the Palace tea rooms at the front of a file otherwise consisting of lists of machinery parts. The folder was marked 'Palace Misc.'. There are a lot of 'Misc.' files. If there has ever been a coherent system it has been lost in decades of randomness. The material she has found relating to the Harpers, mainly book reviews and old photographs of the exterior of High Hob, does little to flesh out their story. If there was a mystery to their deaths she hasn't found any hint of it so far. But Frank was so convinced. Does he know more than he is letting on?

She checks her watch. Eleven thirty. Too early for lunch. She reaches for the handheld temperature and humidity monitor.

She's going to try it out on the top floor this morning, to compare the readings there with the rest of the building. After her conversation with Frank she had explored the two closed floors. It hadn't taken long. There were no hidden bodies. No bloodstains. Neither was there any evidence that the space was unsafe, although the stairs leading up are worn and uneven.

She had raised the possibility of making use of the rooms with Erica again yesterday when she phoned for her weekly update and had been told that it would be 'inappropriate', before the call was brought to a swift close.

Anna considers the word now as she crosses the museum to the stairs. Has she missed something? Manoeuvring round a pile of cotton bales she bumps a table with her hip, almost dislodging a pile of writing slates. This room is too full. A spinning wheel, a milk churn and old maps of the West Riding are displayed alongside cotton bales, samples of woven cloth and part of the mill's Victorian steam turbine, abandoned in the early twentieth century because it was too costly to run. A gramophone player and a metal sign promoting 'Tip Top Teas' represent the mill's later resurgence. All good stuff, Anna thinks, but packed in so tightly together that visitors must leave feeling bewildered and not particularly well informed. If the upper floors were opened, the story could be told more coherently. What could be inappropriate about that?

She ducks under the yellow and black tape intended to prevent visitors exploring the flight of stone stairs. The steps are the whitish grey of old bones, worn into waves by decades of boots and clogs. There is a pair of children's clogs on display downstairs. Stiff leather tacked to the inflexible curve of a wooden sole. Metal plates attached to the heel and toe. The racket they must have made, she thinks, a clattering tap dance up and down the stairs.

She stops on the first floor, once home to the Palace tea rooms, and before that, for most of the nineteenth century, a workshop lined with spinning mules. Men and women operating the machines while children wove in and out and under, piecing together broken threads, gathering up waste, avoiding the shuttering wood and metal. Voices lost in the relentless noise.

There is a thick silence now, so quiet even her breath sounds loud. She continues to the top floor where the stairs open into a large room filled with light streaming through two walls of windows. Unlike the floors of the lower rooms which are pitted and scarred by the long-gone machinery, up here the boards are smooth, a sprung floor laid at the turn of the twentieth century. The gramophone would have been up here playing the latest tunes. Live dance bands on special occasions. Jazz, perhaps, heard for the first time. No wonder the place had been so popular.

A stone shelf juts out from the wall beneath one of the windows. She sits down, ignoring the cold chill through her jeans, and closes her eyes. Strains her ears for the echo of clicking heels, the shuffle of boots, the quick breath of the dancers. Hears nothing, except her own breath and the steady beat of her heart. She imagines the fox-trotters and the waltzers in their holiday best, freed from the long hours of a working week. If she sits here long enough, still enough, might their spirits reappear? What secrets are they shielding? Come on, she urges them, let me in on what Erica and Frank are holding back. If she turns as cold as the stone, will they forget she is there? A dull ache spreads down her thighs to her knees. In her stillness the air around her seems to move.

'You'll get piles if you sit there too long.'

Her eyes spring open.

No impudent ghost. Only Frank Chambers. Hands tucked in the pockets of a quilted green gilet. Corduroy flat cap set at a rakish angle. Enough to disperse a bevy of phantoms.

'How long have you been there?' she asks.

'Long enough to know it's time you shifted your arse while you can still feel it.'

She slides off the shelf, trying to hide the rigidity in her legs and the numbness in her buttocks.

'Is this what they pay you for then? Guarding the windows?'

She rubs at the back of her thighs. 'Members of the public aren't supposed to be up here,' she reminds him.

'Pah.' He sniffs. 'I'm not just any old member of the public, you know. You can't fob me off with a no entry sign and a bit of cheap tape.'

He thrusts an A4 envelope towards her. 'And no need for you to be so hoity. I came up here to bring you these.'

She takes the envelope.

'I'm having a sort out.' He straightens his shoulders. 'Our John's not stopped his mithering about the Halcyon Happy Home. He says Michael's in agreement. Pair of them'll have me conscripted at this rate. I won't be able to take everything with me. The flats are nowhere near big enough for a lifetime's belongings.'

'Do they allow pets?' Anna asks, thinking of Betsy stretched across his feet.

'Aye, well, that's the sticking point. They won't have her. John thinks she's on her last legs but she could keep going for years yet. They're tough, are collies. Anyroad, they haven't got a space for me yet. I let them put me on the waiting list, to keep the lads happy. Death list more like. It's one in, one out. Mind you don't bump into the funeral procession when you arrive with your "Welcome to your new home" balloons.'

Anna laughs, despite the morbid image.

'Photographs,' he points to the envelope, 'of this place back in the day. Shaws and Chambers stuff. It belongs here, by rights, not in a trunk in John's attic in Oz or in the bin, more like, if it was left to Michael. It's writ on the back who's who and where's where. If you need any further explaining you know where to find me.'

'That's great, thank you,' Anna says. 'Would you mind if I scan them into the computer? I'm going to create a website to show the world what we've got.'

Frank makes a humphing sound. 'Please yourself. I suppose even this old place has to move with the times. That's another thing they offer down at the oldies' place. Computer classes. Jim's an inmate there already and he loves all that. Says I could talk to our John and the young'uns on a video link.' He shakes his head. 'Time'll come none of us'll have to leave our houses. We'll just get up of a morning and plug ourselves in.'

'Don't worry, Ackerdean's a long way from that.' She remembers one of her finds yesterday. 'There's a mention in an old account book about a Mary Shaw who ran the tea room. Was that your gran?'

'Aye, that'll be Nana Shaw. Queen of the scones and puddings, Mr Potter called her. I haven't got any pictures of her, mind, nor of my granddad either.'

'I'll let you know if I find anything.' Anna picks up the humidity monitor from where it has been resting on the shelf. Not too much moisture, but very cold. 'Let's get back downstairs.'

'So what have you dug up about the Harpers?' Frank asks Anna, once they reach the relative warmth of the reception area. 'Bet there's a stack of stuff about them in that glory hole of yours that the board won't have on display cos it doesn't fit the bill.'

'There's not as much as you might think. Most of what we have on them is already on display. But the archives are all mixed in together at the moment. Part of my job is to untangle it, although I'm hoping to find connections between the collections too.'

'Aye, well, the Shaws are the ones you want if you're after connections.' He gives her a sideways glance. 'My uncle Billy lived up at High Hob when he were a lad.' He nods approvingly when her eyes widen in surprise. 'Mam said it gave him ideas above his station and did him no good in the end. But Billy told me tales of what him and that lad of theirs got up to. Right pair of tearaways, by his account.'

'Did he work up there?'

'Bed and board and a fancy education, Mam said, in return for keeping the young lad company. Daft ideas some folks have. Don't know why they didn't send him to the village school if he were lonely.' He pauses and seems about to add more, but then purses his lips and shakes his head. 'Never mind that, come on through here.'

He disappears into the Harper Room. Anna has work to do in the office but follows him anyway, curious to hear what he has to say about the writers.

Frank is standing in the recreation of Charles's study. On the solid oak desk a typewriter is flanked by a glazed vase filled with ragged peacock feathers and a stack of travel and natural history books. A curved scimitar hangs in a glass case on the wall above. To the left of the desk stands a life-size model of a Mongol warrior.

The red fabric of the Mongol's robe has faded to pink in parts but the plate of the armour shows no sign of rust. Anna runs a finger over the dull metal surface.

'There were a Zulu one as well,' says Frank. 'They got rid of it back in the eighties. Weren't considered PC.'

'Have you thought of becoming a volunteer?' Anna asks. 'You must have so many stories you could share. You could tell people about your gran and granddad.'

Frank grunts. 'And be told what to do by Trevor Stanhope? No chance. He acts like he's a sergeant major and the rest of the volunteers are his bloody foot soldiers.'

Anna smiles at the image. 'Well technically I'm in charge of the volunteers now, not Trevor.'

'Ha! Bet that's put his nose out of joint. Being demoted, and by a woman too.'

'Let's say we've reached an amicable truce. But bear it in mind. It would be great to have you here. And you'd get a discount in the café.'

Frank shrugs. 'You're missing a trick here, you know. Up at Haworth they've got the sofa one of the Brontë sisters got consumpted and died on. And a hanky spotted with her blood. That's what this place needs. Never mind dusty feathers and books. Where's the bloodstained rug? The murder weapon? That'd bring the place to life.'

'It's not a murder weapon when it's a suicide.' Anna rubs her arms through her jacket. The temperature monitor is registering the lower end of what is recommended. A couple more radiators is what the place could do with, not gruesome mementoes.

'If it were suicide,' says Frank.

'I know you said there was speculation,' she says. 'There always is around sudden deaths.' She can understand the need to question the how and the why. To search for something tangible amid the helplessness of loss. She clears her throat. 'But the coroner was convinced it was joint suicide "while of unsound mind".'

'Aye, well, the unsound bit is true enough. Folk round here knew that Edie Harper were, what do you call it, "troubled". Not what they called it then, I can tell you. Wandering round the moors like a will-o'-the wisp in her underclothes, if you believe the tales. And there's them that claim her brother fathered her son.'

'It's been suggested,' she admits. 'But there's no evidence for it.'

'Hmm. Evidence is all very well. But there's as many theories about the goings-on up there as there are thistles in Bill Turner's bottom field. There's a mystery, see.' He taps his nose with one of his knotted fingers. 'People like a good mystery. But the board will have none of it.'

'Did your mother and father ever talk about the Harpers' deaths?'

'Mam said what went on in other folks' houses were none of our business. She were down at the farm by then. Married my father in 1934. He never talked of it neither. Mind, he wasn't much of a one for words on any subject. And Billy were long gone before it all happened. Went to seek his fortune in London. Well out of it, Mam said.'

On the other side of the room Edie's study is represented by a dusky-pink chaise-longue and her leather-topped desk, with its inkwell and pens and a pile of paper. On the wall above the desk an image of the moor around High Hob has been overprinted with extracts from her final novel. The complete document has never been found but she had sent a chapter to her editor in 1933, which is now in the library of an American university. We should get a facsimile of it, Anna thinks, that shouldn't be too hard to arrange. It would be better than just this scattering of lines taken out of context. She reads some of the sentences out loud:

'"The past had built walls around her. A prison stronger than his arms, fiercer than his passion. Mightier than the winds that battened her inside the house."

'"She knew there was a life for her without him. But she hadn't found it yet."'

'Not what you'd call a cheery tale,' says Frank behind her. 'About what you'd expect, mind, looking at her picture.' He nods over to the far wall, which is covered with photographs and framed

46

documents. One pair of photographs have been blown up and printed on poster-sized canvas. Edie Harper is sitting in a dimly lit room, one elbow resting on her desk, gazing through heavy-lidded eyes at an arched window, a pen poised in her hand. Charles is standing with his hand resting on a mounted globe. A handsome man, Anna thinks as she approaches the picture, although there is something about his half-closed eyes that she mistrusts. Or maybe it's the period of the photo; his slicked-back hair and his thin moustache above a sulky mouth that give him the appearance of a movie villain.

One of the framed documents is a typed letter from Charles to his publisher, in which he complains about the 'frankly ludicrous notion' that has been suggested as a plot line for his next book. He even threatens to kill off his hero if he doesn't get his way.

```
Garth is my creation. If I decide to let him
plunge to his death or be fatally wounded,
you will not be able to resurrect him. Do
not for a moment suppose that he can be
adopted and thinly disguised by another
writer. The public will not be fooled by
rehashed ideas and second-hand words. And
neither will my lawyers.
```

Next to the letter is a film poster from the 1970s, showing a muscled actor slashing his way through a jungle, beneath the banner: 'Garth Winter returns.' And then the report in the Bradford *Telegraph and Argus* from July 1936 that had caught her eye when she was first shown round.

TRAGIC DEATHS SHOCK
LITERARY WORLD

The well-known adventure writer Charles Harper and his sister and fellow author Edie Harper were found dead at their home, High Hob House above Oakenshaw village, early on Friday evening. They were discovered by Miss Harper's son Jasper and the Reverend Anthony Haste, vicar of St John's, Oakenshaw.

The young Mr Harper had just returned from his school in Derbyshire and had fortunately been driven home from Oakenshaw station by the vicar, otherwise he would have made the grim discovery on his own. He is said to be in shock and is temporarily in the care of Revd Haste. Tributes to the writers have been sent from as far away as the United States and France.

The cause of death has yet to be confirmed, although our reporter understands that the police are not looking for anyone else in connection with the deaths.

'"Not looking for anyone else",' reads Frank over her shoulder. 'No mention of who the young lad's father were or where he might be. Or that Charles Harper were a bit of a ladies' man, by all accounts, and who knows who he might have upset. There's too much that gets buried, hidden away. It ain't healthy.' He walks over to the window, peering out at the bare trees bowing in the wind. 'It's getting a mite wild and woolly out there. I'd best be making tracks.'

Anna follows him out into the yard. As he crosses the bridge a string of schoolchildren in bright yellow vests trail onto the cobbles. They are chattering in twos and threes, eyes on each other's hands and faces. Stop, Anna wants to tell them. Stop and look.

'At what, miss?'

At their age she wouldn't have seen it either. It had taken her a few days, but by the end of her first week she had become entranced by this hulk of long-gone industry cupped by the tranquil valley. The woods and river that have watched its heydays come and go and will still be there long after its stones have crumbled away. She is part of it now. Part of its continuing story. Even more of a reason to get the story right.

Back in the office she empties out the envelope that Frank gave her. There are twelve photographs. In one of them she recognises Frank's wife from the picture in his wallet. She is younger here, wearing a loose print dress, standing on the little bridge, the old Pavilion café visible over her shoulder. On the back are pencilled the words 'Ellen, Acker Water, 1962'.

The rest of the photographs are older. A shot of the front of the mill with a small kiosk under an awning advertising sweets for sale and another of a burly man standing against a striped background, his arms wrapped across his broad chest. The writing on the back says 'Mr Peters, The Pavilion, 1938(?)'. Anna compares it with the photo of Frank's wife. In that one the café is a plain drab colour, the stripes must have fallen out of fashion. The building itself had been pulled down in the early eighties.

Another photo catches her eye. It is black and white but she can imagine the colours. Stripes of ribbon spinning out from a maypole while a blur of girls in full skirts skip round. A man and a woman are watching, with a young boy between them. Distracted from the dancers his eyes stare directly at the camera. The sky is bright, almost overexposed as if there is too much light for the picture to hold.

It would look good on display, especially if it was blown up. She checks on the back: 'Maud, Arthur and Frank, Whit Monday 1950'. She wonders who took it.

The maypole triggers a memory. She has seen a box labelled 'Ribbons'. Might they be the maypole ribbons?

The box is on top of a high pile between the coat stand and a tall ornately carved bookcase jammed with box files and books.

She stands on an upturned plastic stacker box to reach it, steadying herself with one hand on top of the bookcase. Instead of the wooden surface she is expecting, her fingers brush against something textured. She stands on her tiptoes. A large flat box, thick with dust, is wedged inside the raised edges of the bookcase top. It is heavy but she is able to lift it over the scrolled edging that has hidden it from sight. She hugs it to her body as she steps down.

The box has 'Swintons, Shirts and Collars' etched in gold on the top. A sweet musty smell is released as she lifts the lid to reveal a leather-bound atlas of the world. As she takes it out the spine loosens and the pages splay open. A sheaf of typewritten sheets slip out. They are bound at the top left-hand corner with a metal clip. For a thrilling moment she hopes it might be part of Edie's lost novel. But the first sheet reads 'Shore to Shore and other poems by C. A. Harper.'

The next page has a dedication: 'For my beloved brother Matthew 1882–1928'. Matthew Harper is mentioned in Charles and Edie's biography, their older brother who died while travelling in South America. Charles Harper, a poet?

The first ten poems, printed one to a page, are collectively titled 'Shore to Shore', and chart the story of a man's life, from idyllic childhood to adulthood, through war service and travels in Asia and Africa. Was this Matthew Harper's story? Seen through the eyes of his adoring younger brother? The time period would fit, Charles himself had been too young to fight in the war. They include two short poems about a soldier's life, each two verses long, called 'Duty Done' and 'Happy Return'.

She flicks back to the title page. They are part of a three-poem section headed 'The Soldier', but the first one, 'Farewell to England', is missing. She reads the other two again. Charles's soldier talks of marching to victory 'With comrades brave, And fellows bold, For country and for God.' In 'Happy Return' the soldier is welcomed home by his family and praised as a hero, with just a passing reference – 'fellows dealt a poorer hand' – to all those who had died. The simple style and rhythm reminds her of something. She catches her breath.

Her copy of *Siblings in Arms* is on her desk. Its frontispiece, the two verses found with the Harpers' bodies, are identical in rhythm and meter to those of the 'Soldier' poems. This has to be 'Farewell to England', the missing poem from the sequence. The title transforms its meaning. It isn't a farewell to a cruel world as the writer steps into oblivion. The second verse:

> *So no adieus or wiedersehens*
> *No coward's voice be heard*
> *A silent touch, a vow unspoke*
> *More telling than a word*

A soldier saying a heartfelt goodbye to his country and his loved ones, and promising to return. Charles wrote it knowing that his brother did come home.

Frank's speculation about the suicides is still in her mind. And now this. She remembers Charles's letter to his publisher, his contempt for 'second-hand words' and 'rehashed ideas'. Edie had once said something similar. Anna flicks through the biography to a quote from Edie's 'Advice to New Women Writers': 'Only you can tell your story. Never settle for other voices speaking for you.'

The verses that comprised their suicide note, their supposed final words to the world, were torn from a pre-existing manuscript on a different subject altogether. 'Second-hand words', 'rehashed' to a new purpose, and in Edie's case, somebody else's words speaking for her.

The Harpers lived by their writing. Surely, when they decided to end their lives, they would have found between them the right words, written for the purpose, to say goodbye.

CHAPTER 5

Billy: 1932

Thursday afternoons Jasper had his piano lesson. A thin-faced man called Mr Planter rode up the path to the house on his bicycle, which he parked up by the wall with his cap on the handlebars. I'd watch from the stairs as Sally led him into the back parlour next to Charles's study. Jasper would be waiting on the piano stool, his face grim as a farm cat. Sally always shut the door tight behind her when she left them and Jasper would never speak about the horror of his lesson, but from the crashing sounds within, I could picture it: Jasper hunched over the piano, his fingers bashing away at the keys while Mr Planter wrung his hands and made polite suggestions on ways he could improve.

While Jasper was fighting with the piano I had musical appreciation with Edie. She would borrow Charles's gramophone but then selected records from her own collection. She listened from her desk while I lay on the sofa that she called her 'shays long'. Her perfume filled the room with the smell of dust and violets and made me want to sneeze. I'd wait for a loud bit of music, a clashing of cymbals, or a thundering voice if she was making us listen to opera, so that I could let it go.

One Thursday, towards the end of March, Edie told me she had a headache and our musical afternoon was cancelled.

'Go for a walk,' she suggested, wafting one hand as the other clutched at her forehead. 'Listen for the melodies in the birdsong. Consider the intonation of the wind.' I didn't need telling twice.

I had a few hours to myself for the first time that I could remember since I'd arrived. No Jasper to watch out for, no minding my Ps and Qs in front of Charles and Edie. I almost danced out of the room I felt that light. And I knew what I was going to do. I needed to see the Palace. Ma wasn't expecting to see me till my birthday, but she didn't even have to know I was there. I'd slip through like a shadow, just making sure it was all the same as I remembered it.

I put on the leather boots Livvy had handed me just two days back, saying, with barely moving lips, 'They were Master Jasper's. The missus says his feet have growed again and they've hardly been worn. You're to have 'em.'

They wrapped round my feet and ankles like gloves. The leather uppers of my clogs were stiff despite all their wear, but this stuff was soft as cloth. The laces took some working out, I was used to my clogs' single buckle. But I wasn't going to be beaten by a couple of bits of string and once I'd fastened them those boots were dandy.

And they showed something; showed that Billy Shaw was doing pretty well. Plus I could copy Jasper and slip my whittling knife down the side. Couldn't do that with clogs.

There was no sound from the parlour as my boots' thin soles swished soft across the hall tiles. Jasper and I had started a game a week or so back that I couldn't stop now even when I was in a hurry. You stepped on black tiles one day, white tiles the next. Today was a white tile day, which was easiest because of the border of white round the edge. I made it across with no one nosing their heads round doors to see what was going on.

On the moor top the buffeting wind snatched at my breath and pushed me back and forth. I imagined the Beast out there lying low among the heather. I prayed it wouldn't catch the scent of me

53

and that if it was nearby the giddiness of the wind would confuse its senses. When I turned down the path to the road the wind fell away and I almost fell with it. The silence hit me and it was like I could think straight for the first time in weeks. Something else had slipped away too as I left the moor – not just the noise of the place but the grip of it. As if that big sky and all it held, High Hob, the Harpers and the lurking Beast, had held me too, but I'd escaped. Then the silence broke and I heard the sound I'd been missing those past weeks, the rush of the river. Not as strong as it can be in the winter but loud enough and never giving up, and I raced headlong down the track to greet it.

I caught sight of the top dam, like a dark penny, and I laughed out loud as a stag and his family took flight not fifty yards ahead of me. The deer often used to spook me. I'd be walking along late in the day, minding my own, listening to the birds and the river and working out a way to get onto the Pav roof without Joseph Peters noticing, or adding up my takings from the weekend, and I'd see these bobbits of white moving about, appearing and disappearing. I'd give myself the willies thinking it was tree spirits or ghosts. Then they'd kick their legs and I'd know what I'd seen was the arse-ends of deer.

Halfway down the hill there's a bend in the road and when I rounded it I stopped. There was the Palace, its back wall to me, the triple rows of windows looking over the bottom dam. The water was like a dirty old rug today, with the sky drooping above. There'd be no trippers about, unless a special party or picnic had been arranged. Peggy would be at school and Ma and Maud would be baking ready for the weekend.

I crossed over to the dam and did my usual walk along its narrow stone rim, and didn't my boots look fine. When I reached the Palace wall I spread my palm flat on the rough gritstone. It was coarse as salt against my skin. Solid walls that hadn't tumbled or crumbled away for the lack of me. Ma and my sisters safe inside. I got a tight feeling in my chest thinking of Ma's face if she guessed how much

I suddenly wanted to not go back to High Hob. After everything I'd promised. Even if I showed her my boots and explained I was just a shadow, not really here at all.

'What're you waiting for?'

I spun round.

Jasper was standing bang in the middle of the track, legs apart as if he bloomin' owned it. A half-eaten apple in his hand, the binoculars hanging from his neck.

'I've never been to a palace before. You'll have to tell me how to behave. Don't want to get sent to the Tower or have my head chopped off.'

'What happened to your lesson?' I asked. His cheeks were pink and his chest was heaving, though he was trying to act all steady. He must have run like the clappers to catch me up.

He sniffed. 'Mr Planter's too clumsy to be a piano teacher. Got his fingers trapped under the lid.' He threw the apple core into the water. 'A couple of them might be broken. I won't be having any more lessons for a while.' He jerked his head towards the mill. 'Come on then. Let's go.'

I belted across the back of the mill to catch him up. At least having Jasper with me showed I was being a good companion and all. Educating him in the ways of the Palace and the valley and the woods. Mebbes Ma would be so pleased to see me that she wouldn't mind at all that I'd come back so soon.

The yard was empty but I could hear a familiar tune coming from over the river in the Pavilion field. David often whistled about packing up his old kitbag when he was working. We'd leave off facing Ma for a bit while I showed Jasper the dragons.

On busy days the field would be covered with people sitting and lying about with their baskets and picnic boxes and rugs. But today there was only the green grass and in the middle, before you got to the Pav, the giant frame of the swingboats and David with pots of paint at his feet.

He raised his eyebrows when he saw me, like he'd been wondering all along where I'd got to.

'Just giving 'em a touch up,' he grunted, pointing his red-tipped brush at one of the boats. 'This'un's taken a right battering. Bloody hooligans barging 'em. Got no respect.'

There were four swings. They used to be all one colour, a sort of mucky yellow. Then David took over the maintenance jobs and got the idea of turning them into dragons. He'd swirled the sides with red and green and at the front each one had staring eyes and flaming nostrils. When they were swinging and the colours and patterns blurred they were magical.

'Your mother'll be glad you're still wanting to hobnob with us down here.' David dabbed crimson paint onto the dragon's tongue. 'That they haven't had your head filled with airy-fairy ways.'

Jasper coughed.

David scrunched up his eyes.

'What's this then?' he asked.

'This is Jasper,' I said. 'He lives up at High Hob as well.'

'Right,' David said. 'Well, pair of you stay clear of the boats for the next couple of hours. Don't want the paint smearing.' He eyed me up and down, lingering on the high shine of my boots. 'I wouldn't want you spoiling your finery.'

Ma was in the kitchen at the back of the tea rooms, bent over a row of pie cases laid out on the stone shelf, spooning in the fillings. I could smell beef and kidney and that rich gravy she did, thick with onions. I was starving; it had been hours since breakfast and there'd been no eggs cos the delivery hadn't come up from Oakenshaw. 'And no explanation neither,' Livvy had moaned. 'Do they think folks up here live on fresh air?'

'Ma,' I said.

'Billy?' Her eyes went wide and she held the ladle in the air as if she was ready to fight someone off with it. 'What are you doing back?' she asked. 'Is everything all right?'

'It's fine. Everything's fine,' I gabbled. She mustn't know about my fears and doubts and how close I was to begging her to let me stay. 'I'm being a good companion. I'm being one right now even.' I paused for a breath. She wasn't looking at me though, she was watching Jasper, and she still had the ladle in her hand.

'Pleased to meet you, Mrs Shaw.' I hardly knew Jasper's voice, it was that polite, as he stepped forward. 'I hope Billy isn't in trouble. It was my idea to come down. He's talked so much about the Palace. I wanted to see it for myself.'

Ma's lips tweaked but it wasn't her usual warm smile. 'I'm very pleased to meet you too, Jasper.' Then she gave a soft shake of her head. 'Come here, our Billy.'

I was round the counter in a flash and she fair picked me up her hug was that strong. Over her shoulder I could see Jasper. He was filching raisins from one of the big jars, but he was watching us too. And he wasn't making a joke of it either.

'These pies'll be ready in an hour,' Ma said when she let go. 'When are they expecting you back up at the house?' She frowned. 'You're not missing your lessons, are you?'

'It's our nature study time.' The fib rolled off Jasper's tongue as easily as it would have stumbled on mine. Though his eyes gave him away, a quick double blink, so quick you'd miss it, if you weren't watching for it. 'We have to observe the native flora and fauna ...' He paused and I thought perhaps his imagination had failed him but then he added, 'And look for signs of spring. We don't get them as much up on the moor, you see, with not so much growing there.'

Ma nodded, though with another twitch of her mouth that this time was a smile. She could see through any lie, could Ma, which is why I'd given up on them so quick. 'Well so long as you won't be in trouble, either of you.' She gave me her warning look. 'I don't want bad word getting back to Mr Nathaniel.'

I couldn't tell her that Charles, who had probably driven Mr Planter to the doctor's surgery, and Edie, having a lie-down with a damp hanky on her forehead, wouldn't even notice we were gone. Then I remembered Edie's words as I left. 'Miss Harper said in particular I was to listen out for the birds and the intonation of the wind.'

'Well you go and do that then.' She dipped her ladle back into the pie filling, which was our signal to be out of her way.

Jasper had spent weeks showing me his world up on the moor, and now it was my turn to be the guide. But as we went round, although nothing had changed, I was seeing it anew, as if through his eyes. Or maybe my eyes had got infected by the Harpers and I wasn't seeing stuff like Billy Shaw any more. The bunting, though it was newly hung, was limp and faded and when we peered through the window of the skating rink shed all was dust and drab. Jasper just shrugged as if he hadn't expected any different and didn't even bother to challenge me when I said, 'It's bright enough when it's filled with trippers. You'll see.'

We did a circuit of the bottom dam and then down to the river and over the stepping stones back to the Pavilion. It would have been a grand day for the swings if only the paint had been dry. There were dippers on the water and I pointed out the small yellow flowers on the banking which were aconites and the bunches of stiff leaves that would be bluebells come May. Jasper said very little, but at least he didn't throw anything at the dippers or trample on the flowers just for the hell of it.

We still had time to spare when we got back to the Palace, so I led him up the stairs to the dance hall. The gramophone hadn't been brought down from the Big House yet, so there was nothing to see but the polished floor. We took off our boots and played slides across the wooden boards. I beat Jasper by a foot and a half but he said I'd had more practice so that was no surprise. On the next go he hurled himself so hard that he barged me against one of the pillars and knocked the air out of me. Then he said we were quits. When we were putting our boots back on he showed me the scuff on the back of one of mine where he'd scraped it on a rock, when they were his.

'Who's that?' He was up at the window, on the yard side. I joined him and peered down. Mr Nathaniel was standing beside the old 'Prentice House. He had his head down so all I could see was the black circle of his hat. His hands were clasped behind his back. He was with two other men in long black coats who had their arms behind them too. All three nodding, like blackbirds with their wings tucked in, bobbing for worms. Then out stepped Lizzie from the 'Prentice House with a grim-faced lass a bit older than her, neither of them talking or taking any notice of the group of men. Mr Nathaniel lifted his head and spread his arms towards the Palace.

'Give us a song!' Jasper shouted.

I got ready to hide if they looked up, but the window was shut tight and they were too far down to hear. Then Lizzie lifted her head. Her eyes squinted and I waved. If she did see us she didn't let on.

'Do you know her?' Jasper asked. I swear I didn't blush but he poked me in the ribs. 'You're sweet on her, aren't you?'

'Don't be daft.' Last thing I wanted was Jasper knowing how much Lizzie meant to me. I turned away and was already half a step ahead as I shouted, 'Race you to the pies' and belted for the stairs. He jostled me all the way down, so we were red in the face and bruised when we leaped the last two steps onto the first-floor landing. He gave me a final push that almost landed me on top of Mr Nathaniel as he appeared at the top of the stairs.

'Billy Shaw!'

I'd never seen him so surprised. You'd think I was a sheep that had appeared on the landing, not a lad who'd lived here all his life.

'Sorry, sir. I'm just back for a visit. A real quick one.'

'Nature study,' hissed Jasper from behind me but I didn't see how we could play that one seeing as we were inside the Palace where the only nature was the bottled fruit Ma put in her sweet pies.

Mr Nathaniel's fingers played a scale in the air that would have been a joy to Mr Planter. 'Couldn't keep away, could you? I was just telling these gentlemen this place is a veritable magnet. Folk just can't resist it.' He squinted at Jasper. 'And this'll be young Mr Harper. How are you liking the companion I found for you? Doing all right, is he?'

Jasper nodded.

'Excellent, excellent. Well, keep up the good work. Next time I see you, Billy, I'll expect some Latin. You are having Latin, aren't you? Verbs and conjugations?'

I bit my lip. We were having more than enough learning, from Charles at least. But this was the first I'd heard of expectations of Latin.

'Amo, amas, amat,' piped up Jasper. Which he later told me was all the Latin he remembered from school. Lizzie, who'd been tucked in quiet by the wall all this time, put her hand over her mouth, not quick enough to hide her giggle.

'Indeed.' Mr Nathaniel rubbed his hands together. 'Well, gentlemen, let us continue our perambulations. You will appreciate the full investment potential when you have seen the upper floor. This way please.'

He led the black coats up the stairs we had tumbled down. The grim-faced lass was close behind, saying, 'Follow me, Elizabeth.' Lizzie paid her no heed, or at least not before she'd skipped over and squeezed my hand. 'Look at you, Billy,' she said. Then she cocked her head as if she'd heard a tread on the stair and skipped off again. And that was it, but it had me grinning till Jasper ribbed me again and pushed past me through the tea room door.

I wasn't going to mention to Ma about Mr Nathaniel but as she scrubbed at the baking trays in the sink she asked if we'd seen him and if we'd been polite to the gentlemen, who, if all went well, were going to help pay for his plans for the Palace.

'What plans?' A new and horrible idea filled my head. 'He's not for selling up, is he?'

'He'd no more sell the Palace,' she said, 'than hire Lizzie out to the circus. Though this place isn't pulling in as much money as it did a few years back.' She sighed. 'Mrs Potter thinks it's but a hobby to him. It makes nothing compared to his farms and her father's mills, and it takes some looking after.' She rubbed at a tray with her brush. 'He says the Palace has to pay its own way. He can't be letting it drain his other interests dry.' She frowned at a stubborn spot on the metal and went at it again with the brush.

I'd have to speak to Mr Nathaniel soon. Remind him that though I was living on the top of the hill for now it wasn't going to be for ever. I didn't want him forgetting those ideas I'd given him, or worse, finding another assistant before I came back.

But, as if she could read my mind, Ma said, 'We're all doing our best to keep from under his feet. He's very busy, not just with the Palace, there's problems over at one of the mills in Nelson and with Lizzie still getting over her fever—'

'Lizzie's ill?' I asked, my mouth half full of the meat and gravy pie.

'She's past the worst of it, though it was touch and go for a while. Comes down for a walk most days with her father or that friend of hers. Recuperation, he calls it.' Ma rolled her eyes. 'She'll be right as rain in a week or so and back at school.'

I knew I'd been away too long, only five weeks but already there were new plans afoot for the Palace and Lizzie had nearly died, all without me knowing a thing of it.

'Should have given her one of your pies, Mrs Shaw,' Jasper said. 'That would have sorted her. They're champion.' He grew this smile I've never seen before, but which turned him into one of those children you see in advertisements with words like 'Wholesome' and 'Good for You' written below.

Ma thanked him but added to me, 'So mind you're not mithering him.'

'I just want to let him know I can help,' I said, wiping the gravy from my chin.

'Best help you could give him is let him see you're making the most of the opportunity he's given you.' Her eyes darted quick to Jasper who was bent over the remains of his pie. I nodded to let her know I understood, and it was the sealing of my promises all over again.

I'd hoped to stay to see Maud who was over at Chambers' farm fetching eggs, and Peggy who'd be back from school before long. But Ma said wouldn't they be expecting us back at High Hob for tea and she hoped the pies hadn't spoiled our appetites. She packed us up a bag of fresh scones, 'Enough for all of you up there.' By the size of the bag she must have reckoned on there being a small army, or at least a football team living at High Hob.

'Those blokes he was showing round. They looked shifty to me,' said Jasper as we climbed back up the path out of the valley. He was picking at his fingernails, examining flakes of what looked like green paint. I swear I hadn't left him alone near them swingboats. David would make merry hell if his artwork was damaged. Maybe he'd blame them hooligans he'd been ranting about.

'He was acting all jolly,' Jasper continued, 'but really he was try-ing to give you a secret message. That stuff about us learning Latin. It was a code. They've threatened to kill him if he doesn't hand over the deeds to the Palace and your ma's secret pastry recipe.' He was grinning, enjoying his story.

They'd looked to me the sort of men who might have plenty of money to spare, with their fine coats and high-polished shoes. Enough money to turn the Palace into a concert hall or an animal park. Mr Nathaniel's cogitations on my brilliant ideas were being distracted by chattering blackbirds that didn't know a single stone or tile of the place. I kicked out at a rock, scuffing the toe of my boot.

'So what was Lizzie doing there?' I asked.

'She was trying to warn you too.' He paused. 'Did she pass you a piece of paper with a message on it when she squeezed your hand?'

'No,' I said, and this time I did blush but he was too busy with his theory about what was really going on at the Palace; a theory that included African diamond smugglers and a torture chamber and a pit of snakes under the mill. That afternoon, crossing the empty moor under a cloud-streaked sky, it sounded a load of non-sense, but better than the probable truth which was that life at the Palace was changing and moving on, in spite of me not being there.

CHAPTER 6

Anna: November

'This is quite a find.' Erica Walker's finger rests on the manuscript of Charles Harper's poems. 'They're not going to knock Ted Hughes off his perch or raise clamours for a posthumous laureateship for Charles.' Her mouth tweaks a brief smile. 'But as you say, a glimpse of another side of the man and of his relationship with his brother. Their mother died when Charles and Edie were very young. Even though Matthew would have been a teenager at the time, it's not too surprising that the siblings had such a strong bond. We'll need to make space in one of the display cases. Lovely to see your work bearing fruit already.' She raises her cup of coffee as a toast. They are having their meeting in the café rather than the office, on Erica's insistence that 'We might as well be cosy.'

Anna had been kept busy over the half-term holiday week. The cold crisp weather had brought out steady streams of hardy picnickers who dotted the grassy areas on either side of the river with blankets and folding chairs, while the length of the river and the woods rang with the shouts of children and the barking of dogs. There were queues for ice cream from the temporary kiosk set up by a local dairy farmer who knew the autumn chill wouldn't deter her customers, queues for the portaloo behind the café and even queues to get into the museum at the end of the week, when the fair weather turned to rain. Throughout it all Charles Harper's poems had nagged at her. 'A gunner's last retort.' It was assumed that Edie had written the suicide note. Her name was signed first after the typewritten text, and she was known to have written poetry, some of which was published in magazines in Paris when she lived there in the early twenties. The more Anna thought about it, the less likely it seemed that Edie would have chosen that poem, those words, as her final goodbye to the world.

'Don't you agree that it casts a different light on things?' she asks now. 'Knowing where the verse originated from.' When Erica doesn't reply, she adds, 'What happened to the note itself? Do we have it in the archive?'

Erica places both hands round her coffee mug. Her skin is veined and liver-spotted. Two heavy silver rings on her right hand, but none on her left. Mid-sixties, Anna has decided, younger than Frank but not by much.

'It's in the possession of a collector in Boston, New England,' Erica says. 'Morbid man. Specialises in the things. He bought it from the family. Money actually changed hands.' She tuts. 'We contacted him years ago with the idea of having a copy of it on display. He sent a photograph, but we chose not to use it: the board decided it didn't fit with the rest of the exhibition. It was too intimate, bordered on disrespectful. Also, he wanted a fee.'

'The photo's in the archive?'

'It will be. Somewhere.' Erica sighs. 'I agree that the note found with Charles and Edie does appear to have come from this,' she waves her hand over the poems, 'and I don't disagree that knowing its context, it was an odd choice. But, Anna,' she places her hand on the table between them and for a moment Anna thinks she is going to take hold of her wrist, 'it all happened nearly eighty years ago. It's rather late to go delving into the how, what and whys. It's not as if anyone could be questioned now about anything that happened back then.' She takes a long drink of her coffee. Avoiding my eyes, Anna thinks. Is she protecting someone? After all this time?

'I've drafted an article for the *Halifax Courier*,' Anna says. 'Not about the suicide note,' she adds as Erica's eyes widen. 'But people will be interested in the discovery of the poems. One of the nationals might pick it up. Or the *Yorkshire Post*, at least. It could boost our visitor numbers over the winter.'

'Indeed.' Erica breaks off a piece of flapjack and pops it into her mouth.

'The poems support the idea that Charles's novels were inspired by his brother's adventures,' Anna continues. 'Charles himself hadn't travelled outside Europe.'

Erica nods. 'Other than their years in Paris neither of them went far from home. Edie, of course, was limited once she'd had Jasper and Charles no doubt had his own reasons for squirrelling himself away up here. Bunty Baxendale hints that he broke a string of hearts in Paris and London. Married women, perhaps. She makes several references to her and Charles's "unmatched intimacy". Her husband was the youngest son of an earl.' She drains her coffee mug. 'No one would bat an eyelid these days, of course, illegitimate children, extramarital affairs. But back then, *très scandaleuse* in any language. There's no knowing if Charles changed his ways when he was here.'

'A motive,' Anna says.

'Sorry?'

'What if Edie and Charles didn't leave that note, and someone else did? To make it look like suicide? What if Charles upset one of the locals? Had an affair with a wife, or a daughter? Drove someone to murderous revenge.'

'Anna!' Erica's finely plucked eyebrows arch sharply. 'I didn't have you down as a fan of soap opera or melodrama.'

'It happens in real life too,' Anna says, suspicious of Erica's quick dismissal of her suggestion.

'Not at Ackerdean it doesn't. Tittle-tattle and speculation will do nothing for our cause.'

'Our cause?'

'Protecting and promoting Charles and Edie's legacy and the many-layered history of our valley.' Erica raps the table with her fist. 'Now, let's get back to business. Your email outlining your proposals for the mill.' She pulls an iPad from her handbag and flips open the cover. 'You mention interactive displays, temporary exhibitions ...'

'All of which would help "the cause",' Anna says. 'Not everyone who walks through the woods goes into the mill, especially if they have been there before and feel there is nothing new to see. There is so much more we could do. It comes down to space, in the end.'

'Well, isn't that the cry everywhere,' Erica interrupts. 'It's a small world. There are too many of us. We all need more space.'

A bit off the point, Anna thinks, but continues on her theme. 'We do have the space, on the first and second floors.'

'It can't be done.' Erica taps the screen.

'The cost, I know.' She isn't giving up. 'And the access issues. But there are lifts that can be installed in buildings like this. We have enough space for it.'

'So now we do have enough space.'

'For a lift, yes.' She pushes a sheet of paper towards Erica. 'I got a couple of quotes, just broad figures to start with. They'd have to do a proper survey.'

'You shouldn't be getting quotes for things without consulting the board first.' Erica pushes the sheet away.

Anna clenches her fist under the table. 'You employed me to "widen the public profile of the collections and improve their accessibility",' she quotes from her job description. 'This could be a landmark heritage centre. Obviously there are costs involved and there would be an impact on car parking but I've had a couple of thoughts ...'

Erica raises her hands.

'No more thoughts please. This isn't a question of logistics. Or even finance. Our capital fund would cover,' she waves her hand at the figures on the sheet, 'all this. But our benefactor didn't want the upper floors to be used.'

'Why not?'

'There was a problem. An accident.' A small crease forms between her arched brows. 'On the stairs, perhaps. I don't know the details. It was in the mid-thirties.' She snaps the cover over her iPad and puts it back in her bag. 'Perhaps someone threatened to sue. Personal injury claims aren't a modern invention. Nathaniel Potter had the top floors closed off. There were wooden boards across the stairs for years.'

An accident, 'on the stairs, perhaps'. For someone who runs a heritage centre, Erica Walker has an astonishing lack of curiosity about the past. Could the accident have something to do with the Harpers? Was it connected to their deaths?

'It was a long time ago. Almost eighty years.' Anna echoes Erica's earlier words. 'Unless it's a specific clause in the bequest, can't we move on?'

'I hoped you understood.' Erica's voice is weighted with disappointment. 'This place isn't just about what we want. Nathaniel Potter left his estate in our trust. It was his wish that the upper floors were not to be opened and I for one am prepared to fight for that wish.'

A fight? Anna holds up her hands. 'The people who lived and worked here are at the heart of what I want to do. I'm not proposing that we disrespect their memory. But we need to use the resource we have to its fullest. Fill it with noise and life, like it was for the first hundred years of its history.'

Erica stands up. 'I'm meeting with the rest of the board on Thursday. I'll show them your proposals and will forward their responses.'

'I want to do a presentation to them.' Anna gets to her feet as well. 'I'm required to deliver regular comprehensive reports to the board. To all of the board.'

'I'll put it to them. Though finding a date might be tricky this close to Christmas.'

It's the beginning of November, Anna thinks. 'I can manage any evening,' she says. 'Between now and Christmas Eve.'

'I must warn you,' Erica continues as if she hasn't heard, 'that the majority will be with me on this one.' She pauses. 'I'd be grateful if you would hold back on any publicity about Charles's poems until I've spoken to the board about that too. We'll need to agree on the wording of any press release. Make sure we're all singing from the same sheet.'

Anna needs a walk. She heads up the unmade road that runs behind her cottage. It's been a dry morning and although the road is soggy from last week's rain, she doesn't have to skip over the small rivers that often run down it. Just past the small, empty car park the road forks into a rough path that winds down to the river upstream from the millpond and a crossing fancifully marked on the 'Ackerdean Walks' leaflet as the Wishing Bridge. To the right a bridleway leads up through the woods towards the old road to Haworth. She stops at the fork and looks back at the mill, breathing in the stillness and quiet. The blank-eyed windows of the back wall are giving nothing away. Holding on to its secrets as tightly as Erica Walker. As tightly too as Frank Chambers who, despite his fondness for sharing stories about his family, seems to be holding something back. Something about his uncle Billy, born at the mill but sent up to the Harpers, part of their household until just before they died. Was the mill closed up before or after that? Was Billy the key?

She turns back to her walk but a loud rustling in the bushes ahead stops her in her tracks. Something is fighting its way through. With a final flurry of twigs and leaves a black bundle of fur hurtles out. Mouth open, ears flapping, tongue lolling, eyes fixed on Anna. A dog in a cartoon dog gallop, more comical than threatening, but still she steps out of its path. It swerves away at the same time and scrabbles to a halt.

69

'Ruby, come here!'

A figure is approaching at speed down the bridleway. A runner, long legs stretching on the downhill sprint, eyes fixed on the dog. Dark-red hair curls under a blue beanie patterned with snowflakes, white headphone leads connect to a device strapped to her arm.

'Ruby, here now!'

The dog hesitates, turns its face from Anna to the runner and back again. The woman slows to a walk and taps her hip. 'Biskie.' The dog gallops back and is grabbed by its collar and attached to the lead hooked at the woman's waist.

'I'm so sorry.' She pulls out her earbuds as the dog leaps and twists on the lead. 'Get down! She's just a bit lively.' She bites her lower lip. 'God, I used to hate it when dog owners said that to me. I'll be saying "she's only playing" next.' She smiles again. 'Although actually she is.'

'It's OK.' Anna returns the smile. 'I'm the new custodian at the heritage centre. I'm getting used to random encounters with dogs. I've met more of them in the last month than I have in the whole of my life, and plenty of them have been less well-behaved than yours.'

'I can believe it. It's Dog Central round here at times. I'm Sam. Sam Klein,' the woman continues. 'I'm staying up at High Hob, the Harpers' old place.'

'The crime writer?' Anna says and the woman nods.

'That's me.'

I must be the only book-reading person in the country, Anna thinks, who didn't know Sam Klein is a woman. 'Anna Sallis,' she says. 'What's it like up at High Hob these days?'

'Bit more stripped down than when the Harpers had it.' Sam grins. 'Not quite so Bohemian. But there are some traces of the Harpers, or of Jasper Harper, at least. He left his mark. And there's still a feel about the place.' She shrugs. 'It's a good place for me to write. Have you settled in OK at the mill?'

'I'm getting there. Though I find myself talking out loud a lot when I'm on my own. I might have to get a cat.' Ruby barks and Anna laughs.

'I know what you mean. Weeks can go by and the only soul I've chatted to is a four-legged one.' Sam ruffles the fur on the dog's head. 'You should pop up to High Hob sometime. We could both enjoy the luxury of conversing with another human being and you could have a good explore of the house. I'm free this Saturday, if you fancy it.'

'That would be great,' Anna replies. 'I'd love to see inside.' And with a crime writer too, she thinks, who might have an insight into the hows and whys of suspicious deaths. 'I'll walk up. Make a day of it.' She glances up the hillside.

'It's a fair trek. An hour, hour and a half maybe. You know where to find us?'

'I've got maps in the office. I could be up at yours for mid-morning.'

'Perfect. We'll see you then. Come on, Roobs.' Sam whistles and with a wave of her hand begins a steady jog down the path to the river, the dog lolloping at her side.

A feel about the place. Anna considers Sam's words and wonders if High Hob will be more generous with its secrets than the mill.

CHAPTER 7

Billy: 1932

Eleven birthdays I'd had at the Palace. Ma always made it special. No chores, whatever day of the week it was, and my choice of cake and butties for tea down by the river if it wasn't raining, which it almost never was.

This year I wanted ham and mustard sandwiches and Ma's burnt-sugar cake with the sticky icing. When I woke up with the sunlight bright on my face, my first thought was the cake. Would Ma remember it was my favourite? Last thing she had said was, 'See you on your birthday' and I'd kept to my word and not been down since. The butties weren't a problem. There was always ham. But Ma needed to know what type of cake to make and left to her own devices she might do me a tea loaf, which is fine most days but no good for a birthday. I knelt up on the window seat, closed my eyes and sent a big hard thought over the top of the roof and down into the valley: burnt sugar, burnt sugar, burnt sugar.

No one seemed to care tuppence up here that it was my birth-day. I wasn't too surprised. Jasper reckoned that though he'd once had a trip to the zoo and another year had gone to a fancy hotel for dinner, Charles and Edie had sometimes forgotten his birthday altogether. Yesterday I'd asked Charles for leave to go down to the Palace after my lessons today. He'd said I was to ask Edie and I must do whatever she decided, 'as must we all.'

Her study, when I went in, was dusky-dark, with the curtains drawn and the only light the oil lamp at her desk. She'd said 'of course', in that voice that made me wonder if she'd properly heard. She was being all writerly, with ink on her fingers and her hair pinned up but managing mostly to be falling down.

When I told Jasper he looked like he was going to ask if he could come too, opening his mouth but closing it before the words came out. Then he said he was going to go and make rubbings of the cup and ring marks out on the rocks near the reservoir. I told him I'd bring back a piece of cake and he did one of his flat smiles and it got my dander up cos maybe he was mocking my ma. But as usual I didn't pick a fight, although I was finding it harder all the time. If he was just another lad at school we'd have had a fair old scrap by now and we'd know how we stood. But I weren't sure that Jasper even knew how to fight fair.

As I knelt at the window, my cake wishes sailing across the heather, I told myself I wasn't bothered that none of the Harpers cared about my birthday. They weren't my family. It just went to show we knew how to do some things better down at the Palace. Once lessons were out of the way, today would be how my birthday should be. Mr Nathaniel would be at the Palace and not distracted by business or by being tortured by diamond smugglers. He'd say, 'Make way, make way,' when I marched over to the swingboats for my birthday ride. I was going to choose the boat David had been painting with the big flaming red tongue. And Lizzie would be there. She'd be done recuperating now, but the sun was shining and even if she wasn't on an errand she might come down after school. I wanted to make her smile with a daft joke and maybe she'd squeeze my hand again and just for a moment nothing and no one else would matter. I sent a big strong 'Come to the Palace, Lizzie' out of the window too, and hoped it would find its way to the Big House where she was probably still fast asleep.

I wet my head with water from the jug I'd fetched up the night before and dragged my hair back with my comb, so in the mirror it looked dark and sleek, not its usually mousy brush. Both of my pairs of trousers were mud-splattered and peat-stained and one had a rip in the backside. Ma would have a fit. We had to be clean and smart on our birthdays. I didn't get that bit. If I got to choose what to eat I should be able to choose what to wear. But there was no point even starting that one with Ma.

I put on the unripped pair and tucked in my shirt that was still white on account of me not having worn it since I came up here. Both the elbows on my pullover were worn thin but there were no actual holes and I turned the cuffs under to hide the raggedy edges. I didn't want Ma faffing with needle and thread and making me stand still on my birthday.

I was all but out of the door when I remembered the catapult I'd finished making the day before. It was champion. Hit on target nearly every time. Jasper had shown me how he cut strips of rubber from the inner tube of the old bicycle in the outhouse. You had to cut it straight and get the length just right. I had the perfect stick, forked at the right angle with grooves notched on the prongs to make the rubber fit snug. Jasper traded me a square of leather from his collection for sitting the stone in, in return for me not telling Livvy that I'd seen him nosing in the chest of drawers in her room. The leather was soft as butter, finer even than my boots, and I wondered if any of Charles's shoes were missing their tongues.

When I passed Jasper's room I heard the rustling of paper, which meant he was sketching. He could spend hours at it, drawing the Beast mainly but machines as well with wings or enormous wheels. He missed lots of mealtimes that way. I'd have to call him down later. We had spellings with Charles at nine and then 'The Rise of Prussia', which unlike breakfast couldn't be skipped.

Livvy shooed me out of the kitchen with a plate of bread and butter and an apple. Said I was under her feet and if I wasn't to be disappointed later I'd best stay away now. I took it as a warning that she was making me a birthday treat, and hoped it wouldn't be scones. I ate my breakfast sitting on one of the stones in the garden, though it was cold and the apple did nothing to warm me. I'd just chucked the core high over one of the stumpy trees when Edie called me from the open window of her room.

'William? What on earth are you doing out there? You'll catch your death. Come to my study, I need to speak with you.' I headed back inside and hopped my way across the hall. Black squares today. I had to cross the double row of white tiles at the edge all in one go, so I landed in the room with a hop and a skip that made Edie declare, 'Goodness, why do you boys never just walk anywhere?'

The room smelled of flowers, though the big vase on her desk was empty. The curtains were all pulled back and the window at the front of the house was open from where she'd called me, but the light didn't seem to reach in and the room was its usual gloomy grey.

Edie's hands were pressed together in front of her chest. 'Happy birthday, William,' she said. For a minute, I feared she was going to start clapping. Being twelve is something, but I didn't want a round of applause.

'Thank you,' I said. Thinking that was most likely all, I stepped back towards the door and was reckoning how to best navigate the white strip again when she raised her hand.

'Your present.' She picked up a flat parcel from her desk and thrust it towards me.

I unwrapped the tissue paper. Inside was a silver bookmark in the shape of a leaf. I'd seen it on her desk many times. I mumbled my thanks.

'I should have waited until the party,' she said.

'Party?'

'You mean Jasper didn't tell you? I told him it was to be a surprise and for once he must have listened.' She took hold of my hand,

75

closing my fingers around the bookmark. Her fingers were cool and so light and soft that I couldn't believe there were bones inside. 'You've made such a difference already, William. Two months and not a single complaint from anyone in the village and nothing of consequence from the neighbours.' She sighed. 'Of course, Mrs Trimmer over at that scruffy farm has her usual grumbles but she'd be hard pressed to lay the blame for all her troubles at Jasper's door.' She stepped back. 'Your mother will be arriving about half-past three.'

'My mother?' I had turned into a parrot and all I could do was repeat what she said.

'Of course,' said Edie. 'I am so keen to meet her. We mothers must show solidarity, whatever other differences life has presented us with.'

'I was going down to the Palace.' My voice sounded tiny in the cold flowery room. 'I asked and everything.'

A small frown appeared between Edie's eyebrows. 'Well it's all arranged now. So let's have a jolly good time.' Her eyes fixed on me and I could see that nothing could be done.

'I'll walk up with her. I'll go down to the Palace after my lessons.' My voice faltered. The word 'Palace' stuck on my tongue. It was like I was talking about a fairy-tale place that I'd invented or dreamed about.

Edie was shaking her head.

'There's no need. Charles will fetch her up in the car.' She glanced out at the shadowed garden outside and shivered. 'We couldn't expect her to walk on a day like this. Not carrying a cake and who knows what else besides.'

I wasn't expecting there would be much else besides. Ma usually made me a vest or pullover. Last year Maud and Peggy had knitted me a pair of socks. They'd made one each, so they didn't quite match, Maud's being all tightly stitched and proper and Peggy's having odd loops of wool and a hole in the ankle.

'Are my sisters coming too?' I asked, not thinking about my

sisters at all but of the picnic by the river and the Easter bunting and the dragon with the long red tongue.

'I expect so. Why not? The more the merrier. I did invite Mr Potter. I thought he might want to see how you're getting along. But he begged other, family, commitments. So we'll just have to soldier on without him.' She clapped her hands now, a quick sharp sound. 'So shoo! Go and get ready for your outing.'

An outing? So I *was* going to the Palace.

Edie was already half-turned towards her desk, leaning with one hand on the back of her chair, as if the effort of talking to me had worn her out. 'There are to be no classroom lessons today. Charles is taking you and Jasper to visit the man at the garage in Oakenshaw, who has a rather splendid engine. Doesn't that sound delightful?'

She didn't wait for a reply, just made a fluttering movement in the air with her hand. 'Run along. Find Jasper. Charles will want to leave straight after breakfast and he hates to be kept waiting.'

The engine was all right. It was big, anyway, and loud when Mr Procter fired it up. Mr Procter had a shed full of engines but the big one was his favourite. He called it 'Lady Bella'.

'Got her from a man with military connections.' He tapped his nose and winked at Charles. 'Diesel power, six cylinders. I'm going to hitch her up to that chassis.' He pointed to a long piece of machinery with bright orange and red wheels. One of his lads was painting them slowly and carefully. 'Ex-army,' he said, and I didn't know if he meant the chassis or the 'prentice.

'Aye, she's a beauty.' He patted the engine like she was an old dairy cow. 'She's going to be the finest omnibus these valleys have ever seen. We'll be running trips to France before the year's out.'

Charles asked questions about horsepower and camshafts and negotiating bends. Jasper begged a ride on the trip to France. Mr Procter said he would send word when it was ready to leave. Then we went to the Drovers' Rest where Charles said it was only right

77

and proper to celebrate my birthday. We sat outside and he had beer and we had lemonade.

'So, boys,' Charles said. 'What do you think of Borneo?'

I slurped at my drink and shifted my eyes to Jasper but he looked as clueless as me.

'Is it an engine?' I asked.

Charles shook his head. 'Dear Lord. Maybe Garth should go back to Brazil, at least everyone's heard of Brazil.'

He didn't usually talk about his books and I hadn't read any of them yet but I knew bits from what Jasper had shared. Garth Winter hunted for lost treasure in faraway places and fought villains, like the diamond smugglers Jasper was so fond of and Big Game hunters who didn't play fair.

'So Borneo's a place then?' I couldn't remember it from the globe.

'Got it in one, Billy-boy,' Charles said. 'A dark steamy place full of wild beasts and exotic women.'

'What sort of beasts?' Jasper was suddenly alert.

'Apes,' said Charles. 'Great orange apes with the faces of men and arms that hang to the floor. Orang-utan, they call them. Means "man of the forest". I've got a splendid recording of one. I fancy pitting old Garth against a pack of them. What do you think?'

We spent the next hour coming up with adventures and dangers that Garth could face with the jungle apes. Neither of them mocked me for my Yorkshire vowels and Jasper said my idea of having Garth swim across a lake of carnivorous fish was brilliant. It was the longest time the three of us had spent together without there being a row. Charles didn't even shout at Jasper when he knocked over his half-full glass showing us how Garth could swing across the jungle paths from tree to tree on the back of an unsuspecting ape.

But the best part of the trip was the car ride in Charles's Crossley Tourer. There and back we raced so fast we were beating the wind. I wanted to halloo but Charles and Jasper were sitting so still and steady. Jasper even managed to look bored. So I pretended to be as calm about it as they were. But my bones were singing.

When we got back Jasper hied off to his room, with something bundled under his jacket. I went off to the kitchen to scavenge for food. I was lifting lids in the pantry when I remembered Ma. Edie had said half past three, which must be about now cos I was starving. As I went back through to the hall with a handful of crackers, I could hear Charles's voice coming from Edie's room. He sounded bored but with a whine that turned it nasty.

'I thought I'd done my bit for the day. Time for the mothers to take over. I do have work to do, you know.'

Edie's voice was quieter and I couldn't make out her reply.

As I climbed the stairs Charles strode out into the hall fastening his scarf round his neck. He ignored me as he jammed on his hat and headed for the front door, slamming it behind him.

When I reached the first-floor landing Edie's voice called up from below. 'Don't go disappearing anywhere, boys. William's mother will be here shortly.'

Jasper's bedroom door was shut tight. It might as well have had a big 'Keep Out' sign on the front. I went up the stairs to my own room. The cuff of my shirt was smeared with engine oil and the patch on my trouser leg where Jasper's lemonade had spilled was sticky. I cleaned myself up as best I could. Combed my hair back down. My pullover hid the oil, so Ma need never know. I scrubbed at the lemonade mark with a hanky but that only made it grubby. I would just have to hope she didn't notice it, or at least didn't make a fuss.

'What you doing?' Jasper had walked in without even knocking at the door. He'd throw a fit if I tried that in his room. Not that I wanted to go in. The smell of long-dead animals was enough to put anyone off. Sally point-blank refused to go in there to clean.

'Aw, leave it,' he said, prodding a finger at the damp patch on my trousers. 'It's your birthday. You can't be scolded on your birthday. It's not allowed.' He sat down on the bed and picked up the silver leaf bookmark, which lay there on its wrappings. He flicked the leaf's tip and dropped it back on the bed, picking up my catapult instead. His had broken a week ago when one of the forks snapped off.

'Haven't got you a present,' he turned the catty over in his hands, 'but I'll let you set the trap later.'

'Ta.' He never usually let me set the trap, or even be the first to check it.

'Wish there were orang-utans in Yorkshire,' he said, jumping up. Over at the window, he pressed his face against the glass. 'Bright orange fur. I bet they glow in the dark. We could hunt them at night. They wouldn't see us but we'd see them. *Pwang!* He turned and pretended to fire the catty.

'Charles said they're twice the size of a human,' I reminded him. 'Stones would only tickle 'em.'

'We'd drive them into a rage,' Jasper countered. 'Until they fell into our pit full of barbed spikes.' He jabbed at the air with the forked stick. 'They'd squeal like dying pigs.' He began a high-pitched keening that made my bones tingle. It was all I could do to stop myself covering my ears.

He hopped down from the window seat. 'I'm going to fetch my drawing things.'

I took his place at the window, glad for the silence now he'd gone. I could see across to the trees at the bottom of the path where Charles parked the Crossley. Jasper came back in and settled himself on the floor. His pencil scratched softly on the paper as I watched and watched out of the window. It was half an hour at least before the red and black of the car slid into the shadows.

Figures emerged from the jumble of the trees and trailed in a procession up the hill. Charles and Ma in front, him carrying a box and her stepping smartly beside in her best coat and the hat with the felt flowers on the brim that she wore for church. Behind them Peggy and Maud were hugging themselves inside their coats. They looked so tiny with the moor spread wide around them. I imagined the Beast in its winged form swooping out of the sky and carrying them off.

80

I left Jasper lying on the rug sketching. He grunted when I passed. He was colouring in a huge orange figure. It was tearing a tree trunk apart in its hands.

I was waiting at the bottom of the stairs when the front door opened and Charles showed Ma and the girls inside. It was still a black tiles day. Ma would give me one of her looks if I hopscotched across the floor to them. I gritted my teeth. It was just a daft game, after all. I stepped out across the hallway, heedless of the black and white, black and white beneath my feet.

'Billy!' Ma's cheeks were all rosy from the wind and from the thrill of the car ride, no doubt. Peggy and Maud had their heads bowed but were sneaking glances round the hall. Peggy's eyes were wide as an owl's.

Ma kissed my forehead and eyed me up and down.

'You're looking well, our Billy.' Then, 'Oh, and happy birthday.' As if it was a strange place to be saying it. Which, of course, it was.

'Happy birthday, Billy.' My sisters stepped forward and kissed me. I'd never known the like from Maud before. Then there was a waft of violets and lemon and in came Edie. She was bright and brittle Edie this afternoon. A small sharp smile and bursts of brisk chatter. She offered one hand to Ma and with the other played with the string of pearls that slid against the silky green fabric of her dress. It was the first time I'd seen her without her grey cardigan. Her bare arms were the same creamy white as her pearls, but covered with soft downy hair and goose-flesh.

'Welcome,' she said. 'Come on through.' Instead of turning to her study she led us into the parlour. As well as the piano standing against one wall, there were some bow-legged chairs and a matching sofa, set next to a small table. A low fire burned in the grate and a laden coal scuttle stood by.

'I'll leave you to catch up,' Edie said. 'Livvy will come through when we're ready for tea.'

The door had scarce closed when Maud hissed, 'Billy, what you done to your hair? You've turned into a right dandy.'

Peggy was straight up at the mantel playing with a pair of china figures like they were dolls. Ma spat on her hanky and advanced towards my legs.

'I don't know, our Billy,' she rubbed hard at the trouser cloth, 'you could get yourself mucky in a snowdrift.' Peggy and Maud started laughing and so did I.

It was grand cos it was like it always was, excepting we weren't at the Palace. It felt so warm and cosy having them all huddled close around me. My eyes went a mite teary but I couldn't let my sisters see so I wiped my nose with the back of my sleeve and blinked my eyes while they were half hid. Ma yelped and batted at my arm, which made my sisters laugh even more.

'What cake have you made?' I asked.

'Burnt sugar, of course. Your favourite.'

So that was all right.

'You mind you only have your fair share,' Maud said. 'It might be your birthday and you might be twelve but we had to be up at the crack this morning to get the day's work done so we could come up this afternoon. Been busy as flies round a cowpat, we have. Thank goodness for Mr Harper and his motor car.'

'It were like we were flying,' said Peggy. 'Ma nearly lost her hat.'

Ma wanted to know how my schooling was going so I told her about our lessons with Charles and how it wasn't just reading and writing and sums, but history as well, and lives of the scientists and geography (that being Borneo and the orang-utans). I told her about Edie's books on art and poetry, but not that she'd giving up on teaching us.

Ma kept scolding me for not saying Mr Harper and Miss Harper but I told her it was no good me trying. I explained how Edie kept trying to call me William. Maud laughed. 'You're no William,' she said. 'Not even with your new dandy hair. You're Billy born and Billy you'll always be.' And I grinned, cos that's how it was.

Then Ma told me about the goings-on at the Palace. How David had fallen out with Joseph Peters over payment for the repair work

David had done on the Pavilion. Joseph, who rented the place in the summer and served up chops and sausages, swore he'd not asked for it to be done. And how the tea rooms had sold out of fruit teacakes early last Saturday and there'd been a near riot of Rochdale Methodists who came in starving after a hike. Peggy said Maud and Arthur Chambers were walking out and old Mrs Chambers had heard the distant chiming of wedding bells. Maud clamped her hand over Peggy's mouth and told her not to gab about something she knew nowt about. But her cheeks were flushed berry-red so I reckoned there was a seed of truth in it.

Ma was smiling her little smile and not saying yea or nay to the story. Instead she reached into her bag.

'Here's a present for you, Billy love. I'm hoping it'll still fit you, what with all the growing you've been doing.'

It was a new pullover, striped with bands of different-coloured wool.

'You'll be needing it,' she said. 'Being out on the moor in all weathers and with the way the wind hurtles around this place.' She held it up against my front. 'That should do you right for a year or more. But you go careful with those cuffs. I don't want this one spoiling. I don't expect anyone up here's got time for mending your clothes.' She didn't need to mention my ragged sleeves for me to know she'd seen them.

Maud pulled out a parcel too.

'Made it ourselves,' she said as she handed it over.

'Maud did the special 'broidery,' Peggy piped up. 'But I did the other stitching and it's mostly even too.'

The feel of it wasn't clothes, so thank the Lord no more of their saggy socks. It was a book, the pages cut and folded from the rolls of mill paper still stored in the old 'Prentice House. Stitched between a cover of green worsted with the word BIRDS embroidered in red wool.

'It's for you to record the names of all the birds and when you've seen them and the like,' said Maud.

'Miss Offat said it were a grand idea,' added Peggy.

'It's champion,' I said.

There was a knock on the door and in came Livvy pushing her trolley, set with the best blue china. Ma's burnt-sugar cake had pride of place in the middle. There were smaller plates below stacked with butties and a rocky crag of Livvy's dreaded scones. Edie and Jasper followed her in.

Edie called, 'Shall I be mother?' and started pouring out the tea.

Ma seemed right at home there in the parlour chatting about the weather with Edie, though she kept patting at her hair, checking its pins were still in place, and every now and then she'd touch the cameo brooch pinned to her chest as if reminding herself she'd put it on. She frowned at Peggy when she squealed at something Jasper whispered. She'd have frowned harder still if she'd heard what he'd said. Edie asked Ma all sorts of questions about her work at the Palace till Ma looked fair flustered but pleased as well. I'd never heard her talk about herself so much before.

Mebbes this birthday wasn't so bad after all. I could always bob down to the Palace later on.

Except that later on, after we'd stuffed our faces with ham and bread and half the cake and our bellies were aching with the weight of Livvy's scones, Ma said it was getting on and, no, I'd no need to walk them back. They'd be fine, them knowing the place like the backs of their hands.

But Edie said, 'Nonsense, it's getting dark, of course Charles will drive you home.' Then it was all of a hurry cos Charles was standing in the hall saying it was no trouble but he had a man to see and if they wanted to go they had to leave right now.

Then they were gone. My cheek still damp from Ma's kiss and the scent of Maud's lavender water hanging in the air. I'd never even had a chance to show Peggy the golden plover nest hiding in the tussocks of cottongrass near the path behind the house.

I stayed at the open door till the little procession of Charles, Ma and my sisters had wound its way down the hill like an adder with four heads, and disappeared into the trees.

When I went back into the parlour Jasper was lying in one of the chairs. He had his feet up on the arm, his grubby socks resting on my new pullover. The big blue plate was empty. There was a hunk of cake in his gob and sticky crumbs on his cheeks. He must've had to ram it all in to make sure he'd had it all by the time I got back.

'You could've left me some,' I said. He grinned, and his teeth were all sponge and brown icing. He mumbled something but that was all cake too. My bird book was splayed open on the floor, a puddle of spilled tea seeping into the cover. I was certain I'd left it on the table. I bent to pick it up and Jasper took the chance to rub his sticky fingers in my hair.

'Get off,' I said.

'Or else?' He'd swallowed the last lump of cake now. His eyes had those dancing lights in them that he gets when he's all up for it. 'Set your mother on me, will you?'

'Don't you say anything about my ma.'

'Your big sister then. Maud.' He drew her name out long like a stretch of toffee. 'I bet she could throw a couple of good punches with those big arms of hers.'

I'd held back from scrapping with him so long. Now he had to go and spoil everything on my birthday when I hadn't wanted to spend it at High Hob anyway. I hurled myself at him. He wasn't expecting it, or not so fast anyhow. He pushed back and we both fell against the table and onto the floor. I grabbed his hair cos it was the easiest part of him to get hold of. His fists made sharp little jabs at my ribs. I tried to throw him off but he was heavier and had me pinned.

His eyes were blazing now, those dancing lights turned to dark fire. He raised himself up as if to get height for his next punch. I took my chance and kneed him in the knackers. He yelled and crunched up and I scrambled to my feet.

'Dirty bloody trick,' he groaned.

My shirt was torn and the cuff hung loose.

'You're the dirty one,' I said. 'And shut up about my family. You're only jealous cos you've not got a proper one of your own.'

'You bloody sod,' he wheezed but he was back on his feet and he lunged at me again, throwing me onto the chair, and holding me down with his knee on my chest. Before I knew it he'd got something round my neck and yanked it tight. I could smell a dry rubberyness. His fist held the stick of the catapult tight to the side of my head.

'Gerroff!'

He twisted it tighter, his face close up to mine.

'Jealous of you?' he growled. 'You big mummy's boy.'

The rubber stretched and pulled against my throat, one of the prongs of the fork sharp behind my ear. My lungs were empty and I couldn't take a breath. My left arm was pinned but with my right I grabbed at the tightening band and held it away from my neck, and heaved in some air. I worked up a fat ball of spit in my mouth and spat full in his face.

'Boys!'

Jasper was yanked away, his fingers releasing their hold on the catty gut. As I scrambled for it, pulling it over my head, I heard the slap of a hand hitting flesh, and a sharp yelp. Edie was holding Jasper by his wrist, glaring at his face, at the scarlet stain on his cheek. The string of her pearls hung broken round her neck, its beads pooling at her feet. Without taking her eyes off Jasper she reached over and grabbed me too.

'Animals.' She was breathing heavy as we were, her nostrils flaring, her whole face tense and hard. Her grip was like an iron clamp. I could feel bruises blossoming on my wrist beneath her fingers. 'I will not have it.' There was spittle at the corners of her mouth. I dared not move though my arm was going numb. Jasper was motionless too, his eyes dulled. 'You will control yourselves in this house. Do you hear me? Now tidy this up.' She released her grip. 'I want it spotless and Livvy is not to give you a jot of help.'

She watched us in silence as we picked up cushions and anti-macassars and placed them back where they belonged. I began to gather up the pearls until she hissed, 'Leave them!' She might have been holding a whip, or a beating stick, for the fear she put in us, but all she needed was that face that threatened worse.

As we worked I ignored the ache at my wrist and my throat, but I swore in fierce words in my head that I'd never speak to Jasper Harper again. I'd go back to the Palace. Go back to my old life and sod High Hob and its fancy parlour and Edie with her pearls and stupid bloody Jasper and the stupid bloody Beast.

CHAPTER 8

Anna: November

Anna emerges from the shelter of the trees as the bridleway meets the old Haworth road that runs along the top of the valley from Sowley. A wooden sign indicates the footpath, over a stile in the wall and up a hillside of pale grass and ragged clumps of bracken.

As she climbs higher gusts of wind steer her along the path, whipping her hair across her face, strands catching in her mouth. The scrubby field opens onto the moor through the broken teeth of a dry stone wall. She reaches a plateau and stops to pull on a bobble hat, smoothing her hair under its edges. From here she can see to the furthest reaches of the moor, wind turbines in one direction and the haze of hills to the other. She realises how restricted her view has been for the last few months. Trevor Stanhope had warned her about 'valley fever'.

'Get yerself up on the tops once in a while, lass, or you'll be forgetting there's life beyond these valley walls.'

It had reminded her of the description in Edie's novel of the walls that imprisoned her narrator. Had Edie felt trapped up on the moor? Bound by the weather, motherhood, her frustrations as a writer? Would she really have chosen suicide as her only way out?

She checks her map. High Hob is a tiny square in a puddle of contour lines. Most of the climb is behind her now. The grey sheen of cloud shifts and scars of silver light appear in the sky as she clambers up another rise.

High Hob is perched on a ridge a short distance away. With its church-like gables it looks out of place in the wild landscape, as if a whirlwind has lifted it from a sleepy village and dumped it there.

A Scooby-Doo house, she hears Dan say in her head. He would have been up for a mystery. Would have listened to her and Frank's theories and added a few of his own. She tucks an escaped lock of hair back under her hat. You're on your own now, Velma, she reminds herself, and heads up the narrow path through the heather to the house.

The rear of the building is in shadow. She follows a wall and a sparse hawthorn hedge round to a gate that opens onto a gravel path. The grey stone of the front of the house is bathed in a cold light that silvers the rows of windows. Like bared teeth, she thinks.

Sam opens the door when Anna is halfway up the path. She is wearing jeans and an oversized thick wool jumper, a pair of glasses perch on top of her head. Ruby charges out, almost knocking Anna off her feet.

'Down, Ruby!' Sam calls. 'You found us OK then. I've put the kettle on.'

The entrance hall is windowless and dim, its shadows untouched by the narrow shaft of daylight through the open door. Sam flicks a light switch but the glow from a heavily shaded overhead bulb makes little difference.

'Sorry,' she says. 'I don't notice the dark so much when I'm here on my own. Must have been horribly gloomy when the Harpers had it. They had oil lamps right till the end. It wasn't hooked up to the mains until their cousin did a refurb after the war.' She leads Anna across chequered tiles to a spacious kitchen that showed little sign of being lived in other than a bunch of keys and a laptop on the wooden table. No pictures or knick-knacks, only a couple of takeout menus blu-tacked to the wall and a crocheted throw on an armchair in the corner. A strip of mullioned windows watches over the moorland Anna has just crossed, her view of it partially blocked by an enormous paper ball lampshade. The main feature is a large cream and black range; Anna can feel its heat across the room. As Sam retrieves a metal teapot from a cupboard the chipped enamel kettle sitting on the hotplate begins to whistle.

'I'm curious about your job,' Sam says when they are sitting at the table with mugs of tea and a plate of biscuits. 'I've not met a custodian before.'

Anna groans. 'Me neither. I suppose they wanted a title that would cover everything, not just managing the collection but supervising the volunteers and dealing with the public. It sounds so stuffy though and doesn't sum up what I'm trying to do.'

'Which is?'

'Create order out of chaos, for a start. There's some great stuff in there but it's never been properly organised. I'm making some progress with that, but I want to make it more accessible too. Bring the place back to life.' She explains about Erica's insistence on keeping the upper floors closed.

'What a waste,' Sam says. 'I'd presumed there was a major structural problem – a hole in the floor or a collapsed staircase. If something happened in the thirties that was bad enough to close the place down, you'd think it would be public knowledge. Have you had a search online?'

Anna nods. 'I didn't find anything, and there's nothing obvious in the archive. I'm going to check the local papers in the library. If I can shed light on Nathaniel Potter's decision it could help my case when I put it to the Ackerdean Board. Although I think nothing less than a visitation from the spirit of the man himself will change Erica's mind.'

Sam grins. 'Nowt so queer as folk, eh?' She drains her mug, and raises it in the air. 'To revolution down at t'mill. But for now, are you ready for the tour?'

'Edie's study?' They are standing in a long narrow room off the hallway. Anna recognises the arch of the window from the photograph at the mill.

'Yes,' says Sam. 'Not many of the original furnishings are left though. All the good pieces are down at the mill and the rest has been replaced with modern stuff over time. I think this dining table might date back to Charles and Edie's time, and that chair by the fire. The company that rent the house out still have some sort of family link to the Harpers, but they've made no attempt to preserve it as a shrine.'

'Do you work in here?'

'God no. The fire's a bugger to light and the shape of the room means it takes for ever to get warm. I'd never get started on a morning. Don't know how Edie managed it. She must have had more than mere mortal blood in her veins. Either that or a set of top quality thermal underwear.'

Bookshelves line one wall. They are empty except for a single row.

'They're among the few remaining genuine Harper artefacts in the house,' Sam says as Anna steps over to take a closer look. 'Not valuable enough to be sold off, maybe they hoped they'd inspire future tenants. I like to imagine that Edie or Charles might have once held them and read them.'

Anna takes down a red-bound copy of *Wuthering Heights*. The cloth cover is worn at the edges, the title on the front embossed in gold. A printed label on the first page reads 'Ex Libris Edina Harper'. The pages have a well-thumbed softness. As she replaces the book her eyes follow the spines across the shelf. They are mainly series of classics in matching covers: blue for Dickens, dark red for the Brontës, and at the end volumes of poetry in a variety of bindings. She takes the poetry books from the shelf one by one.

The anthologies and collected poems of Coleridge, Longfellow and Ezra Pound all have Edie's 'Ex Libris' labels. There is no label inside a slim volume of Rabindranath Tagore's haikus, the first page bears only the title 'Fireflies' and the author's name. She turns it over.

For Beebee
Forever yours
Dec '35

The words are scrawled in looping letters across the top corner. A present to Edie or Charles? But which of them was 'Beebee'? Anna takes a seat on the sofa and begins to turn the pages. Each page contains a single haiku. She is about to close the book when it falls open to where a dried sprig of heather has been used as a marker. The paper is stained from the now grey buds. The haiku is about autumn. Underneath, three lines have been added in the same looped script as the dedication:

My heart's but a leaf
Falling through the air to turn
Upon your sweet breath

'Found something interesting?' Sam asks.

Anna holds out the book. 'A present for someone called "Beebee". It's dated December 1935 so presumably it was given to either Charles or Edie. I wonder who it was from? Whoever it was they sound pretty smitten.'

Sam reads the poem and turns back to the dedication. 'It could be a pet name for either of them, I suppose. But the book's in Edie's study. And she was the poetic one. Can't see anyone trying to woo Charles with poetry.'

Anna hesitates. 'They might. If they knew he was a poet himself.' She tells Sam about Charles's poems, and, encouraged by her interest, explains about the missing poem and the suicide note.

'There's supposed to be a photograph of the note in the archive but I can't find it. I emailed the guy who bought the original asking if he could send me a scanned picture. He's being very possessive about it. Worried that we might try and use it without paying him an extortionate fee. I'm going to keep pestering him. I want to see the original note alongside the poems.'

Sam slides down onto the sofa beside her. 'So instead of writing a heartfelt message to their loved ones before they topped themselves they just used an appropriate poem that Charles had written earlier?'

'But that's my point. It's not even appropriate. It's called "Farewell to England" and it's about a soldier, probably the Harpers' older brother Matthew, saying goodbye before going off to war. We're not talking Wilfred Owen or Siegfried Sassoon here. There's no profound sadness on the loss and waste of life. In the context of the other two poems it's very much about a hero going off on a big adventure. In the next poem he comes home wreathed in glory.'

'He doesn't die?'

'Nope. Matthew fought in the First World War, but he died years later, of a fever in South America. The final poem in Charles's collection, called "Release", is about a man's death.' She closes her eyes, recalling the lines. '"His body stilled, no longer flamed, with passion nor with fevered blood". If they had to choose a poem for their death note at least that one would have been on the right subject.'

'Whoever chose the poem,' says Sam, 'thought it was appropriate because it was about saying goodbye, but didn't bother reading it properly?'

Anna nods. 'Charles knew exactly what the poem was about, and I can't believe Edie would put her name to something that didn't represent exactly what she wanted to say. Saying "farewell cruel world" with a not very good piece of war poetry. It's just not her style.' She is surprised by her own passion.

'It would mean someone forged their signatures,' says Sam. 'Did whatever they could to make it look like suicide.'

'And why would they do that unless they were involved in the Harper's deaths?'

'A cold case murder,' says Sam. 'My favourite kind.'

'Erica's not such a fan. She was very reluctant for me to investigate it any further.'

'Well that's suspicious for a start. Even more reason to dig around. So, Sherlock, who are your suspects?'

'Suspects?'

'The "someone else" who chose the poem, forged the signatures. Did the deed.' Sam gestures to the book of haikus. 'A secret lover, or a secret lover's husband. Always a good bet.'

'You might be right.' Anna repeats what Erica told her about Charles's past affairs and her own speculation that he may have become involved with someone locally. 'Finding out who sent the haiku book and who to would be a start. Though "Beebee" and a date isn't much to go on.' She pauses. 'Bunty Baxendale was a BB.'

'The woman who wrote the biography?'

Anna nods. 'She was a close friend. She hints in her book that there was something special between her and Charles. She calls it "an unmatched intimacy". I suppose the book could have been dedicated to her.' She rubs her hands together, to try to create some warmth. 'But that wouldn't explain why it was still here. And Beebee could just as easily stand for Beautiful Baby.'

'Or Bashful Batchelor,' says Sam with a grin. 'C'mon, I told you we'd freeze in here. Let's move on. It might get our brain cells working better too.'

Before she leaves the room Anna crosses to the arched window. The world outside is a slub of browns and mauves, dotted with pale tussocks of old grass. She can make out a dark band of trees in the distance. She tries to imagine Edie Harper sitting in her chair, poised as she is in the photograph, pen raised as if waiting to catch a word or phrase. It must have been so lonely up here. Did they have guests? Secret assignations? A visitor who had reason enough to want both the writers dead?

'This is my den.' Sam opens a door on the other side of the hall. The room contains a large modern desk and chair and an electric heater and has a large window overlooking the front garden. The wall by the desk is covered with cuttings from magazines and newspapers. As Anna draws closer she realises they are all accounts of crimes, murders and unusual deaths.

'You know about these things,' Anna says. 'Bodies, weapons, locations. Had you ever wondered if it could have been anything other than suicide?'

'I'm always up for questioning accepted stories,' says Sam. 'But until you brought up the whole suicide note/poem thing I'd assumed this one was cut and dried. The coroner sounded pretty convinced.' She gestures to one of the clippings on the wall. 'You'll have seen that, I expect.'

It's a photocopy of a newspaper report about the Harpers. Not the brief notice on display in the museum. This is a longer article from the *Yorkshire Post*, dated a couple of weeks after the deaths.

'No, I haven't seen it before. Where did you find it?'

'Would you believe it was in the welcome pack I got from the letting company? Talk about trying to create an atmosphere.'

DOUBLE SUICIDE TRAGEDY

A verdict of suicide by mutual agreement, while of unsound mind, was returned yesterday at the inquest into the deaths of the authors Charles Harper and Edie Harper who were found at their home, High Hob House, Oakenshaw on the evening of Friday July 17th.

Dr Thomas Darin, who was called to the house when the tragedy was discovered, said that the brother and sister were found in Mr Harper's study, both with fatal gunshot wounds, Miss Harper lying in her brother's arms. A gun was discovered between their bodies along with a note signed by them both. Dr Darin surmised that they had both been dead at least twelve hours before they were found.

When questioned Dr Darin confirmed that Miss Harper had been prescribed various medications for her anxiety and insomnia over several years, including morphia and chloral hydrate. He had on occasion cautioned Mr Harper about his heavy drinking and further, on his recommendation, Mr Harper had recently undergone sessions of hypnosis to treat his melancholia. Evidence submitted by a business associate suggests that Mr Harper had complex financial concerns.

Dr M. S. Wells, pathologist, gave evidence that the time that had elapsed before their bodies were found did not allow for an accurate measure of their blood alcohol levels at the time of death. He reported however that 1/12th of a grain of morphia was found in Miss Harper's stomach.

The coroner summing up declared it was a tragic story of two highly talented people destroyed by a mutual tendency to melancholia and anxiety, and a dependence on alcohol and drugs. Both had died from gunshot wounds, Miss Harper to her right temple and Mr Harper to the throat. Only one gun was found at the scene. The position of the bodies and the gun indicated that Mr Harper had died first.

The jury after deliberating for three quarters of an hour returned a verdict that Mr and Miss Harper both died from self-inflicted wounds and that the acts were committed by mutual agreement.

'"Suicide by mutual agreement",' Sam reads. 'As if they shook hands on it. Makes it sound almost cosy and sensible.' She glances round the room. 'It must have made a horrible mess. This carpet's vile, but I hate to think what stains it's covering up.'

'Does it not feel creepy?' The hairs on Anna's arms had hackled as she read the report. 'Being alone up here. Knowing that they died in this room. Don't you find yourself checking over your shoulder at the slightest noise? Leaving all the lights on. Avoiding shadowy corners.'

'Stop it. I've been fine up till now, thank you very much.' Sam laughs. 'I'm not a big believer in ghosts. What's dead, stays dead. Though I must admit sometimes ...'

'Go on.'

'It's an old house. It creaks, it groans, especially at night. The usual stuff. But yes, OK, I do sometimes let Ruby sleep on my bed. Though how much use she'd be if the spirits of Edie and Charles decided to have a wander I don't know. Now come on before we both get too spooked to explore upstairs.'

On the top landing Sam pushes open a door with frosted glass panes. 'Note the delightful 1970s avocado bathroom suite that someone thoughtfully replaced the original fittings with.'

'Nice.' Anna takes in the two toothbrushes in the holder over the sink, the beard trimmer on one of the shelves. Anna doesn't feel she knows Sam well enough to ask who her house-guest is.

At the end of the corridor Sam opens a door to reveal a narrow staircase. 'The other rooms on this floor were bedrooms but they're just blank spaces now. No clues as to who slept where. This is where it gets interesting. Come on up.'

They reach a small landing with a door on either side. Sam opens the door on the right.

The room is in the gabled roof, the ceiling sloping down from a high peak in the middle to about five feet high at the sides. A dormer window looks out across the moor to the rooftops of Oakenshaw in the distance.

Three of the walls are painted white, marked in places with the grey bloom of damp; the fourth is covered with a mural. A dark scene of jagged rocks topped by a crescent moon. In the foreground a wild creature, orange and shaggy, rears up on its hind legs, the two halves of an uprooted tree grasped in its hands. Its fanged jaws are wide, howling at the moon. Its eyes picked out with red. Two small figures are poised beneath it, brandishing weapons.

Anna kneels by the picture and touches it. The paint is a thick dulled gloss.

'Jasper Harper,' says Sam. 'See, he's signed it.' The initials JH are daubed at the bottom, above a symbol in red, a triangle with two horizontal lines radiating out from each side and two smaller upturned triangles above. 'This was probably his bedroom.'

'Up in the attic?'

'Isn't that how they liked their children in those days? Out of the way.' Sam peers at the painting. 'I wonder who the figures represent?'

'There was another boy,' Anna says.

Sam looks at her in surprise.

'A local boy who came to live here. As a companion for Jasper. He was tutored along with him. Though that must have stopped when Jasper was sent off to school.'

'Was he here when the Harpers died?'

'Apparently not. Though I haven't got an exact date for when he left.'

'Put him on your suspect list,' says Sam. 'He may have come back.'

'He must have had an alibi.'

'Or maybe in all the excitement he was forgotten about. His family quick to say he was elsewhere. He could have been harbouring all sorts of resentments if he was brought up here and then kicked out when he was no longer needed. Don't suppose his initials were BB, were they?'

'Not quite. Which could be a blessing. He was my neighbour Frank Chambers' uncle.'

'Ah, Mr Chambers,' says Sam. 'Ruby took a dislike to his dog one day when we were out running. They had a big ruckus in his yard. He told me I needed to learn to control my dog and called me a couple of choice names. I managed to keep my temper up to the point when he threatened Roobs with a stick.'

'Frank was going to hit Ruby?'

Sam made a 'who knows' face. 'He wasn't that coherent, or that steady on his feet. Think we'd picked a bad time.' She makes quote marks in the air with her fingers. 'I take the longer route now, further up the hill.'

She tilts her head at the painting. 'What do you reckon the big creature is? Some sort of bear? A wolf?'

'Or an ape.' Anna points to the creature's human-like fingers. 'King Kong came out in the early thirties. Maybe Jasper was taken to see it.' She sits back on her heels. 'Whatever it is, I don't fancy those boys' chances against it with a catapult and a sharp stick.'

CHAPTER 9

Billy: 1932

I stayed. Though part of me wanted to run back to the Palace and tell Ma it was no good, I didn't want to learn to be a gentleman if it meant putting up with the brooding threat of Jasper, Edie's different faces and different moods and Charles not seeming to care enough about any of it. I stayed. Not cos Jasper ever said sorry, cos he didn't. Neither did Edie. And not cos of the painting I found on my wall when I went to bed that night.

I'd made my mind up before I even saw it, as I headed up the stairs cradling my bruised wrist. I was going to show them all. Mr Nathaniel was right. This was my big chance. When I pictured my life in the future, away from all this, it wasn't as a shop boy in Sowley or as a hand in a mill. It was me looking down from somewhere high up, a fancy balcony maybe, at my kingdom, the best entertainment emporium in England. And though I'd admit it to no one, I wanted Lizzie Potter to be by my side. I knew that wasn't going to happen till I'd hoicked myself up a few rungs closer to her and her family. This was the one chance I had to learn the stuff I needed to hobnob with the best of them. Charles might not be the greatest teacher in the world, Jasper was far from an ideal schoolmate and Edie was no substitute for Ma. But if I just kept that picture in my head – me and Lizzie on the balcony of Shaw's Pleasure Palace surrounded by bunting and pennants and crowds of laughing cheering trippers – I reckoned it would be enough to see me through.

I knew something was up when I reached the landing, before I'd even opened the door. A smell that didn't belong to bedrooms, that took me back to Mr Procter's garage and his oil cans and barrels of fuel. What had Jasper been doing all that time I was busy with Ma and the girls in the parlour? The door swung open in the usual way and my bed and cupboard were as I'd left them. But the back wall had changed.

I thought my eyes were playing tricks, that the lamplight was casting strange shadows. But as I drew nearer the image on the wall came clear. It was me and Jasper fighting the Beast, me with my catty and him with a sword. The Beast was stretched up on its hind legs and its fur was the shiny orange of the wheels in Mr Procter's garage, its eyes a matching glossy red. Jasper must have had the paint pots hidden under his coat as we sat and drank our lemonade at the Drovers'. I was impressed. Though my arm still hurt like hell and Jasper was still to blame.

Next morning was Saturday and when Jasper said 'Coming to set the trap then?' I went along. It was better than staying in the house, with Edie lurking around in who knows what state.

We didn't talk till we got to the rocks he called the Stag Stones. One of them, Hound's Head Rock, was our main lookout post. The top of the rock stuck out, like the nose of a dog sniffing over to the dark cleft that marked Ackerdean. Jasper got out his chisel and picked up a rock for a hammer. I expected it would be his initials he'd carve on the Hound's cheek, but instead he made the triangles and lines of the Beast face he'd signed his painting with.

When he'd finished he rolled up his sleeve to his elbow. A faint band of purple and blue ringed his lower arm. He said, 'Show me yours,' and I did and it was worse. It didn't make things right, but at least I was closer now to knowing what he was capable of. There'd been a split second while he was tightening that catty band round my neck when I'd seen his eyes. They were blank, no excitement or fear or anger. It was like he wasn't there at all.

It was a while before we went back down to the Palace. I kept away deliberate. This time my promise was to myself. Next time I went back I wouldn't be the old Billy Shaw. I'd show them all, Palace and High Hob, what I had the makings of.

I worked so hard at my lessons that Jasper got to kicking me every time I raised my hand. I paid no heed. We worked our way through the monarchies of Europe, the rise and fall of empires and myths of the Greeks and Romans, as well as algebra and trigonometry. I listened as hard to the way Charles and Edie spoke as I did to what they said. Sometimes my head felt as if it was bursting and I couldn't remember what I'd learned and what I was trying to forget and then I was glad of the release when we left the house and headed onto the moor.

Outside lessons, in the late afternoon and early evening as the days grew longer, and every weekend, we lived on that moor. We owned it, like I'd once owned the Palace. Our territory stretched from the new reservoir out at Walthorpe back past High Hob to the opposite horizon where, from the jumble of stones that Jasper said was an old Druid church, you could see the chimneys of Halifax.

Not even the rain stopped us, though the soft ground turned sodden, with a joyous squelch as it sucked and released our feet. Once, in a lashing storm, we crouched for shelter under an over-hang of red rock that Jasper called the Oxtongue. Suddenly he grabbed my arm. He'd seen something shifting in the rain. Then it loomed at us. A great big gurning face. We both lurched back and I banged my head against the rock as a great fat sheep did a skip and disappeared back into the grey.

Sometimes it was like me and Jasper were each other's shadow, chasing each other short and tall across the day. Mostly that suited me fine, but there were times when I wanted to be alone, with my own thoughts, without his butting in. Even when he wasn't talking, just by being there, he was loud. Though since our scrap something had shifted between us. He jibed me less, his prods and kicks, though they didn't stop, were less sharp. I liked to think it was because I'd fought back, but more likely he was bored or he'd realised that he was better off with me there, as companion, audience, scapegoat, than not. At the very least I was there to share his obsession with the Beast. Though with no new sightings or reports of attacks I began to have doubts. If it was out there wouldn't we have seen some sign of it by now?

Jasper spent weeks collecting animal dung for evidence. I trailed along beside him, making notes in my book, marking the changing season in the call of the birds. The first skylarks appeared not long after my birthday. Their liquid warbling high above as the birds rose and fell. Most of the pellets in Jasper's collection looked like rabbit or sheep, maybe hare.

'You're not looking properly,' he said, teasing them apart. 'See this?'

He'd found a bone. Tiny. Part of the fine wiring of a bird or a small mammal.

'Whatever made this was a carnivore,' he said. 'You don't get this in sheep shit.'

'It's an owl pellet,' I said. 'Used to find them all the time in the woods.' A couple of months ago I wouldn't have dared challenge him. But part of the shift in the way we were was him now admitting sometimes I was right. He grunted and chucked the pellet away, but when he turned back there was a fierceness in his eyes that made my heart hammer. I clenched my fists ready for whatever was to come.

'I've got proof,' he said. 'You've got to swear you won't tell a soul. Not them at home, nor your mother, nor your sweetheart either. Swear it.'

*

It was a skull. He fetched it out from under his bed wrapped in a length of blue silk. Creamy yellow bone, shaped like a rugby ball with deep sockets where its eyes and nose would be. And it had fangs: a long curved upper pair that locked round two shorter ones on the bottom. I cradled it in my hands like it was one of those holy relics they have in big churches.

'Does this mean the Beast's dead?' I whispered. It felt wrong to speak any louder, as if the very presence of the skull made the stinking lair of Jasper's room a sacred place.

He shook his head. 'This one died years and years ago. Our Beast has struck twenty times or more since. This was its father. Or its mother. Like in *Beowulf*. The original monster is dead but its son is still out there.'

We'd been taking it in turns to read out lines from Edie's copy of *Beowulf*. I was pretty certain the hero killed Grendel first before he killed its mother. But now wasn't the time to be right.

'Where did you get it?' I asked instead.

He snatched the skull back, wrapping it in the blue silk till it looked mummified. 'Found it,' he said. 'I've been hunting the Beast long before you got here. See if you can find anything better.'

Charles had a book that showed the anatomy of birds, organs and bones and the structure of feathers. But pictures in a book weren't enough for Jasper, and neither were the carcasses we found on the moor. He had a plan to trap small animals, voles and shrews and the like, to 'examine' as he called it, while they were still alive. Imagine, he said, seeing an actual beating heart. I told him I wasn't having it. Creatures we found dead, fair enough. I didn't mind the dividing up of bones, the rebuilding of scattered skeletons, but I wasn't messing with anything still breathing, not unless it was the Beast itself.

'Fat lot of good you'd be as an explorer, Billy. You'd starve or get eaten yourself.'

'I'd do it for food,' I said. 'I like rabbit stew. I'd eat wild birds even, if I had to. But I'm not doing it for sport.'

'It's not sport, it's science.' He dropped the subject then, started back on how we needed to catch the Beast soon otherwise there'd be no other wild creatures left uneaten on the moor anyway. But just because he wasn't talking about it didn't mean he wasn't planning on doing it anyway.

When the plover chicks hatched I kept quiet. Waited till Jasper was busy inside the house before I went to watch the mother bird fussing back and forth. She wouldn't let me get too near, struck up a fury when I drew close. I didn't want Jasper finding them. The mother bird wouldn't be able to stop him grabbing one of the chicks. I promised they'd come to no harm.

One morning at the end of June, when the curlews were gliding and falling and whistling and whirruping in the wide sky, Jasper led me on a different route across the moor, away from the Stag Stones and down to a valley we'd not explored together before. It was his birthday and he'd chosen a day out on the moor with me over anything Edie or Charles might have offered.

'Where we off to?' I asked. The path was narrow between the heather and if you went too fast your feet tumbled over themselves or you kicked your own calf. Jasper was always that bit ahead and I never saw him stumble at all.

'To see Old Abe,' was as much as I could draw from him till we got there. 'There' being a stone hut huddled in the shelter of a knotted tree that was bent back the same way the wind blew. An old man was sitting outside, both hands clamped round a stick, a black and white dog at his feet. Sheep were scattered across the sloping field in front of him. When we drew close the dog got to its feet, its eyes were all clouded over and misted, but it sniffed the air and barked.

'Sit thissen down,' the old man said and we all did, even the dog.

'When it took a child, that were when folk started payin' notice.' Old Abe pulled the brim of his cap down as if the sun was too strong for his eyes. Jasper and I were sitting cross-legged on tussocks of grass. Jasper was taking his time picking at a scab on his knee. I guessed he'd heard this story before.

'Beast plucked 'im from 'is cradle and none knew till 'twere too late.'

The dog growled.

'Hush, you daft brute, there's nowt tha can do about it now. This were years back, when I weren't much more than a lad missen.'

The sun was warm, but I shivered and checked the sky for a passing cloud.

'What did it do with him?' I asked.

'Ooo knows,' said Abe. 'Et 'im, most like. It's what wild beasts do. Seen it 'appen often enough with a lamb. What's a tiny bairn but a plucked lamb to a wild beast?'

Jasper had lifted the lid off his scab. The skin beneath was pink and speckled with blood. I glanced over my shoulder. The moor was wide behind and around us. We were dots on its vastness.

'Did anyone try to catch it?' There would be farmers with guns, and hunters on horses. A wild chase across the heather. Hooves pounding, horns blasting and the Beast cowering in its lair.

The old man shook his head. 'It left no trace. Not a scent for the dogs, nor a drop of blood to follow.'

'Did the police send a detective?' I'd read *The Hound of the Baskervilles*, I knew how these things went.

'Ah well, it was kept hush, see. Folk'd panic else. Bad enough they knowed it kill't the lambs. Lambs, they can say it were a fox or a big bird. But a child. Taken clean out of his cradle. It weren't a fox. A fox kills on the spot. There were no blood. Summat had picked the bairn up in its jaws and carried it off like it were a kitten. That were the work of the Beast.'

I imagined Ma coming out of the cottage when I was a baby and finding me gone. Snatched from the rug where she'd left me with my rag and my top. Her screams would have filled the valley.

'What about the child's ma and pa?' I asked.

Old Abe shrugged. 'They went back home. They weren't from round here. Out here on a visit from Manchester, or else Leeds. If they'd been local they'd have known 'tweren't safe to leave a bairn out untended.'

There was a long silence as Abe cast his watery gaze over the far hills and Jasper began on a new scab on his shin. I wondered how come we'd never heard tell down at the Palace about a child being taken. Only Peggy's gossip about Jasper being found, a story that sometimes seemed more likely than anything I'd heard about the Beast.

'There's been many a sighting since.' Abe picked up his tale again. 'By law-abiding folk wi' no cause to be makin' tales.' His blue eyes fixed on me as if he had heard my doubts. 'Last summer there were a cow over Ovenden. Lifted clean in the air and dropped five mile away. Same cow, alive but wi' its heart going like the clappers. Ever since her milk has curdled.' He nodded slowly. 'Nowt but the Beast could do that.'

I remembered what Jasper had told me. 'You've seen it yourself?'

He scrunched up his face, etching wrinkles upon wrinkles. 'Aye.'

I searched for the fear that Jasper had promised would be in his eyes but all I saw was a sad dampness.

'Up yonder.' He flicked his stick towards the moor top. 'Lying low. If I'd stepped a yard or more nearer I'd have tripped over him. I were lucky with the direction of the wind. He went off after a whiff of summat else. By hell he were fast.'

'Have you never seen him again?' I asked.

'A couple of times.' He glanced sideways at us. 'Out the corner of my eye. But he's a wily beggar. If he knows tha's looking for him, he can make himsen near invisible.'

'The binoculars,' whispered Jasper. 'I told you.'

'Have you tried to catch him?'

'Nah. I'm no hunter.' He leaned forward on his stick. 'Him that does though, he'll be a hero. Folk'll rest easier in their beds once the Beast is gone.'

I'd hoped Charles might help with our quest for the Beast, what with Garth spending most of his time either hunting down or escaping from wild creatures. Jasper had a pile of the books, the dust covers all creased and torn. My favourite was *Winter in the Congo*. There was a girl in it who wore a big hat that shaded her eyes, so Garth could never tell whether she was being serious or teasing. He whipped the hat off in the last chapter to kiss her. I skipped that bit but the rest was all right. There were plenty of beasts: pumas and cobras and a parrot that squawked 'Danger danger!' whenever a bad guy drew near. The parrot got shot in the end, its final squawk saving Garth's life as it was blown away in a shower of red and green feathers. There was a rhinoceros too. Garth shot it when it charged at the girl in the big hat. If she hadn't been wearing the hat she might have seen it coming and could have saved herself.

Charles had been teaching us about the meerkats of the Kalahari, inspired to the subject by the pouty-faced weasel that stood in the study hearth, its paws raised like a boxer at the ready. 'Meerkats,' he said, 'steal eggs from ground-nesting birds and turtles and eat them whole.'

Thinking it was a good opportunity to enlist his help I asked if there was a creature that might steal a child from its cradle. He seemed to give it serious consideration till I added that it had been Old Abe who had told us about the bairn on the moor.

Charles near snapped the pencil he was holding in two, and I feared he was going to hurl it at my head. 'Abraham Bartlett has spent too much time on his own, out with his flock and in the snug at the Drovers' Rest. If there's been creatures killed you need look no further than foxes and half-starved farm dogs. Nature red in tooth and claw. Nothing supernatural about that.'

Jasper went red in the face and his mouth clamped tight. I waited for him to tell Charles he was wrong. To tell him about the skull. But he kept mum till we were outside, dismissed once more for the day.

'What does he know?' he said. 'He's the one who spends all day making up stories. He'll be sorry when we're more famous than his idiotic Garth Winter.'

Edie hadn't forgotten about our Friday 'book talks', which were her contribution to our education. She had Sally light the fire in her room, which was always a drama as it refused to draw and more often the smoke would pour back out and fill the room. But once it was settled Livvy would bring us tea and biscuits and we would begin. It was there that we discovered Beowulf and Sherlock Holmes and Edgar Allan Poe.

Edie still read us poems, though often she'd stop mid-verse and stare out of the window, so we never got to hear the end. She found me one about a skylark. It went on a bit but it was spot on about the bird's flight and its song. I copied it in my book and learned bits off by heart.

Charles liked to check up on what he called 'my sister's notion of education'. Once I showed him the copy of *Modern English Poets* that she was so fond of. He noted one of the turned down corners and raised his eyebrows. 'Been sharing the joys of James Ross, has she?'

It was the poem about the geese.

'Gifted poet, but a brute of a man,' said Charles.

'Like a dog,' I asked. Remembering how old Abe spoke to his collie.

'God no.' Charles closed the book. 'Dogs can be trained. They're loyal, affectionate, even when they've been beaten and whipped. Ross is a brute, he treats other people like dogs.'

I didn't like to ask him how he knew.

As summer drew on Charles's lessons tailed off until he finally announced that it was the holidays and we were free. Then he added as if it was of no importance at all, 'I've found you a tutor. He's starting in September. God help him.'

*

I held out till the end of the second week of the holiday and then I said to Jasper that I was going to the Palace and did he want to come too? Now it was the summer the whole valley would be teeming. Not only the Palace but all the kiosks and cafés dotted through the woods and up the hillside, and the camping site and the guest houses. Just talking about it made me wish I hadn't stayed away so long.

'All right.' Jasper sniffed the air. 'The wind's no good for tracking today anyway.'

I was right about the crowds. Every inch of grass and rocks was covered with bodies, blankets and baskets. There were kiddies paddling, and on the stepping stones a row of women posed for a photograph, hats held out in front of them like they'd each caught a fish. As always there were couples sneaking off to go courting in the woods, catching hands the minute they thought the trees were hiding them. I remembered how I used to watch them cuddling and kissing. The lasses batting the lads' hands away and squealing if they got mud or grass stains on their clothes.

Soon as I told Jasper about it he wanted to see it for himself. Said it was social anthropology and it would help prepare him for his expeditions in the jungle. We followed one pair up the track behind the Pav, but the bloke kept turning round and squinting at us, so we skipped over the ditch and took a detour through the trees. There was a copse not far off. Lush green grass out of sight behind a great lump of rock. From the other side we heard giggling and the low murmur of a man's voice.

Peering over the rock it was hard to make out at first, the grass was that long and the lass was hidden except for one long leg, her skirt ridden up so you could see her stocking top. The bloke was laid flat, a slab of white cotton and grey serge, one of his hands dark and meaty on the lass's leg. We watched in silence as his fingers left her leg and tugged at his belt and then his trousers, till his great hairy arse was showing. We bobbed down behind the rock clutching our sides. When we peeked back over they were still at it, the white moon of his arse jigging up and down in time to his grunts and the squeaks of the lass that we still couldn't see. Jasper stretched back his arm. I hadn't even seen him load the catapult. He let it go and it struck a bullseye. We should have run. But Jasper shoved me down behind the rock as the bloke roared and the girl cried, 'Shush, shush! Folks'll hear!'

Jasper's eyes were gleaming. Mebbes he thought the bloke would think he was stung or bitten. That they'd carry on when he was calmed. But the next thing was a wrenching of my scalp and a yelp from Jasper, as we were jerked to our feet by our hair. I pulled free and jumped away but Jasper was held tight, the man's sausage fingers clutching his thick curls as he bellowed that he'd smash his bleedin' head in. Jasper twisted and dipped but the man grabbed his ear with his other hand and I expected to see his head mashed against the rock. Then Jasper's right arm flailed and the bloke yelled, flinging him away, and Jasper was past me and running through the trees. I got one last peek at the bloke. His hand was clasping his arm, blood seeping through his fingers, his shirtsleeve blossoming red. Over his shoulder the pale face of the lass, her hair all mussed up, her eyes and mouth wide. Then I legged it too.

'You cut him,' I said. 'You bloody cut him.' Jasper was wiping his knife against the grass down by the river, hidden from the trippers by a thick bush of holly.

'He asked for it,' he said. He inspected the blade and then slipped it back inside his boot. I remembered that twist and dip of his body, not struggling to be free, he'd been reaching for his knife.

'Come on.' He climbed up past the holly, not minding as it caught at him. 'You said there'd be hot potatoes. I'm starving.'

'Let's have a gander at the rink,' I said. We were back in the yard, taties eaten, no sign of the man and his bloody arm. I was twitchy, scanning the crowd for him. Jasper was whistling, showing he didn't care. He said the bloke would be more scared of us. He probably had no right being in the woods with the girl anyway. I thought I'd seen her after. Hair all smoothed, walking along with a dour pair that might have been her ma and da. So maybe he was right.

Still I reckoned the rink was safer than hanging about outside. Only the young'uns went there and close up the bloke had been grizzled, with grey streaking his hair, years older than the lass, at any rate. There was a queue for the skating but if I had a word with Albert we'd be all right.

God love Jasper's eyes when he saw inside. I'd swear he'd never seen the like nor heard it neither. The roar of the river had nothing on twenty or thirty pairs of skates going round on a wooden floor. A couple of lasses were singing 'Nellie Dean' as they circled and a gang of lads in the corner joined in with a made-up chorus that got the girls squealing.

'So, are we having a go?' asked Jasper.

'Course. If you've tuppence for the skates.'

I didn't have tuppence but Albert handed me my skates anyway, with a wink.

Jasper on wheels was like a lamb new born, all legs and tangles. I let him wobble around for a bit then took pity and showed him how it was done. Not that I'm an expert, but I can get round well enough without waving my limbs every which way. It took Jasper a few goes before he got the hang of it. Even then he'd suddenly lurch without warning and grab my arm and all but take me over.

We were leaning by the back wall, him steadying himself after he'd been nearly downed by a pair of linked-arm lasses. He nudged me and tilted his head towards the door. 'Is that your girl?'

Who else could he mean but Lizzie? She was with the same older lass from last time, who shook her head when Albert tried to hand her a pair of skates. She stood at the side watching as Lizzie fastened her skates. Lizzie was wearing a blue dress spotted with white. She was like a skater from a Christmas card, just needing a dusting of snowflakes, and ice, not wood, under her feet. She began a slow circuit of the rink and I half expected her to do a full twirl and a curtsy in the centre, she looked so fine. But she kept steady on, eyes front, arms loose by her sides.

'Lizzie!' I called as she passed us and her skates stuttered and her body arched fore and back. I thought she was gone for certain, but she steadied herself and rolled to the wall.

'Billy!' There was a flush on her cheeks.

'How do?' I said and felt my own cheeks going warm. After all our scrambling in the woods I felt a right scruff standing there with Jasper lurking at my heels. 'This is Jasper,' I said quickly before he had a chance to say anything. 'From High Hob.'

'Oh yes.' That tone of voice that wound my sisters up but which she'd never used with me before. 'The boy who wanted a companion.'

'I didn't want one,' Jasper said. 'It was them that asked for it.'

It? I glared at him but he was too busy trading hoity looks with Lizzie.

'Didn't know you came skating here,' I said. As if I still had a clue what went on day-to-day around the Palace.

'It was Jane's idea.' She nodded over to the lass by the door. Albert had given her a chair and she had her nose in a book. 'She says it will strengthen my calves.'

'Are they weak?' I asked.

'No. But Mother thinks it might improve my dancing.' She crossed her eyes and giggled. I let out a long breath. It was all right. She was still the old Lizzie. She nodded over to the girl Jane. 'She's the daughter of my mother's friend. She's staying with us for a while. She follows me everywhere when I'm not at school. Have you still been going to school, Billy?'

I didn't like the way she said it. As if she was checking up on me.

'We've been getting tutoring.' I wasn't having her thinking I was falling behind or that we were wild savages up at High Hob. 'History and literature and algebra.'

'And natural history, and classical civilisations,' Jasper added.

'But not skating,' said Lizzie, raising an eyebrow at Jasper who was wobbling even though he was holding the rail. She tapped her left toe on the floor. 'Fifteen more laps to go.' A flash of those blue eyes. 'Race you,' and she was off and halfway round the rink before I could move. Then I pushed off, leaving Jasper gawping behind.

I'd been round that rink enough times and I could go fast when I wanted to. I soon caught up and I was going to skate by her side but she pushed forward with a wicked grin and tried to overtake me. I wasn't having a lass, not even Lizzie Potter, beating me. Albert usually blew his whistle or shouted 'Hoi!' if anyone started a race but either he was distracted or he was choosing to look the other way because he didn't dare to shout at Mr Nathaniel's daughter. Either way, no one tried to stop us and the other skaters shifted sharpish as we whizzed by. I lost count of the times I passed Jasper, until Lizzie shouted over my shoulder 'Last lap!' and sped past me.

I pumped my arms, head down and shot by her as we passed Jasper again, catching my arm round one of the pillars when I reached it and spinning round to slow down. Lizzie caught my free arm and we spun together.

'Beat you,' I said gasping for breath.

'I let you,' she said.

'Did not!' But we were both laughing, faces glowing. Locks of her damp hair clung to her cheeks and I didn't care whether she'd let me win or not.

She grabbed my arm with her other hand as she swung in to let a pair of skaters past. We clung to each other still laughing.

A blast of a whistle rang across the rink and I nearly fell on my arse, Lizzie giggling as I grasped at the pillar. But her smile dropped and so did mine as Nathaniel Potter came striding across the wooden floor regardless of the skaters who all dived for the sides or grabbed each other as they tried not collide. He had Albert's whistle clutched in his fist, the red cord dangling loose as if he'd torn it from the old man's neck. His face full as a steam engine about to pop. Nostrils flaring as he took a deep breath, like he was about to yell. Then he huffed the breath out.

'There you are, Lizzie. And Billy. You're here too. Charming, charming.' He stared at the whistle in his hand. His palm was scarlet where it had dug into his skin. 'Youthful exuberance. I understand.' He slipped the whistle into his pocket and fixed his eyes on mine. 'Was young myself once. But we don't want any accidents.' He took hold of Lizzie's hand and pulled her towards him. 'The rules apply to everyone. No racing. No ...' he waved his free hand at me, 'no unnecessary ...' he seemed to be grasping for the right word in the air. 'Spinning,' he said at last. Then he headed for the door, pulling Lizzie behind him, her face confused and apologetic. The other skaters were either staring like dolts or deliberately looking away. I got a full-on scowl from the lass Jane. I guessed she'd be getting an earful when she got home too.

'Blimey,' said Jasper as he wobbled to a halt by the pillar. 'He's an old bear when he's riled. If he doesn't want anyone racing he should put up a sign.'

CHAPTER 10

Anna: November

The stuffed weasel is glowering at her from the corner of the office, its teeth clenched as if they might start chattering at any moment. Anna takes her scarf off the back of her chair and throws it over its head.

Her eyes are dry from staring at the rows and columns in the High Hob household account books. She'd found a pile of them stacked with a collection of hymn books in almost identical bindings. The entries are brief, printed in clear block capitals, headings underlined and unpaid bills circled in red. A bare-bones insight into the High Hob household in the late 1920s and 1930s. Lists of weekly and monthly outgoings, including wages paid to Olive Wilshaw and Sally Marsden. From the difference in their wages Anna guesses Olive was the housekeeper. Then monthly payments to a 'Mr P', who helpfully has 'piano' in brackets after his name in the first entry for him in 1930, and from the end of 1932 a quarterly sum to someone called Sefton although there is no clue as to his role and he disappears from the record a couple of years later. A chauffeur, or a gardener? A tutor? Well paid for his troubles anyway.

Sam had suggested she draw up a list of suspects. Who might

have had reason to kill the Harpers? Someone cunning enough to try to cover their tracks by making it look like suicide. Might there be more than one person involved? Did Charles have an affair with Sally the maid? Did a dismissed and disgruntled Sefton attempt a robbery that went wrong? The last entry in the account books is dated June 1935, a year before the Harpers died. There is nothing there to link the Harpers to the Palace or its partial closure. And no mention of Billy Shaw.

She had spent an afternoon in Halifax library searching through microfiched copies of the *Sowley Gazette* from the 1930s for clues as to what happened at the Palace just before the upper floors were closed. She has a date for her presentation to the board in early December. She needs to be ready. Fully armed, she thinks, remembering Erica's readiness for 'a fight'.

An article in the *Gazette* from October 1936 stated that the Palace was to be closed for refurbishment, and that there was to be a sale of 'equipment and extraneous items' the following month. An advertisement for the promised sale appeared on 10 November and highlighted 'a miniature engine and carriages of interest to enthusiasts and collectors'. In April 1937, it was reported that a Sunday School party had enjoyed the refreshments in the newly relocated tea room in the former Apprentice House. A piece from later in the same year announced that dances at the Fraser Hotel in Sowley were proving popular since 'the unfortunate demise of the Palace Dances, which it seems are unlikely ever to be revived'. There are no references to an accident or other incident at the Palace either before its closure or afterwards.

It could have been a financial decision. The Palace was past its heyday. Maybe visitor numbers didn't warrant it staying fully open. But why would a decision made for business reasons eighty years ago still be valid today? Erica's suggestion that there had been an accident niggles at her. And the closure had begun in October 1936. Only months after the Harpers' deaths.

She puts the account books to one side now and pulls over an old shoebox she found underneath a bundle of bobbins in a crate marked 'High Hob'. The box is filled with C90 cassette tapes.

Each tape is marked with pairs of letters and the date '1997'. Too late for High Hob. Unless a documentary or drama had been recorded up there. She hasn't been able to find a tape player anywhere and a phone call to Erica confirms that there isn't one at the mill.

'Those will be the oral history tapes,' Erica says. 'Nineteen ninety-seven, did you say? That sounds about right.'

'Who were the interviewees?' Anna asks.

'Local people mainly, who remembered the old days at Ackerdean. There was a call out in the *Yorkshire Post* too. Pulled a few in from further afield. It was schoolchildren that did the interviews.'

'Children?'

'Yes. Older ones obviously, we're not talking infants. Part of their Duke of Edinburgh award up at the high school. They put on a presentation as part of the Sowley town hall centenary celebrations. I don't think those tapes have seen the light of day since.'

Transcripts of the interviews would save her having to wade through hours of tape, although if there are any finding them in the archive could take just as long. She will get hold of a tape player from somewhere. She wants voices in the mill. It could be that she has found them.

Frank is sitting by himself in a corner of the café with a large mug of tea and a curd tart, Betsy at his feet. Their usual spot at this time on a Friday. Betsy lifts her head as Anna approaches but doesn't make a fuss, as if she knows she is May's only exception to the 'No Dogs Allowed' rule.

Frank raises one bushy eyebrow when Anna mentions her latest find.

'Ah, you found them, did you?'

'You knew about them? Why didn't you mention it? They're just the sort of thing I'm after.'

'I can't be spoon-feeding you like a sick lamb.' He coughs. 'If you look careful you'll find one with yours truly on it.'

She leans back in her chair. 'Were you being asked about your uncle Billy?'

He frowns. 'Billy? No, why would they ask me about him?'

'The tapes were in a crate marked High Hob.'

Frank shakes his head. 'Weren't nothing about the Harpers. They were dead and gone before I were even born. 'Twere all about memories of the mill and the Palace.' He sniffs. 'I told 'em I were too young to remember them days but when I said about my mam and grandma their ears perked up.'

'Erica said the interviews were done by children.'

'Aye, bunch of schoolkids. An award they were trying for, had to show they'd done summat in the community.' He chuckles. 'They were keen enough, but they didn't have a clue about life here back then. I could've told 'em we ate coal and painted our faces blue for Christmas and they'd have lapped it up.'

'You're not telling me that you made everything up?'

'Nah. You couldn't wind 'em up too much. Wouldn't have been fair. And they were using it for a presentation in the town hall. Didn't want to make myself a laughing stock.' He screws up his forehead. 'I went along to that. They had boxes of slides, old photos and such, and played some of the tapes. Overran a bit with a couple of the old codgers wittering on about "the best days of their lives". And you couldn't hear some of them right well. Still, not bad for a bunch of kids.' He breaks a piece off his curd tart and gives it to Betsy.

'I actually came in to show you these.' She passes him a photocopied sheet of paper. It records two complaints made to Jeremiah Potter by an Archibald Chambers in the early 1900s, about 'Palace trippers' he had caught 'cavorting' and 'consuming spirits' in one of his fields, and another from the same time accusing the Potters of disturbing his sheep with the tooting of the whistle on the miniature railway. It makes Frank chuckle.

'I'd love to have seen that railway. They ripped it out before the

Great War. Ran all along the back there through the woods. Trust Granddad Chambers to make a complaint about drunkards. He were strict Methodist. Not that they were his fields, he were still a tenant then.'

'I thought your family owned the farm?'

Frank shakes his head. 'They paid rent for near a hundred years, to the Hardwicks from over Ripponden way. We didn't own it till I bought it. Uncle Billy left me a pot of money. He weren't a rich man when he died but he'd done all right.' His eyes dart away and he bends to pat Betsy on the back. 'It's what he would have wanted. We'd earned the place, the years of hard work we'd put into it.'

'Talking of hard work...' Anna passes him a photograph. It's the only one she's found so far of the interior of the mill. A tall woman in a cap and apron poses with a tray of sandwiches next to a small sign saying 'Tip-Top Teas'.

'Nana Shaw! It has to be. Well done, lass.' He peers at the photo. 'Got a look of my mam about her. Not a look you'd want to argue with. She could cut through grease with it.' He purses his lips. 'When Nathaniel Potter died she took it right hard, though she had no fondness for the man. He were a miserable old codger by the time he went. He'd locked himself away in that house all on his own for the ten years or more since his wife passed. But when they announced he'd left the mill and the woodland to the society...' He shakes his head. 'I'd never seen the like. Mam beat the hell out of every rug we had. "That place is yours by right, Frank." Those were her very words. She said the least he could have done were leave things straight before he died.'

May appears at the table with a teapot. 'Top-up, Frank? Can I be getting you anything, Anna?'

'No thanks, I just wanted a word with Frank.' She waits until May has poured Frank's tea and returned behind the counter.

'Did you ever ask her what she meant by it?'

'I tried but she clammed up. She were arguing once with my dad about Uncle Billy, about how Potter owed him and if he was a real gentleman he'd pay his debts.' He coughs into his fist and takes a long drink of his tea. 'I read somewhere about a man who lost everything he owned in a game of cards. Mebbes Potter gambled with Billy and lost the mill to him or else sold the mill to him, in secret. Mortgaged it, to pay off what he owed. Who knows?'

'I've not read anything about Mr Potter gambling or having debts,' says Anna. 'But I suppose it's possible.' She hesitates. 'Could it be that she meant the Shaws had earned a share of the mill, through the generations of hard work they'd put into it? Like what you said yourself about the Chambers earning the farm even before you bought it.'

Frank drains his mug. 'You could be right. But I'd like to get to the bottom of it. Set the story straight. It matters. So I can tell my lads, you know.'

'You're right, it does matter.' Her voice falters. 'We all have stories that we're the only ones left to tell.'

'It's hard,' his usually gruff tone now surprisingly gentle, 'when there's times you only shared with one other person and they ain't around no more to remember them with.'

She closes her eyes and her mouth as if to stop a physical out-pouring of the grief that surges up inside her. Every reminder is like a body blow, gradually lessening in intensity, but still enough to unbalance her. Her memory stubbornly replaying the phone call, the words that she'll never forget: *There's been an accident. I thought you should know.*

DECEMBER

'We'd go up to the Palace regular.' The woman's voice is frail but with the lilt of remembered excitement. 'We'd walk up along the river and first thing you saw was the stripes of the Pavilion. It was like arriving at a party. I'd run ahead of my sisters and shout, "We're here we're here!"'

Anna presses the pause button and makes a note on her laptop. She is on the sofa in the living room, having abandoned the office where there are no curtains to muffle the lashing of the rain against the window and only an ancient gas heater for warmth. Here she can snuggle under a blanket, and with the stove banked up with wood she is warm enough, as long as she doesn't stray into the kitchen or upstairs. With no sign yet of any transcripts for the oral history interviews she is resigned to listening to the tapes in full, although she has fast-forwarded through sections in which the interviewees were side-tracked, recalling memories that don't involve the Ackerdean valley. Accounts of war experiences in France and life in 1960s Manchester are fascinating but not what she is after right now. The new tape player she bought online is proving as nifty as she hoped, and its built-in mp3 converter means she can make digital copies of everything.

'It's what we need if we are going to use them for interpretation or to enhance the website,' she'd told Erica, who had agreed and authorised the necessary funds.

It's only mid-afternoon but the unceasing rain has brought an early end to the day. She has all the lights on and the glass pane of the stove glows a comforting red. The old oak clock that she found in the storeroom is ticking time on the mantel. She has covered the scratchy grey fabric of the sofa and chair with blue and red plaid blankets and a woven hanging patterned with rows of colourful fish, bought at the market in Sowley, brightens the chalky blankness of one of the walls. The cottage is beginning to feel more like home.

On her laptop under the interviewee's name, Lilian Atterlee, she adds the time-code and the reference to the Palace pavilion. She is constructing a story arc, linking this excerpt with an earlier one in which an elderly man remembered how as a boy he and his friend would lie in wait round the far side of the Pavilion armed with cow parsley stems and pocketfuls of rowan berries to shoot at the holidaymakers as they came and went. 'You got extra points,' he'd said, 'if you got 'em to turn round. Mind, we had to belt it if we were spotted.'

Anna starts Mrs Atterlee's tape again. The young voice of the interviewer asks: 'What did you like best about the Palace?'

'We used to go skating at the rink.' There is a clinking of china. 'The room that's got them writer's bits and bobs in now. There was a wooden floor and you got a rumble like thunder from the skates. They covered it over later with something synthetic. It was smoother. But I missed that sound.' A pause and more china clinking.

'Is it true the Palace had its own electricity?' the interviewer asks.

'That's right. It ran off a turbine. We used to try and sneak a look at it. It made a right racket. But it were all shut away.'

'I heard that the main switch for the generator was up at Mr Potter's house,' says the interviewer. 'He used to turn it off when he went to bed, even if there were still people dancing at the Palace.'

'If you know so much already what are you asking me for?'

'Sorry, Mrs Atterlee. An old man told us. I thought you might know if it was true.'

'Yes, well, I don't know anything about that. We weren't allowed down there at night.'

The interview ends and the rest of the tape is blank.

Anna opens another cassette case, labelled 'IH, SM, MB' and starts a new document on the laptop.

The interviewer, who again sounds like a young girl, begins by saying, 'I'm at the Sowley Day Centre with three ladies who remember the mill when it was a pleasure palace.' A soft giggle, followed by a shush.

'Eeh, it were the place to be.' The voice is high-pitched but steady.

'Could you say who you are first?'

'If you insist. My name is Ivy Hall and I were down at the Palace every minute I could get. Well, it's where all the young men were.' A coarse chuckle. 'We'd fight to get to the front of the queue for the swings. There were a young lad in charge. What were his name?'

Another voice says, 'David.'

'No, Margaret, the one after him. Young lad. Jack, or John, mebbes. It were after the war but he'd done his bit. Had a gammy arm but he could push like a good'un with the other. Eeh, we went high.'

'Was that the First World War, Mrs Hall?' A boy's voice this time.

''Ow old do you think I am, lad? First World War indeed. I weren't even born then. If you want ancient history you need to talk to Sal. Ain't that right?' The same coarse chuckle followed by a loud sniff. 'No, this were in 1947, maybe '48, I were a young slip of eighteen.'

'You star,' whispers Anna. 'Age and date. Love you, Ivy Hall.'

'The Palace weren't what it had been. No more fancy dances. That were all closed up. But it had a café and the swings, and the rink. We were divvels on that rink. It were a sad day when they closed it.'

The girl asks, 'What do the rest of you remember?'

There is just the low hiss of the original recording equipment, then a quiet voice, hesitant, definitely not Ivy Hall.

'It wasn't just about the lads, not for all of us.'

'Could you say your name please?'

'Sally Marsden. It wasn't the same after the war. The life had gone out of the place. Not like when I was a girl.'

'When was that, Mrs Marsden?' The boy this time.

'Don't tell him, Sally.' It was Ivy Hall. 'You should never ask a lady her age, young man. And she's a miss not a missus.' A pause. 'She's eighty-one next week. You wouldn't know it, would you?'

Sally continues. 'We lived up by Wicken Falls. Summer evenings we'd walk along the river to the Palace. The insects were terrible. Biting at our faces and hands.'

'Did you use the skating rink?'

'No, but we watched through the windows and we had picnics by the Pavilion. There was a man there. He had big arms and a moustache. Used to scare us. We'd scurry home as if he was on our heels.' She is interrupted by Ivy Hall's laughter. 'There was none of that, though, once I started work.' A pause. 'I did go back later. But it wasn't the same.'

'How old were you when you started work, Miss Marsden?' the girl interviewer asks.

'Straight after I left school at fourteen,' the quiet voice begins again. 'Cleaning and helping with the laundry. Hauling in coals and logs of wood for to keep them warm. Not that there was a chance of it up there. The wind howled through them windows like they had iron bars not glass. And the old woman were no help.'

'Your mistress?' the girl asks.

Sally Marsden. The name suddenly registers. The maid at High Hob. Anna presses rewind and then play.

'Your mistress?'

'No. The missus weren't no old woman. She was a lady.' There is a snuffling noise on the tape. 'Aunt Livvy was the housekeeper. I called her Aunt but she was just a friend of Mother's. Said she needed an extra pair of hands so they took me on as well. As a day maid, not live-in. Aunt Livvy couldn't cope on her own with that lad of theirs running wild about the place.' A ragged breath. 'He weren't right. What happened. It weren't right.'

Jasper. A cold tingle runs down Anna's arms as she presses the pause button. She wishes Sam was here to hear this. 'Running wild' she types, imagining the boy charging round the house waving his stick or his catapult, followed, or led, by Billy. But then *He weren't right*. Was Sally suggesting there was more to his behaviour than just boisterousness? The vivid painting on the wall at High Hob. A monster conjured up in a young mind. *What happened. It weren't right*. The house lights flicker. There's been trouble with the supply all week. Erica had warned her to expect occasional power failures. She pulls the blanket closer. Thinks of Sam and Ruby up on the moor and Frank with Betsy lying across his feet. She envies them the shared warmth of another living creature. A sudden splurting of the kitchen tap jolts her, her heart hammering. *Jesus.* She runs a hand through her hair, takes a deep breath. Come on, woman, back to work. Let's hear what else Sally Marsden has to say.

'It was only skivvying four days a week. But the pay wasn't bad and the missus could be kind.'

'Did you have to make fancy dinners?'

'Fancy? Not likely. Not with Aunt Livvy in charge of the kitchen. There's only so much a body can take, she used to say, and her body couldn't take much.' A pause. 'One Christmas there was a bit of a do. They had folk up from London. I was run ragged.' A long pause.

'So ...' the interviewer begins.

'House wasn't fit for entertaining most of the time. In spite of Aunt Livvy's bustling and my scrubbing and polishing. The things I saw in that kitchen, it would make you shudder.'

'What sort of things?' the boy asks, a new enthusiasm in his voice.

'They made an awful mess.' Her voice stumbles. 'The young master, he said it was science and that it was beyond a girl like me. I shouldn't mourn the loss of a chicken in the pursuit of science. That's what him and Master William called their messings, science. There was blood on that table that didn't come from any chicken. I scrubbed it but I never got those stains out. Not properly. Covered it with a cloth but I knew it was there.' Her voice becomes a mumble then rises again. 'Hours he'd spend drawing pictures. Bones and innards all laid out. Scribbling down their secrets. Told me to stop gawping.' Her voice trails off. A doorbell rings insistently in the background. A whisper that picks back up again. '... called me a liar. His breath, in my ear. I was a silly girl. I'd got confused. But I know what I saw. Him and his animal ways.' She is sniffing now as though she is crying.

'Don't mind her.' It's Ivy again. 'She has her moments, don't you, love. Margaret, give her one of your tissues. Don't want these young'uns thinking it was all doom and gloom. I worked in a

bakery over in Rochdale before I got married and we had a riot.'
Ivy's highly coloured reminiscences fill the rest of the tape.

Anna sits back.

'Master William', must be Frank's Uncle Billy. Sally sounded so frightened when she talked about him and Jasper. Even after all those years. Their 'animal ways'. What had she seen those boys do?

CHAPTER 11

Billy: 1932

Our tutor arrived in the middle of September with the rain.

The first half of the month had been glorious. On warm days the smell of the heather was honey-sweet and made my head go fuzzy if I lay in it for long. Once we saw a gang of golden plover, their backs glinting like new brass coins. Their song carried on the wind reminded me of a crying babe, and I tried not to think of the one in Old Abe's story, lost on the moor. Jasper added sketches to my bird notebook, usually with his own elaborations. A viper would hang from the curved beak of a peregrine falcon, or a grouse would have the headless body of a field mouse in its claws. When we weren't out on the moor we were in the woods making rope swings and doing target practice, or bathing and fishing for trout at Wicken Falls.

One night we took the skull out to the barn at Thurcross Farm above Oakenshaw. Jasper lit candles and chanted words that were supposed to call up the Beast. But all that happened was Mr Trimmer came out shouting with a lantern and when we scarpered Jasper kicked over a candle and started a fire in the straw. When the Trimmers came calling the next day Edie swore we were locked up in High Hob all night with the key safe beneath her pillow. It must have been tramps or tinkers. And they couldn't prove it otherwise.

We'd been back to the Palace a couple of times, but with never a sight of Nathaniel Potter or the thug with the bleeding arm. Nor of Lizzie, which wrung my heart. I wanted nothing more than to swing her round in my arms again like we'd done on the rink. I had faith we'd be together again soon though, it was one of those things that was meant to be, like Christmas and sunrise and birds laying eggs. Couldn't be stopped, no matter how hard her father blew on that whistle.

Sums and dates and properties of the elements were the furthest things from mine and Jasper's minds. When Charles announced one day that our lessons were to start the next morning, it was like hearing a great door slamming shut.

Charles wanted his study back for himself. He had another Garth Winter story brewing, so the parlour was to be our new schoolroom. My birthday afternoon in there with Ma and my sisters, the scrap with Jasper, and Edie's broken pearls, all seemed years ago, not a few months.

The sofa had been pushed to one side and a table was set up for us, with a comfy chair by the fire for the tutor. His name was Mr Graham. He was boarding with his sister in Oakenshaw and walked up every morning and back again at night.

'This will do splendidly,' he said when he saw the parlour, rubbing his hands together.

'He's thinking of all the money he's getting for this,' Jasper whispered. 'Reckons he's on to an easy life.'

If he did start off thinking that, he must've changed his mind pretty fast. Jasper had been to more schools than me, and had been chucked out of all of them. From the start he was planning how quick he could make the tutor give up.

First off, he wouldn't sit at the table. He set himself up on the windowsill, knees hunched to his chest, pricking the flesh of his shins with the point of a compass. When Mr Graham, said, 'So let's get started, boys,' I think he truly expected that Jasper would come and sit in his place next to me. But he stayed where he was, his sun-browned legs dotted with spots of red.

Mr Graham laid out sheets of paper on the table.

'We'll start with a couple of tests. So I can get an idea of where you're at. We'll begin with arithmetic.' He cleared his throat. 'Does that sound all right?'

He lasted two weeks.

He left with a satchel full of unfinished test papers and a scar on the back of his hand from when he'd unwisely tried to take the compass from Jasper. He had a twitching under his left eye too that I'd swear hadn't been there when he arrived. I heard him telling Charles, 'That boy needs to be taught a proper lesson.' But wasn't that what he'd been paid to do?

'That should give us a break,' said Jasper. 'The weather's brightening up too. Turned out right nice, ain't it.' Mimicking the way I spoke. The way I used to speak.

But he was wrong on both counts. The clouds had gathered again by Sunday teatime and nine o'clock Monday morning our new tutor arrived.

There was a rumbling outside which had to be thunder because it was two weeks too early to be the coalman. We ran to the door and saw a dark green truck bouncing up the track. It rolled to a halt by the wall. Charles never brought the car all the way up to the house. Said the road would destroy the undercarriage. But this was a military vehicle. Were we at war again? Was it a friend or foe?

He wasn't in uniform but you could tell he was a soldier. The way he walked and stood. His clipped moustache and his voice to match.

His name was Major Sefton. He wasn't in the army any more but we still had to call him Major, Charles said, out of respect. 'He's your new tutor,' he announced. 'And I've given him *carte blanche* to do whatever it takes.'

Major Sefton didn't have time for tests and assessments. He had us doing drills first thing. Marching and turning and running with knapsacks on our backs, filled with rocks.

In the parlour, when we got in there, he didn't waste his breath telling us where to sit or stand. He opened all the windows wide as they would go, then strode round the room smacking a long wooden ruler against the palm of his hand. I thought about the *carte blanche* thing that Charles had given him. Made my mind up not to give him cause to use it on me.

He'd fought in the war and taught at a boys' school and he said there was little difference between the two. There wasn't much he couldn't teach except maybe dancing. That was the only time he laughed: at the idea of the three of us dancing.

At the end of that first day he rapped the table sharp with his ruler and barked, 'Reassemble tomorrow at oh eight thirty hours.'

After the crunch of his polished boots down the path we waited for the rumble of the truck. When there was only silence we went to investigate. The truck was still parked by the wall and a plume of smoke was pouring out of the top. We rushed out of the gate expecting a fire, hoping for an explosion. We found Major Sefton sitting on the footboard of the truck holding a cup of tea.

'This is my bivouac, lads.' He waved his arm at the truck. 'Got everything a man could need.' He winked. 'I'm here to stay, boys. Don't you doubt that for a minute.'

Our school days were longer once the Major arrived. Especially with the added hour of drills and physical fitness exercises.

'Essential,' the Major barked at us, 'for a healthy mind and the suppression of physical urges.' If he meant to tire Jasper out too much to misbehave I'd say he got close. Either that or even Jasper was scared by the threat of *carte blanche*. Our lessons passed calmer than they'd ever done before.

Our weekends were still our own and sure enough I got to see Lizzie again. But she was always with Jane. And I was always with Jasper. It was maddening not to be alone with her. There were things I wanted to tell her. Thoughts, some important, some not, that I didn't want to share with anyone else, that I knew she'd understand. I wanted to hear her talk too, about proper stuff not just lists of the many ways her mother kept trying to keep her occupied outside school or her father's obsession with his new motor car. Her stories were comical and the way she rolled her eyes made even Jane smile, but there was so much more I wanted to hear her say. I knew she felt the same, by the way she looked at me for longer than was needed when she said goodbye and brushed her arm against mine as she walked away.

Maybe it was the shorter autumn days or the Major's drills and exercises but somehow the weeks flew past and then Charles was dragging a fir tree into the hall and Edie was clapping her hands together and saying how we must all welcome in the spirit of Christmas.

'What took you so long?' Jasper asked as the garden gate swung shut behind me. He was lurking like a troll under one of the crabbed hawthorn trees. 'It's been hell here. If that old woman prods me one more time and talks about fattening me up, like she's planning to have me for dinner, I'll bite her.' His hair was slicked back and his face was very shiny. He had on his best long trousers, but had managed to untuck his shirt and there was no sign of a tie.

I'd only been gone a week. Back with Ma and my sisters for Christmas. It was the longest I'd left High Hob for since I'd arrived. The Palace had been closed up for the holidays. Mr Nathaniel had talked in years past of opening up for Christmas week with special dances and festive luncheons and mistletoe bows dangling from the rafters above the skating rink. But then he'd done his sums and worked out the cost of heating the place in December and decided he would never break even.

'In the summer folks don't mind, if the place isn't cosy,' he said. 'But in the winter when you have to drag 'em away from the warmth of their own hearths it's a different matter altogether.'

So 'Potter's Christmas Extravaganza' never happened. Which I was sad for, because he'd promised sleigh bells on the swingboats and carol singers in the yard. Ma had even found a recipe for hot punch. There would have been good takings to be had for me handing out hot taties for folks to put in their pockets to keep their hands warm and, if it was wet, pennies for watching over their brollies and galoshes when they went in for their teas.

Still, I told myself as I ran down the hill at daybreak on Christmas Eve, it would mean there was nothing changed. I had my da's knapsack on my back, emptied of rocks and filled with presents for everyone, and a bloomin' heavy basket swinging off my arm packed with goodies from Edie. She must have worried we'd have a poor Christmas otherwise.

Ma told me not to be ungrateful as she unpacked jars of mincemeat and sauces, a fat plum pudding (bought from Robertsons in Oakenshaw and untouched by Livvy's hand), a tub of goose fat and a big box of sweets. She said gifts at Christmas were always welcome.

Maud and Peggy were proud as Punch of their decorations this year. Peggy led me round as if I was a guest from another country who had never seen paper chains or a holly wreath before. They made the chains fresh every year, alternating the brown mill paper with brighter-coloured stuff that Maud, magpie-like, gathered and saved through the year from parcels and deliveries. She was especially proud this time of the stiff green paper that she had cut into the shape of holly leaves. When she saw the box of sweets in Edie's hamper she straight away bagged the shiny wrappers to put away for next year.

There was a yew bough over the mantel. Ma had saved the decorating of that for when I arrived. I went gathering firewood with Maud first. Breathing in the river-damp air like a parched man downing water. Maud was in one of her good moods and stopped with me by the dam to skim stones. I reminded her how it had been frozen last year and how the stones had rung like metal on metal. She said she remembered the ice being thick and grey as if it held smoke not water below, and I told her she could have been a poet if she wasn't so set on being a farmer's wife. I feared she was going to clout me, but she just said, 'Don't go spouting on subjects you know nothing about, our Billy.' I caught the smile she wasn't quick enough to hide.

When we got back, our sled laden with branches and twigs, Ma had the box of glass decorations out from under the bed. Her and Da had bought them just after the war, on a trip to Blackpool arranged by Nathaniel Potter for his workers. Five glass shapes, though there'd been six once: the one shaped like an angel had broken when I was only small.

My favourite was the trumpet, with its sheen of yellow brass (copper and zinc, I thought, and knew Charles would have been proud). Peggy loved the soldier with his red jacket and for Maud it was the golden harp. We hung them on the yew bough and Ma added the star and the pine cone. In between, Maud wove sprigs of berried holly saved over from the wreath, yelping whenever the leaves spiked her thumbs. As we sat by the fire we remembered past Christmases and Ma told us stories of how it was when Da was alive. How he would play blind man's buff and try to cheat at charades. And how he would say that all you needed for a good Christmas was a handful of Shaws.

'Mr Nathaniel came down one Christmas,' I said.

'No, he never did,' said Ma, adding, 'Mrs Potter would never give him leave, not at Christmas.'

But I remembered it clearly. Him standing in front of our fireplace, looking too big for the room with the evergreen on the mantel sprouting behind his head like bushy green whiskers.

'Maybe he sneaked out while she was minding the goose,' I said. Ma told me to watch my cheek, and at that moment the lights went out.

'That's the Potters off to bed,' she said, as she always did, and stood up to light the lamp.

On Christmas morning we hiked up to Draper's Cross chapel. The school building alongside was closed and shuttered but Miss Offat was one of the first to greet me as we entered the churchyard. I wished I'd brought up my bird notebook to show her. Though Jasper's drawings would have taken some explaining.

The sermon was long and the pews were hard but it was grand to see all the familiar faces. I knew the Potters wouldn't be there. They were High Church and drove over Halifax-way for their worship, even on Christmas morning. But I had a present in my pocket for Lizzie just in case, the poem about the skylark written out in my neatest hand.

Back home we handed out our gifts. Ma said the bundle of clothes pegs I'd whittled was very thoughtful and Peggy loved her carved lion and didn't notice or didn't mention that one of its paws was askew. I gave Maud a pretty sketch of a pair of curlews done by Jasper (another trade, this time for a promise that I'd take the blame next time he broke anything at all). She said it was perfect and she'd ask Arthur to make a frame to put it in. She hugged me, so I knew she meant it.

Then Ma was bustling about the stove and Maud and Peggy were laying the cloth on the table and setting the wreath in the centre with the big fat yellow candle in the middle. There was a goose and slices of tongue. Taties, roasted in the dripping, and a big jug of bread sauce. Ma opened the apple sauce that Edie had sent but she put by the plum pudding for the one she'd made herself. Peggy bit into the sixpence and made a wish, which she told me later was that I would come back home for good.

'Maud's tons nicer when you're here,' she said.

'Crikey, she must be a gorgon when I'm not.' Which made her laugh and then I had to tell her all about the Gorgons and Perseus, making up any bits I couldn't remember right.

After the pudding we took it in turns to pull a motto from the wreath where Maud had hidden them wrapped in coloured tissue. She'd written the verses herself and I said again about how she could be a poet, but this time she did clout me. Peggy said they were all lovely and she'd keep hers for ever.

We went for a walk in the early evening and listened for the calling of the owls. Peggy said it was the saddest sound in the world, never mind that they were calling to one another and making friends.

When we got back Ma made us mugs of cocoa and I must have fallen asleep on the rug by the fire because next thing I knew she was shaking my shoulder, and the oil lamps were lit.

'The Potters have gone to bed,' I said.

'Aye.' Her face was pale and thin, with all the joy and energy of the day gone. 'I reckon they have and we best had too while there's still warmth from the fire in our bones.'

Now it was the first day of the new year and I was back in the garden of High Hob, with Jasper ranting about an old woman wanting to fatten him up for dinner. It was like I'd never been away.

'What old woman?' I asked.

'Boys!'

Edie was leaning from the open window of her study.

I heard Charles shout from inside. 'Will you shut that bloody thing? The fire'll never catch with a gale blowing through.'

Edie took no notice.

'Come on in, you're missing the party.' Her voice lit up and down, like she'd been practising Christmas carols and still had the tunes in her head.

I wondered if she expected us to hop through the window, but then she waved towards the front door. 'Get your outers off, William, and warm yourself by the roaring fire that Charles is making.' She gave us a great big wink before shutting the window. I'd never known her be so playful. She must have been full of that Christmas spirit.

I hung my cap and my coat on the pegs by the door and took a while in pulling off my boots. I wasn't in a hurry to go through to the study, not with Edie in such an odd mood and Charles sounding like he was building up to a storm.

'What's going on?' I asked. 'Is the old woman who wants to eat you in there?'

Jasper nodded, while picking a scab on his knuckle. It was a brilliant one, well crusted. He was lifting the edges with his fingernail.

'They turned up last night. Edie said it's been arranged for weeks but it was the first Charles knew of it and Edie said who else did he think was going to eat the side of beef and the cheese and puddings that Robertsons delivered on Friday. And Livvy said, "Am I expected to work miracles?"' Jasper was brilliant at doing Livvy's flat voice. Last night's supper hadn't been served up till after ten o'clock and the beef was burnt black on the outside and still running blood at the centre. 'And today Sally's been acting half-daft and driving Charles doolally-tap. Anyway,' he finished up, 'they're all in there.'

'All of them?'

'The woman's got this soppy husband and they've been sleeping in my room so I've had to bunk in yours. There's another one who just puffs on his pipe all day long.'

'Boys!' Edie stood in the doorway of her room, arms spread out with a hand clutching each door jamb. Silver fringes hung from the shoulders of her black dress, all a-sparkle with beads. Her voice wasn't so sing-song now. There was a little crease in the space between her eyebrows. 'Come on through, for goodness sake. We've got nibbles and if you're very good we might allow you a glass of sherry. Just this once.'

We trudged through. The sherry wasn't much of a spur. Jasper had pinched the bottle from Charles's cabinet months ago. We'd both felt sick after long slugs of it and had topped it back up with sugar and water. Jasper said they'd never know cos they only gave it to guests and guests were too polite to complain. It might even make it taste better.

Edie's room was filled with a heavy scent, not the usual flowery sweetness of her perfume. Charles was crouched by the fire with

Sally. She had a white pinny tied round her waist and her dark hair was scrunched up under a white cap that I'd never seen before. Charles was telling her to hold up a sheet of newspaper closer to the fire.

'To create a draw,' he said. 'Once the air is through we'll be blazing.'

At that moment the centre of the sheet burst into a circle of flame. Sally yelped and fell backward and the paper floated up, dripping burnt flakes like black snow. Charles lunged at it and flapped it into the fireplace.

'For goodness sake. You silly girl.' He grabbed a fresh sheet of newspaper from the pile by his feet. 'I'll do it myself.'

Sally stumbled to her feet, brushed down her skirts and ran past us out of the room, making a clumsy bob to Edie as she went by.

A man standing by the window was tapping the end of a pipe against his lips, watching Charles. His suit was sharp with coloured lapels and his tie was a bright green plaid. He squinted his eyes as he lit a match and raised it to the bowl of his pipe, sucking in his cheeks and releasing little clouds of smoke.

Among a cluster of chairs by the fire sat a man and a woman. The woman had a fine shawl wrapped around her like a cocoon. Her hair was chestnut brown and she didn't look particularly old, not much older than Edie and definitely not as old as Ma, but when she glanced up I knew Jasper was right. She was the child-eating type. The tip of her tongue ran across her upper lip. The man next to her was pale and limp like a piece of wet haddock, flopped over the edges of the chair.

'Everyone, this is William,' Edie announced. 'Jasper's little friend. William, this is Bunty and George, my two oldest dearest friends come all the way from London to welcome in the new year with us.'

Haddock man didn't stir but the woman smiled. I half expected fangs but her teeth were normal, small and square.

'And they've brought Mr Anthony Hobart with them,' Edie continued. 'Aren't we fortunate?'

Mr Hobart's face was partly shadowed because of the light from the window behind him but he raised his pipe in our direction. I realised the unfamiliar scent was coming from him, though whether it was perfume or his tobacco I couldn't tell.

Lunch was leftovers. I handed over a sweet mincemeat pie that Ma had made and told Edie it could be eaten cold but was best heated through. Edie glanced at Livvy simmering over the meat slices. 'Cold will be lovely, we'll top it with cream.'

The child-eating woman, Bunty, said the mincemeat was 'Full of character' as she picked bits of it from her teeth. Nobody'd ever said Ma's pies were full of character before. I'd make sure to tell her. Though she'd be more concerned that it was full of fruit and good suet herself.

I had a couple of slices of the pie and a stack of buttery biscuits that had been brought from London. We had our promised sherry too. Mr Hobart raised his glass to the light to inspect it. His face was pink and round but his features were all bunched close, as if they had been pinched together in the middle.

'Jolly good vintage,' he declared.

'Best vintage sugar water,' Jasper whispered behind his hand.

I hoped we'd get away after we'd eaten. I wanted to show Jasper my new knife that Ma and the girls had got me. But Edie kept giving us a 'stay right where you are' look.

Jasper got out a pack of cards and showed me a game called gin rummy. We used crackers for stakes and I soon had a fair pile of them but lost them all even quicker. Jasper kept scoffing his takings so there was no knowing who was winning.

Charles tried to teach us tactics to improve our game.

'You watch him, boys,' Mr Hobart said. 'He's a demon on the tables.' But Charles soon got bored with Jasper doing the exact opposite of what he suggested and after saying something in a low voice to Mr Hobart the pair of them left the room. Haddock man was asleep in his chair, or at least his eyes were closed, an unlit cigar drooped in his hand.

I had half my mind on the card game and half on Edie and Bunty who were sitting close together, drinking gin from long glasses packed with slices of lemon. Bunty was chattering like a spring bird but I could tell Edie was only half there. She held her glass close to her nose as if sniffing the freshness of the fruit. She nodded when Bunty described a party she'd been to, but I bet she couldn't have repeated any of the details back if she had been asked.

'I couldn't help but notice.' There was a rise in Bunty's voice that made me look up. She took a sip from her glass and nodded in our direction. 'He has such a look of his father to him. More than just his face. The way he holds himself. That same cockiness. He's still got it, the swine.'

Edie looked more alert now. Her eyes flickered in my direction but then settled on Jasper.

'Bunty, please.'

'Oh, tush. We're among friends here.' She looked at her husband and raised her eyebrows. 'And not even conscious ones at that.'

Edie was frowning, her fingers fidgeting with the fringe of beads at her shoulder. If she rubbed them any harder they were going to come apart and there would be beads everywhere again. But then she stopped and patted her hands together. 'What's this about Robbie Plummer's new play causing a scandal in the West End?'

Bunty had spoken as if Jasper's father was still alive, not dead in France. Might he even have been at that party she'd been describing? Jasper didn't seem to have noticed. He was stacking up his crackers and while I wasn't concentrating had added most of mine to his pile too.

When Charles and Mr Hobart came back through Mr Hobart was talking about a palace. I expected he meant Buckingham Palace where the King lived, so when he started talking about lions I wasn't surprised. They had great big bronze lions in London. I'd seen pictures in one of Charles's books.

'This chap says he can get me a male and a female,' he went on. 'A troupe of monkeys too. I said to him, Barney, you show me the figures. If they add up it's a goer. And while you're at it, find me a lad to shovel up their muck, there are gardeners who'll pay hard cash for the stuff.'

One thing I knew for certain was bronze lions didn't make muck.

'Do you mean real lions and monkeys, sir?' I asked. He looked round as if a mouse had squeaked and he couldn't find it. Then he saw me. 'Well yes, sonny. We could hardly call it a "wildlife enclosure" with stuffed animals now, could we?'

'Are you a zookeeper?' asked Jasper. Mr Hobart pursed his lips.

'I am many things,' he said. 'But a zookeeper is not one of them.' He folded his arms. 'Eastlea Palace and Winter Gardens is London's Premier Entertainment Emporium, of which I am sole proprietor and impresario.'

My mouth fell open. He was talking about a real palace, my kind of palace, and a pretty special one by the sound of it.

'You've got live animals?' I asked.

'Soon will, all being well.'

'And dancing?' I asked. 'And skating?'

'Oh yes,' he said. 'Got a sprung dance floor and next to it the finest rink you'll find in England.'

'We've got a grand rink down at Potter's Palace, sir.' I jumped to my feet, so eager was I to tell him. 'Polished wood floor with pillars in the middle to swing round and there's singing, though you're pushed to hear it above the roar of the rollers.'

Mr Hobart waved his hand for me to stop. 'Not a roller-skating rink, boy.' His voice dripped with something that said he would never set foot in such a place. Beside him Charles chuckled.

'Ice skating is what the customers are clamouring for in the city.' He turned to Charles. 'Doddle to set up and the running costs are minimal. Got brine piped in from the dairy next door. Makes for a surface like glass.' He shook his head at me. 'There's no roar, boy, just the sweet sound of the till roll turning. You must pay us a visit. Any friend of Charles is a friend of mine.' He nodded at Jasper. 'You too, if you fancy it.'

He turned back to Charles and gave him a slap on his back. 'If this wildlife enclosure goes ahead I'll give you a call, old boy. Or rather I'll call Garth Winter. Have you cutting the ribbon on his behalf. Make a speech about the taming of the wild, that sort of thing.'

'You'll be asking me to turn up in fancy dress next.'

'Not a bad idea. Bring one of your guns. We'll mock up a scene from, what was it, *Winter on the Amazon*? A couple of pot plants from the hot house, a friendly chimp clinging to your back.'

'There aren't any chimpanzees in South America,' Charles said, but Mr Hobart wasn't deterred. 'We host a wrestling match first Saturday of every month. Group of lads who'd look good in loincloths. There's your savages for you.'

My head was full of lions and monkeys and a floor of ice. What with that and Mr Hobart's perfume and the sugar water and the butter biscuits stacked up in my belly I was feeling fair woozy.

Then Jasper leaned in and whispered, 'We can go now, no one will notice.' And he was right. The grown-ups were all huddled together with their glasses and their bottles and their smoke.

We went up to my room and I showed Jasper my penknife and he showed me his new watch and pocket compass which he said an explorer couldn't do without, though I saw the way he eyed my knife, with its different blades, and I reckon he wanted that more. He'd added more details to the Beast picture on the wall. It had fangs now, like the ones on the skull, and long claws. I preferred how it was before. The fangs made it more like a creature from a comic book. I didn't tell him though. It was still the holidays and I didn't feel up to a fight.

We talked instead about Mr Hobart's palace and how if Potter didn't want the Beast we would take it to London. We laughed ourselves daft imagining it with skates fastened to its paws and Charles chasing it with his rifle across the ice. It was best when Jasper was like this, though it was rare and never lasted long. I couldn't afford to forget how quickly the darkness could come over him and how swiftly a joke could switch to a threat. We hadn't come to blows again since my birthday, but it never felt safe to drop my guard.

My wooziness passed and I helped Jasper eat some of the cold beef he'd smuggled upstairs. Tearing off chunks and pretending we were hyenas finishing off a zebra. Jasper did the best hyena whoops, copied from one of Charles's gramophone records. It was so loud and chilling I couldn't believe that no one came up to see what was going on. Afterwards he made a nest of blankets and pillows on my floor and I turned off the lamp. He fell asleep before I did, and I lay in the dark listening to the snuffles and whimpers that interrupted his slow steady breaths.

In the morning we woke late and ate the remains of smuggled leftovers for breakfast, before we ventured downstairs. The door to Jasper's room was shut tight and the house was as quiet as Sunday so we reckoned that everyone else must still be asleep. The door to Charles's study was closed, but Edie's was ajar. Inside, a quick shadow crossed the room.

Jasper was saying it was black tiles today, remember, when there was a shout from Edie's study and then smash smash smash like ice stamped underfoot.

The shout was Charles, I was sure of it, but then came Edie's voice, a roll of words of which I only caught half, but I know she was calling him 'stupid' and 'inconsiderate' and 'careless', words usually saved for me and Jasper.

Charles's voice broke through her tirade with a rising growl. 'Are you my gaoler? I'm tired of it, Edie. You can't deny me ...' He let out a yelp that wasn't far off Jasper's hyena call.

'I won't let you, Charles. Not again. Bunty is happy to tattle tales to me so who knows who else she's blabbed to. When will you realise how dangerous, how stupid—'

There was a roar and the door to her room was flung open. Charles filled the frame, head down, his gold and green robe hanging loose to the waist, revealing his chest as dark and hairy as a beast's beneath.

I stared at the thick matt of fur and thought of the time I'd suggested the Beast might be a werewolf. Jasper had said no chance. I tried to remember if it was a full moon now, and were we both about to be eaten alive.

Charles raised his head and I half expected the snout of a wolf or at least a pair of burning red eyes. But it was just Charles, same as always except maybe a werewolf had got him, for below his left eye there was a deep cut and a smear of blood on his cheek.

CHAPTER 12

Anna: December

Subject: Presentation to the Board 1 attachment
From: Erica J Walker 11th December
To: Anna Sallis

Dear Anna

Apologies for the delay in getting back to you after your thought-provoking presentation to the board. Our members are very appreciative of your efforts, both the great strides you have made in organising and promoting the collection, and also your 'blue sky thinking' on the future. I hope we made our appreciation clear.

All the members now have copies of your full proposals to examine in further detail. I know that you had hoped to get a final response before the end of this calendar year, however the Festive Season is upon us and we are all, to a man, and woman, committed to community and family responsibilities.

The New Year will be a more fitting time to look forwards, and I assure you that the board will reconvene at the earliest possibility, once tinsel and trappings are packed away, to make a decision.

Meanwhile I attach the approved form of your Press Release for the *Courier*.

Best wishes

Erica

Halifax Evening Courier
15th December

ANNA UNEARTHS LITERARY TREASURE
Ackerdean Custodian Anna Sallis has found a lost work that sheds new light on one of our local legends

Death-defying chases, narrow escapes and swashbuckling derring-do: the usual elements of a Charles Harper novel, brought vividly to life by 1970s heart-throb Carl Hunter as the heroic Garth Winter in the perennially popular films. But Anna Sallis, who has spent the last few months trawling through the archives at the Ackerdean Heritage Centre, discovered another side to the adventure writer when she stumbled across a collection of his poetry.

'The manuscript has been lost for years,' she explains. 'The poems, which are dedicated to his brother, a real-life action hero, give us a more balanced view of Charles Harper's breadth as a writer and a glimpse of his sensitive side.'

Excerpts from the poems will be included in a new multimedia exhibition at the Centre next spring, created with help from Year Six children from Sowley J and I, and Hillside Primary. 'There are currently no plans to place the full manuscript on public display,' says Erica Walker, Chair of Ackerdean Board, 'due to its rare and fragile nature.'

It's all looking very festive down here at the mill. A big thank you to everyone who joined the Friends of Ackerdean in bedecking the museums, yard and café in their evergreen finery. Special thanks to the Acker Valley WI for the beautiful garlands.

All we need now is a dusting of snow and we will have the perfect setting for our carol concert on Sunday in the mill yard. Sowley Junior Brass Band will strike up at 2 pm and song sheets will be available. Mulled cider and hot mince pies along with May's usual goodies available all afternoon.

Looking forward to seeing you there

Seasons' Greetings
to a Special Daughter

**Merry Christmas, Anna
lots of love Mum and Dad xxx**

ps Looking forward to seeing you on Christmas Eve. Take care when you come off the A9, your Dad's worried about black ice

From: Anna Sallis

1 attachment

To: Sam Klein

23rd December

Merry Christmas!

Sorry you missed the carols. It was lovely despite the lack of
snow. Hope you had a productive time in London.

Thank you for the card and invite to your New Year's Eve party.
Sounds good fun and I will do my best to be there – as long as I
don't end up snowbound in Scotland or made comatose by too
much of Dad's homemade beer or Mum's sloe gin. Since they
took early retirement and moved north of the border my folks have
turned into drink producers on a grand scale. I'm expecting news
of a new distillery any day now!

I have attached a small Christmas gift. I found this interview
with Charles Harper in an old magazine in the files. It's from just
a month or so before he died. Planning to work it into the new
display, but meanwhile thought you might like to read it (after you
saying how much you hate giving interviews!) so scanned you a
copy. He sounds as though he had plenty of plans for the future.
Not that I'd expect him to confide suicidal feelings to a journalist,
but still.

Will be in touch when I get back.

Best

Anna

BTW Also have some juicy oral history excerpts about High Hob
– from the Harper's maid, no less. Would love your thoughts on
them – will fill you in when I see you.

A 'WINTER' TEASER by Robin May

Garth Winter's latest adventure *Winter in the Alps* is to be published this month. His fans are agog to discover what dangers and excitements our hero will find himself embroiled in next after his recent tussles with a tribe of orang-utans. I asked his creator Charles Harper: What has Garth got coming his way this time?

'Elephants,' he told me. 'A whole herd of them. Garth sets out to imitate Hannibal, transporting a dozen elephants over the Alps. No mean feat but one that he is obviously equal to.'

'Aha, hence the title. But is it merely a publicity stunt? Doesn't sound like Garth's usual style.'

'No, for him it's just another job. But the businessman who's contracted him will certainly be hoping to get some publicity from it. They're part of his big show that he is taking on tour over Western Europe. Crossing the Alps is only the start.'

'And I imagine something or someone tries to get in Garth's way.'

'Of course. Where would the adventure be without the bad guys? A rival showman hears about the scheme and decides to try to shoot it in the foot. The elephant's foot.'

'Sounds like it could get dangerous.'

'It does. But Garth thrives on danger, he'd be bored without it.'

'And the beautiful lady?'

'Garth and the elephants are accompanied by the animal trainer Selima Whittaker, a bewitching half-Indian girl with a scandalous past that is about to catch up with her.'

'Sounds wonderful, Mr Harper. I'm sure your readers are on the edge of their seats in anticipation. Once he's recovered from this adventure, any idea where Garth will be heading next?'

'Well there's a whole world out there for him to explore. Australia may well be calling. The parched desert, the perilous outback, and the prospect of a sun-drenched goddess or two. Could be just what he needs.'

'Indeed. Sounds like Garth Winter's idea of heaven.'

CHAPTER 13

Billy: 1933

The snow came in February, thick and wild, like swarms of pale bees. We were trapped inside for days; explorers holed up in the Antarctic with only our wits and Major Sefton's improvised 'indoor drills' to help us survive. Outside lesson time, when we ran out of games, we turned to a stack of American magazines Charles had been sent. Full of stories about creatures from outer space. Long-legged aliens and robots now occupied more of Jasper's drawings than the Beast. I would catch him staring up at the snow-laden sky as if he was wishing for some strange being to tumble to earth. Probably so he could dissect it and draw its insides.

At the end of February word reached us Old Abe had taken ill and was being cared for by his sister Dolly over in Haworth.

'He's the last one who'll ever know the full truth,' said Jasper. 'It's down to us now to carry on the hunt.' But the hunger for it had gone from his eyes. He'd got bored of things before, abandoning ideas halfway through and moving on to something more interesting, but this was the first time I'd seen a hint of him losing faith in us catching the Beast. It didn't help that we spent so much time indoors and when we did go out the air nipped hard at his lungs. He'd never admit it but it was there plain on his face when he couldn't catch his breath and he'd bend double or squat on his haunches pretending to inspect the ground. The doctor called it asthma and said it was nothing that fresh air wouldn't cure. I heard him telling Edie that it was common in children who'd lost their fathers; that they would make themselves ill with the sadness of it. Edie gave him short shrift. Told him Jasper had all the family a boy could need.

The snow had cleared by Easter and the moor was waking up, the curlews marking out their territory and lone buzzards on reconnaissance missions, spying out unwary rodents in the heath. When I heard the piping of a meadow pipit I knew spring was here to stay.

My thirteenth birthday was Easter Saturday. One of the busiest days at the Palace. Ma and my sisters would be all hands on deck in the tea rooms. I was torn between wanting to go down and help, throw myself back into that world, and yet not wanting to, cos I was feeling more and more distant from it all. Before I came to High Hob, my life and the life of the Palace had been one rollicking stream but now it was like I'd snagged on a rock and I was 'Billy-in-between', not really belonging to either place, and aiming in the end for somewhere else altogether. Lizzie was part of it. Part of me wanting to get it right. To not mess up or let myself down.

When Charles suggested going out in the car on my birthday like we had last year, but a longer trip this time to the Dales, I said yes. It's not as if Ma and the girls would be able to come for tea. They'd be buttering bread and scones for the trippers till dusk fell. They sent me presents though, delivered by a flush-faced Arty Chambers who said he was doing it as a favour to Maud. There was a card with blue and purple pansies pressed and dried and glued to the front. One of my sisters, Maud probably because it wasn't at all smudged, had printed 'Birthday Greetings' underneath. There was also a short note from Maud. She wanted me to hear it from her before anyone else that her and Arty were engaged to be wed.

Major Sefton took us camping the week after. Jasper had seen the scout tents up on the hillside above the Palace and said it looked like a right laugh. The Major seemed set on showing us it was anything but. It was hard work, especially in the rain. But we learned to skin a rabbit and cook it over a fire and on the last day we shot at targets with his air rifle. He said he'd make men of us yet.

So we missed Easter at the Palace but by the time Whit weekend came rolling round in June I had an ache to go down, Billy-in-between or no. Just the thought of bumping into Lizzie in the sunshine, among the ribbons and the bunting, was enough to push my doubts away.

'It'll be busy as hell,' I told Jasper.

'And will your girl be there?' he asked, as if he could read my mind. I ignored him but he added, 'Better not let Potter see you. He doesn't fancy the likes of you for his daughter.' We both called him Potter now and I'd even stopped thinking of him as Mr Nathaniel in my head.

I brushed off his teasing. Said instead that there'd be a few bob in it for us, if we played it right. I told him of the ways I used to earn tips from the trippers. Although we wanted for nothing up at High Hob there was never any harm in putting a few pennies by.

'You sound like Mr Hobart,' said Jasper with a sly look.

Aye, or Nathaniel Potter himself, I thought.

Folk must have been marching up the road since the first train got in. The place was jam-packed when we got there just past eleven o'clock by Jasper's wristwatch, though I was glad to see the old clock still said twenty past four. There was a queue for the swing-boats already. Each boat was only built to take two but there were three or four people in each one. The chains were groaning and the faces of the dragons strained with the effort as they lunged for the sky.

The maypole was fixed up with its rainbow ribbons, ready for the dancing. The rowboats were tied in a line at the edge of the bottom dam and a banner said, 'Regatta. All Welcome. 1s 6d per boat. Big Prize'. One of Potter's new ideas, because I'd never heard of a regatta before. Jasper said it meant a boat race and chaps waving their hats and people cheering. There'd been one on the river at his last but one school, but he hadn't been allowed to take part.

The crowds were heaving like a nest of snakes. There was extra bunting out in every colour, hanging in two rows criss-crossing above the yard, fluttering in the breeze like strings of butterflies. The air was filled with the hot smell of the taties singeing in the oven on the hawker's cart and fried onions from the stall at the entrance to the yard where they sold faggots and peas for them that didn't want to sit down and eat inside. There was a richer and meatier smell too and I guessed Joseph had got a hog roast going behind the Pav. My mouth was watering just thinking about it. But first, so as not to miss a trick, we set about offering to fetch hot drinks for the picnickers and we soon had a pocketful of ha'pennies each.

We were standing in the yard, backs against the rough wall, hot taties in our hands. The insides were fluffy and buttery and I'd scooped all mine out and was about to start on the leathery jacket when I saw Lizzie.

Her hair was hid mostly by her hat pulled low on her head, but the bits that showed were as shiny and slick as feathers. I checked quick behind her and over the bridge but there was no sign of her father. She was talking with Jane, all serious, then she looked up, straight at me, and laughed out loud. I nearly dropped my tatie. She whispered to her friend who glanced over to us and then quickly away.

'What's biting you?' Jasper asked. His mouth was full of potato and there were creamy flecks of it in his curls.

'Nowt.' My cheeks felt hot, but I couldn't blame the baked tatie.

If he knew it was cos of Lizzie I'd not hear the last of it. I'd been so keen to see her but now there she was looking all fancy and me with the tatie carcass in my hands and my socks and boots all wet from when I'd slipped off the stepping stones before.

'Let's go and see my mother,' I said and we crossed the yard and tucked through the door. I caught a glimpse of Lizzie frowning before we were safe inside.

There was a steaming crowd in the tea rooms. Every table was full with people squeezed in on extra chairs that had been brought down from the dance hall. Cake stands were piled with scones and slices and slabs of pie were stacked alongside plates of ham and cheese and jugs of cream. My sisters were weaving in and out with trays.

Ma gave me a smack of a kiss on my head. 'Well, aren't you a sight for sore eyes, our Billy. You too, Jasper. You're both looking grand.' Jasper let her pat him on the arm. 'Go make yourselves up a plate each in the back. But be good lads and stay in there. There isn't a seat to spare or air left to breathe out here.'

At the far side of the room the windows looked out over the dam. It would have been the best place to watch the boat race later, but it was separated off by a wooden screen that Maud kept slipping behind. That was the first-class section where all the nobs ate. When I was a tiddler I used to think they ate different from us and were embarrassed to be seen at it. Maybe they got on all fours and lapped their tea like dogs, or used their feet instead of their hands. I was sore disappointed, when I plucked up the courage to peek, that they ate no different and no better nor worse than anyone else. They got the First Class Service though, which Ma said was basically thicker slices of ham, an extra pot of hot water for their tea and making sure Maud's cap wasn't skew-whiff.

I knew I shouldn't have told Jasper about it. When we'd finished off our plates he said he had to have a look, to be certain the First Class nobs weren't space aliens in disguise. He pressed himself flat against the wall next to the screen and sneaked a peek behind. Then he dropped on to his hands and knees and crawled out of view. I imagined him under the tables in amongst the stockinged ankles and polished boots. Even I'd not done that. Then he was back out again and up on his two feet and leading me to the stairs.

Once out in the yard I followed him round to the dam at the back. The race was due to start in half an hour. A group of blokes by the boats were haggling over which was likely to be the fastest. A couple of them had oars raised, acting like they might come to blows. David was there with a bag over his shoulder collecting their coins and shouting, 'Keep it friendly, lads.'

Jasper led me away up the path to the ruins of the top pavilion, which had been closed since the war. We climbed through the long grass to the back of it where the smell of rotting wood was strong. The paint had all weathered away and the planks were like matted straw.

Jasper pulled his jacket open and a fox's head snarled up at me, its teeth bared.

I pressed back against the crumbling wood, thinking he'd caught a live fox and fearing that if he loosened his grip it would leap at my throat.

He waggled the head and barked, 'Arf arf. Hello, Master Billy.' And I saw it was a fox fur looped round his neck, the head and tail hanging over his shoulders. He fastened his jacket back up.

'Where did you get that?'

'One of the nobs,' he said, pinching my word. 'She'd dropped it so that means she didn't want it any more, right? She had enough flesh to keep herself warm, she didn't need Mr Fox.'

'What are you going to do with it?' I stared at the bulge under the wool of his jacket.

'Dunno. Beast bait maybe. It's worth a go.' It was the first time he'd suggested Beast hunting for ages and though I didn't think a long-dead fox would help much I was glad he seemed keen to get back on its trail.

*

Shouts from the Palace drew us back to the dam, where the race was about to begin. As we elbowed our way through the crowd I lost sight of Jasper. When I reached the front there was a jostling to my left, someone pushing their way through. I felt a warm hand on mine and Lizzie whispered in my ear.

'Bet you a penny the pair in the yellow caps win.'

Ma had told me gambling was a sin and worse it drove honest men to drink and destruction. But Lizzie's face was so close to mine, I could see myself reflected in the shine of her eyes. I looked back at the boats. One of the men who'd had his oar raised earlier had his shirtsleeves up, and was flexing his muscles. At the front of his boat his mate was sat in place, eyes already fixed ahead.

'The boat with the green band,' I said. 'It'll take yours by half an oar's length.'

'Show me your penny,' she said.

I rummaged in my pocket and held up two ha'penny bits.

David shouted for the rowers to get in position. He blew a whistle and there was a scuffle and splash of oars and a roar from the men in the boats as they set off. The race was to the far side and back. My blokes were leading as they reached the end and started to turn. Jasper was at the edge there, his eyes wide, fixed on the rowers, face red as he yelled. The turn was tight, with boats bumping and oars clashing. The man with the muscles in the back of the green-banded boat stood up with his oar and clouted the man in the next boat, who roared and clouted him back. My man wobbled and the boat tipped and emptied them both in. Above their shouts and splashing there was a cheer as the two blokes in the yellow caps won the race.

Lizzie's fingers closed over the coins in my hand. She leaned in to me as the crowd pressed from behind and I could feel the warmth of her body. The smell of her so close was like spring blossom. I slipped my arm around her waist, and she didn't move away. We stood like that not speaking as the crowd billowed around us and then started to drift away. Across the dam I spotted Potter scanning the crowd. Behind him Jane, frowning again now. Potter squinted in our direction.

'Bye, Billy.' Her lips so close to my ear, I felt the words as much as heard them. Then she was gone.

'Next year, you and me we'll whup them.' Jasper red-faced, his curls a wild mop. 'We'll need to practise though.' He was eyeing up the boats. 'Did you see that bloke fall in? What an idiot. If you're going to sab the other team you have to be more subtle than that.' I nodded though I scarce took in his words, my whole body still aglow with Lizzie.

Jasper started to walk round the edge of the dam, tapping at the stone edge with a stick, talking about race tactics and the importance of the turn. I followed him. The crowd had cleared on the other side. There was no sign of Potter or Jane. I wanted to see Lizzie again. Wanted to be certain I hadn't dreamt her being there.

We circled the dam, ending up by the side of the Palace on the old bridge. Our cottage sat neat as ever across the yard. Jasper hurled his stick far as he could down the river. A duck minding its own business lifted its wings in alarm and I saw the flash of greeny-blue feathers. What did Lizzie think when she passed our cottage? Did she ever peer in through the windows? I smiled at the image of my sisters squawking like startled chicks in a nest if they ever spied her face pressed against the glass.

'I've got a fishing rod in my old room,' I said, remembering. 'I'll fetch it for next time we go to the falls.' I nodded towards the cottage. 'You can come in if you want.'

'Nah,' he said. 'I'll stay here.' He hoyed another stick but the duck was now beyond his reach.

The front door was locked. Ma didn't trust that trippers wouldn't wander in. But I knew where she hid the key under the stone by the step. It was quiet inside, the thickness of the walls dulling the outside noise to a buzz. I climbed the stairs to the room at the front that I had shared with my sisters. My bed was still there but spare linen from the tea rooms lay in neat piles on the blankets. I knelt on the boards and reached under the bed, my fingers finding and closing on the pole of the fishing rod and line that used to be my father's.

As I passed by the open door of Ma's room I spied the trunk at the end of her bed. The lock had been broken for years and the lid lifted with a creak. A couple of blankets lay over a thick wodge of old clothing. Da's best worsted suit was there. Ma said she'd alter it for me when I was tall enough and in need of something dapper. Underneath the heavy wool were Da's medals in their boxes and at the bottom, wedged in the corner, a soft leather pouch. I eased it open and out slid the silver pocket watch on a chain. Ma said it belonged to my granddad, my da's father, and one day it would be mine. On the back it was engraved with the words 'For devoted service' and then the date '1897'.

It weighed heavy in my hand, like the perfect smooth stone you always hope you'll find in the river. There was a bar at one end of the chain to slip through a buttonhole. I couldn't imagine Da wearing it, nor his father either, even though he was foreman at Ackerdean before he died. It was all engraved with flowers around the face. Maybe he kept it for Sundays.

I put it back into its pouch, then, I dunno why, but I slipped it into my pocket. Maybe it was because of Jasper taking the fox, though this was different as the watch was to be mine one day anyway. I put all the clothing back in, with the suit at the bottom. Chances were Ma wouldn't look beyond the blankets for a long while. That's what I told myself anyway as I left the cottage, though by the time I reached Jasper on the bridge I was of a mind to run back with it or at least tell Ma that I'd taken it. But Jasper grabbed at the fishing pole, saying we should go and try it out now.

Then I heard Potter calling my name as he pushed past a crowd of trippers on the riverbank. Maybe he just wanted to say hello, or maybe he wanted to find out what me and Lizzie had been talking about so close. He hadn't minded us being pals while we were both kids at the village school, but now she was growing up a young lady he wasn't so keen. It made my bones ache to know he thought so little of us Shaws.

'Come on.' I grabbed back the rod. 'We'll give it a go up at the falls.' I led the way through the ginnel between the Palace and the cottage, and up the track. All the while the smooth stone of the watch in my pocket banging time against my side.

Jasper couldn't resist prodding and poking at dark places. Starting the scrap with the bloke in the woods, stealing Mr Fox, filling jars with different types of animal blood that he got from who knows where. He had his reasons every time, why he was in the right and the rest of the world was wrong, but they were reasons that stood solid only in his own head.

Major Sefton, for all his strictness, liked this side of Jasper. Once, mid-lecture on the amphibian reproductive cycle, the splayed body of a dried Australian tree frog in his hand, its bulging eyes permanently startled, he was stopped by Jasper thrusting his own hand in the air.

'Could you keep it alive?' he asked. 'I mean, open it up and investigate its workings while it was still breathing?'

The notion of sticking a knife in living flesh made me squirm, though I wouldn't admit it to either of them. I wasn't even keen when the creature was dead as a doornail. But Major Sefton rubbed his moustache slowly as if giving it serious consideration.

'It would depend very much on your skill. Soon as it registered what you were doing it would die of shock. If you could do it undetected. Swift.' He flicked a finger over the carcass of the frog. 'And precise, not even disturbing it with your breath. It might be possible.' Then he explained to us in great detail how a traitor in the past would be disembowelled and his private parts removed while he was still living. 'So he could see his innards spilling out without the relief of dying first.'

Details enough for Jasper to reproduce the scene of the con-demned man in hideous detail in his sketchbook after supper that evening, while I lay on my bed trying not to picture the contents of my own stomach.

As the days got longer we started going down to the stretch of river near the Palace after our lessons. There was better fishing there than up at the falls though it could have been the new rod that made the difference. Sometimes, when we were there, especially if we ended up by the top dam lying against the rocks, watching the pond skaters and minnows, we'd meet Lizzie. Her own companion Jane never far behind.

Lizzie's father didn't know she was there and she said her mother was so busy now with her charity work and Ladies' Meetings that so long as she kept up with her schoolwork and had Jane to chaperone her she'd let her be.

We weren't bothered too much by Jane. More often than not she abandoned us to sit some distance away, on a rock or under a tree to read a book or fill pages in her diary.

Jane's parents were in India.

'They wouldn't take her with them,' Lizzie explained. 'They said she would wilt in the heat and catch every disease going.' She sighed. 'Just let Mother and Father try to keep me in England if they ever decided to move to India. Imagine missing out on seeing monkeys and tigers and riding on elephants and meeting maharajahs?'

I thought a maharajah was a tropical creature too, till she put me right, said it was a handsome prince with eyes like chocolate. I took against him straight away until she said that when she and the other girls at school played a game called 'The Maharajah and the Lady' she was always the prince not 'the swooning lady'.

The woods grew busier and the Palace was open more often and for longer, catering for parties in the evening and for the holiday-makers renting cottages or camping on the hillsides around. Packs of cyclists arrived in the evenings, racing up and down the track, some of them making a circuit along the top road and down to Sowley, then back to Ma's tables for their tea at the end. They fancied themselves, did the cycling lads, in their caps and blazers, and the lasses liked them too. There was that much hallooing and whooping, it was as though a flock of wild birds had set to roost in the valley.

When the summer arrived good and proper, Major Sefton went away on his travels. He was going to visit his fallen comrades, he said, and I didn't dare to ask whether he meant the graves of soldiers who'd died or those still living who, like him, had left the army once peace came.

Lizzie disappeared for three weeks visiting relatives with her family down Birmingham way. I missed her more than I expected. I'd got used to our easy conversations and trying out new ways to make her smile. Made me realise how much hard work Jasper was: it felt so comfortable being with someone and not having to worry if their mood would suddenly snap or that they'd be waving the innards of a baby rabbit in my face. When Lizzie came back she said she never wanted to see another Rutherford, that being her mother's family, as long as she lived. She declared that she intended to spend the rest of the summer as a wild creature of the woods.

That was fine by us. Charles and Edie, used to us being occupied by the Major during term time, didn't seem to notice that we were suddenly unsupervised. Edie was busy writing. Hiding herself away in her study more than ever. Like a hibernating animal only coming out to forage in the kitchen, fidgeting with tins and packets. She sat down with us one lunchtime and took one of Jasper's butties. Nibbled at the bread like a squirrel with a nut. She was staring at Jasper and I thought he'd done something wrong. He probably had, but I mean I thought he'd done something wrong and she'd found out. She put down the butty and her hand went out to his face. I was certain he was going to get a slap, though Jasper didn't flinch. But she just touched his cheek with two fingers, then stroked the side of his face down to his lips and rested them there. Then she snapped them away and rubbed at the crease between her brows.

Charles kept mainly to his routine of staying in his study all day and 'being allowed out' as he called it to the pub of an evening. One Thursday morning he announced he was going to London for the weekend and if Edie wanted to stop him she'd have to chain him up or barricade us all in the house. She did neither, but she did sulk from the minute he was gone. Doors were slammed so hard I feared the plasterwork might crack. Charles came back in a foul mood, with shadows under his eyes and his suit creased as if he'd slept in it. It was easiest if we kept out of their way.

One August afternoon, Lizzie and I were sitting by the steps that led up to the top dam. Her father was away on business for a week and her mother was helping to organise a flower show. It was the third day in a row that she'd been able to come down to meet us. Jane had stormed off upstream, complaining she'd had enough of Jasper's teasing, which mainly consisted of a song he'd made up about 'Plain Jane who died in the rain'. He didn't even have to sing the words, just whistling the tune was enough to make her angry. Not angry enough yet to tell tales to Mr and Mrs Potter, so I reckoned she valued having the freedom of the woods too. I saw her cross the old wooden bridge that led to the stone fisherman's hut where she'd gone before to write her diary 'in peace'. Lizzie and I were sitting close on the step, our knees touching, though I dared not put my arm around her while Jasper was nearby.

Along from the top of the steps a narrow stone wall overlooked the water below. Jasper was slowly making his way along it, one careful footstep at a time. I pointed out to Lizzie the spot on the opposite side of the pond, where I'd seen a kingfisher the day before perched on an overhanging tree branch.

'In the spring it had a nest in the river banking, just before the bend. I saw it go in and out.'

'Best not let on to my father. He collects birds' eggs.' She sighed. 'He has a whole cabinet full of them arranged from biggest to tiniest. I don't think he has a kingfisher's.' She tugged a long piece of grass from the ground, and pressed it between her thumbs. 'Is this right?' she asked. I knew she was only teasing. She could make a blade whistle as well as Jasper or I. She was about to raise it to her lips when she dropped it and grabbed my arm.

'There's that bird again,' she said. 'The daft one with the bobbing head.'

'It's a dipper,' I said. 'It's not daft. It's catching flies.'

We watched as it nodded its head and then flew low, skimming the top of the pond. I wanted the moment to stretch on and on, me and Lizzie holding on to each other and the rest of the world shut out. The bird tapped the water with its belly and took off again, grabbing a fly in its beak mid-air.

From above us Jasper shouted, 'Oy!'

In the middle of the wall there was a gap where the water overflowed down a stepped slope to the bottom dam. A wide horseshoe of metal stuck out over the drop, part of an old sluice no longer used. Jasper was standing at the furthest edge of the hoop. Not even making an act of having to keep his balance. Just standing there. Arms crossed. Being Jasper.

'Dare you!'

It was me he was daring but he was staring at Lizzie.

I didn't want to stand on the stupid bit of metal. I wasn't scared, though it was a long drop. I was just fed up of his daft challenges. Now that he knew I could outrun him and match him shot for shot with my catty he was always trying new ways to prove he was better than me. If he wanted to stand there gurning like the gargoyles on Oakenshaw church, that was his choice. I wasn't doing it. Lizzie stood up.

'You get down first. There isn't room up there for both of us.'

'He didn't mean you,' I said. But she ignored me and ran up the steps.

'All righty!' Jasper hopped back to the wall, passing her with a nudge on his way down the steps. Lizzie unbuckled her boots and as we stared pulled off her stockings. She put them in a neat pile on the wall. Without another word or glance at us she stepped onto the hoop. She winced as the cold metal touched her skin. Her feet were tiny and pale as china. I watched them, not the rest of her, as she made her way along. I might have forgotten to breathe cos when she got to the far end I let all the air out of my lungs in one go.

Lizzie held her arms out from her sides. She was staring dead ahead, her body so slight that I feared a gust of wind might blow her away.

Jasper started a slow clap and then a chant. 'One leg. One leg.'

Lizzie didn't blink. She stood there as if frozen. Maybe she was; the metal so cold it had seeped into her bones. Then she lifted her left foot and pointed the toes.

'Elizabeth!' Jane's shriek made me jump and Lizzie jolted too. I leaped forward with my arms stretched wide. Don't fall, please don't fall. The drop was down to rocks and boulders and the concrete slope of the sluice. She hung there for what seemed like for ever, her arms mirroring mine, ready for flight. I blinked and her raised foot was back down on the metal. Her arms back by her sides. Her face was lily white as her dark eyes found mine.

'Would you catch me, Billy, if I fell?'

'You won't,' I said. But I kept my arms ready as she stepped slowly, one cold foot in front of the other round the hoop of metal. As she stepped safe back onto the wall I dropped my arms and my shoulders ached as I let them go as if they'd borne the weight of her after all.

I was pushed out of the way as Jane charged past. 'Elizabeth Potter, if you've harmed a hair on your head while in my charge . . .'

I wanted to let out a huge bellow of relief to clear the image that had flashed into my mind, of Lizzie broken on the rocks. Nothing ever making her smile again. Her voice never again saying my name.

But already I could hear her gently chiding Jane, with 'I'm fine, stop fussing'. And her eyes when they caught mine were sparking and alive.

CHAPTER 14

Anna: New Year's Eve

'Five, four, three, two, one ... Happy new year!' Sam releases the cork on the bottle of champagne.

I should spend New Year's Eve with strangers more often, Anna thinks, as her arms are linked on either side and she joins in a chorus of 'Auld Lang Syne'. The walls of Edie's old study flicker in the light of the many candles that Sam has lit. It hasn't been the worst start to a new year ever. That would be last year's, three months after Dan's death. She hadn't been able to face renditions of 'should old acquaintance be forgot' and had been in bed, alone, long before midnight.

Sam has three friends up from London: Ben and Marie ('started dating when we were at sixth form together, had a huge wedding last year') and Jenny ('former flatmate, twice divorced, runs her own business making pincushions that look like famous politicians'). They are enthralled by their friend's very own 'Wuthering Heights' and intrigued by Anna's job at Ackerdean. Jenny has spent much of the evening speculating about the likelihood of ghosts at both places, only to be mocked by her friends. Anna laughs it off too, not wanting to admit that she has wondered the same herself.

Their evening had been interrupted at ten o'clock when Ruby's frantic barking in the hallway alerted them to the arrival of Sam's brother Carter. He'd flown into Manchester from Hamburg that afternoon and was clutching a bottle of duty free vodka. 'Happy Christmas, New Year whatever,' he said as he handed over the two-thirds empty bottle to Sam. 'Can you sub me the taxi fare, sis? The driver's getting a bit antsy out there, reckons that last bit of track to the house has knackered his exhaust.'

Without waiting for introductions he had fallen asleep on the sofa and wouldn't move despite frequent nudges and pinches from Sam. He snored his way through the midnight chimes and not even the popping of corks and raucous singing had roused him.

Sam adds more logs to the fire. 'I had my doubts,' she says as the others settle on to cushions on the floor. 'But getting in that chimney sweep was definitely worth it. Makes this room almost cosy having a functioning fire.'

Carter's snores can be heard behind them. Ruby has joined him, curled up in the gap between his body and the sofa back. Sam apologises again for her brother's behaviour.

'It's no excuse, but he is going through a horrible divorce. From a lovely woman, who deserves better.'

When Anna raises her eyebrows, Sam says, 'As a brother I love him dearly, but he's toxic in any other relationship. Don't be fooled by his sweet face and glib patter.'

From what Anna has seen so far he looks anything but sweet, having scowled throughout the five minutes or so before he fell asleep. Now curled up on the sofa around Ruby, only his close-cropped hair, the same dark red as his sister's, is showing.

Sam has switched off the lights. Their faces are lit by the flickering glow of the fire.

'We should tell ghost stories,' says Jenny. The hairs on Anna's arms prickle.

'Please no,' protests Marie. 'Some of us are hoping to get to sleep tonight. It's bad enough knowing those writers killed themselves here. No offence, Sam.'

'None taken,' says Sam. 'But I promise there are no ghosts. Ruby would have snuffled them out by now if there were. Dogs,' she adds with a grin. 'They see dead people, you know.'

There is a tap-tap-tap at the window and Marie gasps.

'It's just the wind blowing the branches of a tree against the glass,' says Ben.

'Except,' says Sam. Everyone turns to look at her. Her eyes are wide and dark. 'Except that there are no trees that close to the house.'

Marie shrieks as the tapping starts again and hides her face in Ben's shirt. Anna hugs her knees to her chest watching Sam whose face is making strange contortions, which resolve into a grin.

'Got you,' she says. 'It's just a bit of wiring from an old phone extension or an aerial. It's hanging loose outside the window and it makes that noise whenever the wind gets up.' Marie throws a cushion at her and Sam grabs her wineglass. 'Watch it. But to be fair it freaked me out too till I worked out what it was.'

'More fizz,' demands Marie, holding out her glass. 'At this rate I'm going to have to be unconscious before I get any sleep tonight.'

'Here you go.' Sam passes her a half-full bottle. 'Have the lot if that's what it takes. I don't want to be woken by screams in the middle of the night.'

'What about your mill?' Jenny looks at Anna. 'Any ghosts down there?'

Anna shakes her head. 'Sorry. None there either. As far as I can tell.'

'But there is a mystery,' says Sam. Anna mouths 'no' to her friend, thinking she is about to tell them about the suicide note and Charles's poems.

'The mystery of the Forbidden Floors,' Sam continues.

'And a bloody frustrating mystery it is too,' Anna says with a grateful smile to Sam. She outlines the problem to the others.

'I'm sure the rest of the board can see it makes sense but when I broached it with them last week they all kept glancing at Erica, as if she was a wicked witch who would expelliarmus them if they said a word out of turn.'

'Maybe she *is* a witch,' says Ben. 'Upstairs at your mill is where her coven meets.'

'Don't be daft.' Marie jabs him with her elbow.

'OK, so not a coven,' says Jenny. 'But maybe she uses it for activities she doesn't want you to know about.'

'Waltzing with the ghost of a lost lover,' says Sam. 'Or holding séances or practising her roller skating or ...'

'Stop.' Anna smiles. 'It's far too cold to do anything up there. Even roller skating.' She pauses. 'But you could be right. Maybe it is something personal.'

'Like what?' asks Sam.

'I don't know, but I've been assuming it was to do with the Harpers because that's her big obsession. Other than that I know very little about her. Although I'm pretty certain she's not a witch or a spiritualist.'

'Maybe something happened to her up there,' suggests Marie. 'Could she have had a traumatic experience when she was younger? Would it still have been open then?'

'It's been officially closed for eighty years, but that doesn't mean people haven't got in there.' She remembers Frank's confidence and familiarity as he strode around. 'Erica will have had access to the key ever since she joined the board.'

'Maybe she had a dangerous liaison up there,' says Ben.

'A sneaky shag?' says Marie. 'That would fit. If something happened there that she regrets or wants to forget she could just be using the old owner's "wishes" thing to protect her own feelings.'

'It's not matching up with what I know of her,' Anna says. 'But you never know. If it is a personal issue then it would give me stronger grounds for overriding her. Thanks.' She raises her glass. 'You've given me something new to go on.'

'Great,' said Marie. 'Now can we please talk about something, anything, that doesn't involve ghosts or witches or things that go bump in the night. Please.'

'Up before ten o'clock on New Year's Day? What's wrong with you, woman?' asks Sam. She is sitting at the kitchen table playing with a pincushion in the image of Tony Blair. 'I have to be up and ready with eggs and coffee and Alka Seltzer for my guests. What's your excuse?'

'I woke up and it's a beautiful morning,' says Anna. 'The view is amazing across the moor.'

'I know. I've become more of an early bird since living here too. It seems a shame to miss it at its best.' Sam yawns and props the pincushion against a salt pot. 'I'd prefer Thatcher, and I have never pinned or sewn anything in my life. But it was a nice thought. The likeness is uncanny. Coffee?'

Anna nods in reply.

'That stinky brother of mine is still flat out on the sofa.' Sam fills the kettle. 'He uses this place as a bolt-hole when things get too difficult elsewhere, so he's often the worse for wear when he arrives. He'll pay for it later: he can peel the spuds for lunch. I'm glad you're staying to help us eat that enormous piece of beef. You can get to know my friends when they're not loaded with wine. Sorry about their ghost fixation.'

'No worries,' says Anna. 'It was useful to talk about the mill with them.' She picks up the pincushion and starts to rearrange the pins. 'I just need to work out how to poke into Erica's private life without her clamming up on me.'

'That reminds me,' says Sam. 'I've got you a pressie.' She leaves the room, returning minutes later with an unwrapped book. 'Here you go.'

'Thanks,' says Anna. '*Great Expectations*. Lovely.'

'Not the book, though you're welcome to it. It's one of Charles and Edie's. But open it up and see what's been used as a bookmark.'

Anna tilts the book onto its spine and it falls open about two thirds of the way through. A black and white photograph marks the page. A headshot of a soldier, in a peaked cap. He is looking directly at the camera. A short message is printed in plain blocky letters at the bottom – 'So you don't forget, B.B. x'

'You found Beebee,' says Anna with a smile.

'It would certainly make sense of the nickname.'

'If this is Beebee, and the haiku book is dedicated to him, that means it was a present to him, not to someone at High Hob.' She frowns. 'From Edie, perhaps. Do you think he might be Jasper's father?'

'It would fit, wouldn't it? If he was a soldier in the First World War, met Edie in Paris shortly afterwards. She and Charles were there about 1919, 1920?'

'He may have been a regular visitor to High Hob. Returning to see his son, and Edie. The coroner said that on the night they died, she and Charles had been drinking heavily. Maybe the soldier was there too. An alcohol-fuelled argument?'

'But to kill them both?'

'I know.' Anna picks up the photo again. 'We could do with a photo of Jasper. See if there's any resemblance.'

'All we know of him are his "animal ways",' says Sam. Anna had told her about Sally Marsden's revelations in her oral history interview. 'Any more luck with finding those transcripts for the tapes?'

'Nope. But the permissions forms turned up, well, most of them. Sally Marsden's and a couple of others are missing. There's a chance they never signed them. I think Sally was still afraid. Even allowing for the frailty of age, her voice on the tape sounded so scared.' She purses her lips as she thinks it through. 'The verdict of suicide wasn't challenged at the time. And now the only ones who knew what really went on up there aren't around to tell it.' She pauses, the photo still in her hand, the young soldier's long gaze seems to be trying to see into his own future. 'Charles and Edie had so much to live for. Their lives cut short—' Her voice catches and she stops.

'Are you OK? Is it ... ah shit, your boyfriend? You said there was an accident. He must have been ... I'm so sorry.'

'It's OK. I don't really want to ...' Anna takes a long breath, steadies her voice. 'So, the haiku book. If it was a Christmas present from Edie to B.B. in 1935, why is it still here at High Hob? Unless she didn't have a chance to give it to him. Perhaps she was hoping he would visit and he didn't.'

'Or maybe, like you said, he did visit,' says Sam, to Anna's relief not pursuing the conversation about Dan. 'Not at Christmas but six months later. On the night they died.'

'Who died?'

Carter Klein is leaning against the door jamb, in a T-shirt and boxers, yawning.

'The Kraken wakes,' says Sam. 'I'd better get it a coffee.'

At lunch, which is later than planned and lasts most of the afternoon, Anna sits between Marie and Carter. Marie, nursing an aching head, is quiet throughout the meal but Carter makes up for her. Keen to hear about the mill and in particular its potential as a gallery for his photographs.

'Huge stark walls are just what I need,' he explains. 'I mainly do post-industrial landscapes. This area is a goldmine for them. The juxtaposition of the wild landscape and the remains of the labour-intensive industry that once dominated it. Your mill would be an ideal setting for an exhibition.'

'You're right.' Anna imagines the walls of the first floor covered in photographs. 'It would be perfect.'

'Great. When can I come and have a look?'

He has leaned in towards her and his eyes are teasing. Is he interested in more than the art space? Or is he just flirting for the fun of it?

'There's no guarantee I'll be able to persuade the board,' she says, trying to ignore the invitation in his dark brown eyes.

'Surely a woman of your charms will have no problem winning

over a load of stuffed shirts,' he persists. Sam raises her eyebrows and Anna bites her lower lip to suppress a grin.

'I'll let you know,' she promises, moving her chair back a little. 'If my plans are given the green light then I'd love to include a photography exhibition in the mix.'

After the meal, while Anna is helping to make coffees, Sam says, 'Can't say I didn't warn you about him.'

Anna adds a chipped milk jug to the tray alongside the sugar bowl. 'He's not all talk. He showed me some of his photos on his phone. They're amazing.'

'He makes a living from it, and he's internationally renowned, if his blurb is to be believed,' Sam says. 'Even won an award or two. If he wants an exhibition at the mill he could be useful to have on your side against the board. What Carter wants, Carter usually gets.'

It is late when Anna drives home. As she leaves the brightly lit main road for the track to the mill, the darkness closes in, with only a half-moon to light her way. There is something comforting about this dark though: the lines of trees guiding her way on both sides and the pale path ahead leading home. It makes her think of the day trippers who after a day of dancing and skating would walk this long trail back to the town and the railway station, arms linked, bodies swaying in time to remembered tunes.

She parks up by the end of the cottage and stands for a moment, listening to the evening: the murmur of the river, the soft movement of the trees in the wind, her ears ready for the hooting of owls. The cold air brushes her cheeks. It brushes the stones of the cottages, the rocks by the river, the bare branches of the trees. She is part of this place now; it is a kinship she hasn't felt for anywhere for a long time.

She looks up at the mill. There is a blur of movement in a top-floor window, a white shape that makes her start, her heart racing. It moves again, and she realises what it is: a reflection of the night sky, where pale clouds flit across the moon.

CHAPTER 15

Billy: 1933-34

We'd been exploring a patch of bog over by Abe's hut, where wide hollows were filled with weeds. It was the end of August and most of the grass and heather was pale and brittle. We were seeing whose boots made the best sucking noise when they were submerged and then pulled out of the boggy ground. Major Sefton's truck would be rolling back up the hill any day now and we were determined to make the most of every remaining minute of the summer. We ignored the dark clouds building up in the sky. It wasn't till the first fat blobs of rain landed on us that we started to leg it home. Jasper still lost his breath if we ran too hard so we stopped every now and then for him to recover, even though it meant us getting soaked.

As we raced into the house Jasper charged past me and up the stairs. We'd given up our game of hopscotching over the squares and his muddy boots left marks on black and white squares alike. As I peeled off my own sodden boots, Edie peered out from her study.

'There you are,' she said. 'Come on through.'

'I'm all wet,' I said.

She shook her head. 'That can't be helped.'

I followed her into the room, expecting a telling-off. But instead there was Lizzie and her mother, who I'd only seen before from a distance, sitting on Edie's chaise longue, nibbling biscuits and drinking lemonade. Lizzie held a tall glass to her lips, which failed to hide her smile. It was a month since I'd last seen her, a whole month since her almost-fall. I felt the swoop of it again in my stomach and a settling glow of joy that she was sitting here safe and sound. I looked away from her with a daft grin, my rain-drenched hair dripping water on my neck, to see her mother peering down her long nose at me, which considering as how I was standing up and she was sitting down was a pretty smart trick.

She gave me a nod as Edie did the introductions calling me 'William, Jasper's little friend'. I mumbled an apology for being late. I didn't know if I was or not but as I often was, it was worth saying. Lizzie jumped up, almost spilling her lemonade, and shook my hand. 'Pleased to meet you, William,' she said, all polite. Mrs Potter told her to sit down and stop being silly.

'I believe you two already have a passing acquaintance.' She was still doing that peering thing. 'Your mother is Mrs Shaw at the Palace?'

I nodded.

'And you were a Draper's Cross boy?'

I nodded again and helped myself to a biscuit, glad to see they were shop-bought not Livvy-made, and tried to stop stealing glances at Lizzie. How much had Jane let on about our days together by the dam?

'Do sit down, William,' said Edie, and though her voice was light her eyes were keen, taking their turn with each of us. The heron waiting. Though I didn't know what for.

My trousers were damp from the rain and what I wanted more than anything was a towel to rub dry my hair. But Lizzie was here. So I did as I was told and we sat drinking lemonade and being polite and not taking the last biscuit. All the time Mrs Potter watching me, like I was an insect under a microscope, and Lizzie pulling faces and trying not to laugh.

'Children,' Mrs Potter said. We all looked at her. 'They grow up so fast, don't they?' Her mouth quivered but didn't quite smile. Edie murmured in agreement. 'It seems only months,' Mrs Potter continued, 'since Elizabeth was but a babe in my arms.'

I sucked in my cheeks to stop myself laughing at the thought of Lizzie as a baby. In return she crossed her eyes. Neither Mrs Potter or Edie seemed to notice.

'She forgets,' Mrs Potter continued, talking for all the world as if Lizzie wasn't there, 'that she is not a little girl any more. She'll be fourteen in the new year, a young woman. She can't be hobbledy-hoying in the woods with all and sundry.'

My cheeks blazed and Lizzie put down her glass and glared at her mother. So that's what me and Jasper were, was it? 'All and sundry'? First Mr Potter gets all snobby about me and Lizzie being friends and now here was his missus calling me and Jasper names. Words filled my head. About how I was going to be equal to, if not better than Mr Potter one day. That for all his land and property he was Ackerdean valley born-and-bred just like me. There was nowt but hard graft between me becoming a bigger success in the entertainment business than he could ever hope for. And when Lizzie was grown she'd make her own decisions. Then I realised I was imagining me and her in the future together right in front of her and her ma and my cheeks blushed even hotter and my mouth clamped and refused to let the words come out.

I expected Edie might speak up for us, but she just said, 'Would anybody like any more lemonade? The jug's empty but Livvy could be called upon to produce more.' Mrs Potter shook her head and dabbed at her mouth with a napkin.

Then Edie did her starting-a-sentence-part-way-through trick. As if she thought she'd spoken the first part out loud but had actually only said it in her head. 'Bringing three children up, all on her own, while running that café almost single-handed must have required such strength of character. Don't you agree, Mrs Potter?'

She was talking about Ma. Was this Edie's way of saying I was more than all and sundry? Because Ma was so strong and full of character, just like her mincemeat pie. What business was it of theirs how Ma had brought us up?

Lizzie made a polite little cough and passed the biscuit plate over to me. 'Would you like another biscuit, William?' she asked.

'Yes, thank you, Elizabeth,' I said in my very best High Hob voice. 'I do believe I would.' Past her arm her mother was still considering me down that long nose.

'The working woman,' Edie continued, 'is often forced to draw on resources the rest of us can only imagine.'

'Indeed,' Mrs Potter said, answering Edie but her eyes never leaving me as I reached to take the last biscuit. 'One can only imagine.'

Major Sefton came back from his holidays with a stack of textbooks that he said we needed to work our way through if we had any hope of taking our education further than the High Hob parlour. This was new. There'd been no talk of our learning taking us anywhere before.

The weather turned bad again and stayed that way so we mainly kept our weekend rambles close to home. I was glad of the excuse to steer clear of the Palace and the chance of bumping into a disgruntled Nathaniel Potter. We saw Lizzie, briefly, one late autumn day when, making the most of a cloudy but dry morning, we went down into the valley to look at the rain-swollen river. She was walking along the path with Jane who scowled at us and marched on ahead. Lizzie and I held hands as we walked behind her. I didn't care that Jasper could see us plain as day. Neither of us mentioned that teatime at High Hob, or what her mother had said. She told me she was boarding at school during the week now and her mother had her helping with the Women's Institute most weekends. She joked that we'd never get a chance to see each other unless I started hanging about in Sowley Community Hall pretending an interest in quilts or crochet. But the heat of our palms told me we'd find a way.

I had Christmas back at the Palace without sight or sound of a single Potter. Ma said they'd gone down to Birmingham again and I felt sad for Lizzie spending the season in company she hated.

As winter wheeled round into spring and Easter and my birthday approached I began thinking on whether I would soon be sent back home. If I wasn't going to see Lizzie so often for a while I needed to use the time to plan for the future and make sure she was part of it, whether her parents liked it or not.

There'd never been any talk of exactly how long I was to be a companion, but I was coming up fourteen and most of my old school pals would be leaving Draper's Cross to help their families on their farms or getting work in town or in the mills. With Potter being so off with me there seemed little opportunity for me at the Palace for the time being. Charles had mentioned his friend Mr Hobart again. Said he'd asked after me last time they'd met up.

'Took a shine to you, Billy. Thinks you have the making of something.' Though like Miss Offat back at school he didn't explain what that something was.

I should have asked then about how long I'd still be with them, but I didn't want to sound ungrateful or put the idea in his mind of sending me packing just yet. But then suddenly the decision was made, and me and Jasper played our part in the making of it.

Easter was early that year, so it sneaked in a good while before my birthday. We had a whole two weeks without the Major who went off to stay with his sister in Norfolk. Lizzie was home too. On the first Monday of the holiday, with her father in Manchester on business and her mother supervising the redecoration of the Big House, she and Jane came down to the Palace. They met us by the wooden bridge, where we were dithering about whether to head upstream to the falls or downstream to the dam.

It was almost like the old days. But better because Jane was in a decent mood and Jasper for once gave off teasing and instead set himself the challenge of trying to make her laugh or at least smile. Lizzie and I caught up properly on what we'd been doing in the ages and ages since we'd last spoke. There was plenty of not talking too. Just looks and hand-holding that gave me hope. I expected we'd have more afternoons like that, and we might have done too. If it hadn't been for the Scouts.

They had their camp as usual on the hillside overlooking Ackerdean, below the Big House. Every Easter the tents covered the grass like white flags. Some mornings at the Palace I'd heard the Scoutmasters bellowing from as soon as the sun came up.

From our viewpoint with the binoculars on the other side of the valley Jasper said the Scouts looked a boring lot.

'Following orders from someone who isn't a soldier or even a policeman. In the holidays too. Pack of duffers.'

The middle of that first week the tents took a right battering with a night of such wild winds that I feared the roof of High Hob itself might lift off and leave me in my bed staring at the stars. But still the Scouts were out the next morning, clearing up the mess and fettling the canvases and frames. It wasn't much fun just watching them and getting whipped by the tail end of the storm. Jasper said we should go over and say hello.

'Going over and saying hello' didn't necessarily mean to Jasper what it did to other folk. I might have tried to put him off, but he'd picked on a sore spot with them Scouts. The couple of times I'd run into them they'd been a snooty lot, acting so clever with their maps and whistles.

It was a fair hike, down into the valley bottom to the wooden bridge and then up again on the track towards the Potters' place. As we reached the fields, Sally Marsden came walking up the track, heading towards the Big House as she always did on Fridays. She hurried on when she saw us, as if she was late. I'd half a mind to catch her up and give her a message to take. But she would scarce meet our eyes lately and scuttled out of rooms when we came in. I blamed it on the chicken Jasper had gutted in the kitchen two weeks back.

He swore he'd found it dead out the back of Thurcross Farm. But as I was coming down the stairs that morning there had been such a racket from the kitchen that I thought Charles was playing one of his wildlife recordings in there. The chicken was splayed open on the table, its innards mottled and gleaming. Jasper was standing over it with a bloodied kitchen knife, his fingers already probing the exposed organs, while Sally cowered on the floor by the stove. The squealing I'd heard had been her, sure enough, but I'm pretty certain she wasn't the one who'd been clucking and squawking only minutes before.

If I gave her a message for Lizzie, I wasn't sure I could trust her not to say anything to Mrs Potter.

The Scout field was down a path past a sign saying 'Private'. There were six or so white tents pegged out in rows and one big marquee. The Scouts were by the tents messing with bits of rope and wood. Some of them were only about ten or eleven but each group had an older lad in charge, who must have been seventeen or more. Next to the marquee, six lads were washing pots in a bowl set in a wooden frame.

'Got 'em doing chores,' said Jasper. 'Wonder what they did to deserve that.'

Before we even had the chance to say hello a big lad put down his scrubbing pad and came over. He crossed his arms over his shirt below his neckerchief. 'What do you want?' His accent had a flat twang like the trippers from Burnley and Rochdale. 'You're trespassing.'

'It's not your field,' Jasper said right back.

'Is so. It's for Scout troops only.' He checked us up and down with a sneer on his face. Making it clear we didn't measure up. He was joined by a scrawny lad whose hair stuck up in blond tufts.

This one screwed up his nose as if he could smell something bad. His front two teeth sticking out made him look like a rat.

'Clear off.' His voice was a rodent squeak. 'This ain't no circus show.'

'Are you sure?' said Jasper. He was standing with his shoulders dropped, hands deep in the pockets of his shorts. 'You look like a bunch of freaks to me.'

The bigger boy lunged forward but stopped at a shout from the big white tent. A tall man in a uniform that was just a bigger version of the ones the lads were wearing strode over. Jasper said 'Good morning', as polite as could be, and told him we were thinking of joining the Scouts and were wondering what it was all about. The man, who had spotty cheeks and one eye that wandered skywards while the other was staring straight at you, was eager enough to tell us what a wonderful organisation the Boy Scouts was. He told us about Queen and Country and duty to God, and 'working together against adversity with the resources to hand', till Jasper interrupted.

'But what is it that you do?'

So he told us about knots and orienteering and bushcraft. All the time behind him the Scouts casting us looks and making gestures that said they wanted to show us their skills in giving us a good thumping.

'And there are the night marches, of course.'

Jasper's eyes sharpened and he leaned towards him, his hands clasped behind his back like the Major when he was reciting tables. 'You go marching at night?' he asked. 'Don't you worry about anyone getting lost?'

'We're well prepared.' The man had a smug smile on his face. 'Looking forward to Saturday night's march, aren't you, boys?' He noticed then that they had stopped their work and he shooed them back to the pots.

'Well, that's very interesting,' Jasper said. 'I'll be sure to tell Mother. I do hope she'll let us join up.'

The spotty bloke beamed, convinced he had two new recruits.

'We're First North Manchester. You'll be wanting nearer. Give Halifax a shout. They've a good Scoutmaster over there.'

On the way back I tried to get out of Jasper what he was plotting. I was pretty certain it wasn't us joining the Halifax Scout troop. But he clammed up and said, 'Just leave it.' I knew I'd find out before long.

We were crouched in the trees by the field on Saturday night when the Scouts came back from their march just after midnight. We'd crept out of the house straight after supper. Edie's assurances to the Trimmers that she kept us under lock and key at night had no more truth in it than our denial that we'd ever been in their barn.

No one had been left on guard at the camp. Even the younger ones had gone on the march. They were yawning now and plodding their feet. The Scoutmasters, the spotty one and two others, were chivvying them along.

'Too late for a campfire,' one of them shouted. 'But we'll strike up the primus stove and have hot chocolate before we turn in.' The Scouts settled themselves on a semicircle of logs in front of the marquee, while the masters sorted kettles and pans. The stove glowed and before long we could smell the chocolate. There was some singing of songs, a lull while they drank their chocolate, and then they started to head to their tents. One of the masters stayed by the stove finishing his brew. We waited. It was cold among the leaves and twigs. Stray scraps of cloud crossed the moon, but there was no breeze. My legs were aching from being in the same position for so long. Jasper was coldly calm, focused on the scene.

A scream erupted from one of the tents. A small lad came peeling out in his pyjamas. He was grabbing at the back of his neck and spinning round. Jasper didn't move. More Scouts emptied out of the other tents. One of them rolled on the floor, another ran, yelling, hands rubbing feverishly at his face, straight towards the light of the stove. The spotty Scoutmaster's face was lit by the stove's glow. His mouth opened. I heard a shout. He lunged at the boy and pushed him to the ground. Jasper rose to his feet beside me. An acrid smell rose with him. The rasp of a match being struck. He reached his arm back and then lobbed something high and bright into the air. I followed the trail of its glowing light as it arced towards the marquee. There was a whoomf and a spume of flame. Silence and then cries that could have been horror or pain. I didn't have a chance to find out. Jasper grabbed my arm and dragged me away through the trees. The noise we made not mattering in the mêlée we left behind.

Nobody died. We found out the full tale, earwigging by the kitchen door, as Sally told it breathless to Livvy, while Livvy chopped carrots. The marquee had been destroyed. One lad's hair got badly singed and the flames had caught the leg of a Scoutmaster. The camp had been cut short and the Scouts were heading back to Manchester.

If it had just been the wood ants we'd put in the sleeping bags we might have got away with it. I hadn't known till he chucked it that Jasper was carrying a bottle bomb. He'd siphoned petrol from the Crossley. Soaked the rag wick in paraffin stolen from Livvy's kitchen supply. He told me all this afterwards, reciting his method as if it was a recipe for a pie or instructions for mending a bicycle. When I said that someone could have been killed he replied, 'But no one was,' as if he'd made sure of it. But I was certain he hadn't cared where the bottle had landed. It was like a game I'd read about in one of Charles's novels, Russian roulette – maybe someone would die, maybe they wouldn't.

One of the Scouts had seen a figure rise up from the shadows in the seconds before the bottle hurtled towards the camp. It was too dark for him to identify the thrower but the Scoutmaster started asking around about the two boys who'd been up to the camp earlier in the week, and he was sent in the direction of High Hob. When he turned up asking to see Charles, Sally fled to the kitchen. Her face flushed, eyes not daring to meet ours.

It must have been the spotty master who was burned. This one had never seen either of us before. There was no proof, only speculation. Nothing left of the exploded bottle except shattered glass. Only an empty tin found abandoned on the track by the field that Livvy confessed did look like one of hers, but last time she'd seen it, it had been full of best tea. Last time I'd seen it, it was full of ants.

We denied it all, though the tin was sitting on the table in front of us. Jasper said he'd heard camping stoves could be dangerous things. Wouldn't go near one himself. He mentioned we'd seen Sally heading over that way a couple of days ago. She'd been hiding something under her jacket. 'What do you reckon, Billy?' he asked. 'Could it have been a tin of Livvy's best tea?' My shrug might have been taken for a no as much as a yes. But later I heard Livvy scolding her.

'Just watch yourself. They were lucky no one was killed. It's your word against theirs, you daft lass.'

The Scoutmaster left and whether he was convinced of our guilt or innocence we would never know. But Charles wasn't taking any chances. It was almost a week before we found out what our punishment would be.

'Major Sefton has been given his marching orders,' he said. 'He won't be returning to us.' We waited. And then it came.

'Congratulations, Jasper,' he said. 'It appears that there is one school left in the country that's prepared to take you. Though not one in Yorkshire or even Lancashire. So you'll be boarding. And yes, they do know your history. Simmonds House has a reputation for remoulding the most recalcitrant of wills. They're eager to meet you.'

'I'm not going to no school,' Jasper said as we crossed the hall. 'Thrown in with a load of stuck-up boys and lunatic masters wielding canes. They can't make me.'

But it turned out they could. The next week was a bustle of laundry and packing and the arrival of parcels, including a new blazer and long trousers, and a cap and tie. A silent bustle, though, as Charles refused to speak to either of us and there was not even Sally's chatter as she stayed at home with a stomach ache that seemed likely to last until Jasper was gone.

Edie was quiet too. More disappointed than angry, shaking her head and saying, 'Oh, Jasper', as if she'd given up on his fate. If she hadn't wanted him to go she could have stopped it. She could usually make Charles do as she wished.

Of my fate nothing was said and I took it that I'd be going home. Home being the Palace though it felt odd now to think of it so. Livvy must have expected it too, cos she washed all my things ready for packing.

I had to make plans for what I was to do till I was old enough to seek out Mr Hobart in London. Mr Procter at the garage in Oakenshaw might take me on as a 'prentice. Knowing about engines would be no bad thing and, if I showed him I had a good head for figures, he might teach me accounting and books. Failing that, there might be something going down in Sowley. I could move back in at the Palace and pay towards my keep. It was a good plan. One even Ma might approve of, though my heart chilled at the idea of her finding out about the part I'd played in getting Jasper sent away and ending my time as a companion.

But I was never called to tell her, though the valley being as it was I knew she'd have heard a version of the truth. A week before Jasper was due to leave for school Charles called me into his study. Time for my marching orders now, I thought, but I went in with my back straight, eyes fixed on the stuffed weasel, daring it to mock me. When Charles said, 'So, Billy, how do you fancy a couple more years at school?' I felt like I'd been kicked in the back of my knees.

'Draper's Cross won't have me, sir. I'm fourteen next week.'

'Not the village school,' he said. 'Funds,' he lingered on the word, 'a scholarship if you will, have become available. You will be accompanying Jasper to Simmonds House.' He scratched at his chin. 'You should fare well enough there if you keep your head down and don't rile the masters.' He tapped the bowl of his pipe against his desk. 'I've little hope that Jasper will manage the same. It's all arranged.' Though I'd not answered his question about how I felt about it. 'I'll drive you both down at the end of the week. Between now and then feel free to go home to say your goodbyes to your family.' He chuckled. 'It's only Derbyshire, not the colonies, but the term times are long. It'll be summer before the pair of you are back here. Damn, the place'll be quiet.' He looked almost sorrowful. 'So off you go and break the good news to Jasper.' His mouth twisted into a half smile. 'I'm sure he'll be overjoyed. Which is the only flaw in the plan, as far as I'm concerned.'

CHAPTER 16

Anna: January

On Anna's desk several folders are ready for cataloguing and next to them the High Hob copy of *Great Expectations* and the photograph of 'B.B'.

Who are you? She taps the photo. She had sent a scanned copy through to one of her former colleagues in Tyneside who specialises in military history. His reply had been swift.

'An officer in the Warwickshire Fusiliers. Their regimental museum might be able to help. But without a name you're in needle in a haystack territory.'

No name, just his initials. She takes her copy of *Siblings in Arms* from the shelf above her desk. Bunty was married. Could her husband be B. B.? If Bunty shared an 'unmatched intimacy' with Charles, did Edie have a similar relationship with Mr Baxendale? And was he ever a fusilier? Anna finds him mentioned early in the book. 'My long-suffering Georgie', and a reference to his father, Thomas, who was an earl. In the small selection of pictures in the centre of the book there is one of the author and her husband. Definitely not Beebee, she decides, comparing the picture of the soldier with the pale, long-faced man with drooping eyelids. Georgie looks long-suffering indeed.

A ping from her computer alerts her to a new email. It's from the University of Central Virginia. A professor in the Women's Studies department thanking Anna for her interest in her work and confirming that the department has the original copy of the sole surviving chapter of Edie's novel. She has attached a scan of the pages, but warns that they mustn't be used or distributed without obtaining further permissions.

Anna opens the pdf. Ten pages of neatly rounded handwriting. She enlarges the document to read it more easily. The passage that fills her screen focuses on an unnamed working woman burdened with chores and childcare. There are closely observed descriptions of her dry and worn hands, the dowdiness of her clothes, *the damp felt of her hat* and *a single piece of jewellery* that *pinned her femininity to her chest*. She stops reading as a realisation dawns. She takes the book of Tagore's haikus from her drawer and opens it at the dedication. Those narrow loops and flourishes don't match the writing on the screen. Edie didn't write the dedication or the haiku about the falling leaves. If not Edie then who? Charles? He had typewritten everything, the only example of his handwriting she remembered seeing was the angry scrawl of his name at the end of the letter to his publisher. Who else could it be? Jasper and Billy Shaw were still schoolboys. Was the haiku another example of Charles's poetry? Was he gay, with a secret lover who was a soldier? She sits back down. What else didn't the world know about Charles Harper?

Her thoughts are interrupted by a knock at the door. Frank peers round. 'Little monsters all gone, have they?'

Anna had been working with a class of Year Sixes all morning, showing them samples of fleece and raw cotton, and answering their questions about how Ackerdean had risen from its decline as a mill to become a 'fun palace'.

Sharing history with children was one of her favourite parts of her job. It was how she had met Dan, when he brought his Year

Four class to visit the People's Museum. The head of his school had described him, in the local paper, as 'An inspirational teacher who would be sorely missed by pupils and staff alike.' His class had sent a beautiful wreath to the funeral.

There were always going to be reminders. She had watched the children chalking their names or pictures on the slate boards she had provided. The anger was gone now, and the initial engulfing grief. But still those waves that hit her unexpectedly. The kids they'd talked about having one day. They'd even argued about names. She'd had to steady herself, one hand to the rough stone wall, and ask the child who was asking her a question to repeat what she had said.

'They're gone for the time being,' Anna replies to Frank now. 'But they'll be back. I'm giving an assembly to the whole school next week. I want to find out what sort of activities they'd like to see here.'

'Oh aye.' Frank steps into the room. 'Taking the mountain to Muhammad, are you?' He pauses. 'Are you allowed to say that these days?' He shrugs. 'Anyroad, this is Jim,' he adds as another man follows him in. He has a younger face than Frank, but his back is stooped and he leans on a stick with an ornate curved handle.

'Sorry to be disturbing you.' Jim touches his cap.

'Nonsense,' says Frank. 'She likes a bit of company, don't you, love?'

Anna shakes the man's offered hand. 'Nice to meet you, Jim.'

'The Halcyon warders have let him out for an airing,' Frank says. 'Told him about what you've been up to here. Wanted to have a gander for himself.'

'I used to come here when I were a kiddie,' Jim says. 'It were all shut up then. Even the café in the end. But we'd have a walk in the woods after popping in to see Nana Shaw.'

Anna raises an eyebrow at Frank.

'Did I not say? Jim's my cousin. Auntie Peggy's eldest. I thought maybe you could have worked that out.' He turns to Jim. 'With all the technology the young'uns have these days, I forget they don't know everything.'

'It must have been very different when it was all closed up.' Anna turns to Jim. 'Even compared to now.'

'Oh aye,' Jim agrees. 'Still got them big-eyed windows, mind. When I were a kiddie I wouldn't look at them. Thought they were staring at me the way the teacher did when he knew I was up to summat. Had me frit, it did, about what were going on behind 'em. That and Ma's story about the angel.'

'I'd forgotten that,' says Frank. 'Aunt Peggy's angel. Tell her about it, Jim. She's after stories.'

Jim shifts from one foot to the other, leaning on his stick.

'Would you like a seat?' Anna offers him her chair. 'I'd love to hear your mother's story.'

'Aye, why not. Might as well be comfy.' He settles into the chair and rests the walking stick across his knees. 'Mam's angel.' He pauses, blinks. 'Have you ever looked up at them windows and seen scraps of white, like rags, floating across the windows?'

Anna nods, remembering how she had scared herself at New Year.

'I thought it were ghosts, when I were a little'un,' Jim continues. 'Later I knew it to be clouds mirrored in the glass. But in between Mam told me that what I were seeing were angels. The spirits of the mill girls and the dancers and the skaters, come back to watch over the place.' He leans forward and lowers his voice. 'She swore that one day she'd seen one. Not just a flicker, but a full-blown angel. She always made sure her mother were out of earshot when she talked about it. Nana Shaw wouldn't hear of angels or spirits. Her being a Methodist to the bone. We had to wait until she were having her nap by the fire. Mam would take me up to her old bedroom and we'd press our faces to the window and she'd tell me what she'd seen.'

He flexes his fingers on the walking stick. 'She were a young woman when it happened, teenager I suppose, and high with a fever. Her mother had dosed her with Epsom salts and goodness knows what else and said she must stay in bed till it passed. But she were so hot and she pressed her forehead against the glass to cool it. That were when she saw the angel dancing on the sill of one of those windows.' He taps his stick on the floor. 'I told her it sounded like a ghost but she said no it were an angel and she'd grip my hand hard. A shining angel, its head bowed behind the swoop of its raised wings. And for all her naysaying her mother saw it too cos she heard her cry out from the yard and they were all standing there, gawping up.'

'Why did she think it was an angel?' Anna asks.

'Because it flew. Its feet did a little skip, she said, and then it leaped out into the air as if it were flying into the arms of another.' He shakes his head. 'Makes you wonder, doesn't it, about medicines in them days. What had they given her, eh?'

Frank rolls his eyes. 'What do you reckon, Anna? Will there be room for angels in the new and improved Ackerdean?'

Anna's skin had tingled as Jim told his story. His mother had seen her angel from the window of the room that was now Anna's bedroom.

'It's such a vivid image,' she says. 'Is your mother still alive? It would be lovely to record her memories.'

'You've just missed her,' he says, as if she has popped out to the shops. 'She were a good age. Ninety-four when she passed two winters back.' He glances up at Frank. 'Them of us that are Yorkshire born and bred'll outlast them that aren't. Ain't that right?'

Frank frowns. 'Don't talk daft.' He nods at Anna. 'This'un's a Geordie and she's as strong as an ox, and that's only after a couple of months of Yorkshire air.'

Anna follows the two men outside, deciding she will have lunch in the relative comfort of the cottage. As Frank's Land Rover drives away, jolting onto the main track, it passes Erica Walker's smart little sports car. Erica parks up by the cottage and gets out. Instead of her usual suit she is wearing walking trousers and a sky-blue fleece jacket. She has a rucksack on her back.

Anna glances at the black clouds that are gathering overhead.

'The forecast isn't great for this afternoon,' she says, walking over to greet her. Erica's face is strained as if she'd rather not engage in conversation at all. Probably not the best time, Anna thinks, to break the news that Charles Harper may have had a gay lover.

'It can't be helped,' Erica says. 'It's rarely ideal walking conditions at this time of year.' Adding, as if in recognition of Anna's concern, 'I'm not going far.' She gestures up to the main track towards the fork in the road by the car park. 'Mother had a favourite spot where she liked to sit by the Wishing Bridge. She took me there sometimes when she was still mobile.' Her eyes flicker towards Anna. 'It's where I scattered her ashes.'

After lunch Anna is reluctant to return to the office. The storm clouds have broken and the rain is lashing down. But she wants to see if she can track down any more examples of Charles's handwriting. It is a distraction from her cataloguing work, although, she tells herself, it's all part of the Harper legacy. As she dashes over to the mill she notices that the little sports car is still parked up and she hopes Erica has found somewhere to shelter while the storm passes, although it doesn't look as though it will be letting up anytime soon.

It's almost five o'clock when she switches off the computer and stretches out her arms. It is dark outside and still raining. Sinewy rivulets pour down the window. Water worms, Dan called them, repeating something one of his pupils had written in a poem. Her reflection in the window blurs. She suddenly sees Dan's face through a rain-streaked windscreen. She blinks and it's gone.

As she locks up the mill the wind batters against the doors. Over the stone bridge on the other side of the river trees are bent almost double, thrashing back and forth. Erica's car is still by the cottage. *Damn*. She tries to recall what Erica had been wearing. A fleece but no waterproof, unless there was one in her rucksack. She hadn't noticed what she had on her feet. The river path would be treacherous in this weather.

She dives into the cottage to swap her trainers for her wellies and to collect her waterproof jacket and the lantern torch that Trevor had given her in case of power cuts. Thank God Erica told her where she was going.

A stream of water crosses the main track above the car park and pours down the narrow path that leads to the Wishing Bridge. Anna picks her way carefully down, her torch a steady beam picking out tree roots and rocks ahead. The path meets the torrent of the river, a roaring yellow of froth and scum. Twigs and broken fronds of bracken tumble past. She stops by the water's edge, her eyes following the race of the water. A rush of dizziness forces her to take a step back and to look away. The path continues along the river edge. Anna's boots slip in the mud and on hidden slabs of stone. Her jeans are soaked through and water drips onto her face from the peaked hood of her jacket. She presses on, scanning her torch beam over the path and the river and the sloping hillside to her right. She calls Erica's name but her words are whipped away by the wind.

There is a flicker of blue ahead on the left. She casts her torch back over it. Something caught in one of the overhanging trees on the other bank. Blue fabric swaying.

Her fingers slip on the wet torch as she focuses the light. The rain cocoons her. It's as if air itself has turned to water and she wonders for a moment how it is that she can still breathe. The torchlight picks out the words 'Layers Pellets', white on blue. It's a feedbag, blown down from one of the fields. She wipes the rainwater from her face and turns back to the path.

Minutes later she reaches the Wishing Bridge. There is no sign of Erica but a huge shape looms by the side of the path. The squat stone structure that the locals call the fisherman's hut. Anna hurries towards it, the beam of her torch bouncing over the reaching branches of trees. The entrance is as dark as a cave.

Erica is sitting inside on a wooden bench, a waterproof cape covering most of her body. She shuffles up to make room for Anna.

'It was ten years ago today that Mother died.'

'I'm so sorry, I didn't know ...'

'She wasn't able to look after herself towards the end,' Erica continues. 'Dementia.' She almost whispers the word. 'She became a different person. More like a child.' She pulls her gaze away from the rain, her usually neat bun has loosened and strands of grey hair stick out from her head like the fronds of a plant. 'Sorry, I'm forgetting my manners.' She reaches inside the rucksack on the floor and produces two mini bottles of prosecco. Anna laughs with surprise and Erica smiles in return. 'Mother always liked a drop of fizz. I usually bring a mini bottle to toast her memory with. They were three for two in the Co-op today.' She passes one of the bottles to Anna and untwists the lid on the remaining one, raising it in a toast. 'Cheers,' she says. 'Sorry about the lack of glasses.'

'She was a founder member of the Ackerdean board, you know. And its first chair.'

They have both almost emptied their bottles, and Anna suspects Erica had the third one before she got there. 'She was close to the Potter family, particularly Nathaniel's wife Cassandra. Her confidante, if you like, despite the difference in their ages. Mr Potter left Thornleyroyd to my mother in his will.'

'He left her his house?'

Erica nods. 'She'd lived there with them years before, while her own parents were abroad. But she sold it straight away. Used the money to buy the house I live in now in Savile Park in Halifax. It was a wise investment. Thornleyroyd would have been an albatross round her neck. She was a very practical woman. She'd been active in the Literary and Scientific Society for years. Practically ran the Sowley Museum single-handed.' Erica's voice falters but then picks up again. 'When Mr Potter left the Ackerdean estate to the society, he knew it would be in good hands. Mother knew what he would have wanted. How the story of the mill should be told.' She drains her bottle before dropping it back into her bag.

So she had been right. Erica did have a personal connection to the mill. It wasn't only Nathaniel Potter's, but her mother's wishes and memory that she was protecting. Preserving their version of the mill's history. She thinks about her conversation with Frank about setting stories straight.

'Those who are left behind,' she says, 'pass on the stories that make up how a person, or a place is remembered. We weave a myth that those who weren't there can't take apart. It's a way of coping.' The bottle is cold between her fingers, the taste of the wine stale on her tongue. 'Sometimes it might be better if we confronted the reality instead. Who they were, their flaws and mistakes and regrets.' Her mouth feels dry. She wishes there was more wine to wash away the bitterness in her mouth. 'We risk making them unreal,' she continues. 'Denying who they were.'

There is silence except for the drumming of rain on the roof of the hut. Erica seems to be lost in her own thoughts and Anna realises she has wandered too far into her own buried past.

'What are Ackerdean's myths?' she asks, hoping to bring the conversation back round, though she decides against mentioning Peggy Shaw's angel. 'Are there any local legends and tales we could incorporate? They can be a good focal point in a heritage building.'

Erica pulls herself up straight, in full Chair of the Board mode, despite her unruly hair and voluminous cape.

'It's not something we encourage,' she says. 'It can lead to mis-understandings and exaggeration. We had enough of that with that ridiculous television fiasco.'

'Ackerdean was on television?'

'Thankfully no, we managed to stop it. It was years ago. 1993, maybe '94. I'd not been chair long. It was when Mother first became ill. I took a brief sabbatical. Left another board member to run things day to day. Thought he could be trusted. He was a retired butcher, for goodness sake. Next thing I know it's on the front page of the *Courier*, "Ghostly Goings on in't Mill".' She pauses to gauge Anna's reaction. Anna keeps her face straight, murmurs something that might be an agreement of disgust.

'A group of so-called ghost-hunters had turned up. Made what they had the cheek to call a documentary.' Erica gives a dismissive wave with one hand. 'My deputy obviously didn't have a clue what they were up to. Just took their money and left them to it. They had all their facts wrong, and the bits that were correct were all mixed up. They thought that because the Harper archive was there that must mean they had lived in the mill. They had a young woman dressed up as Edie wailing on the stairs.'

'But there's not even any evidence that Edie ever visited the mill. Why would she be haunting the place?'

'Exactly. But the truth wasn't what mattered. They just wanted a good story. It took me months to sort out all the hoo-ha afterwards. That was the last time that butcher was given any responsibility, I can tell you. So we will have no talk of ghosts or legends, if you don't mind. Apart from anything else, it's disrespectful to the dead.'

Outside the hut the rain is easing off to a light drizzle. Erica gathers up her rucksack and gets to her feet. She gestures to Anna's torch. Its beam of light is beginning to flicker. 'Let's just hope and pray that thing lasts until we get back to the mill.'

The next morning the phone rings as soon as Anna enters the office. It's Karen Barker, the schoolteacher who organised the oral history project at the High School in 1997.

'Luckily for you I have twenty-five years' worth of Duke of Edinburgh box files in my cupboard and I've got the transcripts you're after. The kids had to write up the interviews as part of the project though I don't think they've ever been looked at – they've certainly not been marked or commented on. Pop by the school and pick them up anytime you like.'

'That's fantastic,' Anna says. 'I'm still missing a few of the per-mission forms, I don't suppose you have copies.'

'Not that I know of. It wasn't the most organised of projects. I was the overall DofE supervisor but I gave this one to one of our history teachers to manage. His heart wasn't really in it though. He left teaching shortly after. The kids did a presentation with a slide show of photos, but they couldn't use some of the tapes because people refused permission. One lady asked to hear the tape played back and then complained it didn't sound like her voice. That wasn't how she talked, she said. As if they'd got an actress to do it. She denied she'd said half the things.'

Voices, Anna thinks that afternoon as she opens up the box file that Karen had handed over and starts to read one of the transcripts. After her conversation with Erica yesterday she is more certain of her chance of winning her and the board over if she can prove to them that she has no intention of exploiting or despoiling memo-ries of those linked with the mill. Karen's mention of a slide show has given her some ideas. She could project photographs from the archive on one of the large white walls while extracts from the tapes were being played. The key was going to be piecing the extracts into a compelling narrative, and finding the best photographs to accom-pany it. At least now she has the interview transcripts she won't have to listen through all the tapes to find out what they contain.

The first interviewee is a man called Fred Parker. According to the transcript, after recollections of his life in the Merchant Navy he begins to talk about the walkers' café in the old Apprentice House in the early fifties. She finds his recorded interview on her mp3 player and fast-forwards through to the relevant point. She is about to press PLAY but then stands up and pulls on the heavy jumper that she keeps on the back of her chair. She wants to get a better feel for how this might work. With the box file of transcripts under one arm she picks up the player and heads up to the first floor of the mill.

'Nowt better,' Fred Parker says, in response to the interviewer's question about the café. 'When you've walked fifteen miles, half of 'em through thick mud and the other half down rivers of rocks that'd twist your ankle without a warning, nowt better than a strong cup of tea and an egg butty made with real butter. None of your vegetable-spread muck.' He'd been a member of a cycling club as well, which had used the field over the bridge for their picnics. 'Nice old lady lived in the mill cottage. Used to run the café but she'd handed it on to a young couple by then. Always happy to see us, she was. Let us refill our water bottles from her tap when the café was closed. Buggered if I can remember her name though.'

Looking out of the first-floor window, Anna can picture the cyclists streaming down the track and curving into the yard and over the bridge. Jumping off their bikes and throwing themselves on the grass. Not ghosts. Echoes. Like Peggy Shaw's angel. A man is crossing the yard with a pair of Labradors. If he glances up now and she waves, what will he think he's seen?

Fred Parker continues to reminisce about how the spring water from the hillside above the mill tasted better than lemonade.

Anna highlights the sections in the transcript with an orange marker pen and scribbles a note about a picture she has seen of cyclists from around that era. She moves on to the memories of a woman who had been sent to Ackerdean as an evacuee. Her parents were killed in the Leeds blitz in 1941 and she never went home. 'First time I saw a sheep,' she says, 'I thought it was a bear. Wouldn't come out from under my bed unless someone promised to shoot it. Eeh, I was daft.'

Before she leaves to go back to the office, Anna settles on the floor by the window to read the transcript of Sally Marsden's interview. It will be so frustrating if she can't use her words because of the missing form. One of the board members is a lawyer. Perhaps he could advise her on tracking down lost relatives, or on the legal risks involved in using interviews without permissions.

The transcript is very long and badly punctuated as though it has been typed in a hurry. In a few places the text is broken up with dotted lines and question marks, where the transcriber has been unable to make out what is being said. Anna flicks through the pages. After the section in which Sally talks about High Hob and Ivy describes her adventures as a factory girl in Rochdale there are the letters 'CONTD' in capitals and then Ivy Hall starts up again. This hadn't been on the tape.

IH: We all did as we were told in them days. No
    answering back. Not like you lot are allowed.
    We'd have been walloped wouldn't we, Sally?
SM: I was never hit. But there were harsh words.
IH: By 'eck there were. Boss at the factory
    had a tongue on him like a whip and he was
    generous with it. Mind, I was never in service
    like Sally. Treated you all right, didn't they,
    love. Working with the gentry.
SM: The missus gave me a petticoat once. To keep,
    not just to mend. Though it needed mending.
    The lace all hanging off. I kept it for best.
    What ever became of it? - [Voice very quiet.
    Couldn't hear what she said] - A bad do. The
    poor missus.
Q: What kind of work ...?
SM: It was light early, it being high summer, and
    I was up first thing to clean. I normally did
    my sewing Fridays but Aunt Livvy being ill they
    needed me extra. The hens was Saturdays. Bless
    them [... eggs ... pennies or something ...]
    The missus, legs all pale and her pretty
    face spoiled. The master kneeling [some
    mumbling] ... master, his eyes gaping like a
    codfish on the slab. Go away, Sally, he said.

Stupid little girl. Little girl? And him ...
(hungering? *words unclear*) Closed the door.
Told me I wasn't needed. I said but the poor
missus and he [*more mumbling*]. He said no one
would believe a liar [*whispers something about
being a liar*]

[Pause]

I wasn't needed no more. The house was closed
up. Everybody gone. After that it was just the
sewing and the hens until I started at the
vicarage. I was happy there.

Anna's heart is beating hard in her chest. A summer morning at High Hob. The missus '... her pretty face spoiled'. The house closed up afterwards. Sally never went back.

What had Sally Marsden walked in on that morning? According to the coroner, the position of their bodies showed that Charles had killed himself first, followed by Edie, by 'mutual agreement'. Could Sally really have witnessed Charles very much alive, angry and threatening, kneeling over the body of his dead sister?

CHAPTER 17

Billy: 1934-35

I only got Jasper's version of why he was chucked out of his other schools, which may have been worse or less bad than the truth. But the masters at Simmonds House had the full story from Charles and they were ready and waiting for him.

He was treated different from the others. A joke from another boy might raise a smile from a master, but from Jasper resulted in a charge of 'Disrespect' and a punishment of lines, or if it was Mr Sedgwick, the Latin teacher, a caning.

I expected Jasper would fight back like he had done before, but they outnumbered him. Like the gang of tomb-robbers in Bolivia who all turned on Garth Winter at once so he didn't stand a chance. Not a single one of them of a like mind as the Major who for all his strictness and discipline had called Jasper's cheek 'spark' and his pranks 'the sign of a lively mind'. Though we never got to hear his opinion on Jasper's bombing of the Scouts, and even he might have blown his top if Jasper had made a campfire under another boy's bed, as he did in our first term at Simmonds House. I thought for certain he'd be sent home for that, and he hoped so too. But he was made instead to face the wall outside the headmaster's study all the next day to contemplate his actions and the welts on his behind left by the cane. No doubt he spent the time plotting who to target next.

I didn't much like the school, but I didn't want to get kicked out neither. I missed Ma and the Palace with an ache like nothing I'd felt at High Hob. Up on the moor I'd known that home was just a walk away and that the sky above my head was the same one as over the Palace. Some nights, lying in my narrow bed at Simmonds House, I felt like a spaceman in one of Jasper's science fiction comics, who'd crashed on a strange new planet, cut off from my own kind and having to learn how to adapt to a whole new world. A world where the aliens were stalking masters in black cloaks, with canes instead of ray guns for weapons, and boys who spoke a language I could barely understand. I'd never felt more alone. But Simmonds House was a fancy school with a crest and a motto and pupils whose fathers were businessmen and bankers. It's where you need to be, Billy, I told myself, like it or lump it.

I kept my head down and got on with my work and tried not to get riled into scraps. The other boys mocked my accent, which even after three years at High Hob stood out like a clog in a slipper rack. They found out soon enough that my father had worked in the mills and that my mother served teas. I suspected Jasper for letting on.

They waited for me to prove I was stupid in class, to wipe my nose on my sleeve or scratch myself for lice. I didn't give them the satisfaction. And they started giving me a wide berth once they'd encountered the full force of Jasper. He got into a fight every day for the first few weeks. He usually came off best but he was rarely without a blackened eye or a fat lip. The other boys said he didn't fight fair, but he didn't care. There were rumours that he'd flashed a knife or another weapon that sounded to me like his stone-carving chisel. But nothing was found when his clothes and bags were searched.

Being the companion of the most feared boy in the school gave me some protection. It also meant that I made very few new friends.

The schoolwork was tough. There were plenty of gaps in what we'd learnt at High Hob. I spent my spare hours doing extra study. It earned me jibes for being a swot, but friendship too of a sort from boys who needed help with their work. Jasper got by all right, but he saved his true brilliance for his pranks and wind-ups. He attracted a different group of pals. Boys who wanted the admiration and protection that came from being with him. They tolerated me, but called me 'mill boy' when Jasper wasn't around.

The holidays back at High Hob were like coming up for air after you'd had your face plunged in the washbasin too long, which happened to be one of the ways the fifth formers liked to entertain themselves with the younger boys. We were back home for seven weeks for the summer. I felt dizzy stood out there at the Hound's Rock with Jasper for the first time after so long. There were hills and moors above Simmonds House but they might as well have been stars and moons for all we got to touch them. It was only on the cross-country runs, which Jasper was excused because of his asthma, that I felt anything near like alive.

That first day back, Oakenshaw Moor smelled freshly painted, the air thick with sweet heather and the sharp blood-smell of the peat. I breathed in and in and never wanted to breathe out again.

'What you doing, you daft bugger?' Jasper pushed me off the rock I was perched on. 'You look like a ruddy great rat that's got the scent of bacon.' But he must have felt it too, because he howled and whooped like I'd not heard for all the months we'd been away.

The first time Edie saw us again, it was like she'd forgotten who we were.

'The boys are back,' Charles said in a hale and hearty way that wasn't his usual style. Edie smiled sweetly and nodded as if she'd been introduced to a couple of young princes from Timbuctoo. She asked why wasn't there any tea, could she please have some tea.

Sally, who was hovering by the door said, 'Yes, mam, right away, mam,' and scuttled off like she was glad of something to do.

We sat in Edie's room with tea and scones, but it was a ghost of the times we'd shared in there before; the fire unlit as always but Edie's face with no light in it either. Afterwards, Charles said we weren't to bother her. She'd been unwell. An old friend had died, and she was taking it badly. The doctor had prescribed special pills and she'd be right as rain before long. That hale and hearty voice again. He was an unconvincing liar, unlike Jasper who gave a glowing report of our first term at school. Unfortunately, Charles had received our actual reports in the post. He agreed that he couldn't fault our academic effort – 'You're both getting by' – but he needed to have words with Jasper about his behaviour. The words took hours and were spoken in his lowest most serious tone; I couldn't make out a single one of them even with a glass between my ear and his study door.

Our Maud's wedding was at the end of July. She rode to Draper's Cross in a cart all covered with paper flowers pulled by the Chamber's old mare Jenny with a garland round her neck. They were to live in the farmhouse with Arty's parents, who were getting on a bit, and it would be theirs alone one day. Though she told me that bit in a whisper and a quick smile to her in-laws to show she wasn't wishing them dead and gone just yet.

It was hard to picture Ma in the cottage with only Peggy for company. Though Peggy was less silly now she'd finished school and was working full time at the Palace. She said her and Ma rubbed along fine.

There was no sign of Potter or of Lizzie. They were off on their holidays, Ma said, though this time she didn't know where. It had been months since I'd seen Lizzie and I had so much I wanted to tell her. I feared she was slipping away from me. Off on new adventures more exciting than my own, meeting new people and maybe forgetting about Billy back at home. I couldn't tell anyone, not even Peggy. I just hoped the Potters' holidaying would come to an end soon.

I slept solid back in my bed up in the attic. Bliss to be in a room that wasn't filled with the scratching and sniffing of other boys. But one night, a week or so before we were due to return to Derbyshire, something wakened me. Made me slip out of bed and look out of the window. The moon was up. One of them enormous cheesy moons when it gets so big it looks like it might drop out of the sky. I had a clear view across the moor. Something billowed white amongst the heather, a sheep perhaps, or a wandered off cow. But then the shape turned and lifted its face up to the sky and though I couldn't make out her features, I knew it was Edie.

It must have been the door closing behind her that had wakened me. Maybe she had done it on other nights, but more quietly. I remembered what Peggy once said, about Edie being seen wandering the moors in her nightie, *trying to catch summat romantic to die of.*

She'd been pale and mopey for weeks, still full of sadness for her dead friend and the pills not seeming to make things better. A chill could do for her. I should go and fetch her in. But before I had made up my mind what to do, another figure appeared. Moving towards her. As the two figures met, the second one wrapped something dark around Edie, covering the pale nightdress. Together they walked back towards the house. Charles. Looking out for his sister, and guiding her home.

It was the day before we headed back to Derbyshire. Trunks packed and in the back of the Crossley. We'd said goodbye to the Stag Stones and had visited Abe's hut, now in a poor state, with the roof caved in. We still had a couple of hours before we were due back for our farewell tea prepared by Sally and Livvy.

'Let's bob down to the Palace,' I said. I'd said my goodbyes to Ma and Peggy a couple of days before. We'd had supper with Maud and Arty at the farm, with me and Peggy kicking each other under the table at the sight of our big sister clucking round the kitchen like she'd been a farmer's wife all her life. But I wanted a final look at the Palace. To get it fixed in my head proper, to think on when school got too tough.

I hadn't dared hope to see Lizzie but there she was by the Upper Dam. On her own, though she said Jane was lurking somewhere nearby. I wanted to hug her and I knew by the way she leaned against me when we were talking that she was feeling the same. But Jasper hung as close as a shadow, though a loud and solid one, so we never got a chance. I said I'd wanted to write to her from school, but our letters were read by the masters and we were only allowed family correspondence. She said her school was the same but she knew a way round it.

It was the letters from 'Your cousin Elizabeth', and my replies signed 'Cousin William', that got me through the roughness of the next couple of terms. There'd been complaints from parents about Jasper, so now we had a junior master, Mr Rawthorne, assigned to our dorm. It meant that the nights were peaceful but the other boys just hated us more. They didn't dare take it out on Jasper, so I got it instead. Small things. Missing pens, blotted and torn exercise books, my vest and shorts dragged through the mud before games. Enough to make the masters irritated by my carelessness, enough to make my days more of a chore. But I had the solace of Lizzie's letters, deciphering the hidden meanings behind her sedate lines – *How I miss sitting on the riverbank with the warm touch of the sun on my arms* – and responding in my own similar code. It was as though with every letter I was transported briefly to Ackerdean, with Lizzie close by my side.

Though the days at Simmonds House seemed long the terms passed quickly. I couldn't credit it, as we travelled back to Sowley on the train that Easter, that we'd been at school for a whole year. Jasper couldn't believe it either, though mainly he couldn't understand why he still hadn't been expelled, even after at least three other boys had left on his account.

It was my fifteenth birthday a couple of days after we arrived back. There was no question of me not going down to the Palace. Jasper was sulking. His end of term report had sent Charles into such a rage I could see the veins bulging at both temples like all the words he wanted to shout were fighting to get out. Staying behind on my birthday was just one of Jasper's punishments.

It was too quiet. I could tell even before I reached the yard. There were trippers about, but with long gaps between them and they seemed distracted, as if they were no longer having the time of their lives and were wondering if they should have tried elsewhere instead. Ma said more of the mills were closed and folks were moving further afield to work. Them that stayed behind had less money to spend on jollity. David had a different explanation.

'Call of the ocean waves, Billy,' he said. 'They're buggering off to the seaside instead.' I found him having a smoke round the back of the Pavilion. He offered me one of his Woodbines. But I said no, not knowing right what to do with it, though some of the boys at school had smokes and Jasper often joined them.

'Fancy a bit of sea air myself, I do.' He sniffed. 'The smell of something other than the bloody trees and the river.'

I didn't get that. What better smell was there? The painted boards of the Pavilion were warm against my back. I could smell the linseed in the wood and David's baccy, but underneath it the solid smell of the peaty orange water over the river stones and the spring leaves all soft and new. I felt dizzy at the thought of being without it ever again. Though I knew that the stink of dusty floors and old textbooks and the rancid odour of the dorm lay only a few weeks ahead.

'The boss reckons the seaside is just a novelty what they'll tire of. Nothing there that we don't have here. 'Cepting the sea, of course, and the sand.' David scrunched up his face. 'Hope he's right. We're running the place close to the bone as it is.'

*

I nipped back across the river on the stepping stones, balancing myself as the stone second-but-one to the end gave its familiar wobble, glad that some things hadn't changed. As I approached the yard, Ma was looking out from an open window on the first floor. I waved up at her, but I felt unsteady for a minute and stopped in my tracks. The whole of the Palace was laid out in front of me, with Ma at the centre. It was like looking at a picture and if I wanted to be part of it I would have to believe in magic and step into it, like that *Alice Through the Looking Glass* that Lizzie was so fond of. I almost expected some sort of jolt as I stepped forward, but there was nothing. I just kept walking until I was in the middle of it all, the scattering of couples walking arm in arm, the bunting, tatty but brave, fluttering above the splash and shouts of lads mucking about in the river. I was in it but it was all happening outside me.

'You all right, Billy love?' Ma held me at arm's length after she'd hugged me. She put the back of her hand to my forehead to check for a temperature.

I dodged away. 'I'm all right, Ma, don't fret.'

'Good. I don't want any of your birthday treat going to waste. Come on, Peggy can't wait to see you.'

'Don't you have to be working?' I asked.

Ma shrugged. 'I can spare half an hour. I've got Mabel Askwith on the counter. She should be enough cover for the slim pickings we've got today.'

Peggy came out of the kitchen. Her hair was up like Ma's, not tied in the pigtails she'd been wearing the last time I'd seen her. But her cheeky elf grin was still there and she half skipped across the room to me.

'Billy, have they not been feeding you? You're skinny as a rake.' She linked her arm in mine and led me over to the table where plates were set with sandwiches and a double stand of cakes sat in the centre. Peggy was full of her usual banter, telling me I'd turned into a proper young gent since I'd been at school and I'd have to watch I wasn't getting too high and mighty for Ackerdean. I tried to avoid using any new words or turns of phrase I might have picked up at Simmonds House, but then I said, 'The Latin master is ghastly' and Peggy squealed, 'Get you, our Billy.'

I asked Ma about Potter. Whether he was likely to be around today. Partly out of wonder at how he'd react to seeing me, something near to a proper gentleman, but mainly cos I was hoping Lizzie would come down with him, knowing it was my birthday. There had been one, too-short, morning over Christmas when we'd gone nature watching by the frosty banks of the river, our ever-present shadows in tow. Though our talk was of the bare branches of the trees and the ice on the rocks, it was the sharing of our voices that counted. We'd talked more over the past year in written words than we had in spoken ones and I longed to hear her say my name again.

'They've gone to the Highlands,' Ma said in a voice that sounded unimpressed, as if she'd heard they were spending the afternoon in the laundry.

'The Highlands?'

'It's in Scotland,' Peggy said.

'I know,' I growled and Peggy kicked my foot under the table.

'Lizzie was down here the day before they left,' Peggy said. 'She's got a new sketchbook and a box of coloured pencils. They're staying in a castle near a big lake that's got a monster in it.' Peggy spread her arms wide in the air. 'It's a giant snake or a dragon mebbes and she's going to draw it and tell me all about it when she gets back.' She paused. 'She's not near as stuck up as she used to be. Not like some,' she added, sticking her tongue out at me.

There was a hollowness in my chest. All week I'd been imagining me and Lizzie flying in one of the swingboats. Her face grinning down at me and teasing me to go higher and calling me sweet cousin William. Now it wasn't going to happen. Worse, she was off hunting real dragons, hundreds of miles away, without me.

I wished Jasper had been able to come down with me after all. Ma was wiping her hands and adjusting her cap getting ready to go back to the counter and Peggy said she had pots to put away.

Someone cleared their throat behind me and at the same time Peggy's mouth fell wide open.

I twisted my chair round and saw why Peggy was gawping. It was Edie Harper, in what she called her 'finery'. Not the woolly greys and browns that she usually wore at home. Her dress was shiny and the blue of a kingfisher's back and a fox fur lay over her shoulders. It still had its head and brush and I recognised it, from the glint in its eye, as Mr Fox from First Class. She had one hand to her throat, twirling a length of clear beads round her fingers. Her head was half bowed so you could see the dark blue feathers on the crown of her little hat.

'Miss Harper,' said Ma, like she was the person she most wanted to see in the world. 'How lovely of you to come down. What can I be getting you?'

'Thank you, Mrs Shaw. A cup of tea would be lovely.' Edie lifted her head and there was a wicked twinkle in her eye the like of which I'd never seen before.

'Have you left me a slice of cake?' she said, taking the chair next to Peggy as Ma went to fetch her tea. She reached for the last piece of the Dundee. It was one with plenty of cherries in it, thank goodness. Peggy just kept gawping at her. I could swear she squeaked when Edie leaned towards me, put a hand on my trouser leg and said, 'I couldn't bear to miss your birthday treat. I hope you don't mind me joining in.'

Her words were blurred at the edges with the lemony gin I could smell on her breath.

'No,' I said. 'I mean, you're welcome.'

She'd powdered her face. The fine grains rested on her skin. Her lips a deep red with a smudge at one corner. She blinked and her eyes seemed to brim, but then she looked away.

'Fabulous,' she said. She finished her slice of cake, hungrily like it was the first thing she'd eaten that day. 'So what's the plan?' She brushed the crumbs from her fingers. 'Fun and games?'

Peggy jumped up. 'Sorry, miss, but I have to go and help Ma.' She scuttled off but glanced over her shoulder as she reached the kitchen door, as if she'd rather have stayed behind.

'So, William, just you and me.' She shuffled her chair closer and there was something about her eyes, like she was seeing me through liquid. 'What shall we do with ourselves?'

'Well, there's the swingboats,' I said. They were what had been most on my mind.

She clapped her hands like a little girl. 'Sounds like an excellent place to start. Lead the way.'

It wasn't exactly what I'd had planned. Me and Edie Harper in a swingboat. It should have been me and Lizzie. But it was fun, of sorts. Edie kept calling for me to pull harder on the rope and at the top of each swing she lifted both arms in the air like she wanted to take flight.

She took me home after in the Crossley. I didn't even know she could drive. She went faster still than Charles and going round corners through Sowley I hung on to my seat. When we reached the copse at the end of the track to High Hob she pulled on the brake and sank back, looking out of breath as if she'd run all the way. As we started up the track, she announced she had a headache and was going to bed and marched on ahead. I let her go. Jasper was in the garden, chucking stones at a row of empty tin cans he had lined up on the wall. 'Have a nice party, did you?' he asked, hurling a stone and missing the tins completely.

'It was all right,' I said.

He chucked another stone and this time hit his target. 'Shall we go out to the Hound's Head,' he said, 'see if there's any new Beast spoor?'

I pictured the dragon boat and Edie's arms lifted to the sky. Lizzie in the turret of a Highland castle with a spyglass trained on the still waters of the lake, waiting for the monster to emerge.

'Aye,' I said. I picked up a stone and hurled it at the cans, catching one that toppled and knocked down the rest. 'Let's.'

CHAPTER 18

Anna: February

What I know

1. Someone at High Hob, probably Charles, had a romantic connection with an officer in the Warwickshire Fusiliers known as Beebee / B.B.

2. Edie and Charles didn't write the 'suicide note'.

3. Sally claims Charles was still alive in the morning. Told her to go away. Called her a liar.

4. If she's telling the truth then the coroner was wrong about Charles dying first. Did he kill Edie and then himself? But who left the note? Not Charles — it's a poem about his brother going to war.

5. Sally a suspect? Killed Charles when she found him with Edie dead? Made it look like suicide. [Would explain her fear.] Could she have done all that on her own? Was she in cahoots with Billy Shaw? Was B.B. involved?

6. What does this mean?????

Anna stretches her back against the cushions of the armchair and watches the flicker of the flames in the stove. It means, she thinks, that eighty years ago, someone may have got away with murder.

If Charles and Edie didn't kill themselves then it changes their story. She runs over again the conversation with Erica. The revelation that her mother was a close friend of the Potters. Erica's palpable fear of scandal and misrepresentation. But still no adequate explanation about the closure of the mill. *She's still holding back.*

I need one of those boards that they have in police dramas, she decides, putting her notebook on the arm of the chair. Then she thinks – Sam. She has more insight into the workings of the criminal mind than anyone else she knows, perhaps she could make sense of it. She hasn't spoken to her since she'd rung her a couple of weeks ago to tell her about Edie's handwriting not matching the haiku dedication, and her conclusion that Beebee was more likely to have been Charles's lover than Edie's.

Sam's mobile goes straight to voicemail. Anna hesitates but doesn't leave a message. It's too complicated. She'll try again later.

If only she could find the rest of Sally's interview, listen to it for herself. But so far her trawl through the tapes has been fruitless and she still has hours of recordings to hear. It might not even be there. Sally could have asked for the tape to be destroyed.

The wind rattles the cottage window as if reminding her that it's a Sunday and she had planned to go out today. A walk might help to sort out the tangle of facts and speculation in her head.

It is wilder outside than she expected. The rattling of the windows should have been more of a warning. The trees are shimmying to the rhythm of the wind. The river water looks solid: smooth muscle and sinew twisting round rocks and fallen branches, reaching down the cleft of the valley and through the arc of the bridge. It reminds her of the molten glass she and Dan had watched being pulled and shaped at a workshop in Cornwall two summers ago. She'd bought a small glass seal, its skin speckled with bubbles, its head reaching upwards as if stretching the glass, still holding on to some of the liquid movement it was born from.

As she crosses the bridge Anna's hair whips across her face, in her mouth and eyes. She grabs it into a bunch at the back and twists a rough plait, tying the end with a piece of twine from her pocket.

When she reaches the gate to Frank's farm she sees him crossing the yard, his body stooped. As she draws nearer she can hear him whistling, a trill, like birdsong. He stops when he sees her and raises his hand.

'Just passing through, are you?' he asks. He is wearing a thick jumper, his padded gilet on top and a woollen scarf knotted round his neck. 'Or is this an official visit?'

Anna smiles. 'I fancied a walk and realised I haven't seen you for a while.'

'Aye, well, I've been girding my loins, haven't I.'

'What for?'

'It's official. This place is on the market and as soon as there's a room free I'm moving in to the Bungalow of Eternal Rest. It's one in one out so I'm waiting for someone to die. Mind, I could be dead myself by then.'

'Cheerful for a Sunday afternoon.'

Frank pulls out a handkerchief and starts to cough, waving her away with his other hand when she asks if he's OK. 'It's nowt but a winter cold. It'll pass by the spring. Come on in. We'll have a drop and a warm. This wind'll nip the living breath out of you.'

'Do you have any milk?' she asks.

'If you insist.'

'How's it going?' Frank passes her a mug of brick-coloured tea and balances a plate of fig rolls on the arm of her chair. He sits down on the sofa opposite, his scarf still fastened round his neck, fingerless mittens on his knotty hands. Betsy settles across his feet. 'Have you managed to drag the place into the twenty-first century yet?'

'Getting there,' says Anna. 'The Ackerdean Heritage Centre is now part of the World Wide Web.'

'Blimey, how did you do that?'

She tells him about the baker in Sowley whose son is a web designer. 'Family connections,' she says. 'His great-granddad used to sell hot food at the Pavilion. The family have always had a soft spot for the place and the son said it was the least he could do to "knock us up a website". His words, not mine, though it took him less than a day. It's mainly the catalogue of the collection at the moment, which itself is a work in progress. But I've uploaded lots of photos and I'm writing a blog.'

Frank furrows his brow.

'An online diary,' she explains. 'About my work. I'll be adding more photos, scans of important documents as I go along. Maybe even some of the oral history interviews.'

'What's Erica Walker's opinion on all this?'

'She loves it. She had lots of ideas for the layout and colour scheme though thankfully Josh, that's the baker's son, kept pretty much to my brief. I'll show you it next time you're down.'

'Aye, you could do that. Or I could look at the actual displays and have an actual conversation with you about what you're up to. "Blog",' he huffs. 'Sounds like something you'd use to clean the lav.'

Anna grins. 'I think Erica would prefer it if the whole collection was on the Internet – exhibits and all. Let the public explore it from the safety of their own homes, no grubby fingers, no fear of breakages or compensation claims.' She rests back in the sofa. 'It will widen our audience, but the museum can't survive without footfall. We need to draw people in. Make proper use of the building.'

'Still got her back up about your expansion plans, has she?'

Anna nods and helps herself to a fig roll.

'I've got my fingers crossed for the board though. There were some sympathetic responses at my presentation. By the way, I thought you might like to see this.' She passes him a black and white photo she had found yesterday. It was taken near the Pavilion. The central figure is a woman in a dark dress smiling up at the photographer. To her right, caught by the camera and oblivious to it, stand a boy and a girl. He is pointing at the sky and she is looking up in the direction of his hand. Anna had recognised Frank straightaway. The same intense gaze that he has on the family photo he brought her. His sandy hair tufted at the front, his firm mouth and sharply defined chin.

'How old were you, about fourteen?'

Frank studies the picture for a while, 'That ain't me, lass. How old do you think I am? That were taken back when the Pavilion was still striped, before they made it all over camo-green during the war.' He points at the picture. 'Haven't a clue who the sweet-faced lass is, but the lad is Uncle Billy.'

He sinks back in his chair, still holding the photo. 'My mother loved Billy. Though you'd be hard put to know it when he was around, which wasn't often. "Once in a blue moon," she used to say. She talked to him like he was a naughty schoolboy, when he were a grown man. But when he went to leave she'd be hugging and kissing him and telling him not to leave it so long next time. He'd done all right for himself. Ran a pleasure gardens and a couple of theatres. Hosted a boxing match that was in all the papers. He called it his empire.' He lays the photograph on his lap and stares at the glowing bars of the electric fire. 'Billy could've made summat of the old Palace, given the chance.'

'Did he ever get involved in it?' Anna asks. 'I know most of it was closed down before the Second World War, but afterwards when there was still the Apprentice House café and the roller rink?'

Frank shakes his head. 'Nah, he wasn't on speaking terms with Nathaniel Potter. Some kind of falling-out was all Mam would say, just before he cleared off down south.'

A falling-out between Mr Potter and Billy Shaw, shortly before the Harpers died? Once again, Anna wonders about Billy and his role up at High Hob. Could he have been involved with Sally

Marsden? Might he have been an accomplice to whatever happened that night? Was his departure connected to the closing up of the mill?

'Do you have any other photographs of him?' she asks.

'A couple.' He begins to rise up from his seat, but then sinks back down. 'My back's giving me gyp today. There's an album in the top drawer of the dresser. Fetch it over, will you?'

The drawer is stiff, she has to yank it open. Inside there is a white-bound photo album and a jumble of documents, including a passport and an envelope marked 'Marriage Certificate'. From underneath peeks the creamy white of a birth certificate: the red ink across the top reads 'Registration District: Bethnal Green'. Jim's jibe about *Them of us that are Yorkshire born and bred*. She knows she has no right to look, but quietly she pushes the passport and envelope to one side.

'When and where born: 17th March 1942, Bethnal Green / Sex: Boy / Name: Francis William / Name and Surname of Father: William Shaw / Name of mother: Catherine Shaw, formerly Sanders.'

Anna picks up the photo album and shuts the drawer.

Frank takes the album from her and makes room for her on the sofa. She watches his face. His likeness to the photo of the young Billy had been uncanny. She'd known he was holding something back. Part of the puzzle slots into place.

Frank has opened the album at the first page. A single photograph is positioned in the centre, the date '1946' handwritten above. A young man in a pinstriped suit sits on a bench, a pint of beer on the table in front of him. Hair combed back, a handkerchief peeking out of his breast pocket. Looking at the camera uncertainly, one arm around a young child bundled into a bulky smock coat, trousers and boots. A flat cap on the child's head and a drinking bottle grasped in both hands.

'That's me.' Frank points to the child. 'Billy was up for a visit. It's the beer garden at the King's Head in Sowley. Mam called the picture "Frank's first pint".' He moves through the album to two wedding photographs in faded colour. In one a bride in white satin clutches a bouquet of yellow flowers and next to her the groom is a young Frank in a suit and tie. In the other the bride and groom are talking to the vicar. Over the bride's shoulder a man faces the camera. Billy Shaw. Older now, but still recognisable from the earlier photograph.

'He was there,' Frank says. 'For my wedding.'

She looks from Frank to the photo and back.

'You haven't changed much.' She means it. The still-sharp angles of his jaw, the steady gaze of his eyes, the long nose only slightly more bulbous now with age.

'Happen,' he says. 'Though the mirror tells me different.'

'You were very alike,' she says. 'You and Billy.' He flashes her a look that makes her wonder if she has pushed too far. Then he sighs and puts the album down on the table.

'Technically, it's none of your business,' he says. 'But it's not exactly a secret. More of on a need-to-know-basis.' He coughs into his hand. 'Maud and Arthur Chambers, God bless them, they were my mam and dad in every way that mattered. They wanted a bairn badly, wanted a whole brood of them, but not one came along. Didn't have all that fancy science and test tubes in them days. If you couldn't make a baby the way nature intended then it was hard luck.'

He frowns at the photo album as if searching for the rest of the story.

'They adopted you?' Anna asks. She picks up the original photo that Frank had identified as Billy.

'He wasn't my uncle.' He lifts his head and there is a hint of pride in his voice. 'Billy. He was my dad.'

'Have you always known?'

'They didn't tell me for years. My mother died when I was born and Billy he was in no state to care for me. It was during the war and all his businesses were in London. No place for a baby, he said.

So he brought me up here and gave me to his sister.' He wipes his mouth with his handkerchief.

'He left everything to you,' Anna remembers.

'Aye, I couldn't have bought this place without him. Makes it harder for me to let it go.' He reaches into his pocket and pulls out a cloth pouch. 'I'll always have this though.' His crooked fingers loosen the cord at the neck of the pouch and he shakes out a silver object onto his hand.

'Gave me this one of the last times I saw him. He was getting on then. It was the 1980s, bloody Thatcher's Britain. Billy was all right though, retired in comfort in his own house, bought and paid for. The watch was his granddad's, my great-granddad's. Here, have a look.'

Anna takes it from him. A silver pocket watch, engraved with loops and swirls and still showing the right time. She turns it over and reads the inscription and date on the back. '"For devoted service, 1897",' she says. 'Was it a gift from the mill owners? Or was he in military service?'

'The mill, I think. He must have done summat right. Don't get that kind of kit for just turning up and doing your job. I told you. Shaws were the backbone of that place.' He takes the watch back and puts it in its pouch. 'I'll have to keep it locked up at the old folks' home. Billy said it was all he had of his dad's side of the family and I was to keep it safe. Pass it on to my young'uns when the time comes. I've got my granddad's medals, too, from my mam but Billy wanted me to take special care of this. "Part of our heritage, Frank," he said. "Yours and mine. Pass it on, so it's not forgotten." He was all for family and remembering where and what we came from, despite him haring off to London first chance he got.'

On Thursday morning, when she opens her emails there is a short message from her mum with some photos attached from Christmas. And an email from Erica.

Dear Anna

The board met again last night to discuss your presentation and report. Please accept our apologies for the time taken for our response but there were many implications, moral, legal and financial that had to be given serious consideration before a decision could be reached.

I was surprised I have to say by the strength of the other board members' feelings. There are, it appears, no legal or financial obstructions to your plans going ahead. On these grounds the majority of the board voted for your proposals, including the refurbishment and opening up of the upper floors of the mill, with only a few minor changes detailed in the attached.

You know my feelings on this. However, the board is not and never has been one person and I must abide by what the majority decides. Our treasurer Mary Lewis will be in touch today to discuss how next to proceed.

Best wishes

Erica

She has to read it through twice. They've said yes.

She's going to be able to do it. Create the exhibition spaces that the generations of Ackerdean's inhabitants, workers and visitors deserve. The history they deserve. There is no mention in the email of the conversation she and Erica shared in the fisherman's hut. But she wonders if it made a difference.

She needs to tell someone. She rings Sam's mobile, but again it goes to voicemail. This time she leaves a brief message. She could phone her mum and dad. They'd be pleased for her about the opening up of the mill, but it wouldn't be the same as talking about it with someone who knows the place. Carter's business card is propped up on the shelf above her desk. He would be excited about her news and he might be able to put her in touch with Sam.

'Crime writing festival in Copenhagen,' he says. 'Did she not mention it? It's one of the highlights of her year. I'm squatting at High Hob in the meantime and picking her up from Leeds Bradford in the morning. Anything I can help with?'

'No, I'm fine, thanks,' she says. 'I just wanted to share some news.' She tells him about Erica's email. He suggests that they go out and celebrate.

'Maybe when Sam gets back,' she says. 'I might have more details about what's happening next by then.'

Six down, four to go. Anna is in the cottage, working her way through the tapes that she hasn't listened to yet, although she has read through the scripts. She picks up the next cassette, hoping the batteries in the player will last. The electricity went off in the cottage and the mill an hour ago. It's the second time this week. 'An intermittent fault caused by the storm,' she's been told. 'Our engineers are working on it.' She has the player hooked up to a mini speaker and is listening to the tapes in a cocoon of candlelight. In the silence between each interview the only sounds are the gentle dripping of the leaky gutter outside the front door and the barely audible tock-tock of the mantelpiece clock.

She has been listening to the disembodied voices for hours. Her feet are numb from being curled beneath her, but she is reluctant to move from under her blanket. The stove is unlit and the log bucket needs restocking from the pile outside. If I go out, she thinks, I might as well get in the car and drive into town. Sit by a functioning radiator in a brightly lit pub, eking out a glass of wine and some crisps. Spend a couple of hours among the warmth and fug of other people, surrounded by the voices of the living, not the dead.

Her toes tingle as she stretches out her legs. She could phone her mum, or one of her old friends in Newcastle. More disembodied voices, still no one she can reach out and touch. A draught causes the candles to flicker, fingers of light and dark play across the wall. 'Half sick of shadows,' she whispers aloud.

The tape she has picked up is Frank's. The transcript of it is several pages long and the interview is recorded on two sides of one of the original tapes. It is mostly about his life as a farmer but she has highlighted a section towards the end when he talks about how he had helped his grandmother with the chickens she kept after the Palace closed.

She listens to his account of a harsh winter at the farm, followed by his memories of the mill yard filled with hens and his gran shooing them out of her kitchen. Perfect, Anna thinks. The young interviewer says, 'Thank you, Mr Chambers', and there is the familiar clunk of the original machine being switched off. Anna is about to press stop when there is another clunk and a woman's voice begins.

'We all did as we were told in them days. No answering back.'

It's Ivy Hall. The rest of the interview in the retirement home, recorded on the spare space at the end of Frank's tape.

She turns up the volume and focuses on the old lady's words. Sally Marsden next, talking about the petticoat the 'poor missus' had given her. Her voice fading in and out as though she is moving back and forth from the microphone. The interviewer begins to ask another question about her time as a maid.

'What kind of work ...?'

'It was light early, it being high summer, and I was up first thing to clean. I normally did my sewing Fridays but Aunt Livvy being ill they needed me extra.'

Anna closes her eyes and listens hard.

'The hens was Saturdays. Bless them. Plenty of eggs but I only got pennies.' Her voice is a whisper. 'The missus, legs all pale and her pretty face spoiled. The master kneeling by her side. Crying, he was. Just crying. The young master, though, his eyes gaping like a codfish on the slab. Go away, Sally, he said. Stupid little girl.'

Her voice is so quiet. Anna rewinds the tape, turns up the volume, strains to hear through the hiss of the tape.

'Stupid little girl. Little girl? And him younger'n me. He closed the door. Told me I wasn't needed. I said but the poor missus and he said no, you're wrong. He said no one would believe a liar.'

'Are you all right, Sally love? I think she's had enough for today.'

'I wasn't needed no more. The house was closed up. Everybody gone. After that it was just the sewing and the hens until I started at the vicarage. I was happy there. But I don't want to talk about it today. Will you go away now please.'

There is a silence, a low hiss and the recording stops. Sally's words seem to hang in the air like smoke.

Anna checks the transcript. The writer had got it wrong. Sally Marsden didn't describe Charles Harper, 'the master', telling Sally to go home. The person who was gaping like a codfish was 'the young master', younger than Sally herself. But Jasper hadn't been there 'first thing' that day. He had been away at boarding school and returned to Yorkshire late on the Friday afternoon. The vicar drove him up to the house from Oakenshaw train station. And they found the bodies together. The only other 'young master' at High Hob was Billy Shaw. Sally's voice was scared, even after all this time. He'd said no one would believe her. She'd said he was the liar.

In the official accounts there is no mention of anyone else being at the house that day. No reference to Sally Marsden. Or to Frank's father, Billy Shaw.

The sound of a vehicle engine rumbles into the yard and comes to a stop. She checks the clock. Nine forty-five. She pulls herself up from the chair, her feet still tingling as she crosses the dark room to the window and peers outside. Sam's Volvo, she must have got back early. She opens the door, to find Carter Klein with one fist raised about to knock.

'I just popped into Sowley for a teatime pint,' he begins. 'Ended up being dragged onto a pub quiz team.' He shrugs. 'We were losing by half-time so I did a runner. Who'd have known Argentina was bigger than Peru? Thought I'd check up on you on my way back.'

She can smell the beer on him and feels nostalgic for nights down at the pub with her friends in Newcastle. Memories of the one time she and Dan were on a winning quiz team.

'Check up on me?' she asks.

'Yeah. That, you know, you're all right here on your tod.' He peers into the candlelit room. 'Christ. I haven't interrupted a seance, have I?'

'Powercut,' she says. The night air makes her shiver.

'Not to worry.' Carter sways. 'I come bearing gifts.' He pulls two bottles of beer out from under his coat, clinks them together. 'So we can celebrate your news.'

For a moment she is confused, thinking he means her new discovery from Sally's tape.

'Your victory,' he says. 'The mill and stuff.' He is smiling like a child expecting a party.

How much has he had over his original pint?

'Sam would kill you if you pranged her car or ran it into a sheep.'

He shakes his head again. 'Nah, I'm all right. And if this tips me over,' he raises the bottles, 'I can always walk. Lovely night for it.'

She should tell him to go. But the prospect of sharing a couple of beers in celebration is appealing. She could leave her thoughts about Billy and Jasper and Sally until the morning when she is less tired.

'Come on in, then,' she says. 'But you should call for a taxi if you're planning on having another one. It's a long walk to High Hob in the dark.'

'Yeah, yeah.' Carter follows her into the cottage. 'Which one do you fancy, Old Chomper or Stumbling Badger? They're both local and highly recommended by the cheery bar staff of the King's Head.' He places the bottles on the table. As Anna picks one of them up Carter moves closer, his arm resting against hers. Before she realises what he is doing he has pulled her close to him, his head nuzzling her shoulder.

She pushes him away.

'You're pissed,' she says.

'Only a bit.'

His breath is warm and sweet.

'You're very lovely.' He wraps both arms round her again.

He might be pissed but he is also very attractive. Amusing enough when he's not being sarky. Not a man she's likely to lose her heart to. He wouldn't be her first brief encounter since Dan. He lifts his head from her shoulder. As she raises her face his lips twitch a smile. What Carter wants, Carter usually gets. Anna shakes her head and tries to push him away. For a moment he resists, but then he steps back, palms raised. Still that half smile, that 'Come on, you know you want to' look in his eyes.

'It's getting late,' she says. 'I'll pass on the beer.'

He lowers his hands, shrugs and reaches for one of the bottles.

'I'll put the kettle on,' Anna adds, thankful, not for the first time, that the cooker hob runs off bottled gas. 'While it's boiling I'll ring for your taxi. You should have time for a cup of tea before it arrives.'

CHAPTER 19

Billy: 1935-36

It was the start of the long summer holidays with close to two months before we were expected back at Simmonds House.

We'd been out at the Stag Stones. Jasper wanted us to burn our ties as a symbol of the end of the school year. I argued that we would need them again in September but he said we could say they were lost over the holidays. He was burning his blazer too, said it was getting tight across the shoulders and he'd need a new one next term anyway. But I shoved mine at the back of the wardrobe. Ma would have a fit if she heard of us burning clobber that still had good wear in it.

The ties didn't take well to the flames that had licked their way through the heap of dry heather, and when Jasper threw his blazer on it he all but put it out. Then he threw on a lick of paraffin from the can Livvy kept in the back kitchen store. There was a whoompf and angry flames leapt up and ravaged the cloth. I hid the shudder that came with the memory of the fire at the Scout camp, the horror that was, and the worse horror that might have been.

The blazer was still smouldering when we headed for home, though Jasper had peed on the fire to try to put it out. Edie had a visitor coming and had made us promise we'd be back for high tea in the parlour, and no grubby paws.

We were late. Edie was waving her guest goodbye as we ambled through the front gate. It was the Reverend Haste from Oakenshaw. What tales he'd heard of us up at High Hob I don't know but he put his hand to his heart when Jasper lurched forward to say hello, his hair a riot of black curls and the stink of the fire on him still, as if he'd just popped up from hell. Edie managed to do two faces at once, one all warm for the vicar, while staring ice at us.

The Reverend had come to invite us to the church fete. Although we weren't, as he put it, 'regular' members of the congregation, we would all be welcome. Something about past transgressions being forgiven. His voice was hesitant as if he regretted the invitation now he'd met us again in the flesh. I could still smell the paraffin like a mist around us and I wondered if the Reverend could see the flames of our burning ties flickering behind our eyes.

We never made it to the fete. Edie forgot all about it the minute the vicar left, and we weren't up for reminding her. We had other things to do.

Abe Bartlett had died. It made Jasper keener to find the Beast than ever before. Maybe he wanted to be known at Simmonds House as the Big Hunter; maybe he hoped it would be his ticket out of ever going back. I went with him sometimes, but more often than not I made excuses and he went off on his own. The honest truth being that I'd rather be down in Ackerdean.

Lizzie and I had kept up our letters and our charade of being cousins. I'd read and reread her words every night under the thin covers of my dorm bed. She'd told me she was to be away later in the summer (in Devon this time, visiting another relative. Mrs Potter must have sisters and cousins in every county of Britain), but she would be around for a few weeks at the start. We made sure to meet. By accident, it would seem, to anyone taking notice. Me visiting Ma or strolling along the river to Low Farm to see how Maud was enjoying married life. Jane usually dropped well behind us and let us talk and walk without hanging on to our every word.

'She's got plenty to occupy her mind now she's got a beau,' Lizzie told me. 'The son of one of Father's friends. He's in carpets.' Lizzie pulled a face. 'Mother's determined to have her married off in a year or so.' I couldn't imagine sour-faced Jane being all soppy about a man, but if it meant Lizzie and I could have a bit of peace it suited me fine. I couldn't always express what I wanted to say properly, whether it was about the valley, or school or my plans for the future, but she understood, even when I didn't get the words right. I didn't have to spell out my feelings, because more often than not she'd had the same feelings too. I loved hearing her stories about her travels, her mimicking of her horrendous relatives and her dreams of being a teacher one day in a school for children who couldn't afford to go to stuck-up places like ours. By the time it came to Lizzie having to leave for the south I had memories enough stored away to see me through to when we could start writing to each other again.

Jasper would come back with fresh reports on the Beast. He'd been talking to the local farmers, he said. He'd been down to Oakenshaw too and made enquiries of the butcher and the local bobby. He'd had it confirmed that lambs had been taken that spring and a cow had been found dead in the river down at Wicken Falls. He even had a newspaper cutting of a man over at Haworth who'd taken a photograph as evidence. The picture was smudged and creased from being in Jasper's pocket. It showed a large dark shape against a slightly lighter background under the headline, 'Killer Kitty?'

'They know nothing,' said Jasper. 'If it was just a cat we'd have had it hung, drawn and quartered months ago.'

But despite his investigating and plotting and me joining in again once Lizzie was gone we returned to school with the Beast unseen and uncaught. Once there he never breathed a word of it or showed anyone the clipping. Until he had physical proof the other boys would only use it to rag him.

Edie and Charles's friend Bunty came to High Hob for Christmas, but this time without her wet fish of a husband, who it turned out was now a member of parliament. And without Mr Hobart too which was a bitter disappointment. The adults drank a lot in Edie's study and I didn't feel I was missing much when I went down to the Palace for a few days.

When I came back the house was in silence, no one rushed out to greet me. I took my bag up to my room and after a quick wash and brush headed back down the stairs. Jasper was standing on the first-floor landing. His finger to his lips. I could hear voices in the hall. He motioned for me to follow him and we crouched together by the banister and peeked through the rails. Charles and Bunty were below, standing close together by the little round table on spindly legs that wobbled if you caught it when you went past. It was as if they were trying to hide, though the plant on the table was too scrawny to give cover to a crow, never mind two full-grown humans.

'Please, Bunty.' Charles was holding a book out to her, but she had her hands clasped behind her back.

'I can't,' she said, but then she reached out and took it anyway. She started turning the pages, making a clucking noise like a hen ready to lay. 'Love poems, sweetie. Isn't that a bit obvious?' She handed the book back. 'You might as well draw a heart on your sleeve with initials entwined inside it and be done with it.'

Charles's hand on the book was so tight I could see the bone of his knuckles. Then he slapped it down on the little table and put both his hands onto her shoulders. Their faces were so close, they were eyeball to eyeball. I thought my own eyes would pop out of my head and my neck ached from stretching to have a good view. Jasper was tense beside me. Neither of us daring to breathe and me trying not to remember that I needed to pee. I was certain Charles was going to kiss Bunty right there in the hall. Neither blinked for the length of a prize-winning stare, then she let out this big breath and gave a tiny shake of her head.

'I'm sorry, Charles. But I can't. You're putting me in an impossible position. George's political career would be scuppered at any whiff of a scandal.' She pushed him away. 'Have you learned nothing?' Then she went back into Edie's room, leaving Charles standing there looking mournful after her.

Later, when we were safe outside chucking stones at old plates for targets, Jasper didn't want to talk about it. He said if I was interested in cissy stuff like that I should be reading girls' books and maybe I could borrow some from my sisters next time I went to visit.

It was the beginning of January and we were due back at school in a few days, when we heard the big news.

A little lad had gone missing from one of the houses on the edge of Oakenshaw village. The house backed onto the hillside and the moor above. Livvy said it was likely the tinkers. Jasper said it was obviously the Beast.

'He's beyond catties and sharp sticks,' he said. He was up in my room and had brought the skull on a rare outing. He was stroking it as he spoke. 'We were idiots to think that would be enough. He needs hunting down proper. We'll take the Baker rifle and the Webley. Charlie doesn't need to know.' He'd started calling Charles 'Charlie' since we'd been at school, though not yet to his face.

I'd given far more thought to Lizzie than to the Beast for months now. But I still felt a stirring of excitement at the thought that we might have a chance to catch it. Lizzie might even be impressed by a show of heroics, though only if we caught it alive, not killed it.

'They're not loaded,' I said.

'They can be,' he said. It dawned on me that he'd had this in mind for years. He'd once persuaded Charles to demonstrate the workings of the guns in his collection. Military studies, Jasper had said, it's part of learning history. And he'd been an eager student when Major Sefton gave us target practice with his air rifle.

'We'll lie in wait, all night if we have to,' he said now. 'Jacob Trimmer's got a handful of sheep out on Old Laithe Flats. They're the perfect bait.'

Charles was away the next night, down in London. There was some crisis over his next Garth Winter book. The publisher wanted to bring it out five months earlier than planned. It had put him in a foul mood for weeks: which meant the sound of him bashing away at his typewriter at all hours, and a pile of empty brandy bottles by the kitchen door.

His study was always locked when he was away but Jasper had long ago pinched the spare key from the small red and gold jar on the windowsill, and so far Charles hadn't noticed. I refused to carry the rifle so Jasper decided to just take the revolver. 'A rifle's better over a distance,' he weighed up the two options, 'but I'll be quicker with this.' He posed with the pistol pointing at the weasel in the hearth. 'I'll get him right between the eyes.' Before we left he took a silver flask out of the desk drawer. He unscrewed the lid and sniffed. 'Not his best stuff but it'll keep us warm. It could be a long night.'

The weather had been grim for days, a low bloated sky and a bitter wind that cut like gorse against any skin you were daft enough to leave exposed. But the heavy clouds had gone when we stepped outside just after midnight. A plump half-moon bobbed low in a clear sky. We were swaddled in scarfs and hats and had blankets from our beds draped over our coats. My body was warm enough, especially when we got moving, though my nose and cheeks soon felt numb..

Instead of a weapon I carried a torch, though Jasper made me switch it off as we approached the Flats. He guided me to a raised knoll where we spread out one of the blankets, laid on it on our stomachs and covered ourselves with the other. Credit to Jasper, he'd thought his through. No point us freezing to death.

Jasper laid the pistol in front of us. He'd loaded it back at the house and it made me shiver to look at it. He took a nip of brandy from Charles's flask, then offered it to me. In the grey night his eyes were hollows that I couldn't read but there was an urgency in his voice.

'Go on, Billy. You'll be glad of it.'

I took a sip. It was harsh and burned my throat but the heat was welcome.

I couldn't see anything down on the Flats at first, but when my eyes got used to the dark I could make out the pale shapes of what must be sheep, no more than eight or ten of them, sometimes moving, but mostly still.

We lay there for an hour or more, sipping at the brandy. I was feeling drowsy and I'd got myself nestled nicely into the tussocky grass beneath the blanket. In spite of the cold that nipped at my nose I could have slept blissful as a babe.

Jasper's hand on my arm jolted me awake. Confused by the dark sky above and the dark ground beneath us, for a moment I couldn't tell movement from stillness. Was that just the wind ruffling the grass? There was a change in the air. A thickening of the darkness. Down on the Flats something moved among the pale mounds of the sheep. It was huge and swift for its bulk. Jasper lifted himself into a squat, pushing off the blanket and reaching for the pistol. 'Follow me,' his hand already on my sleeve pulling me forward. Half crouching, half falling, we stumbled down the slope. As we reached the Flats Jasper's voice rang out clear.

'To the right. To the right.'

I ran across his path. A snuffling nearby, louder than my ragged breath. My foot hit something solid. I skipped and veered left in a wide arc. My right foot caught the back of my calf. I tripped and stumbled forward, arms flailing. There was a screech and the air flurried in a whirr of feathers. It was above me. All around me. A crack of thunder and I staggered back. Teeth like ice, like fire, sliced into my leg. The agony drawn out as a wild howl filled the air. The Beast had me tight in its jaw. My leg sacrificed to its hunger. The rest of me floating on a crest of heather. Buffeted by waves of pain.

I didn't know if my eyes were open or closed but above and around me the black night sparkled and exploded with a billion stars. I was sinking and the unbridled howl was following me, down and down and down.

I'd have a scar for life, Dr Darin said, and the nerve damage might be permanent. Only time would tell. Twelve stitches it took to close the gash in my shin made by the steel jaws of the trap. A quick sew-up job, he called it. Could have fooled me. It seemed to go on for ever, even with the morphine he gave me which made the room loop and fold so I was afeared where his needle might go next.

'Once the bruising and swelling have gone down it won't look half as bad. Have you moving about again in a jiffy. You're a lucky lad.'

He said Jasper had probably saved my life. He'd tied my leg with his scarf above the wound. I would have lost too much blood without it. Saved my life right enough, but only after he'd nearly ended it. There was no Beast. Not that night. Only the bulky shadow of a cloud crossing the moon and the rising of a startled grouse. The safety catch on the Webley loosened in anticipation and Jasper's finger too eager on the trigger. But it wasn't the bullet that did for me. That had flown high and wide and was lost in the heather. It was the steel trap he'd filched from one of the farmer's barns and set up earlier in the day. Set it up and not thought to tell me. First I knew of it was when it caught me in its jagged grip.

Edie said what was lucky was that we had a competent surgeon nearby. One that could be trusted not to go blabbing to all and sundry about our goings-on. As I lay on the chaise longue in her study, covered in blankets, my leg raised and throbbing, I heard her explain to Dr Darin that she didn't want to worry Charles with the full story of what had happened. She didn't want him charging around questioning the local farmers, trying to work out who was to blame. It would only lead to bad feelings amongst neighbours. In all likelihood the trap was one that had been lying there for years and forgotten about.

The doctor agreed but only after she'd assured him that we would all take more care out on the moor and wouldn't go wandering about in the dark. He was watching her closely and I wondered if he knew of her night-time excursions and was as worried for her as he was for us.

At my bedside Jasper told me how he'd thought he'd never get me back, my feet stumbling next to his, my body near enough a dead weight. How he could scarcely breathe and he'd thought we were both going to die. Certain the Beast would take us in our weakened state. I listened but I was all fuzzy, awash with the morphine, so I just nodded and shook my head.

Nothing was said of the gun. But Edie had seen it. When she flew down the stairs in answer to Jasper's shouts, and found us in the hall. He was waving it in the air, as if it was part of him. In a moment of bright clarity I saw her eyes switch from the gun to the bloody mess of my leg. I thought she might faint, but I beat her to it, sinking onto the cool tiles. The next time I saw the pistol, months later, it was back on the stand in Charles's study. Whether it was Edie or Jasper who put it there I didn't know.

Edie and Livvy watched over me, checking my temperature. As they talked during their vigils, I picked up that blood poisoning was the main danger. If I got through the first few days I should be all right. After that it was rest and more rest and then exercises, gentle to start with, then picking up steam.

'It's like an engine, lad,' the doctor said when he came to check up on me. 'Your leg is a piston that needs a bit of oiling to get it running smooth again.'

He could talk about machinery all he liked, but I couldn't believe my leg would ever work right again. It was stiff and heavy and any weight I put on it sent pains shooting through to my hip. I drew on the morphine and in my delirium believed it was the oil my leg needed. If I could just draw in enough of it. Instead it sent me to sleep.

Jasper showed me his latest sketches and described a story he was writing about a race of beings that lived under the sea, but he avoided being there at the same time as Edie. She never let on, but I know she didn't believe for a minute that the trap was an old one, left lying there by accident. All she said was that we had enough on our plate without anyone poking their noses into our business. So there was the unspoken truth of what happened, and the version that everyone else, including Charles and Ma, were told.

Ma clucked and fussed when she turned up at High Hob. Her cheeks flushed and her hair wild from her trek up the hill. She wanted me to come home. Said I'd be better cared for there. At which Edie bridled like a cat over its kittens. I lay there watching them and wanting to laugh. But that might have been the morphine lightening things for me.

It was the doctor's word that swung it. He'd said I mustn't be moved and Edie promised Ma could visit as often as she wanted. She'd always be welcome. And that was that.

I was furious with Jasper for what he'd done but that was between him and me. It had been an accident, no matter the stupidity, of which I was part, that had led to it. I didn't want the farmer he'd pinched the trap from getting into trouble, but no one stepped up to claim it and there was talk in the end of it being one of Old Abe's. Neither of us rushed to defend him.

Then the news came that the little lad we'd thought taken by the Beast had been found. Drowned in a pool in an old stone quarry above Oakenshaw. For me, at least, our quest for the Beast was over. If Jasper still thought it was out there he could go and look for it on his own.

When Charles returned from London he hovered in the doorway to Edie's study where I was still laid up.

'Bad luck, Billy-boy.' He shook his head, his eyes watching Edie as she wiped my brow with a damp cloth and raised the cushions beneath my foot. She had been playing the nurse with such sweetness that I started when she raised her head and said, 'See what happens when you leave us to go gallivanting? And stop "Billyboying" him. It's not decent. He's not a child any more.' Then as if by saying it she had released her anger, she bent back to her tending. Charles waited for a moment by the door and I willed him to say something, about what did it matter what he called me and how could him being in London have changed anything at all? But he turned away, his only response the slamming of his own study door.

Jasper once said Lizzie was one of those people who always got what they wanted. He said it with a grumble, as if she had a secret power he could never have. Maybe he was right. Because she managed to persuade her mother to come and visit me, and to bring her too.

They didn't stay long and Lizzie sat all the time by the side of her mother. But she talked aplenty, asking gentle questions about my health and how was I bearing up, and giving me such encouraging smiles that Edie exclaimed, 'My dear, you are quite the little nurse!' And all the time our eyes were having their own private talk with not a word of it being spoken. As they were leaving, Lizzie bent and brushed the hair from my temple and kissed me, light as a falling feather. I don't know what Mrs P thought of it. I didn't dare to glance her way. But I saw Edie's eyes narrow, and maybe a tiny shake of her head.

When the new term at Simmonds House started Jasper left without me. I was to rest for at least another six weeks. Edie said I couldn't be left up in my attic room all day. She would worry and Livvy would have to traipse up and down the stairs to check on me. For their sake as much as mine I was to spend the daytime downstairs.

So for much of the day I lay under my blankets as she wrote.

Watching the shadows change on the ceiling and reading my way through the pile of books she left by my side. She and Charles were on friendly terms again and at four o'clock Charles would join us and Livvy brought us a high tea. I was pretty certain they hadn't had this habit before my accident but I didn't question it. Especially as they mostly kept it jolly, even when Charles was grumbling about changes to his manuscript and Edie was 'tearing my hair out, darling' over the ending to her novel.

One afternoon, while she was pouring tea and Charles was buttering a scone, I asked her about what she was writing. I knew all about Garth Winter and his adventures, but I hadn't a clue what any of Edie's hundreds and thousands of words were about.

She took a while to answer, Charles had already eaten half his scone, but finally she said, 'It's about a woman's quest for fulfilment and the forces that thwart her.'

'Pretty much like *Winter in Arabia*,' Charles said, licking crumbs from his fingers. 'But with lust and betrayal in place of the snakes and tigers, and the villain's a married man wielding lies instead of a sabre.'

'Charles!'

Charles shrugged. 'There are only so many stories,' he said. 'No matter how you dress them up.'

'My writing is honest, at least,' said Edie.

The temperature in the room was never high at the best of times, but at that moment it dived like a peregrine falcon.

'Since when did you want honesty from me?' Charles stood up and his left hand was trembling. He looked down at it as if in surprise and stuck it in his pocket. 'Isn't my honesty the thing that you fear most?' He cocked his head to one side. 'Just imagine it, dear sister. *Winter in Soho*. What larks Garth could have.' He left the room without a word, and that was the end of our afternoon teas.

CHAPTER 20

Billy: 1936

And then he only blooming well took me to London.

I'd moved out of the study, although I still found the stairs a strain. I couldn't put my full weight on my leg, but I was building up my walks outside longer and longer each day. Edie in the throes of some dramatic event in her novel spent a lot of the time pacing up and down. Her study wasn't a relaxing place to be.

There was no talk yet of me returning to school. I knew they were planning to keep Jasper there for a couple more years if they could, but I'd be sixteen in April. Never mind the school crest and my classmate's successful fathers, I knew that more schooling at Simmonds House wasn't what I needed. Once I was fully fit I wanted to be ready to work.

One afternoon I'd come in from a turn about the moor. I'd been hoping to get as far as Owd Jenny, but my leg started to ache so I headed back. The curlews were going mad and I wished Jasper could have been there to see them. I imagined how he'd draw them in his sketchbook, wheeling and swooping dragons in flight.

I was sitting on the stairs taking off my boots when Charles came out from his study.

'Billy!' His voice was overloud as he greeted me and I guessed that early though it was he had been drinking. There was a crash from Edie's room and her door flew open. She stalked out with a wad of papers in her hand. She stopped when she saw us, raised her arms and hurled the whole lot into the air. Sheets and sheets of paper fell, covered in lines of her neat script, skimming the tiles and settling like snow. She marched back into her study and slammed the door behind her.

Charles acted as if nothing had happened. 'I'm off to London in the morning,' he said, still too loud. 'Meetings and whatnot. Mind the fort while I'm gone, won't you?'

I don't know where my words came from. One minute my head was full of wheeling birds and the next all I could think of was London streets, and London buildings and London people.

'Take me with you,' I said. He frowned and I knew I'd have to be quick. He'd have a dozen reasons why I couldn't. 'It would be good experience,' I said. 'To see the city. I won't get in your way. I'll just watch.' At that moment there was another crash from Edie's room and we both flinched.

'Is your leg up to it?'

I nodded and he wrinkled his nose. 'Why the Dickens not? I'd hoped to meet up with an old pal, but he's let me down.' He folded his arms. 'You're not quite his calibre but as aides-de-camp go I could do worse.'

We made an early start in the Crossley on Friday morning to catch the first train out of Leeds. The station was all steam and smoke and people shouting and I couldn't imagine that London could be bigger or dirtier or busier. The carriage trembled as we set off and there was nothing outside the windows but steam. It was like a magic trick and we were being disappeared, because once it had cleared we were in a different place. Green fields and hedges and cows ignoring us even with the racket we made as we roared past. Charles said they called it the Breakfast Flyer because it was so fast.

We spilled out of the train at King's Cross station where Charles hurried us into a taxicab. I felt I had landed in another world. My clothes were wrong, my face, even the way I spoke. I couldn't make out what the cab driver was saying or the market traders calling their wares in the street where he set us down. I waggled my finger in my ear to try to clear it out, but it made no difference.

I sat through Charles's first meeting with a man he called his financial adviser, in an office not much bigger than the High Hob larder. Me perched on a footstool in the corner, while Charles and the bloke were huddled over a grubby table. The adviser spoke English clear enough but with his 'accumulators', 'daily doubles', 'pointspreads' and 'arbitraging', it might as well have been all in foreign. Next, Charles had an interview with a magazine about his new novel *Winter in the Alps*, but he checked his watch and said we had time first for a snifter. He took me to a pub. Said if anyone asked it was my eighteenth birthday. He got himself a whisky and me half a beer. It tasted like dirty water, with a bitterness that left me chewing my tongue.

'God, I hate these interviews.' Charles swirled his second whisky round his glass. The pub was dark, the light from the street filtering through yellowed net curtains. Ma would have a fit if she could see the state of them. She'd be whipping them all off, plunging them in a bucket of hot water and vinegar and pegging them out on the line.

'I'm a writer not a talker, as you may have noticed, Billy.'

I said nothing because to my knowledge Charles was a man who loved the sound of his own voice. Especially when he had an audience who didn't dare tell him to shush.

'Why can't they leave me alone to write?' He drained his glass. 'I feel such a damned idiot sitting there saying Garth did this and Garth did that, and well, now, you ask if Garth were to fall off a cliff he would ... As if anything Garth Winter does matters.'

He was staring into his glass. He'd said once that Garth was the one thing that stood between him and financial ruin. But now was probably not the best time to remind him.

He lifted his gaze up to the bar as if considering whether or not to get another drink. My glass was still half full. The taste of the beer hadn't improved as it got flatter and warmer.

'Drink up,' he said, pulling himself to his feet. 'Best get this over with.'

His meeting with the magazine journalist was in a tall red-brick building on a busy street. I was about to follow him in through the tall etched-glass doors, but Charles stopped me and said it was best if I didn't.

'Might give the wrong idea. You know what these hacks are like.'

I didn't but I waited outside anyway. Preferring the feel of the city air on my face to the mustiness of another cramped office. When Charles came back out he was rubbing at his palms as if trying to rid them of dirt.

'Right, that's that,' he said. 'Should whet the public's appetite for Garth's next foray. Lord knows how much of what I said will make the article, but he seemed a decent chap. Now let's investigate another one of this fair city's fine hostelries for a spot of lunch courtesy of Mr Anthony Hobart.'

'Mr Hobart?' This was better than I'd hoped for. I'd not asked if there was a chance of visiting him at the Eastlea Palace, not least because Charles kept muttering about being on a tight schedule.

It turned out that the London pleasure palace wasn't Mr Hobart's only concern. Charles said he had his fingers in many pies, by which he meant businesses, and one of them was a small literary press.

'I was at college with Hobart,' he said. 'Quiet chap, hardly shared a word beyond "Good morning". Who could have known that all the time he was plotting the building of an empire? But credit where it's due he's not afraid to get his hands dirty.' He squinted at me. 'You still fancy yourself as a bit of an impresario, Billy? Like your old whatsit, Old Potter? Hobart could be the man to know.' He sniffed. 'Watch him though. He hasn't got where he is without squishing a few lemons.'

I had no idea what lemons had to do with it, but my heart

quickened at the prospect of meeting Mr Hobart again. I hoped he'd remember that he'd invited me to visit his palace one day.

The second pub was an improvement on the last. Better lit and cleaner, the curtains might even have passed muster with Ma. The man at the bar scowled at me as we entered and Charles scowled back as he led me over to a far corner. He said we'd hold off ordering drinks until Hobart turned up.

'Does Mr Hobart publish your novels?' I asked. I hoped not. Charles was always having arguments with his publisher about deadlines and advances and Charles's repeated threats to kill his hero off. He brushed at invisible crumbs on the table.

'Good God no. My Winter novels are way out of Hobart's league,' he said. 'He's started a small poetry imprint, which can only mean he thinks there's either money or kudos in it.' He tapped his fingers on the tabletop. 'I've sent him a few verses and he seems to like them.' He cleared his throat. 'At least, he's not said that he hates them. I'm hoping he might put out a volume. Nothing too weighty, but decent enough for a debut.'

Charles wrote poetry! It was the first I'd heard of it. I smiled at the image of Garth fending off villains with a spellbinding sonnet. 'Shall I compare thee to a charging rhino?'

'Ah! There he is.' Charles raised his hand and nodded in the direction of the door.

'Charles, my good man, and one of your boys too. Delightful.' Anthony Hobart was much as I remembered. Flush-cheeked with tiny round spectacles balanced on his pug nose. 'Not drinking?' he asked with a frown and then a bellowing laugh and a slap on Charles's back. 'Only teasing. My round. Whisky?' he asked.

Charles nodded saying, 'And half a light ale for the boy'.

I didn't want another beer. Charles had promised lunch, but I should have known by now that his idea of lunch and mine weren't the same thing at all.

Mr Hobart brought a plate of pickled eggs with our drinks. As they talked I helped myself to one. The vinegary claggyness helped hide the taste of the ale.

'Dreadfully close for October,' Mr Hobart was saying. 'But that's London for you. Must get myself up to your Yorkshire pile again for more of that bracing air and that big wet sky.' He winked at me. I had a mouth full of egg so I just nodded with what I hoped was the right amount of enthusiasm.

'Been consoling myself with the theatre,' Mr Hobart continued. 'Though that's not hitting the spot like it used to. Saw a heap of tripe at the National last week. Three hours of it. My customers wouldn't put up with it. They want an hour, hour and a half tops, of quality entertainment. Any longer than that and they don't linger at the bar afterwards, and that's where the profit's to be made.'

I wanted to ask him so many questions. I wished I had pen and paper with me to take notes. As it was I just sat quiet and listened.

Charles murmured in agreement as Hobart talked. He signed some pieces of paper he passed to him and made notes on the back of a beer mat when Hobart gave him a horse-racing tip.

'A dead cert, madness not to put a ton on it. The same again?' he asked, tipping his glass towards Charles who nodded. I took hold of my glass and said, 'No thank you, I've plenty left.' Mr Hobart opened his wallet and produced a pound note. 'Be a good man and fetch them will you Charles. And make them large ones this time.'

'So,' he said, when Charles had gone, 'it's Billy, isn't it?' I nodded and took a gulp of my beer to clear the last of the egg. 'How's life up at the madhouse? Surviving all right? Have you made your escape plan yet?'

'I want to have my own palace,' I said, deciding nodding again wouldn't be enough. Mr Hobart raised an eyebrow. 'I grew up in one,' I continued. 'I know the ropes and I've got heaps of ideas.' He raised the other eyebrow and waited. 'A miniature railway,' I said off the top of my head. 'Where you can pay extra to be the guard and a dance competition where you don't have to turn up with a partner because you pick one out of a hat.' I stopped and swallowed hard. His eyes were black beads. He blinked.

'Ideas are good. We wouldn't be anywhere without ideas. But have you got the capital?' He rubbed his fingers and thumb together. 'The hard cash to underpin your fantasies. To purchase your site, fit out your buildings, pay your artistes, and your miniature railway engineers, before the ticket sales start rolling in?' He paused while I struggled for an answer. 'No? I thought not.' He glanced over his shoulder at Charles who was still at the bar. 'Can't expect much from that direction. Any rich relatives you can squeeze?'

I thought of Ma's savings tin on the top shelf of the larder.

He shook his head before I could reply. 'No. But if that's your dream,' he sniffed, 'and you haven't got a nest egg to float it on, you'll have to work your way up.' A quick glance over at the barman. He lowered his voice. 'How old are you?'

'Fifteen, sir, nearly sixteen.' I remembered standing before Potter four years ago answering the same question and it made my head spin to think how my life had turned.

'You come and see me in a couple of years. I'll see what I can do. Might have a position for you. Get your foot on the ladder. I can always do with someone with experience and ideas onboard.'

I was all aglow and it wasn't the beer or the heat from the fire. My first step up. Never mind that it might be a tall blooming ladder and with all my years at the Palace I'd still be starting near the bottom. I'd have to be apart from Lizzie, unless I could persuade her to come too. There must be plenty of schools for poor kids in London where she could do the teaching she was so keen on. I stuck out my right hand. Mr Hobart looked surprised, but then he chuckled and took it in his warm grasp.

'That's right, let's shake on it. A gentleman's bond.' He winked again and I just stopped myself from winking in return.

'What are you two plotting?' asked Charles as he placed two glasses and a pile of change on the table.

'Nothing to worry yourself about. It's private business between me and the boy.' He raised his glass to the light and his eye swelled through the ambered glass, like the startled eye of a tree frog. 'There's nothing finer than a good malt.' He took a sip and smacked his lips. 'So, Charles. Your poems.' He took a wad of paper out of his briefcase and slapped it on the table.

Charles seemed to be holding his breath as he watched Mr Hobart take another drink. His own glass was untouched.

'They're interesting,' said Hobart. 'Very ... raw.'

Charles frowned and Hobart held up a palm.

'Raw is good. The reader likes raw. In art they call it "naïve", I believe. And what's good enough for a painter is good enough for a poet, in my book. I can see the reviews now. "Fresh," they will say, "an endearing simplicity". Now, as far as publication goes ...'

'You want to publish them then?'

'But of course. Did I not say? The public interest will be huge. You'll have all your usual Garth Winter readers giving them a try even if they're not usually poetry bods, and then the rest will be baying for a read at the mere prospect of the adventure writer turned versifier. The reviewers will lap it up.'

'Garth,' Charles muttered, 'I was hoping perhaps to use a pen name. C. A. Harper, perhaps, or my mother's maiden name ...'

Mr Hobart wafted the sheets of paper in front of his face. 'Nonsense. You can't buy the type of publicity that Garth will elicit. Now, we're talking an initial print run of a thousand copies. That's a bit more than I'd usually chance on a first timer but you being who you are there's no real risk. It's a safe investment.'

'An investment? Not a very poetic sentiment?'

Hobart shrugged. 'What can I say? I'm a businessman with the heart of a poet, or a poet with the heart of a businessman. Either way it's getting the balance right that counts. I'll need a hundred pounds from you up front and then another hundred closer to actual publication date. Then we can—'

'Two hundred pounds? You want me to pay you to publish my poems?' Charles clenched his fists and I held my breath, waiting for him to slam the table.

'It's not exactly payment, Charles. As I said, it's an investment. Fair's fair, poetry is a tough old game.'

'Do all of your poets fund their publications?'

Mr Hobart dabbed at the corner of one eye with his finger. 'It varies. Every writer is different. You'll have to trust me on this.' He finished off his whisky. 'After all, to a man of your means, what's a couple of hundred pounds?'

Charles had his glass half lifted from the table and I was certain this time he was going to slam it down. His knuckles were streaked white. But he just drained his drink, grabbed the bundle of paper and said, 'Billy, we're leaving, now.'

We got the next train back to Yorkshire and Charles never spoke a word, all the way home.

I wasn't going back to school. The trip to London and that silent train journey back made my mind up for me. If I was going to be a businessman, I needed to learn about business, not Latin and algebra and the laws of physics. Charles was beyond discussing anything, but I fancied Edie might understand. I picked a day when there'd been no crashes or door slammings all morning.

'A correspondence course?' she said. 'What a splendid idea.' But she dismissed the rest of my plan, which was to go back to the Palace and balance my studies with a job in Sowley, doing anything that would cover the cost of the course and my books. 'We can set you up in that corner over there, behind the screen, if you prefer. Your own study within a study. Let's hear no nonsense about you having to get work. Your school fees fund can be diverted. It makes perfect sense for you to stay. All three of us busy as bees in a hive.' She paused and then added as if as an afterthought, 'And when Jasper comes home for the holidays he will expect you to be here.'

But just before the end of term Jasper wrote to say he'd been invited to stay with a friend over Easter. It was the first I'd heard of any such friendship. Jasper would have his reasons and I thought I could guess what they were. The boy Spencer was in the year above, weedy but very clever and rumoured to have the wealthiest parents in the school. Edie shrugged when she read the letter and said she wished the Spencers and their home good luck. Her eyes showed her disappointment though, either at Jasper's absence or his choice of another family over his own. What Charles thought of the arrangement was more difficult to say. Locked away in his study all day, writing or drinking or both. In the evenings there would be the slam of the front door as he went off, stumbling down the hill and driving off in the motor car. Once he told me, on his way out, that I must never have anything to do with Hobart.

'Bloody philistine. Can't think further than his wallet. If he doesn't want my poetry on my terms, I'll find another publisher who does.'

Edie was spending less time writing and more time staring out of the window, occasionally getting up to pace the length of the room, or pulling on a pair of Jasper's wellington boots and going outside for 'a turn' around the house. Her great pile of a novel was almost finished, but was 'lacking something'.

'It will come,' she said. 'It has to.'

I suspected she was drinking, on top of her medication, which she called her happy juice though it never seemed to lift her spirits for long and brought dark sombre days in its wake. She had taken up smoking and often lay on the chaise longue until late in the evening, reading letters from her friends in London, the long cigarette holder trailing from her hand. I had nightmares of waking up in the night and finding the house in flames.

Left on my own I read and walked, got my old birding notebook up to date and started a new one, waiting for my materials to arrive, when I could at last begin to study Business and Financial Management. My leg no longer gave me pain, though I was left with a stiffness that gave a jolt or a limp to my walk and made running near impossible. I held this against Jasper more than anything.

Lizzie had left school at Christmas and in the New Year, just after her visit to my sickbed with her mother, she was sent down south to stay with an aunt. I'd not heard a peep from her since. The silence was unbearable, but there was nothing I could do. I could hardly haul myself up to the Big House and demand that her father gave me her address. But she had kissed me. That meant something. Just wait till she heard about my plans for us in London.

I went down to the Palace less, finding the going hard, especially on the way back up. But Ma and Peggy visited a couple of times and one day Maud and Arty came up. Maud had broadened out and clucked at me as if she was twenty years older, not four and a bit. I expected they'd be having bairns of their own soon, though there was no mention of it. She looked at me with an odd expression on her face as they were leaving and, unusually for Maud, reached out and touched my face. Said I was growing up right fine and was a credit to the Shaw name. I reckoned she was thinking of her bairns that were to come, that would be Chambers, in name at least, not Shaws.

Then my course started and I spent the next few months learning everything there was to know about managing a business. I was sent fat grey books and exercises on balance sheets and investment ventures. I recognised terms and phrases that Potter had used over the years and wished I could have gone to him with my plans. But I decided to wait till I was up to scratch, when I could prove to him that I was worthy of his daughter.

One Monday morning, early in May, Sally came into the study and passed me a note, 'from Miss Potter'. Sally still did sewing up at the Big House. She told me in that quiet voice of hers that Miss Potter had come home last week and had slipped the note to her on Friday and asked her to please deliver it as soon as possible. I expect she also gave her some coins for her trouble but she didn't say so. Lizzie's note said that she would be down at the Top Dam tomorrow morning and would see me there unless she heard word otherwise. There was a PS: 'Jane in India until July.'

The next morning as I strode out, with polished boots and a new neckerchief that I fancied gave me the air of a gentleman, my leg felt easier than it had for weeks. The clouds were faint chalk streaks in the blue sky, the air scented with honeyed heather. The very light seemed keener and new. As I crested the hill and the treetops of the valley came into view, I heard above me the burbling trill of a skylark. He was up high and hanging still, the whole world spread below his wings. I wanted to call up to him, 'You and me both, mate, happy as the day, you and me both.'

It had been four months since Lizzie and I had last clapped eyes on each other, and longer than that since we'd been alone together. When I spotted her waiting by the dam she appeared so poised and elegant, still slim but with curves held snug beneath her dress. And there was me, a good head taller than her now but listing over on my good leg to give the other a rest. She looked at me so serious when she saw me, as if she was trying to divine if I was still the same boy. But then her face widened into a huge smile and I knew inside we were the same Billy and Lizzie that had played daft games on the river and talked about whatever came into our heads.

We sat on the dam wall holding hands and I told her about my trip to London and my business studies and hinted at the future I was hoping for. She said she was proud of me and that one day there'd be people lined up calling me 'Mr Shaw' and 'Sir'. And shyly added that teaching in a school in London would suit her just fine.

I asked if her folks knew she was down here with me and she shook her head.

'They think I am at Draper's Cross meeting old school friends.' She blushed at the admission. 'I'm sorry Father took against you so. He's always been so fond of your mother and the girls. Maybe it's the Harpers. He can be harsh about them.'

'What does he say?'

'Just gossip. About their drinking. About Miss Harper not being married, but having Jasper. Father can be so precious about his business and his reputation.'

But I knew it wasn't the Harpers. It was me. I gazed down the track towards the Palace. Just wait. One day I'd make him an offer for the place. An offer he couldn't refuse. I'd own the Palace and the millponds and the woodland either side. And I'd marry his daughter. Then let him try and say we weren't equals.

'You all right, Billy?' she asked.

I didn't say anything in reply. Just took hold of her hands and brought them to my lips.

'Do you remember,' Lizzie said, her eyes on my lips, 'the day when Jasper dared me onto the overhang? It was a stupid game, but I couldn't let him crow.' Her voice fell to a whisper. 'I knew that you would catch me if I fell.'

I remembered being unable to breathe as I watched her poised in the air above me. I felt the same now, as she leaned towards me, our foreheads touching. I fancied I could feel her heartbeat next to mine. She lifted up her face and I let my breath go with the sheer joy of seeing her smile. Then I kissed her. Gentle, because I'd never put my lips on the lips of a girl before and I was scared what might happen next. What happened was she placed her hand in the small of my back and I linked my arms behind her. And it was as though the world beneath us disappeared and we were a pair of larks spiralling in the sky.

CHAPTER 21

Anna: February

When Anna heads over to the office the morning after Carter's unexpected visit, Sam's Volvo is still in the yard. By the time she comes out to make her lunch at the cottage, it has gone.

Her first thought when she woke up hadn't been Carter's drunken advances, but Sally Marsden's revelation about what she saw up at High Hob. One of the 'young masters' was up there on the morning after Charles and Edie were believed to have died. Jasper had a solid alibi, with the vicar as his witness. But what about Billy Shaw? She tries to imagine Billy's life with the Harpers. Frank said he'd done well for himself. His time spent with them may well have given him the springboard he needed. What motive would he have for killing them?

She looks at her to-do list for the afternoon, then puts it to one side. Frank's photo album is on her desk. She has promised him she won't hang on to it for too long. If she scans the photos in now it's a job done and then she can focus on the oral history tapes. She flicks forward to the picture of Frank on his wedding day, with Billy behind him, and the later one of Frank with his grandchildren.

Next to it, slipped inside the album, is the photograph in which she had mistaken Billy for Frank.

She has already scanned in several photographs for the archive. She opens them up on the screen as a slideshow now. They are grouped thematically and she wonders where best to include Frank's. A 'Shaw/Chambers' file might not be a bad idea. She could include the one of Mary Shaw. There are already a couple of other 'family' collections, including one for the Harpers, which only has a couple of photographs, and another for the Potters and Thornleyroyd. Some of the Potter pictures were taken up at the house and others at the mill. At the end is a formal photograph. A gathering of the Sowley Literary and Scientific Society under a banner that reads '1898–1948'. Nathaniel Potter stands in the middle of the group, next to the mayor. It's the only picture of him looking directly at the camera. Anna pauses the slideshow. She enlarges the image on the screen, then opens up the album at her side. She doesn't trust her eyes.

The ringing of her phone jolts her. She is still processing what she has just seen as she answers it and Sam's voice declares, 'My brother's an arse. What else can I say?'

'You're not his keeper.' Anna turns away from the computer screen. 'And don't worry, I got rid of him sharpish. Thank goodness for an efficient local taxi service.' She hears Sam chuckle.

'Yes, well, I owe you a big thank you for saving my car from his drunken driving. Sod his safety. If he'd marked her I'd have leathered him. Thankfully, both are still in one piece, though Carter is pretty shamefaced. He confessed all on the drive back from the airport. Making sure I heard it from him first. But on a happier note, and maybe to deflect me from his bad behaviour, he also told me your brilliant news about the mill. Well done!'

'Thanks. It is fantastic and I've got lots to set in motion as a result. But look, I've just found something. I could do with a second opinion. It might have implications for the story of the Harpers' deaths.' She pauses. 'And Billy Shaw.'

'Exciting. Why not come up for lunch tomorrow? Carter has slunk back to London with his tail between his legs. I'll make soup and we can get started on the box of fancy Danish biscuits I brought back. They were supposed to be a present for my darling brother. But he doesn't deserve them now.'

'This,' says Anna, 'has got to stay between the two of us, for now at least.' They are sitting in Sam's kitchen. Used soup bowls in the sink and a plate of spiced biscuits and a pot of coffee on the table between them. Anna takes her laptop out of her bag. 'I should really take it to Frank first but I wanted an objective opinion. I don't want to be suggesting way-out ideas that might upset him if I'm wrong.'

'Scout's honour.' Sam grins. 'Not that I ever was one, or a Guide either.' She reaches for the cafetière. 'Let's have a top-up before we start.'

Anna glances over at the window. It's a blur of white, as the snow that had started falling overnight continues. The mill yard had been thinly blanketed with it as she left this morning. 'Promise you'll help dig my car out of a snowdrift if this gets any heavier.' She takes her refilled cup. 'It wasn't forecast to be this bad.'

'This moor doesn't take notice of weather forecasts,' says Sam. 'Come on. What have you got that's for our eyes only?'

Anna turns the screen of her laptop towards Sam. 'Look at these photos. Tell me what you see.'

'A group of men in suits. Oh, and a token woman.'

'Erica Walker's mother, no less,' Anna interrupts.

'Is that what you wanted to show me?'

'No, keep looking.'

'OK.' She clicks to the next photo, the one of Frank with his son and grandsons. 'That's our very own Mr Chambers, isn't it?'

'It is. But can you see anything else?' Anna clicks back to the first photograph. 'Nineteen forty-eight. The fiftieth anniversary of the Literary and Scientific Society, the founders of the mill's local history collection, precursors of the board. Check out the man in the middle.' She enlarges the picture.

'The big shot with the fancy waistcoat?' Sam asks. 'Who is he?'

'Nathaniel Potter,' Anna says. 'The man who left the mill to the society. Now look back at Frank.'

Sam flicks between the two pictures, her eyes widening as she makes the connection. 'Hang on a minute.' She taps at the keyboard. 'That's better.' The two photographs are arranged side by side on the screen. 'That jawline and those eyes. That's what you mean, isn't it? Frank Chambers and Nathaniel Potter. They've got to be related.'

Anna nods. 'I'm glad it's not just me that can see it.'

'It can't be coincidence,' Sam says. 'They're of a similar age in these pictures, aren't they? Sixtyish. But they're almost identical. The more you look at them. Even the shape of their noses. I get the feeling,' she narrows her eyes, 'that you're holding something back. Come on, what is it?'

Anna opens another file. 'Meet Billy Shaw.' The wedding photograph that Frank loaned her appears on the screen. 'The High Hob companion.'

Sam whistles. 'Not so obvious, but if you compare them the same look is there. It's not too surprising, I suppose, that Frank resembles his uncle?'

'Not his uncle.' Anna has decided that the only way this is going to make sense is if she tells Sam everything. 'His father.'

Sam's mouth falls open.

'Frank told me himself,' Anna continues. 'After I'd done a little sneaky snooping.' Sam raises an eyebrow but Anna carries on. 'I think Nathaniel Potter was his grandfather.'

'Isn't that a bit of a long shot?'

'If it was just the photos, perhaps,' says Anna. 'But Frank's got an old watch that Billy claimed belonged to his great-granddad, with an inscription and the date 1897 engraved on the back. This was in the archive.' She takes a slim book out of her bag. '*Sowley*

Town Hall 1897–1997: a Centenary Celebration. I don't know how many copies were made but I'm pretty certain Frank Chambers has never seen it.' She opens the book at the beginning. 'It's here in the first chapter.'

On the morning of the opening of the new building, on 14th July 1897, a grand procession paraded through the decorated streets of Sowley. This was followed by an open-air service in the Market Square, at which a children's choir sang hymns.

After the cutting of the ribbon and a speech by the local MP, Sir Ernest Greenhead, commemorative silver pocket watches were presented to the Mayor and four members of the council in honour of their efforts in bringing the plans for the new building to fruition. The recipients are pictured below with, inset, a close-up of one of the watches now in the possession of Samuel Baskerton, the great-grandson of Mayor Baskerton.

Rumours that the Prince of Wales might put in an appearance, following his celebrated attendance at the opening of Halifax Town Hall 34 years previously, were sadly unfounded.

'It's the same watch,' says Anna. 'And the five men who were given them are named. No Shaws or even Chambers. But one of them was Jeremiah Potter.'

'Nathaniel Potter's father?'

'You've got it.'

'So Billy's granddad was Jeremiah Potter. He was Nathaniel Potter's son. His illegitimate son, right? Potter was married?'

Anna nods. 'Cassandra Potter was wealthy in her own right, may well have kept her husband's businesses afloat.'

'Meanwhile, he was having it away with, what did you say Frank called her? The Queen of the tea rooms?'

'Something like that.'

'Where does that leave us in terms of Billy and High Hob?'

'He might have been sent up there to be kept "out of sight, out of mind". Hardly the ends of the earth, but less chance of Mrs Potter seeing him regularly and people noticing a resemblance. Maybe there was a touch of philanthropy about it too. A chance for Potter's by-blow to move up in the world.'

'But Billy never knew?'

'I think he did in the end. When he gave the watch to Frank he made a big thing about it belonging to his granddad. Maybe he wanted Frank to inherit something of the Potters. This was the 1980s. The mill and estate had already gone to the board. The official line is Potter had no living family when he died in 1963. His wife was dead by then and they'd only had one child, a daughter. She had a disability. There's a passing reference to her in a newspaper cutting from the forties about a charity gala and a shot of a young woman in a wheelchair. If she'd still been alive you'd think she would have contested the bequest. Frank's mum, his adoptive mum, once told him the mill was his by rights. If he was Potter's grandson, she was telling the truth.'

'Are you going to tell Frank?'

Anna taps her fingers on the sheet of paper. 'He might deny the resemblance in the photos but he'd have to accept the origins of the watch. He's very proud of his Shaws and his Chambers. He's not going to take kindly to hearing he's a Potter instead, and an illegitimate one at that.'

'Could this tie in with the Harpers' deaths?'

Anna takes a deep breath. 'It might do if Sally Marsden's testimony is added to the mix.'

'Her testimony?'

By the time Anna has finished explaining Sam is shaking her head. 'It's not looking good for Billy, is it? But I still don't see how it gives him a motive. Even if he found out that Nathaniel Potter was his father, that wouldn't give him a grudge against the Harpers.'

Anna folds her hands together and taps them against her chin. 'What if the Harpers knew about Billy being his son? They could have been blackmailing Potter. And Billy found out.'

'I like it,' says Sam. 'I mean, obviously, it's horrible, blackmail and murder. But it fits. According to the reports, the Harpers had financial problems. It's feasible they might have tried to extort money out of Potter. Billy finds out, rises to the defence of his natural father, and ends up killing them. First Edie and then after he gets rid of Sally, Charles too.'

'He sees the poem,' Anna continues, 'spots that line about saying farewell. He knows more about swingboats and tea rooms than he does about poetry. Forges their signatures, and makes it look like suicide. Maybe Potter was there too, only Sally didn't see him.' She sinks back onto her chair. 'Frank Chambers thinks he wants the truth.' She shakes her head. 'He might wish he'd never asked.'

'Are you going to share this with your boss?'

Anna groans. 'The slightest whiff of a scandal could have her threatening to pull the plug on the mill expansion. I just wish the finger of guilt wasn't pointing at Frank Chambers' dad.'

'It might put our handsome fusilier in the clear.'

'B.B.? Hmm, I still want to know who he was, other than potentially Charles Harper's secret lover. The regimental museum have been very helpful, but there were thousands of men in their ranks during the First World War. Initials aren't much to go on. I could request a list of officers whose surname began with a B. But it's still a long shot.'

Sam glances at the window. 'Hey, the snow's stopped. I need to take Ruby for a walk. Do you fancy a quick stomp across the moor to clear our heads? I've got something to show you too.'

'It's a bit of a trek,' Sam says as they set off over the snow, 'but there's a cluster of rocks about half a mile over that way.' She points north-east from the house in the direction of Ackerdean valley. 'They're pretty impressive and ...' She let it hang in the air. 'Well, you'll see when we get there.'

The sky is clear now, a sharp blue, and the air is spring-water cold. The moor lies still and featureless under its white covering. Their feet crunch and squeak across the newly settled snow. Sam gathers up a handful and packs it into a ball. 'Fetch, Ruby,' she calls as she sends it flying ahead.

Ruby races off and then runs round and round the spot where the snowball has hit, burying her nose in the snow.

Anna laughs. 'That's cruel.'

'No it's not, she loves it.' Sam throws another one and Ruby races after it. 'See? It's her new all-time favourite game.'

'Here we are,' she says as they approach a cluster of rocks that rise metallic against the winter sky, the lichen etched like rust beneath a shallow cap of snow. 'This one's supposed to look like a dog's head though personally I see a ship, the prow of a galleon, perhaps.' Sam tilts her head.

Anna squints at the rock. 'It probably depends on the angle. But nope, I'm seeing dog.' She moves round it. 'And from here? Yup, still dog.'

Sam gestures towards the horizon. 'There's another group further on that have ancient carvings on them. Rings and cups. It's a fascinating landscape. Centuries of history all piled on top of each other, ancient markings, abandoned lime kilns, stone quarries, outlines of long-gone farm buildings. I'm not surprised Carter's enthralled by it.' She hesitates. 'He's a clumsy oaf. I warned him that it wasn't long ago that you lost your boyfriend.' She leans back against the rock with her hands in her coat pockets. 'He expects everyone to be as resilient to life's knocks as he is.'

There is a long silence. Time to set the story straight, Anna thinks. My story this time.

'It's been a year and a bit since Dan died,' she says. She takes a deep breath and as she breathes out she feels as though she is letting something go. 'But he left me three months earlier.'

'Left you?'

It's easy now that she has started. It had just needed that one statement. The one truth.

'He'd met someone else.'

'Ah.'

'Then three months later there was the accident. The road was wet and another car came round the corner too fast. They were head on. A farmer was sitting on his tractor in a field. Witnessed the whole thing. There was nothing he could do. Dan's new girlfriend, Lauren. She rang to tell me.'

'Oh God, and you …'

'I was still at the hating him, hating her, wishing them both dead stage.' She scrapes a thumbnail down the gritty rock. 'We never married. But we'd been together for seven years. Lauren arranged the funeral. Invited me, of course. She could hardly not.'

'Awkward,' says Sam.

'Very. I was mourning him but who was I? Not his wife, not his lover. I'd spent the last seven years with him. She'd been with him for three months. All I could think was, if only he'd waited, if only he'd put off leaving for a bit longer. If he'd given us a chance, or even carried on having his sordid affair behind my back, for another few months. He'd have died and I'd have been none the wiser.'

'Would you really have wanted that?'

She shrugs. 'Then, yes. Now? No, probably not.' She leans against the rock beside Sam, her arms hugged across her chest. 'It's made me cautious about getting involved again. Trusting again.' She hesitates. 'No offence, but I don't think Carter would be an ideal option for me just now.'

Sam snorts. 'My brother should come with a government health warning: "Approach with Caution".'

'You wanted to show me something,' Anna says.

Recognising that Anna wants to drop the subject, Sam leads her round to the other side of the rock and squats down. There is a shape etched into the rock. Three triangles and two pairs of parallel lines. Anna squats beside her. The image tugs at a memory.

'Jasper Harper,' says Sam. 'It's his signature. The one he left on the mural at the house.'

'Of course.' Anna traces the shape with her finger. 'They must have spent hours running and exploring around here.' She stands up and looks out at the vast expanse of the moor. 'What a playground.'

'Everything must have seemed possible.' Sam follows her gaze.

Anna shivers and pulls her coat tighter. 'Everything,' she agrees.

The only photograph of Nathaniel Potter on display in the museum was taken at Thornleyroyd. The large stone house fills the background. Mr Potter is talking to a woman in a flowery dress. The photographer has pressed the button a moment too late, the board's benefactor had turned his head away and his face is a blur. He could be anyone. A stocky man with a rim of white hair around a bald dome. We should replace it with the anniversary picture, Anna thinks as she straightens the frame. Make a feature of the board's own history.

In her hand she has the postcard that arrived this morning. A picture of the Tower of London and on the back to the left of the address (given simply as 'Anna, The Old Mill / Museum, Ackerdean, West Yorkshire') were the words 'Sorry' and 'Carter'. Not one for the collection but another note in her own history.

There is a cough behind her.

'Ow do?' Frank is brushing snowflakes off his coat.

'I was just thinking of you,' says Anna.

'Good thoughts, I hope. Cos I've all but thrown off that cold. You'll have to put up with me a mite longer.' He removes his cap and shakes off the drops of melted snow. 'It's coming down thick and fast out there.'

'I can't believe it's waited until the end of February. We're practically into spring.'

Frank chuckles. 'Not here, we ain't. When I was a lad it was regular on my birthday that we'd go out with our sticks checking in the drifts for sheep and pulling them out. And that's in March. Things haven't changed, never mind your global warming. Couple of years back we had three days of snow and it was nearly April. Drifts half a man above your head.' He sucks on his lower lip. 'What you doing in here then? Planning on chucking some of this stuff out?'

'Are you offering to take it off my hands?' She smiles, then realises she hasn't seen him since she got the good news. 'We're expanding,' she explains. 'Into the upper floors. There'll be room for some of the less well-used bits of the collections. More scope to tell stories.'

Frank rubs his hands together. 'You've got them to pay attention. That's champion. Drag it all out into the open, that's what I say. Never mind them keeping stuff squirrelled away.'

She should tell him now, as they stand in front of Nathaniel Potter's photograph. But instead she finds herself saying, 'Where was Billy in July 1936?'

She hadn't meant to be so direct, to make it sound like an accusation. But Frank doesn't seem to notice. He is peering at the leopard skull she has recently added to Charles's study area. She'd found it in an unmarked box, but the initials MH and the date 1926 printed on the base suggest it may have been a present from Matthew Harper.

'London,' he says. 'He'd had an accident. Walked with a limp after. The Harper lad didn't need a companion any more. Billy got a job down there. Far as I know that was the end of him and the Harpers.' He turns away from the photograph, and in that moment Anna fancies she sees it in his face, that look shared by Nathaniel Potter and Billy Shaw, through differences in ages and decades. All of the same line.

'What did he think of Nathaniel Potter?' she asks. 'Did he ever talk about him?'

'Just the once.' Frank shuffles forward and leans on his stick. 'It was after Mam had her rant about this place being mine by right. I asked Billy, "Uncle Billy" I still called him, about it. He said, "We don't need him or his kind, lad. Us Shaws can make our own lives without them." Those were his very words. So if you're asking, I'd say he didn't think much of him at all.'

CHAPTER 22

Billy: July 1936

'Like a pair of peas, you and Elizabeth Potter.' Edie's voice was thick, her words syruping out as if she were tasting each one and couldn't stop them if she tried. I wondered what she had been drinking. What medicine she'd mixed with it. There was a glass with a chunk of lemon in it next to an opened parcel on the table by the stairs. A book lay on the brown paper wrapping.

I didn't want to stop and talk. Hadn't intended to see or speak to anyone between me leaving the woods and getting to my own room, closing the door behind me, lying on my bed, closing my eyes. Lizzie.

She'd been late to our meeting spot. Ever since we'd first kissed we'd met every other day on the small grassy field by the river. There were flat stones to sit on and the privacy of the trees over-hanging the water's edge made it cosier than the dam. I thought someone at the Big House would suspect if she kept disappearing but her father had been ill and was busy catching up on business he'd neglected, and her mother was dividing her attention between the Halifax Children's Welfare League and the town's Operatic Society. (Lizzie did a wonderful imitation of Mrs Potter singing.)

Even Jane, who had arrived back from India at the beginning of July, was too caught up with the plans for her wedding to resume her role as Lizzie's constant shadow.

I'd almost given up on her that morning, but I'd lingered to watch a goosander floating on the river. The ruff of red hair at the nape of the bird's neck and her slender beak gave her a cross look and I fancied her mate would be in trouble if and when he appeared.

'Billy!' Lizzie scrambled down the steep slope from the footpath a few hundred yards above, sending stones tumbling. I jumped up and the goosander ruffled her feathers and sailed away.

Her face was flushed and her eyes were red and raw. Her hair, which she'd taken to wearing curled and pinned, was loose. A streak of dirt mingled with the roses that patterned the skirt of her dress and there was a long scratch on one of her legs.

'What's happened?'

'It's Father. He knows about us meeting. Someone must have been spying and has told tales.' She glanced around her as if expecting to spot the sneak hiding in the bushes. 'I don't know all he's been told.' She blushed and I took hold of her hand. 'But he looked as though he was going to explode. I've never heard him say such foul things before about you and the Harpers and your father and even,' her voice lowered, 'even your mother. He said I was never to come down here again. He locked me in my room but I got out of the window and onto the laundry room roof. He won't know I'm gone for ages yet.'

She reached out and touched my face. Her palm was hot against my cheeks. 'He doesn't know a thing about you, Billy. He doesn't know how good you are and how you're making plans for your future. I tried to tell him but he wouldn't listen. He said he didn't want your name spoken in our house ever again. He said ...' She gulped and I drew her to me. She laid her face against my neck. 'He said if he saw you he'd skin you like a rabbit. Father's never skinned an animal in his life, not even a fish, but right there and then I believe he meant it. I feared he might drive straight over to

High Hob and have it out with you. I was so scared. I prayed I'd find you safe down here.'

I took hold of both her hands. 'We're both sixteen,' I said. 'We can do as we please.' Her hands tightened on mine. 'No one will be able to stop us. And,' I swallowed hard, the strength of her grip made me bold, 'if you want to become Mrs Lizzie Shaw we'll go to Scotland and be wed and there's nothing they can do to stop us.'

I felt light in the head, like I was hovering above watching my lips moving, my fingers stroking Lizzie's hands. And then her arms were around me and her lips urgent against mine, and I pulled her down, or we fell, onto the grass.

On the long walk back to High Hob part of me had been watching out for Potter but the rest of me was soaring up in the sky singing with the larks. When Edie greeted me with words about Lizzie my first thought was that Potter had been there, might still be there. I felt as though I could take on the world, never mind just Nathaniel Potter, even with a skinning knife in his hand.

'Potter?' she said when I asked. 'The blustering idiot. Puffing and panting about rights and wrongs as if he has any moral high ground to talk from.' She was standing in the open doorway to her room, arms raised with her palms on the doorframe. I had the image of her again as a heron, as I'd first seen her, but now at the point of swooping on her prey.

'I bet you make a lovely couple.' A syrupy laugh. 'Peas in a pod. Potter's peas.' She lowered her arms and began to sway towards me.

'That girl ... she loves you ... course she does. Natural enough. That man. Sowing his peas. In the right light you can see it. The wrong light. Cut of the chin. Gleam in the eye.'

What had Potter told her about me and Lizzie? Or was it Edie who had found out, or guessed, and told him? I started up the stairs, not wanting to hear. I expected her to drift away back to her room but she leapt forward and grabbed my arm. Her grip was strong and bony as ever.

'You're no better than the rest of them. You take what you want and are blind to the consequences.' She was staring at me as if she was trying to see into my soul. 'Sweet sixteen.' Her voice was a flat monotone. 'And blind.' She was so close I could feel the heat of her breath on me. Her face softened and she half closed her eyes. 'Oh, sweet William.' Her hand was trembling as she reached up to touch my cheek. I flinched. I couldn't help it. I didn't want her hand touching my skin where Lizzie had touched me only an hour before.

Her hand flew into a slap and I yelped.

'Bastard!' she shrieked. 'You can't help yourselves, can you?'

'What in God's name is all this racket?' Charles threw open the door to his study.

Edie yelled at him to go back to his hellhole. He answered with a string of curses, worse than even Jasper had ever spilled. I would have fled upstairs but Edie still had me in her grip. I was stronger than her. I could have thrown her off, but despite her words and the sting of her slap, it felt wrong to fight back. I wanted to know what I had done wrong, although, watching her turn on Charles, I was sure this was an anger against him as much as it was against me. This one had been brewing for weeks, fuelled by Charles's frequent trips to London. Each time he returned Edie grew darker and moodier. Let them yell, let them clear the air. I part blamed Livvy for falling ill. She'd gone to stay with her family to be nursed and hadn't been at High Hob for over two weeks. There was something about her presence that put a cap on their rows. Maybe they were worried about her carrying tales back to town. With her gone there was nothing to hold them back. They obviously cared little for what I thought.

Charles stormed back into his study and Edie let go of me to run after him. I should have left them to it but still I needed to know why she had included me in her rage. And what she had meant about Potter.

They were standing by the hearth, Edie with her back to Charles, who was speaking softly, barely a murmur. 'I'm sorry,' he was saying. 'Please.' His hand hovered, not quite touching her shoulder.

Edie was silent, though her chest still heaved. She was lifting peacock feathers one by one from the tall blue and white vase. The one Charles said was over six hundred years old.

I waited for Charles to tell her to put them back. He had lectured us on how fragile those feathers were. They came from India. Arrived wrapped in silk and scented with exotic perfumes whose names were like poetry: sandalwood and lotus flower, and attar of roses. Now Edie was wafting a handful of them in front of her face and Charles said nothing.

'It came today.' Her voice was quieter now but broken up, as if there were scratches between the words. 'James's *Collected Works*. Bunty, generous as ever, "knew you'd want a copy, sweetie". No dedication, of course. You can't write a dedication when you're dead. But a touching foreword by his darling wife.' Her fingers worked at the feathers. The fine strands falling at her feet. '"A fitting memorial to a monumental poet, a loving husband and devoted father."' Edie spat the final words. 'Did she think no one ever saw her bruises? Did she really not know about his lovers? About his bastards.' Her voice cracked properly then.

Charles laid his hand on her shoulder but she twisted away.

'You're no better,' she snapped. 'Just because your tastes are different. You're still a man. With a man's willing blindness.'

'There's been nothing ... No one ...'

'Oh, shut up. There are plenty of little birds in the city only too eager to twitter about your not-so-secret other life. You idiot.'

The letters she received from her London friends. Full of gossip and scandal, she said. Fluff and nonsense. It wasn't fluff and nonsense that had got her into this state.

'You haven't given a thought to us, have you? Me and Jasper. What we have here?'

'What we have here?' Charles's voice was incredulous. 'This isn't a safe haven, Edie. It's a prison. Jasper is never going to call this place his home. He has too much of his father in him to settle for a life confined.' Edie seemed about to interrupt but he waved her aside. 'As for my so-called mistakes. Let me make them. You want me to face the consequences, well I will. Anything would be better than this.' His voice could've cut paper. 'Hobart crushing my work, the public baying for more pap, and you telling me to live a lie. For the sake of what? Consequences? Let them fall.'

'You think this is a prison? Your consequences when they fall will put you behind real bars. You wouldn't survive that.'

My jaw dropped. What had Charles done that risked him going to gaol? I remembered the grubby office in London and the financial adviser with the shiny spiv shoes. Had I been a witness to a crime?

'Hard labour, too,' Edie continued. 'That's what they sentence your sort to. It would break you.' Tears spilled onto her cheeks. She was looking at Charles now with so much tenderness. Her eyes soft and pleading, like they could sometimes be with Jasper, reminding me she was his mother. All that anger and spite, turned to love.

'I'm already broken, Edie. Can't you see that?' I thought he was about to weep too.

I half turned to leave but Edie's voice, cold again said, 'Wait, William. There's something you need to hear. While we're talking consequences.'

I knew this had to do with her early rantings about me and Lizzie. About Potter. I turned back.

Edie's face was half hidden now by the two feathers she still held, a pair of blue green eyes under her own.

'Why don't you tell him, Charles? Man to man.'

'Edie, let's leave Billy out of this. I don't really see—'

'But of course, Charles, you haven't heard the news. Your darling Billy-boy has lost his heart and who knows what else to Nathaniel Potter's daughter.'

'What?' Charles said. 'But ...'

The expression on Edie's face was triumphant.

'They don't know?' he asked.

'Know what?'

Charles was pale. Edie tilted her chin.

'How about I fix us all a drink,' said Charles. He put one hand to his forehead and smoothed back his hair. 'Then we can sit and discuss this like grown-ups.' I could feel Edie's eyes on me but I wouldn't look up. Didn't want to see whatever darkness was spilling out of them.

There was the clink of glass as Charles prepared our drinks.

'He's got your best interests at heart, of course, Sweet William. Nothing to do with Potter confiding his big secret to us, and my brother's promise not to tell tales to his wife so long as Potter slips him a bundle of notes now and again.' No syrup now, her voice dripped venom.

Charles had his back to us, busy over the decanter and glasses.

'Are you blackmailing Mr Potter?' As I spoke the words I felt like I'd slipped into a Garth Winter novel. A story spilling into real life. If we played it right, found the book it had escaped from, could we tuck it all back in again and get back to normal?

Charles turned, an empty glass in his hand.

'Who do you think paid for your education, Billy? Schools like Simmonds House don't come cheap. We could only send Jasper because of a legacy from his great-aunt.'

'My scholarship,' I said.

'Ha!' Edie began to dust the mantel with the peacock feathers.

'God knows how Potter accounted for it in his books,' Charles continued. 'But he managed to get that and sundry allowances for you out under the nose of his wife. And yes,' he glared at Edie, 'he has from time to time helped pull me out of a couple of financial holes. But I assure you there was no coercion on either side.'

'But you asked for me,' I said. 'Child Companion Wanted. Mr Nathaniel showed me the advertisement.' I reverted to the name I'd called him long ago, when I was surer of the world and where I stood in it.

'Oh, that was genuine,' said Charles. 'A desperate attempt to pull Jasper back from the brink. Potter saw an opportunity to palm you off. We made a deal and here you are.'

'A deal?' I said.

Charles sighed. 'That's life, Billy. A long series of deals.' He slumped down in the chair. Rummaged his fingers though his slicked-back hair, ruffling it into feathers. 'Edie thought it would help her finish her novel, keeping Jasper occupied. A deal she made with herself. Novel first, only child second. You and me, we're well down on her list of priorities. Isn't that right, darling?'

He ducked as a carved jade frog that had sat undisturbed on his mantel for all the time I'd known narrowly missed his ear. Edie's lower lip stuck out, her arm still half raised.

'Charles Harper,' she said. 'Knight in shining armour. Our very own Garth Winter. Is that how you see him, William? The man who is going to lift you from your humble origins and hand you the golden keys to the bright lights and streets paved with gold? What has he promised you? Glittering London contacts and the goodwill of Tony Hobart and a string of other impresarios?' She raised an eyebrow. 'He no longer has any of that to give.'

Charles was staring at the empty glass in his hand, turning it as if trying to catch the light in it.

I ignored Edie's words. I had a deal with Mr Hobart that had nothing to do with Charles any more. I focused instead on the other niggling doubt, the one that I was trying to push down but which rose up again stronger each time.

'It was good of Mr Nathaniel to find me a place here and to pay for my schooling. More than we would ever have asked for.' I was thinking out loud, my lips forming the words before they had time to settle in my head.

'He didn't do it out of the goodness of his heart, sweetie.' Edie's voice was sinuous and it wound its way round my head, reaching for the realisation growing right at the back of my mind.

Charles placed his glass on a small table. 'You're Potter's bastard.'

'His what?'

'You know what it means, don't act stupid now.' Edie sounded tired. 'He's your papa. Your "da". Your mother went to him for support and consolation when her husband came back ruined from the war. Potter consoled her all right. And nine months later out you popped.'

My palms tingled and I felt bile rise in my throat. 'You bitch,' I said, and she flinched but the word felt right so I said it again. 'You can't say that about my ma.'

'It wasn't your mother's fault,' Edie said. 'She did what she believed was best for her family. And there's no saying there was no attraction.' She fluttered the peacock fan. 'Wealth, power. Both famous aphrodisiacs.' She lowered the feathers. I expected a mocking smile but her face was sad, regretful, as if what she was telling me pained her as much as it pained me.

'You really had no idea?' Charles asked. 'I thought you must know, at some level. That was one reason why he sent you up here. Didn't want his wife seeing you round the mill all the time. Though chances are she knew all along. She's not a stupid woman.'

'She might throw him out,' Edie sighed as she inspected the fingernails on her left hand, 'if he insisted on parading his bastard in public.' She nibbled at one of her nails. 'There was lots of blah blah blah as well about giving you the opportunity to become a gentleman.' She yawned. 'As if High Hob was a magical portal and you were going to enter it a mill boy and emerge as a prince. We all have our dreams.' Her look at Charles right then, like he was some injured creature, beyond her help. 'But we have to live in the real world.'

'Liars,' I said. 'You're twisted, the pair of you. This is all lies.'

'Stop now, Edie. You've said enough.' Charles stood up and put his hand on her arm. His eyes were pleading but hers were hard.

'Get your hands off me.' She hissed the words. 'I've saved your skin by keeping you here. And even that's not enough. Can't keep your sticky hands off what you can't have. How is darling Bertie these days? Welcoming, was he, last time you paid a visit? Did he tell you about his fiancée? Pretty little thing, apparently. Bunty is to be their matron of honour. She says they make a beautiful couple.'

Charles's chest rose and fell with his deep breaths, but the rest of him was still until that final sentence when he roared and pushed her away.

Edie fell back against the desk but seemed to rebound off it and threw herself at him, thumping at his unresisting arms without aim or directed reason.

I shouted, 'Stop it! Both of you. Stop it now.'

Charles fell or lunged backwards, his arm catching against the cabinet at his side. As he turned to duck one of Edie's blows his hand knocked the Webley pistol off its stand.

I pushed him aside and grabbed the gun. It was heavy and I jerked my hand upwards to steady it. They both froze. I had them. Their full attention.

'You knew and didn't tell me.' I wanted to say more, a torrent more, but the pain in my throat was too harsh. 'You didn't tell me.'

I tried to focus on them, to focus on the fear in their eyes, but my own eyes were wet with tears, blurring my vision. I could see four of them, eight of them. The searing pain in my throat was blocking out the message that was trying to crawl to the front of my brain.

'It wasn't for us to tell,' said Charles. His shoulders slumped. 'Put down the gun, Billy. It's not even loaded, for God's sake.'

My fingers felt clammy and my arm trembled but I kept the gun raised and pointed at them. It was keeping me focused. Focused on what was important.

Edie's face was white as chalk. Charles sighed, 'Did your mother never even hint at it?'

Hint? Hint that my da wasn't my da and that Nathaniel Potter was? I thought back on my days at the Palace and now it was all skewed. I couldn't see it straight any more. Everything I'd believed true. Ma and Da. My sisters. Then it was like I'd been plunged in the millrace. Deep and cold and then dragged out and thrown on the banking. Nathaniel Potter was my father. Like the spreading of cracks on ice, the image of me and Lizzie this morning rolling in the grass began to break apart. Me and Lizzie. Lizzie. My sister.

CHAPTER 23

Anna: February–June

Humphrys and Jackson Ltd
Universal Elevator Works
Baxter Lane
Bradford
BD35 1SD

24th February

Dear Miss Sallis,

LIFT CONSTRUCTION AND INSTALLATION:
FORMER ACKERDEAN MILL

I am writing to confirm that as discussed with
you and the Ackerdean Board Treasurer and in
accordance with your acceptance of our quote
(attached for your reference), we will be able to
begin work at the mill on the 1st March with an
estimated completion date of 2nd July.

Your sincerely

Roger Humphrys

'Hi, Sam it's Anna.'

'How's it going?'

'Great. Still hectic but all heading in the right direction. I really appreciated our wine bar outing last week, by the way. An oasis of calm in the madness. Look, I feel an idiot for not thinking of this before. I've had a sift through the books in Charles's section of the Harper collection.'

'His novels?'

'Not just them, the travel books and natural histories.'

'And? I can tell there's an "and?".'

'We don't have any examples of his handwriting because he typed everything. But he annotated his books. Scribbles in the margin, cross references. Underlinings of bits he probably intended to use in his novels. The handwriting matches the dedication and the haiku in the Tagore. I'd thought it likely but this is the proof I was looking for.'

'It was Charles who wrote the love poem to the fusilier.'

'Erica talked about him breaking hearts and hiding himself away in Yorkshire to avoid his romantic entanglements. It was the 1930s. Homosexuality was a criminal offence. He was hiding from more than just someone's pissed off father or husband. He was hiding from the law.'

Halifax Evening Courier
25th March

WE WANT YOUR MEMORIES
It's all change down at Ackerdean and custodian Anna
Sallis wants you to be part of it.

Later this year Ackerdean mill will embark on the next stage of its varied history as the heritage centre expands into the upper floors of the building that in its past have housed weaving looms, a bustling Edwardian tea room and what was once the most popular dance hall in the valley. Custodian Anna Sallis who is overseeing the redevelopment has set out her plans for the new centre, to be called simply 'Ackerdean Mill'.

'I want people to be at the heart of it,' she explained. 'If you or your families have photographs, first-person accounts, letters or journals relating to the mill, to the Acker Valley or Sowley, or the surrounding moors and villages, we would love to hear from you. Your memories and family histories can be part of the Ackerdean experience. Our new displays and interactive exhibitions will shed a more personal light on the history of the area and the people who made it their own, at work and at play.'

If you want to keep track of what's happening Anna will be posting up pictures and stories on the 'Mill Memories' section of the Ackerdean website (www.ackerdean.org.uk). You can also read her blog there or follow her on Twitter @annacustodian2017.

'View from the Mill' : an Ackerdean blog
Monday 13th April
by Anna Sallis

Thanks to all who came along to our Easter Extravaganza. The volunteers' hard work really paid off and the egg hunt in particular was a great success. Well done to Marilee from Bradford who won first prize.

Work on the mill refurbishment is well under way. We are planning a whole range of events and activities around the launch of the bigger and better Ackerdean Mill in July so Watch This Space.

Meanwhile, don't forget to send us your stories and pictures for our <u>Mill Memories</u> pages. And a final reminder for any 11–18-year-olds planning to enter our logo competition. The deadline is 1st May and you can find all the details by clicking <u>here</u> ...

Barry Clarke
Clocks Made and Repaired
23 Church Street,
Cleckheaton,
W . Yorks

```
RECEIPT                              30th April

One Smith and Baker exterior clock (c.1865)
Parts and Repairs  £235
Paid with thanks
A Sallis on behalf of Ackerdean Board
```

Hey Sherlock. Tried ringing no answer.
I know who BB is ☺

> About to have meeting with Erica
> But go on – who is BB?

Albert 'Bertie' Baxendale
Bunty's brother-in-law

> Wow! How?

Some nifty searching in one of the newspaper
databases I subscribe to. Former Warwickshire Fusilier
implicated in a case of 'gross indecency'
in 1938. Minor scandal – he was married and

his dad was an earl. It's the same photo.
Have copied and will email it to you.

Charles and Bertie!
We're going to need a whole
new section on 'Charles
Harper and his world' ☺

Good luck getting that past
Erica ☺ ☺

30 Hungerwood Lane
Leeds
30th June

Dear Miss Sallis

I was forwarded the article from the *Halifax Evening Courier*
about your work at Ackerdean Mill and thought you might
be interested in some papers left by my father Jonathan
Netherwood. He was the vicar at St Michael's in Halifax
and for many years had regular correspondence with the
Reverend Anthony Haste at St John's in Oakenshaw.

They had studied together before they were ordained.
Their letters were mainly about their sermons, sharing ideas
and so forth. My father had hopes of publishing a collection
of sermons and examples of their advice to each other,
as guidance for the newly ordained. They were both very
eloquent men and widely read. The best of their sermons are
quite exceptional.

He died before he was able to bring this to fruition and it
has not been something I have ever felt capable of tackling.
However, I have kept the letters. I am sure that my father

would appreciate these becoming part of what you are doing at Ackerdean. The Revd Haste often commented on his daily life in Oakenshaw and the surrounding valleys, to which my father was also a frequent visitor. They both drew on the bleakness and beauty of the moors for their words from the pulpit. As men of the people it is fitting that their correspondence should be part of your 'people's history'.

If you are interested please contact me on the number above and we can arrange a convenient time for you to collect.

Yours truly,

Neville Netherwood

Join Us for the Grand Reopening of Ackerdean Mill

1920s Tearoom and Tea Dance
Exhibition by Award-Winning Photographer Carter Klein
Poetry by Valley Verses
inc. readings from poems by Charles Harper
Sowley Junior Brass Band and Acker Ladies Morris
Swingboat Rides and Rowing on the Mill Pond

Saturday 11th July from 12 noon

Family Announcements: Obituaries

GREENLY James. On 2nd July, Jim, aged 72 years, passed away suddenly at Halcyon Haven in Sowley. Beloved husband of the late Joan, much-loved dad of Graham and Rebecca, much-loved Granddad of Eddie, Poppy and Joe, dear cousin of Frank. The funeral service and cremation will be held at Park Wood Crematorium, Elland, on Thursday, 9th July at 2.45 p.m. Family flowers only please, but donations can be made to the RNLI c/o Crasters Funeral Service, Wood Road, Sowley.

CHAPTER 24

Billy: 1936-42

I left High Hob with my knapsack stuffed with what little I owned: my clothes, my knife, and my notebooks. And the silver fob watch I'd taken from Da's chest. Ma said it belonged to my granddad. But I wasn't sure who she meant any more. I added it to my bag, not knowing what I'd do with it but not wanting to leave it behind. Whatever the truth of what Edie and Charles had told me, fact was they believed it. There was no place for me in their home any more.

They were still arguing as I left. They'd forgotten me the minute I'd flung the pistol on to the table and ran out of the room. I fancied I could hear them shouting as I started across the moor, but it might have just been the wind. My leg was aching from already having climbed the valley once that day and I made my way slowly, heading for the Palace, and Ma. Who else could I trust to tell me the truth?

But when it came to it I couldn't face her. Couldn't repeat those vile words. In the empty yard I pulled out the watch from my knapsack and laid it on the step of the cottage. Then I was over the bridge and heading up the other hillside, and the slow climb up to the Big House.

Potter was in the driveway. Polishing the mirrors on his fancy car. I didn't dare to look at the house. Didn't want to see the twitch of a curtain. Lizzie's face at a window. He stopped what he was doing when he saw me and stepped forward, but I didn't give him a chance to speak first.

'I know who you are.' I couldn't say the words 'my father' and I couldn't name my mother but he understood. I swear he shrank back. If he'd been raging earlier he was a different man now. I felt what it must be like, to be a beast with a creature under its paw.

'Billy lad,' he said. 'I only ever wanted what was best for you.' His eyes kept darting to the house. Scared that Mrs P might spy us and ask what I was doing there.

'Right,' I said. 'And not letting me know who I rightfully was. That was for the best? Well that's not how it's turned out, is it?' We locked eyes and I saw my own face reflected back. Lizzie's name hung unspoken between us.

How could I ever have thought he was a grand man? He looked so pathetic now. The shammy-leather in his hand and nothing to say for himself. There was nothing he could say that would change what had happened.

'I'm going,' I said. 'And I ain't coming back. But I needed to know for certain.' I no longer had any doubt.

I glanced up at the house then. How could I leave without seeing her one last time? Was she lying on her bed remembering this morning? That million years ago morning. What could I say? That I was her brother and we could never be together? That we never should have been together. How could I watch her turn from me once she knew the truth? She would blame her father. My mother too. Better that she hate me, the person she should never have loved, than to hate her father who at least could protect her and love her once I was gone.

'Tell Lizzie that I'm gone to London,' I said. 'Tell her I'll write. Tell my mother too.' Was I taking the coward's route? God help me I truly believed I was doing what was best.

Potter drove me to Leeds. Left me at the train station with thirty pounds in my pocket and not a word. Nothing. I'd felt no more like his flesh and blood sitting next to him in that car than I did to the nameless people in the streets we passed through.

London was the only place I could imagine going. I had a deal with Mr Hobart and I knew where to find him: Eastlea Palace and Winter Gardens. On that summer evening, when I got off the train at King's Cross, I had no other choice. I had nothing left. Not Lizzie, not Ma, or at least not the ma I thought I knew, and my sisters who I didn't even share a father with. Even my friendship with Jasper was based on lies. It was the first time I'd thought of Jasper all day. What would Edie and Charles tell him when he came home? I should write to him. Tell him my version of events. I spent that night on a bench in a park, lying awake making plans. Felt the weight of Potter's money in my pocket and counted sums in my head. I told myself I would survive. With Hobart's help or without it.

Mr Hobart remembered me all right. 'Had enough of the mad-house?' he said. 'I don't blame you.' I told him I wanted to take him up on the offer he'd made. It was sooner than he'd suggested but I couldn't wait to get going. He warned me I'd have to start right at the bottom but I told him I wasn't afraid of hard work. It was the right answer. He patted me on the back and said, 'You're in.'

When the news came of Charles and Edie killing themselves, I took it at first like news from another planet. About people or creatures I'd heard of but never really knew. But after, I felt the loss like another page had been ripped out of my life. I wasn't a big one for crying but I had to stop and take big breaths at the memory of a word or a look of them. And what about Jasper? What would he do now?

Mr Hobart said he'd seen it coming. I didn't ask, if that was the case, why hadn't he stepped in its way? 'They leaned too much on each other,' he said. 'For all their fighting theirs was a love that ran deep. Charles felt smothered by it, at times, but Edie had looked after him ever since their mother died. And then she went through hell with that bastard who fathered her son. Nasty piece of work. It was her turn to rely on Charles. But he was swimming in dangerous waters by then. They fled to Yorkshire. Thought running away would solve their problems.' He peered at me then through his little round spectacles. 'It very rarely does, you know.'

He believed me when I said I'd left them both alive. He didn't ask me for more details of what I'd done that night. Neither did the police or the papers. I saw the headline 'Double Suicide Tragedy' and it was weeks before I could bring myself to read the rest. And then a wave of relief that my name was spared.

Hobart's empire was huge and I was his errand boy to start with. Helping keep all the parts running smooth – the palace and gardens, the poetry press, a music hall, theatres, imports and exports. The faster I ran for him, the more work and responsibility he sent my way.

It seemed like a different world down there until you got to the nuts and bolts of it. Then you sussed that people wanted the same thing, north or south, middle of Yorkshire or middle of the Big Smoke. Trippers, at the end of the day, are trippers. You put on an entertainment and if you get it right, they pay their cash and they leave smiling. Everyone's a winner. What could be better than earning a crust making people happy?

Even the birds were no different, for all their city cockiness. Sparrows chirpy as barrow boys and the pigeons, all them bloody pigeons, half of them walking wounded, they still added a song to the air and a vision of flight that could lift your heart at the end of the day.

I didn't write to Jasper, nor Lizzie either at first. I couldn't find words around the truth and I couldn't bear to lie. It was from

Maud that I learned about Lizzie's illness. The scarlet fever that had struck our Peggy bad, but Lizzie worse. I wanted to go home then, to see her, even just as a friend. Especially when Maud told me she was in a chair and couldn't walk. But it was almost two years before I made it back for a visit.

Ma and me didn't speak of what had happened. She laid on a feast fit for a birthday and treated me like a prince, but made no fuss when it was time for me to go. Except that she pressed a small parcel into my hand, wrapped in cloth. I recognised its weight.

'It was your grandfather's.' She looked at me straight so we shared the meaning behind the simple words. 'I have no use for it. It's yours by right.'

She was a beauty, my mother. I didn't know it at the time. She was just Ma and of course she was beautiful. But after, I saw it. Potter called her his star, his queen. She shone in that old mill. Even with her golden hair tied under a cap and her apron on. Flour on her hands and on her cheek, where she'd brushed back a stray curl. She should have been painted by a great artist, hung up on the wall of a gallery. She spent her whole life at Ackerdean. I wondered if she loved Potter at all, or whether she just felt she had no choice.

I made it up to the Big House on the Sunday afternoon before I had to head for my train. Walked up to that front door like the big man I was after my years in London, and shrank to Billy Shaw from the Palace as soon as Mrs Potter was called to the door. Elizabeth was out visiting with Jane, she said, and wouldn't be home till late. But I could leave a message. I said to please tell her that I had called and that I wished her well. Wished her well? As if that could cover everything, or even anything, I was trying to say. As I left I glanced back and scanned the windows but there was no movement, nothing at all.

I tried to write to her after that. Started a dozen letters or more. But it all sounded too cold and bare set down in black and white. Every time, I screwed up the paper and threw it on the fire.

*

My gammy leg spared me the war. When the lads who lived through it came home, along with stories of the ones they'd left behind in France, I felt like I'd skived, not done my bit. But someone had to keep the folks back home happy, keep their spirits up. It wasn't easy, but we did our best, making do with what talent we could find and hoping the Palace and Gardens wouldn't catch the eye of a German bomber. It wasn't the same as getting a medal though.

'You big jessie,' Jasper would have said. After all that time it was still his and Lizzie's voices I heard in my head. When I was faced with anything new or strange Lizzie or Jasper'd pop up and give me their opinion on it. Nine times out of ten I'd agree.

I met Catherine in London at the beginning of the war and though it wasn't the love that I'd had for Lizzie, that first sweet love, it was still good and true. Her family were wiped out in the Blitz. She was a survivor, she said. She was small and strong. But she lost the fight when our baby was born. Little Frank, named after her father.

I'd have been lost without Maud. Peggy had married a chap in Sowley. She was run ragged with him and her brood of children that soon filled their narrow terraced house, which had no room for visitors, not even her brother all the way from London. It was Maud I stayed with on my trips back to the valley. She was so steady and straight. Her and Arty running the farm every hour of the day, with their sheep and their chucks. When I turned up that day with Frank not more than a few weeks old, she clucked and she fussed and when I saw that baby in her arms I knew that was where he belonged. Her and Arthur would bring him up right, under the same Yorkshire sky that had watched over me.

CHAPTER 25

Anna: July

The upturned faces watch the hands of the clock. They have started their vigil too early, Anna thinks. Still a minute and a half to go. There is fidgeting among a group of elderly people hemmed in the middle of the crowd. Eddies of children buffet the edges.

The mayor is standing on a small platform, flanked by Erica on one side and on the other Carter, dressed in a black T-shirt and jeans and looking as though he'd rather be anywhere else. As the two hands of the clock finally slot together over the number twelve there is a loud cheer.

'I am delighted to see so many of you gathered today for this auspicious occasion,' the mayor begins.

Anna knows she should pay attention. It is her auspicious occasion, after all: it has taken so many months of hard work to get to this point. But now it is here she feels distanced from it, eager to move on to the next stage, whatever that might be.

The mayor begins to wind up his speech. Carter catches her eye. She smiles and he raises his eyebrows. Since his apology they have progressed to a cautious friendship. Anna is happy to keep it that way. For now.

'With no more ado, I declare that Ackerdean Mill is now open.' There is a tiny cheer and then not so much a surge as a coordinated amble as most of the crowd head towards the entrance to the mill. On cue the brass band begin to play 'The Floral Dance'. Carter jumps down from the platform, followed more sedately by Erica who takes his arm and guides him towards a small group of women. Anna recognises the president of the WI among them.

Instead of following the crowd Anna slips away, past the café where May's assistants are ready to serve any visitors who choose not to sample the 1920s-style tea room in the mill. She stops at the river's edge. The orange-tinged water bubbles over the rocks and weaves through the stepping stones. A couple of yards downstream a grey heron, poised on one leg, watches and waits. On the water's surface long-legged pond skaters dance, and above them dart the sharp blue of damselflies. It could be a hundred years ago.

Voices call from the opposite hillside. The echoes of workers arriving at the mill, their clogs clattering against the stones; mer-rymakers ready for a day at the Palace, picnic baskets swinging be-tween them; centuries of walkers passing through. Anna looks up as a family emerge from the trees. T-shirts and jeans, Dad wearing a baseball cap, a teenage girl all in black trailing behind, headphones over her ears. A dog barks, running among their legs, managing his flock.

At the far end of the grassy green picnic field the slender bodies of red and green dragons rear into the air. A farmer had rung her six weeks ago to say he had the old swingboats in one of his barns.

'Sixty-odd years they've been sitting there,' he said. 'My father bought them off Mr Potter. Don't know what he thought he were doing with them. Saving them for the nation, probably. He never could bear to see owt thrown away.'

The freshly painted boats, hanging on new chains, have already attracted a long queue. Children are swinging back and forth under the supervision of one of the volunteers. One small boy squeals every time his boat swings up. As Anna heads back across the yard to the mill his voice follows her, carrying over the field like the call of a wild bird.

In the mill, in the corner of the museum formerly occupied by the old steam turbine, there now stands a cotton loom, on long-term loan from a heritage mill in Cheshire. Trevor Stanhope is addressing a small crowd, explaining how the weaving industry in the valley was transformed first by the spinning jennies and then by looms like this one that brought the spinners and weavers out of their cottages and into the mills. He introduces the two 'hard-working mill lads' by his side. Anna recognises Fahim and Alfie, two boys from one of her school groups, grinning from under their caps. As Alfie scrapes his clog over the flagstone, Trevor points out that in a busy mill, with the air filled with cotton dust, the men and women who operated the looms would have to work barefoot for fear that the sparks from their clogs could start a fire. Alfie stops his scraping and puts his feet together.

'I have to be here at six o'clock every morning ...' Fahim begins.

When Trevor and the boys have finished, Anna follows a trail of people up the stairs. Past the notice warning that the stairs are worn and uneven and anyone unsteady on their feet should use the lift.

'Well, you've stirred things up good and proper, lass.' Frank appears at her side as she enters the room on the first floor. 'Erica Walker must be putty in your hands. I overheard her talking about fitting solar panels on the roof next.'

'I can't take any credit for that,' says Anna. 'It's Erica's idea. Now she's embraced the idea of moving the mill forward there's going to be no stopping her.'

Anna had accompanied Frank to Jim's funeral the day before, although he'd told her there was no need, that she should be getting ready for her big day, not saying goodbye to an old man she barely knew. But at the crematorium Frank had leaned against her and she was glad she was there.

'What do you think Jim would have made of this?' she asks, gesturing at the room. People are clustered around the formerly blank walls and temporary partitions, now hung with Carter's photographs: remains of the valley's industrial heritage set in scenes of its most stunning natural beauty, an old limekiln with skeletal hawthorns on either side, a blackened chimney with a flock of white birds flying across it, the scars of a railway running through a coppery beechwood. The central third of the back wall is clear of pictures and is displaying projected images of photographs from the museum's collection. A bank of headphones allows people to listen to excerpts from the oral histories. In one corner a dummy is dressed and poised as a 1920s skater, the original roller skates strapped to her feet: on a board on the wall beside her are the words of Ivy Hall describing the roar and thunder of the rink.

'Reckon he'd have liked to see the old place woken up again. You've flushed out all that doom and gloom. And not an angel in sight.' Frank's voice wavers and he coughs as he fumbles for his handkerchief. 'The bugger. He was determined to get me in that bloomin' sheltered housing. Reckon he was in league with our John. Dying was a bit bloody extreme though. One in, one out. So I'm in.' He sniffs. 'I suppose they'll need someone to keep the old biddies in line now Jim has gone.' He suddenly jerks his head at the projection on the far wall.

'There she is.'

Mary Shaw is standing with her laden tray, white cap perched on her head, a curl of pale hair escaping at one side. Frank stops a man passing by. 'That's my grandma, that is.' He points at the image. The other man smiles and nods.

'She looks like a grand lady,' he says.

'She was. Queen of the scones and puddings, they called her.'

'You must be very proud.' The man shakes Frank's hand before walking away.

'Have you been upstairs yet?' Anna asks. The top floor has been temporarily transformed into a between-the-wars tea room, with vintage china hired from a local company and a CD player disguised as a gramophone playing tunes of the era. Visitors can dress for the part if they want to, choosing from a rail of frocks and jackets and a variety of hats. There is even a fox fur, complete with head and feet. The floor will be partly cleared later ready for the tea dance.

Frank chuckles. 'Local teenagers in pinnies and mob caps balancing china cups and saucers? It's not bad,' he concedes. 'Don't know what Nana Shaw would have made of it though. Now, you'll have to 'scuse me, there's a couple of folks over there puzzling over how to work them headphones. I'll put them right.'

Sam waves to her from the other side of the room. She is standing by one of Carter's photographs, a close-up of a rough-hewn millstone, white and purple flowers growing through the central hole.

'This is amazing,' Sam says when Anna joins her. 'Well done. People are loving Carter's pictures, but it's the location that's setting them off so well.' She glances over to Frank who is helping a grey-haired woman adjust the volume on the headphone set.

She lowers her voice. 'Have you said anything to Frank yet about you-know-what?'

Anna shakes her head. 'I'm waiting till this is all over. He's been so excited about today. It would have taken the edge off for him and he's a bit fragile with his cousin dying.'

'You're prevaricating,' says Sam. 'Not that I blame you. But he's still got plenty to be proud of. Who knows, he might be chuffed to add the name of Potter to his family tree.'

'Hmm. But at the expense of taking out the Shaw,' says Anna. 'And there's still the great unknown. We're certain one of the boys was present between the death of Charles and the death of Edie and probably faked their suicide note. It gives me the shivers, the idea of telling Frank his father might have been a murderer.'

Later, in the yard, a small train of boys and girls steams past Anna and into the ginnel between the cottages and the mill. Moments later Alfie, still in his mill-boy outfit, dashes over the small bridge, his arms going like pistons. A fierce look on his face.

'Have they been past, miss?' He hops from one foot to the other. 'Tell me, tell me. Please.'

'What's the game?' she asks. 'Hide and seek? If it is, I can't say. That would be cheating.'

'Aw, c'mon, give us a clue.'

She glances at the entrance of the ginnel.

'Knew it,' he says. 'Sign of the Catface.'

'The what?'

'The Catface. You know.' And he is off.

She follows him to the narrow entrance. The unmade road and the trees behind it are visible at the end. The tunnel of light is broken as a small figure peels away from the wall two-thirds of the way down and darts out of the far side.

Alfie bellows, 'Seen you, Rose,' and charges down the passageway.

Anna follows him in. Where the girl had seemed to emerge from the wall there is a small alcove, just deep enough to hold a hiding child. The light from that end picks out the contours of the stone.

The Sign of the Catface. Anna sees it as she is about to walk on. She runs her fingers over the lines carved into the recessed stone. The initials JH and next to them the same crude shape made of triangles and lines that she had seen up at the Stag Stones. Of course it was a cat. She can see it now, eyes, nose and whiskers. Below it two sets of initials lie close together. She crouches to see them better. 'BS' and 'LP'. Cut less deeply than the ones above. No date but they've been here a long time. Carved not scratched and the soft fuzz of lichen spilling into the grooves. Her fingers follow the cut lines, Billy Shaw? And LP? Another friend at the Palace?

'Anna.'

Erica Walker is standing at the end of the ginnel. 'I was told you were last seen disappearing down here.'

Anna steps out into the light.

'Well it's all going very well,' Erica says. 'There's been a lot of interest in the tea dance. A lady from the local salsa group has asked if they can hold a couple of sessions here. Could we accommodate that?'

'Of course,' says Anna. 'It's what the dance floor was made for.'

'Exactly.' Erica shifts the strap of her bag on her shoulder. 'I know it's going to be a busy day but could you spare me an hour when it's all over? There's something I want to show you.'

By six o'clock the last of the cars are leaving the car park and the remaining visitors who came on foot are heading up the track.

Sam and Carter are among the last to go. Carter is beaming with the success of his exhibition and is full of praise for the WI.

'Turns out it's not all jam-making and crochet. They want me to do a photography workshop, down at the old silk mill on the other side of Sowley.'

'Sounds like material for another exhibition,' says Sam. 'Meanwhile, Anna, you're invited up to High Hob next Sunday for drinks and nibbles, before I scuttle off back to London. I've braced myself for another winter here, though, so I won't be away for long. If you ask nicely Frank Chambers might even give you a lift up.'

'Frank's invited?'

'Turns out he's one of my biggest fans,' says Sam. 'The prospect of getting an advance copy of my latest even prompted him to apologise about his outburst over Ruby. You will come?'

'Of course.' Anna catches Carter's eye.

'I haven't had my invite yet,' he says.

Sam tells him to stop being an idiot and pushes him towards the car park.

'Very smooth,' Erica says, as she and Anna step out of the lift on the top floor of the now deserted mill. 'And it seems to have dealt admirably with today's crowds.' She looks around. The vintage crockery and costumes have been packed away. The gramophone is silent. 'In all the fuss I didn't make it up here earlier,' she continues, as they sit down at one of the empty tables. 'But I've been told the tea room was very popular. We could investigate the possibility of making it a regular event, although of course the usual café is more practical on an everyday basis.'

'It would be great to run it alongside some more tea dances,' Anna says. She tells Erica about her idea for a vintage weekend at the end of the summer.

'Splendid. Between us we've proved that this mill has got a few decades of life left in it yet.' Erica is fidgeting with the buckle on her bag. It is large and made of stiff brown leather.

'Is that vintage?' Anna asks.

'I suppose so. It was my mother's.' Erica seems to make up her mind about something and undoes the fastening.

'I told you about my mother living with the Potters. She was company for Mrs Potter and acted as a chaperone to their daughter Elizabeth.'

'I knew there was a daughter,' says Anna. 'But there's very little about her in the records.' She mentions the picture of the woman in the wheelchair.

'Scarlet fever. That was the official story,' Erica says. 'Left her unable to use her legs, and there was a problem with her lungs. She was relatively young when she died.' She pulls out a dark-covered book from her bag. 'My mother used to talk about Elizabeth. But it always ended in her being upset. When she died, I found her diaries, including this one.'

Erica pushes the book towards Anna. 'Mother said that after what happened, what Mr Potter really wanted was for the mill to be closed up for ever or pulled down completely. But he could never bring himself to do it. Torn between hating the place and not being able to let it go. That's why he left it to the Literary and Scientific Society rather than letting a company or a developer take it on. In the end he wanted it to be preserved. It was a memorial, you see.'

She leans over and opens the book. On the first page in neat handwriting are the words 'Jane Thomas, Thornleyroyd, West Riding of

Yorkshire'. Erica flicks through the pages and then smooths them open. 'October 1936. My mother was 21 and engaged to be married to Robert Charlton, son of a big carpet manufacturer in Halifax. The wedding was set for November when her parents were due back from India.'

Monday 9th October

The worst day. And the very worst of it is that I can speak to no one about it, not even Robert.

E was insistent she go to the Palace on her own. But I followed. She met the Harper boy on the steps near the dam. It must have been arranged. I thought we wouldn't see his face again, not after what happened up there. But I expect E wanted word of Billy. She has carried such a burden these last months. Not even shared with me though I've guessed it and wished I could tell her I knew.

They spoke for a while and then, suddenly, she slapped his face. He didn't move. I ran towards them not caring that they would know I'd been spying. But she pushed right past me saying only, 'He's a liar. A filthy liar.'

Him looking at me through that wild hair like a dark-eyed animal. He teased me first as is his wont but then he told me what he'd told E. About why Billy wouldn't be showing his face here again. I didn't want to believe him. Knowing what E was carrying.

I raced back along the path knowing I must find and comfort her. It being Monday there was no one in the yard, but the door to the Palace was flung open and above, the windows were wide open for airing.

Mr P stepped out of the Shaw's cottage, with Mrs S close behind. And I felt sick to the stomach that there was indeed truth in Jasper's filthy words.

Mrs S went pale as ash and all our faces turned like hers upwards to the mill. E was at the first floor window, stepping out onto the sill. Mr P shouted, 'Lizzie you get down here'. Mrs S clutching his arm. I didn't know whether to run up the stairs or shout up from below. E looked at her father and lifted her arms to the heavens. Then she fell.

I thought she was dead. Mrs S sobbing and saying fetch the doctor. There was blood on the stones. I said she shouldn't be moved. But Mr P and Mrs S they carried her to the motor car. It would be quicker, they said.

E is in her room with her father and the doctor. I must go back to Mrs P. She will not stop wailing.

Friday 13th November 1936

E is awake but in great pain. The doctor has given her morphia but she cries out in her sleep. He says she may not walk again. Nobody has mentioned the baby. Whether she is still carrying it, or if it was lost. But all that blood.

Anna looks up from the book. 'Elizabeth Potter was pregnant?'

Erica nods. 'She was sixteen or thereabouts. It sounds as though only my mother knew. Until the accident, at least. She appears to have lost the baby in the fall, so the doctor must have realised then. Her parents too. But they wouldn't want anyone else to know.'

Anna feels a shiver. 'She mentions a boy called Billy,' she says. 'Would that be Billy Shaw?'

Erica nods. 'Frank Chambers' uncle. She names him earlier too.' She turns back the pages of the diary.

Friday 17th July
E still refuses to leave her room. I can hear her through the door, saying his name over and over. Ever since her father told her he'd put the Shaw boy on the train to London last night. Gone to seek his fortune without leaving her a single word of goodbye. I tell her to hush. Her father mustn't hear. Mustn't know that the boy's leaving has broken his daughter's heart. How I hate him. I hope for all our sakes that he never comes back.

'BS' and 'LP', the initials together on the wall, with JH gouged above. Elizabeth, 'Lizzie' Potter had been carrying Billy's child. And the 'filthy lie' that Jasper told her? The truth, that even Jane recognised when she saw Nathaniel Potter and Mary Shaw together in the yard. That poor girl. And what about Billy, did he ever know?

'We can't assume she jumped,' Erica continues. 'It could have been a fall. Trying to shock her father, punish him with her daredevilry, and she slipped. I suspect Nathaniel had paid Billy off. He was hardly a suitable match for his daughter. No wonder the girl was so distraught. Abandoned by the father of her unborn child. Lord knows what that brute Jasper Harper said to her.'

Anna is shocked by the venom in Erica's voice. She's talking about a teenage boy. No, she's talking about Jasper Harper, she reminds herself. One more malicious act laid at his door. I can't tell her, she thinks. The full story of what her mother had helped to cover up. That Billy and Elizabeth were siblings as well as lovers. Not until I've spoken to Frank, at least. She looks at the date of the entry again. Friday 17th July 1936. The Harpers were thought to have died during the night of the sixteenth to the seventeenth. Sally had seen Charles alive with 'the young master' at High Hob early on the morning of Friday the seventeenth, when Billy would already have arrived in London. Had anyone ever tested Jasper's alibi?

Erica slots the diary back into her bag, but her fingers linger on the clasp, stroking the metal. What is she still not telling me? Anna thinks.

'I understand now,' she says, 'your reluctance to open up the parts of the mill that Nathaniel Potter had closed. Knowing the burden of sorrow and secrecy your mother shared. What happened to Elizabeth Potter was a tragedy. But you changed your mind. Why? Was it just the pressure from the rest of the board?'

In the silence that follows the room itself seems to be waiting and listening. The stone walls and bright squares of glass. The smooth boards beneath their feet. The stories and lives they have witnessed over two hundred years. Just one more to add, and not the last.

'That afternoon in the fisherman's hut. On Mother's anniversary.' Erica clears her throat. 'You talked about the myths we create around those who are no longer with us. The stories we want heard and the ones we submerge. You said something about it being better that we face up to the reality of who people were. What they did and ...' she hesitates, 'what was done to them.' She stops playing with the clasp and focuses on Anna. 'I was worried that if the upper floors were reopened it might trigger questions, reawaken memories. But you made me realise that by keeping them closed I was denying those memories their existence. Submerging the reality of the people involved. I wasn't being true to the memory of my mother or of Elizabeth Potter. Of what they went through.'

Anna is holding her breath. The wrong question now and Erica might clam up completely. 'What happened?' she asks. 'To your mother?'

Erica's folds her hands together on the table. 'After Elizabeth's accident, she broke off her engagement. Devoted herself to helping

297

the Potters, and stayed with them even when her parents returned to England. Later, perhaps when they needed her less, she threw her energies into running the museum in Sowley. Some of it I know from her diaries, she told other parts of it to me herself. Not always coherently. When her mind started going, that's when she revealed the most. It was hard for her. Hard for me.' Anna recognises in Erica's voice the release she had felt herself when she had started to tell Sam the truth about Dan.

'Mother's work at the museum was voluntary, but it gave her such a sense of purpose. Helped her move on from the Potters and their closed world. She got married just after the war. Tony Walker was a science teacher at Sowley Grammar, as it was then. He encouraged her work, tried to persuade her to take a professional training course. When the Harpers' cousin decided to donate Charles and Edie's papers and possessions to the museum in 1948 she wrote in her diary that it was the pinnacle of her career. It was one of the last diary entries she made.'

Erica seems unable to go on.

'You said before that she was involved with the Literary and Scientific Society when Mr Potter left them the mill. She must have played a vital role in getting the heritage centre established here,' Anna says. 'You must be very proud of what she achieved.'

Erica is clasping the fingers of her left hand so tightly Anna is afraid she might dislocate a joint. She waits. The centuries-old dust and air of the room waits.

'It was much, much later when she told me. I had to piece it together from her disjointed memories. I didn't want to believe what she was telling me. Wanted to blame her confusion, her failing mind. But she repeated the same things over and over until I knew they must be true.' She pauses, but only to release the grasp on her hand. She flexes her fingers.

'He heard about the donation to the museum. He came back.'

He? But Anna knows who Erica means. The fear in Erica's voice, echoes of Sally Marsden.

'Jasper Harper came to the museum one evening when she was there alone. I don't know what he wanted. Mother didn't know or couldn't tell me. He raged through the place, she said, "like a mad dog."' She swallows hard. 'I don't think he found what he was looking for. In his fury he took what was there instead. My mother.'

A chill suffuses Anna's entire body. Jasper Harper is a presence in the room. The violence and rage embodied in the Beast he painted on the attic wall. Sally's lasting fear of his 'animal ways'. The stench of him.

'When I was born,' Erica continues, 'her husband, Tony, knew I wasn't his. They'd been having problems. With the physical side of things. Long before ... long before Jasper Harper did what he did.'

Erica clenches her palms together until her fingers whiten. Anna reaches out her hand and gently covers them.

'Tony stayed around for the first year but then he walked away. After that there was only me and Mother, right up until the day she died.'

'But she continued to work with the Harper material,' Anna says. 'She established the Ackerdean board and you took it on yourself after her. It must have been a constant reminder.'

'Of Charles and Edie Harper.' Some of Erica's usual stridency has returned. 'Their legacy was their work. Not that boy.'

In Erica's face Anna glimpses Jane, the loyal companion, defending and protecting the Potters, and ultimately Edie and Charles Harper too. Your grandmother and your great-uncle, Anna thinks, a fierce pride that overrides the horror that links them to you.

'Sometimes we have to walk away from the past.' Erica finally closes the fastener on her bag and sets it on the floor. 'The mill should be a living memorial to those that have passed, not a mausoleum. You deserved an explanation.' Her voice is brusque. 'But we don't need to go public with the intimate details. We can keep it on a need-to-know basis.'

Layers of family secrets, Anna thinks. We each choose how much to reveal. Has Erica made the connection between Mr Potter and Mrs Shaw? Was there more in those diaries that she was unwilling to share? Does she suspect that Billy was Nathaniel Potter's son?

Anna thinks about the silver fob watch. The one thing, along with a determined chin and a steady gaze, passed down, from Nathaniel Potter to his grandson Frank. Via Billy Shaw who lost everything else, and made a new start on his own. She imagines the watch one day turning and glinting in the Australian sun.

'A need-to-know basis,' she agrees.

CHAPTER 26

Billy: 1957

It was 1957 when I next and last saw Jasper. I was working fourteen hours a day trying to keep the Eastlea Palace on its feet. Old Hobart had left the running of it pretty much to me by then. Postwar London wasn't the easiest of places to keep an entertainment emporium open. People still wanted entertaining, but the war years had opened up new windows on the world. It led to a taste for different things, new diversions.

The flicks nearly did for us, with cinemas popping up all over. Till we had the canny idea of fitting up one of our own. We had to experiment a bit with what we showed. 'Give the trippers what they want,' straight out of Nathaniel Potter's handbook. I'm not saying I'm proud of some of the films we put on. But we made sure the customers knew what was what and nobody wandered in unsuspecting. And it drew them in. Men exhausted after a week at work. Lonely men with no home to go to as well as those with families, that for whatever reason, they weren't ready to face for a couple of hours. Specially on winter evenings when they could slip in unnoticed in the dark. It was my idea to install a side door down the alley, so people weren't put off when the nights got lighter.

But that wasn't the sum total. We did matinees as well for the kiddies and romances for the sweethearts. You've got to cast your net wide if you want to haul in the fishes. Always be looking for new markets. Keep 'em happy. If I was going to add a line to the Potter handbook it would be that: 'Keep 'em happy.'

It was through our pocket cinema that me and Jasper met up. Horror was big then. Scarier the better. Turned out that Jasper was in the business. He'd gone to America. Made a new life for himself. New name even, he was 'Jaz Bartlett' now. Found what they call 'his niche'. He set up his own company with some family money and started making horror films. *The Devil's Changeling* and *The Thing from the Crypt*, they were both his. And of course *The Beast*. Came over to promote them in England and set up a meeting. When he told me about *The Beast* I said we had to show it at Eastlea. He shook my hand and we agreed on a whole run of Bartlett Horrors. They were patchy. Moments of brilliance, shots and scenes when it was like looking in Jasper's old sketchbook. *The Beast* was one of the best, or maybe I'm biased. Gave me the shivers, it did, watching the hero track the glowing red eyes across the dark wasteland. We did a fair bit of business with that run and I wrote to say we'd be up for more. But he never got back in touch. I asked around and was told he'd moved into television.

So, 1957. Me and Jasper sitting in a pub off King's Cross. Both only a few years off forty, not the boys we used to be. He had the same wild head of curls, mind, threaded now with strands of grey, and the same dark eyes. Before any talk of films or screenings there was Edie and Charles.

'God's own, Jasper. When I left them they were both alive. Both breathing hell at each other. The gun was on the desk. But I never stopped to think. I had other stuff to deal with.'

'I know,' said Jasper. 'I was there.'

'No you weren't. It might have been nearly twenty years ago but it's not a day I'm ever going to forget. Believe me. You weren't there.'

'I came home,' Jasper said. 'The upper school had Friday off while the next year's prospective new boys were given the tour. Didn't want us hanging around spoiling the view. So we got a long weekend. They encouraged us to spend it away from the school. Spencer and his father were heading up to the Lakes, Thursday night. I didn't fancy it. Some lark with tents and campfires.' He shot me a quick glance and I smiled. Because after so many years that's what that dreadful night in the Scout field was, a lark.

'I took up their offer of a lift though,' he continued. 'Got them to drop me at Leeds station. I'd missed the last train to Oakenshaw but I said I'd kip in the waiting room, spend the next day exploring the city before heading for home. Worse ways to spend a holiday and I was in no hurry to get to High Hob. Spencer's father said it showed I had a good spirit of adventure, though I think he was just relieved I hadn't asked him to drive me all the way home.

'I got kicked out of the waiting room by a porter who said there was no overnighting under any circumstances. I thought I might have to rough it in the streets of the city, when who did I spy but old Potter. He was acting a bit shifty. Said he'd been seeing off a business colleague, and did I need a lift home?'

I wondered if Jasper had seen me boarding that London train. I half expected him to ask, an arch 'Was that you?' But he took a sip of his drink and carried on.

'I expected he'd drop me off in Sowley, and I'd have half a night's walk ahead of me, but he took me to the Palace. What business he'd be having at the Palace at that time, gone midnight it was, I don't know.' Though his quick sideways look said he had an idea. 'Just as well there was a decent moon and I knew the route up like the back of my hand. When I got there, High Hob was in darkness. I thought I might be spending the night sleeping rough after all. But the door was unlocked.'

He paused and stared at his whisky glass. I imagined him stepping into the hall, the moonlight through the door lighting up the chequerboard floor.

'I couldn't see the point of waking any one, so I went straight up to bed. Should have slept through till noon, but I woke only a few hours later, thirsty and famished, and went downstairs to see what I could scavenge. The door to Charles's study was half open and I heard a noise from inside. I thought I'd best let him know I was there. In case he cared.' He paused and the silence lasted so long that I wondered whether he wanted me to guess the rest of the story, to write the ending myself.

'She was on the floor,' Jasper said. 'Lit by the morning light through the window like a scene from a painting.' He took a deep breath. 'She had a red circle the size of a penny on her forehead. Blood in her hair and on the floor. Charles was slumped in his armchair. Looked like he'd slept there all night. He was awake now, though, eyes open, staring at Edie. The gun was on his lap, resting innocent as a kitten. He looked up and I don't know if he knew it was me or if he imagined I was a policeman or a priest. He said, "I just wanted her to stop. To shut the hell up." His voice was pleading for me to believe, his eyes scared as a trapped rabbit's. "I didn't know," he kept saying. "It was loaded. I didn't know."

'Edie knew it was still loaded, from the night you shot my leg,' I said. I remembered her chalk-white face and her eyes locked on the silver chamber as I waved it at them, never intending to press the trigger, although the tremors were running right down my arm to my fingers. She knew. But she didn't say.

'Then he told me you were gone,' said Jasper. 'As if he'd shot you too. But then he said, "We broke his heart and he won't be coming back." He explained how "she" – that's what he called her as she lay there, her blood soaked and dried into his precious silk rug – how Edie had made him tell you. About Potter.' Jasper looked for my reaction. I just nodded, and he sniffed. 'It explains a lot.' He took a sip of his drink. 'I knelt down to Edie. Of course she was dead. All that blood. But I still needed to know for certain. Her skin was so cold. There was nothing. Nothing of her left. She'd been dead for hours. Charles slid down to the floor beside me. He was blubbing like a baby.'

'And then?' I prompted. In my head, the image of Edie dead, her story already finished but Charles at this point still alive, in shock but still alive.

'Then bloody Sally barged in. All ready to do her daily chores. I sent her away. Don't think she saw anything, but I told her to keep her mouth shut if she didn't want a reputation as a liar. That she'd never get another job without a reference.' His voice was vicious. 'When I'd seen her off I went back in. He was still kneeling next to Edie on the floor with the gun in his hand.'

Jasper ran his fingers through his dark fringe of curls, a twist of his head as he did it. Reminded me of a Canada goose stretching its neck. He blinked, a quick double flicker of his eyes.

'Then the gun was at his throat and bang.'

As if he couldn't help himself, Jasper pointed his two fingers below his chin, and made a popping sound with his lips. 'Lying there his blood all fresh and red next to the dark stain of Edie's.' Another sip of his drink. 'That's why I had to leave them for a bit. Make it more convincing, that they'd died together.' He paused. 'For Edie's sake. She was always so careful about keeping things amongst ourselves. Even if it was an accident. She wouldn't want the world knowing what Charles had done.'

'What about the note?' I asked.

He looked up, his eyes sharp.

'There was a note,' I said. 'They'd both signed it.' I'd read about it in the papers. 'A tragic farewell' the papers called it, the Harpers' final words to the world.

'Yeah, well, he must have done it while I was seeing Sally off.' His dark lashes fluttered. 'Scribbled both their names on, so it looked like it was Edie's decision too.' He sniffed again. 'I didn't bother to read it. It was all lies anyway. She didn't want to be dead.'

I had watched Jasper fibbing from the age of eleven to the time just after his fifteenth birthday when he'd tried to convince Livvy he hadn't been using her bread rolls as missiles against the crows. His black curls might be closer trimmed and peppered with grey but he couldn't hide that quick betrayal of his eyes when he was twisting the truth.

He took out a packet of cigarettes and offered me one but I shook my head.

'I laid low all day and then showed my face in Oakenshaw just after the five-thirty train got in.' He lit a cigarette and inhaled. 'Got myself a lift up to the house with the vicar, no less. Spun him a tale about my day sightseeing in Leeds. Slipped in that I was worried about Edie's state of mind. He was keen as mustard to come and minister uplifting words. Heartbroken to discover he was too late.'

The cold matter-of-factness chills me. Were you heartbroken too, Jasper? I wanted to ask. Instead I said, 'It must have been hard for you. To lose them both.'

He shrugged. 'I've done all right for myself.' Which wasn't what I meant at all.

'I covered your back, Billy,' he continued. 'Put you in the clear. Spoke to your mother. Her and Potter between them had their story straight. That you'd gone down to London the week before, after Livvy got sick. There was no one to counter it. Except Sally, and I made sure she kept quiet.

'I had a word with Lizzie too, later,' he added with a shake of his head. 'She took it bad when I said you wouldn't be coming back.' He touched the side of his face. 'Swung for me, she did. Said she'd have given me worse if I hadn't just been orphaned.' His fingers holding the cigarette trembled. I wondered how much he knew. How much he wasn't telling. One thing I knew for certain, he was getting nothing more out of me.

He leaned forward. 'You remember Bunty?'

'Edie's friend from London?'

He nodded. 'She was a friend of Spencer's family too. Stayed at their place that same time as I did over Easter. She was fond of her gin, was Bunty. She snuggled up to me on the sofa one evening, all cosy, and said I had a right to know about my father. Started off waxing on what a literary legend he was. I half thought she meant Charles at first. But no, turns out he was this poet, James Ross.' He looked at me but I shrugged. 'He's pretty famous,' he continued. 'We did some of his poems with Edie. They met in Paris, he was married, didn't want to know when she told him she was up the duff. Blah blah blah.'

He stubbed out his cigarette in the ashtray.

'He was the love of her life, according to Bunty. I was a poor substitute. Edie was always vague about my father to me. Sometimes he was a god-like genius, other times he was a cruel and selfish monster.'

Sometimes winged and glorious, I thought, sometimes fanged and clawed. I almost reached out to him then, across the table. But he'd never been one for physical affection and would no doubt have pulled away.

'He died a year before Edie did. Liver cirrhosis or pneumonia, or a combination of the two.'

He began to whistle under his breath. He checked his empty glass and stood up. 'I'll get us another round in, then we can start talking business.'

I watched him walk to the bar. The same old Jasper swagger. I imagined him twenty years ago. Discovering the truth about his father. Returning home a few months later and finding his mother dead and Charles holding the gun. Charles in horror and remorse killing himself too.

That quick flicker of Jasper's eyes as he told me his tale suggested another scenario. Charles admitting his guilt, kneeling beside the woman he had killed and Jasper picking up the gun and shooting him dead. Making it appear to be suicide by adding a note. Jasper had read enough novels to know there was always a note. He'd have no trouble copying their handwriting, as easy as sketching.

Jasper returned with our drinks and handed me my glass. Did I ever really know him? I once thought I knew what he was capable

307

of. Now I wondered if I'd only guessed at a fraction of it.

He raised his glass. 'All right, Billy?' And he grinned.

It was the grin of long summers chasing the Beast across the moor, as the heather brushed our shins, of battling the wind and sheltering from the rain. Firing catties and setting traps, hiding from diamond smugglers and plotting against thieves. The roar of the rink and the rush of the river, the dares and the scraps, and the sharing of scars and of so much more, of lies and betrayal, and of the knowledge of fathers lost and found, and lost again.

Our glasses met across the table, the soft clink of glass on glass, a swirl of amber.

'We're all right,' I said.

CHAPTER 27

Anna: July

Frank has combed his hair. The white strands lie in defined rows across his bare scalp. In his carrier bag, Anna knows because she has peeked, are seven Sam Klein novels.

'I don't know how she does it,' Frank says as he manoeuvres the Land Rover up the track towards the house. 'She has me grabbed from the first page to the last.' He sniffs. 'No excuse, mind, for not being able to control her bloomin' dog.'

Betsy, who is sitting in the back of the Land Rover, makes a soft rumbling sound as if in agreement.

'When Betsy comes to live at the mill,' says Anna, 'she and Ruby will have plenty of chances to become friends.' Frank had begrudgingly accepted her offer to take on Betsy, 'So long as you bring her in to see me regular, and don't let her turn into a lap hound. She's a working dog, remember.'

He gestures now to a tattered cardboard box next to the dog. 'I'll drop that off at yours on the way back. Odds and sods of Maud and Arthur's mainly. Farming stuff. But I know how much you like old bits of paper. Nearly killed meself getting them down from the attic.'

'Frank!'

'I know, but I don't want anything left behind for the new folk to be sticking their noses into. There's some of Billy's papers in there too. Sent up from London after he passed. Business documents, publicity leaflets, letters from suppliers and the like. Might be something for your archive, seeing as how he was in the same business.' He glanced up at her. 'No deeds to the mill in there, mind. I've already checked. Don't worry about making it a priority, I expect you'll be busy for a while trying to raise that money for Edie Harper's novel.'

Anna groans. 'I just hope we get it. Funding bids are always tricky, but it'll be a travesty if it's sold to someone else.'

The phone call from Professor Jackson at the University of Central Virginia had come out of the blue. The excited academic explained that a researcher from a specialist film archive had been in touch.

'He was cataloguing a new acquisition. Original scripts and sketches left by Jaz Bartlett. Cult film-maker from the fifties. B-movies mostly, slasher horrors and the like. In the middle of it all, there it was. Edie's lost novel. Complete anomaly. It was hardly likely to be something Bartlett would make a film from. I've been able to confirm it's genuine. The bad news is the film archive is short of cash. They're going to want a lot for it.'

Anna has done some research into Jaz Bartlett. When she saw the cat-faced logo of his company, she understood. Was that what Jasper had been looking for when he visited Jane Thomas? Edie's novel? Did he find it then and rape her anyway as a parting gesture? Or did he take it with him when he left High Hob? Was his visit to the museum that night an attempt to retrieve Charles's poems, which might cast doubt on the suicides and incriminate him if they were found? Either way, she is determined to bring the novel to Ackerdean.

*

310

Sam is waiting at the gate to High Hob.

'Not quite ready in here. Carter is putting cheese cubes on sticks as we speak.'

'Can we do anything?' asks Anna.

'No need,' says Sam. 'One glamorous assistant is enough. Why don't you two go for a walk? Make the most of this glorious weather.' Her eyes catch Anna's and flicker with the relief they'd both felt since Anna's phone call last night.

'It's the closest we'll get to knowing what happened that night,' Anna had said when she told Sam about her find in the newly acquired letters from the Reverend Haste.

Haste briefly mentioned the Harpers' deaths when he asked Reverend Netherwood for advice about his memorial service sermon. But it was a letter he wrote in 1948 that held the key.

Oakenshaw Parsonage
7th March 1948

Dear Jonathan,

My apologies for the tardiness in my reply. Mary sends her love to you and Janet, and thanks you once again for your thoughtful gift. She says the cushions are perfect for the parlour.

My new married life aside, my thoughts this week have turned to forgiveness and I have found myself reaching for St Matthew.

'For if you forgive others their trespasses, your heavenly Father will also forgive you, but if you do not forgive others their trespasses, neither will your Father forgive your trespasses.'

It will be my theme this week and yet I find the words hard to form. To convince myself as well as my congregation. It is hard, is it not, when the effects of a sin have repercussions long after the fact?

Sally, my housekeeper of many years, decided not to stay on after the wedding. She and Mary have not always seen eye to eye over domestic matters. She has found another position in Sowley

311

in a large family that I am sure will suit her. On her leaving she asked to speak with me in private.

What she said was in the form of a question. About forgiveness. How could it be right, she asked, to forgive someone for an act of evil, and then forgive them again, for a lie that covered up that evil, and for holding a person under such a cloud of fear that they would not dare to reveal the truth?

I quoted St Matthew and reminded her that when Peter asked Jesus how many times he should forgive a brother who sinned against him, suggesting 7 times. Jesus replied 70 times 7 times. At this she said, 'No matter how great and mortal the sin?' I nodded though there was despair in her eyes.

Before I had a chance to say anything more she said, 'I saw him. He thought I'd gone but I was at the window and I saw it all. He found me, later, said what he'd do if I ever told. I cannot forgive him. His own flesh and blood. I hope he burns in hell.'

As I write this I tremble, for I fear I know to what she was referring and to whom, yet she would tell me no more. She left without another word. I dare not articulate my suspicions even to you, although I will say that it relates to the shocking tragedy which struck our community many years ago.

I feel a burden of guilt, I confess, a wish that I had been able to see more clearly at the time. For I too feel I have been deceived, the truth clouded not by fear but by a misplaced trust and the belief that a person could change.

Sam had whistled down the telephone line. 'Sally nails Jasper right there, "His own flesh and blood". He must have been one hell of an actor, that boy. Involving the vicar in his somehow faked alibi.'

Anna has not told Sam about Erica's revelations. It is not her story to tell. But the Reverend Haste's words are enough to condemn Jasper. Which will make her own revelations to Frank easier to face.

'I used to come up here all the time when I was younger,' says Frank, as they follow the path through the heather, Betsy trotting along behind.

'Grouse beating,' says Anna.

'How did you know?'

'The oral history tape. You mentioned it.'

'Good memories.' He nods.

They are heading along the path towards the Stag Stones.

'I've found something else,' Anna says.

'About me?'

'Yes. About you. About Shaws and Chambers.'

'I'm all ears.'

'Did you know,' she asks, 'that Billy was friends with Nathaniel Potter's daughter, when they were growing up?'

Frank shakes his head. 'Can't say I did. Never heard much about her. She was an invalid, wasn't she? It's not impossible, I suppose. The Palace will have attracted her as much as the other kids.'

They reach a low flat stone. Its surface is warmed by the sun, but Frank refuses to sit down.

'Five minutes sat there and I'd never rise again.' He leans on his stick as Anna tells him about the initials on the mill wall and mentions that Erica's mother knew Billy and Lizzie when they were children. She stops short of the full story, about the extent of their relationship. It isn't what he needs to know.

'This is really what I wanted to talk to you about, though.' She pulls out a set of photographs from her bag. Shows him side by side the pictures of Nathaniel Potter, Billy Shaw and himself at his wedding.

'What are you saying?' Frank asks, although she is sure he can see it too.

'I think Nathaniel Potter was Billy's father.'

'His father was William Shaw.'

Anna shakes her head. 'It's not just the photographs, although the resemblance is incredible. Nathaniel Potter paid for Billy's school fees, through regular payments to Charles and Edie disguised as "brokering services".' She had found the figures in the household accounts, identical amounts paid in and out. 'Which,' she says as she can see he is about to object, 'could just have been generous philanthropy. But then there's the silver fob watch.'

'My great-granddad Shaw's watch?' There is uncertainty in Frank's voice.

'Can you remember what Billy said when he gave it to you?'

Frank screws up his eyes. 'That it had belonged to his granddad and it was all he had from him and I was to keep it and pass it down to my sons. So it's not forgotten.' He nods. 'Them were his exact words – "so it's not forgotten".'

'The inscription on the back,' Anna says. 'There were five watches engraved with those words and presented to the five men whose efforts led to the building of Sowley Town Hall in 1897. None of those men was a Shaw, but one of them was Jeremiah Potter, Nathaniel's father.' She hopes it will be enough. She is determined not to break Erica's confidence and tell him about Jane's diary and what happened to Lizzie.

'JP,' he says. 'Aye, that fits.'

'JP?'

'On the little bag Billy gave it me in. Them's the letters printed on it. I thought it was the maker's mark, if I thought on it at all.' He inhales deeply. 'Mebbes I will have a sit down after all.'

Anna makes space for him on the stone. He stares at the photos on her lap, his eyes tracking from one to the other, following the lines, the similarities. Eventually he lifts his head. The set of his face as he scans the wide moor tells her that what she has said fits with something he has always known.

'"Yours by right",' he says at last. 'It's what she said, "Yours by right". She knew all along.' He is silent for a while, gazing out across the heather. Pieces of a century-spanning jigsaw slotting into place.

'Don't change a thing though, does it,' he says at last. 'In the end. We are who we are. I might be Nathaniel Potter's grandson. But I'm still and always will be Francis William Chambers.'

Frank's right, and he has his story straight, Anna thinks. Does the world need to hear the rest? Sam has emailed her a proposal for a book: 'A joint project, I couldn't put it together without you.' A reassessment of the Harpers' deaths using the evidence from the archives to flesh out their theory that Jasper killed one or both of them, that it wasn't mutual suicide. 'Like you said,' Sam wrote, 'it's important to set the story straight.'

But it's not a straight story, Anna knows, and once one part of it starts to get untangled it would reveal the rest. The true stories of Edie and Charles, Billy and Lizzie, Mary Shaw and Nathaniel Potter, and Jane Thomas who lived with their secrets all their lives. Would it be worth exposing those stories, changing how they were remembered? For the sake of a theory, no matter how compelling the evidence? Or should we, Anna thinks, join their ranks, and remain silent?

Frank reaches out his hand and Anna helps him to his feet. The moor is spread out before them, Ackerdean valley and the mill hidden below.

'Shaws, Chambers *and* Potters,' Frank says.

'They won't be forgotten.'

'Aye, you'll make certain of that, I'm sure.' He pauses for a moment and then straightens his back, whistles Betsy to her feet. 'Come on, you daft hound, let's go and meet your new playmate, and see what sort of party that pair have cooked up. I'm hoping there's a bottle of beer with my name on it at the very least.'

He clears his throat as they begin to walk. 'If you don't mind me asking. How are you and Mr Happy Snaps Klein getting along? Any budding romance there?'

'Not at the moment.' Anna smiles. 'Too much baggage.'

'His or yours?' When she doesn't answer he adds, 'Only my youngest Michael is paying me a visit next week. He's talking of spending more time up this way. Seems to think I might be in need of company. I've told him all about you and he's very keen to meet you.'

'Frank ...'

'There's no harm, is there,' he pats her arm, 'in making new acquaintances. Never say never. And he's got my good looks.' He stops as a bird breaks into song above their heads. Anna shields her eyes from the sun. She can see the glint in the air.

'"As up he wings the spiral stair, a song of light, and pierces air",' says Frank.

The words are familiar. 'Meredith?' she asks.

'Some Victorian bod,' says Frank with a shrug. 'Great long poem. Couldn't tell you the rest of it. It was one of Billy's favourites. Though I don't think he had more than a couple of lines of it himself. I always remember that bit when I see a lark spiralling up. Reckon he got it just right.'

CHAPTER 28

Billy: 1960

Remembrance Sunday, 1960. I was up at the farm for the weekend. Maud and Arthur were walking up to Draper's Cross chapel with Frank and his girl, so I tagged along. I was never a big one for churchgoing, but it was a special service, with the promise of one of Maud's big dinners after. They'd invited Ma along but she wasn't feeling up to it. Still living in the cottage at the mill, with a growing collection of cats and hens. Arthur promised he'd fetch her afterwards in the Land Rover to join us for dinner. 'Can't have you missing out on Maud's Yorkshires,' he said. Him and Ma were right fond of each other. I was grateful every time I saw them together that he and Maud lived close by.

A troop of Scouts led the way into the church. All solemn-faced and smart behind their leader. Did me and Jasper really fill their beds with wood ants and almost send their camp up in flames? It seemed like nothing but a story now.

It was on the way out that I saw Lizzie. She was sitting at the back in a wheelchair, a stocky but handsome bloke beside her, with one hand on the back of the chair. She must have spotted me earlier, because there was no surprise on her face when our eyes met. She'd had time to prepare, unlike me who gawped like I'd seen a ghost.

After 'Hellos' that seemed like wasted words and an introduction to the stocky bloke – Richard – she said maybe we could have a moment to talk outside. She was talking as much to Richard as me. He nodded smartly, though giving me a wary once-over first. He whirled her chair round and out of the door as if the metal frame and wheels were made of feathers.

It was cold outside but bright. Maud and Arthur were talking to friends, Frank and his girl had wandered off, arm in arm, heads close together. He was a joy to my heart, was Frank. He'd a quick mind and was such a mimic. Got all the birdsongs off to a T before he was ten years old. You're a bloomin' mynah bird, I told him, and his eyes had filled with wonder when I told him of the parrots that flew free in the roof of the Winter Gardens. And there he was now, a man, maybe thinking of starting a family of his own before long.

Richard left me and Lizzie by a bench in the sunshine just off the main path. A last warning look and a promise that he'd be back soon. The air was sharp with the tang of mouldering leaves.

'Father's at the big service in Halifax,' Lizzie said. I remembered her mother had died a few years back and mumbled my condolences.

'Are you warm enough?' I added.

'Perfectly,' she said and shook her shoulders as if shaking off a shawl. 'I'm glad to be out in the fresh air. Why do churches always smell of old paper?'

'All the hymn books, I suppose.'

'I used to think it was the bones,' she said. A familiar smile on her lips. 'All those dead bodies buried under the flags crumbling to papery dust.'

'Nope, definitely hymn books,' I said, my own lips responding to her smile.

'Spoilsport.'

I half expected her to stick out her tongue. But instead she bowed her head and pulled a handkerchief from her pocket.

'Richard's a helpful chap,' I said, hoping it didn't sound as mocking to her as it did in my own head.

'He's a teacher,' she said, her blue eyes scolding me. 'I visit his school twice a week to read with some of the children who are struggling.'

I nodded. Chose silence over saying something else wrong.

'I make him laugh,' she said with a defiant tilt of her chin.

I bet you do, I thought. I bet you make him laugh and smile, and you lift his heart till it's singing like a lark. Because that's what you did to me.

What did we talk about in those minutes, no more than ten, fifteen of them, encased in my memory in a glow of autumn light? None of the things that needed saying. Nothing about how she'd once been my world, and I'd hoped I was hers. About me disappearing out of her life. My silence in the years since. Not about the Harpers. Nor of her illness, except for me asking how she was and her saying that she got by but had to have an operation next year. I could tell she didn't want to go into the details so I left it at that. She was pale, that china-cup whiteness I recalled from times past when she'd been cold or sad. But she still had a quickness about her, especially when we talked about the daft times we used to have.

'When we were children,' she said. And I felt the years stretch away like a catty band. An unreachable image of us playing, innocent, blissful, aged twelve or thirteen. So distant, so small.

I wanted to say sorry for leaving, for not trying to find another way through it all. But she stalled me as soon as my tongue began to tangle the words. 'It was for the best,' she said. And I knew then that at some point she'd learned the truth. A truth that neither of us was going to say out loud. She took my hand as if to seal a pact on it and her calm eyes and her cool palm on mine told me it was too late for 'sorries' and 'I wishes'. Those tiny figures of Billy and Lizzie, and Jasper, climbing over the rocks by the river, balancing on the wall, skimming stones on the pond: they were too far away to hear.

Then she glanced over my shoulder and a new smile lit up her face. Richard had returned to take her home.

Maud telephoned one grey morning in February. Lizzie had had her operation, but there were complications, an infection. She hadn't been strong enough to fight it off. The thought of Lizzie not being strong enough to win a battle, even with Death itself, tipped me over into a grief that felt like it had been waiting for me for twenty-five years.

And twenty-five years too late, I've finished my letter to Lizzie. Like the others that I started years ago that ended up in pieces or in flames, this one will never be sent. But it's the writing of it that matters. Too much is lost – thoughts and feelings and experiences. All that life and energy gone when we die. What can we hope to pass on to the next generation who are all so busy living their own lives, with little time for the passions and joys and fears and regrets of those who went before?

I'm not a poet or a sculptor. I've got my palace and the gardens but what do they say to the world about Billy Shaw? That he was a success? That he fulfilled his dream? Even Frank only knows a fraction of it. Maybe this letter will survive. Maybe one day he'll read it and even just briefly know me better, understand me more.

Dearest Lizzie

I wish I could paint what I want to say. The colours are there in my head. The moss-black of your hair, the deep blue of your eyes. I'd paint you a bird of such beauty and grace in joyous flight and I'd say that's you, Elizabeth Potter, you and my love for you combined.

I cannot be ashamed of what we meant to each other, when we didn't know. When we were just Billy and Lizzie, without Shaws and Potters tangling up the lines. But I'm sorry beyond anything that I ran away. I didn't even know what I was running from at first. The horror of what I'd found out? The aching grief of knowing we could never be together? Maybe I thought that if I left it all behind I'd be free of it. But of course I never was.

It was cruel and unfair to make that decision without you. We could have worked something out if I'd stayed. If I'd come back. We could have started again as brother and sister. As friends. But then I heard about Charles and Edie's deaths and everything changed again.

I was a coward. No matter what other things I might have been, might still be, at that moment I knew I was a coward. I was there that night. Held that gun in my hand, though I swear I did not pull the trigger. But I was so angry, my mind blinded with fury and focused on the people who had unleashed it within me. It would have taken just a moment of pressure from my finger.

I could have been a killer that night. What if the police questioned me and saw that guilt, not guilt of actual murder but the guilt of knowing how close I came to it? Opportunity, motive, my fingerprints on the weapon. So I stayed away and was thankful for every day that passed without a knock on my door. Even after the inquest and the verdict of suicide. Verdicts can be overturned, and once Frank was born I had more reason to make sure my name was never linked to what happened that night. Even now I avoid the eyes of policemen in the street.

Did you know Frank was my son? Maud and Arthur told him when he turned seventeen. It's not really changed anything. We see each other so rarely, they're his real mother and father in every other way. I keep hoping he'll visit me in London but his heart is firmly in Yorkshire, especially now he has a sweetheart of his own. There's so much of my life that I wish I could share with him, but so much too that I don't want to pass on.

I took him up on Oakenshaw Moor once, to the Stag Stones and Hound's Head Rock. He can't have been more than twelve, near the age I was when I first went up there. I told him about me and Jasper and the games we had. I showed him the sign of the Beast marked on the stone.

It was a clear blue day and there was a lark singing in the sky above. As we looked up, our eyes fixed on the bird, it seemed that time stood still. All our lives, all our stories, yours and mine and Jasper's and Frank's, Charles and Edie, our mothers and fathers and theirs before them, and all the bloomin' trippers and hillwalkers too, they were pinned right there to the earth by that bright song of light. Always and for ever.

Yours,

Billy Shaw

ACKNOWLEDGEMENTS

Thank you to everyone at Orion, especially my editor Laura Gerrard whose enthusiasm for *The Companion* and her brilliant editing have made this book possible.

I would like to thank my amazing family for their love and support and patience. Particularly my husband Tim Brooks and daughter Eliza who may sometimes have felt supplanted by Billy and Jasper and Anna, but brought me tea and cake and hugs anyway. And to my Dad, Bill Dunnakey, whose childhood photos of when he was 'young Billy' were beside me on my desk as I created his namesake in this book.

I am very grateful to the friends who have put up with me wittering away for years about 'my book'. In particular Rebecca Yorke and Sakinah Haq who have cheered me on and bolstered my confidence on many occasions. Also to the Monday morning coffee crew, Tuesday night book clubbers, the writing groups that have come and gone, my fell-running buddies and the Friday night 'cheeky teatime pinters' – thanks guys!

Huge thanks must go to Stephen May. A wonderful author but also an inspiring and generous writing teacher, who helped me to write more freely and find my voice. Stephen introduced me to my agent Lucy Luck, for which I am eternally grateful. Lucy's unstinting support and hard work have been a crucial part of *The Companion*'s journey.

I would also like to thank New Writing North and Arts Council England for the Northern Writer's Award that helped me financially and encouraged me to carry on writing.

This novel was inspired by a real place – Gibson Mill in Hardcastle Crags, near Hebden Bridge, West Yorkshire: originally a cotton mill, then an entertainment emporium and now a National Trust property. I have drawn on its stark beauty, stunning setting and multi-layered history to create my fictional Ackerdean Mill and the valley and moors around it. I owe a debt of gratitude to Abraham Gibson and his family who built and developed the mill, to the workers and trippers who have populated it over the centuries and to the National Trust whose renovation has enabled its story to continue.